Burn Out

Pat O'Keeffe's first novel was
Thermal Image

'O'Keeffe brings an authentic feel to his descriptions of fire
fighting, and the plot, involving arson and murder, is skilfully
brought to an exciting climax.'   *Sunday Telegraph*

'This first novel from Pat O'Keeffe is truly gripping with
plenty of twists and turns in the plot . . . a book that is
virtually impossible to put down.'   *Irish World*

'I hope he is planning more murders and more fires for his
hero to fight his way through.'   *Scotsman*

'Pat O'Keeffe has written an intelligent and thoughtful
novel that rises far above the typical arson terrorist adventure
novel . . . *Thermal Image* is a successful debut novel and
worthy of a reader's time.'   *Deadly Pleasures*

'A promising start . . . this first-time novelist draws on his
own experiences as a London firefighter to bring to life the
dangerous world of firefighting.'   *Hello*

By the same author
Thermal Image

About the author

Pat O'Keeffe, an Operational Station Officer in the London Fire Brigade, is also the holder of a 5th degree black belt in Karate and fought twenty-eight times as a kick-boxer. His opponents included three world champions and Nigel Benn, who later went on to become the world middleweight boxing champion. He is a kick-boxing commentator on the Sky Sports television channel and has written a book on the subject, *Kick-Boxing: A Framework for Success*.

Burn Out

Pat O'Keeffe

NEW ENGLISH LIBRARY
Hodder & Stoughton

Copyright © 2002 by Pat O'Keeffe

First published in Great Britain in 2002 by Hodder and Stoughton
First published in paperback in Great Britain in 2003 by Hodder and Stoughton
A division of Hodder Headline
A New English Library paperback

The right of Pat O'Keeffe to be identified as the Author of the Work has been asserted
by him in accordance with the Copyright, Designs and Patents Act 1988.

1 3 5 7 9 10 8 6 4 2

A CIP catalogue record for this title is available from the British Library

ISBN 0 340 82018 7

Typeset in Plantin by Hewer Text Ltd, Edinburgh
Printed and bound in Great Britain by
Mackays of Chatham plc, Chatham, Kent

Hodder and Stoughton
A division of Hodder Headline
338 Euston Road
London NW1 3BH

This book is dedicated to three Station Officers
who were worth their pay and more
George Brown – Silvertown, Jim Strange – Lambeth and
Tommy Hansen – Bethnal Green

ACKNOWLEDGEMENTS

My sincere thanks to my friend and colleague Myles O'Reilly for his technical advice on Urban Search and Rescue and for his loyalty, when it mattered most.

1

I left Romford later than I'd planned.

It was a hot, sticky afternoon and the noise of the traffic and petrol-wrapped heat had seeped through the windows, slowly tightening my mood.

I'd been fighting myself the whole day; one part wanting to go, to flee and leave all the bad blood behind and one part feeling the seductive pull of the past: the emotional investment that had held me, but had also left me strung out and on the verge of nervous collapse.

I couldn't put it right. No amount of soul-searching, of revision, could bring my leading firefighter Sandy Richards back to life or return Jenny to me, warm, beautiful, prepared to be faithful.

Too much and too deep.

In my urge to burn bridges, to create a barrier between the past and some kind of future, I had decided on an act of myopic symbolism. I was leaving the flat for good.

Chris Adamou, the fire brigade union rep, had said that there was a place in Mid-Wales, a therapy unit that specialised in trauma cases like mine. It was a new place, partly sponsored by the union.

What she didn't say was that it was highly political: a thorn in the side of fire authorities who had failed to respond to the increasing numbers of emotionally damaged firefighters.

I had no wish to be a pawn in their games, but with a discipline tribunal hanging over my head it made sense to jump through this particular hoop.

It seemed everybody in the Brigade knew that I was going to the unit.

Many thought I was responsible for Sandy's death, that my lack of foresight had contributed to the tragedy, and many others just repeated the rumours out of ignorance or for want of something better to do.

Either way it was the time to go, to disappear off the scene, until time softened the edges of the lies and friends had a chance to tell it like it really was.

Leaving later meant that I hit the escaping city traffic on the far side of the M25. It stayed that way until Oxford; compressed into a segmented blindworm that moved fitfully and exuded the sour odour of exhaust fumes.

Alex McGregor had lent me his Shogun to replace the one I'd written off.

That too was unfinished business.

I travelled south of Birmingham, on to the M5 and then the A5, making better time as the cars and lorries thinned and the road stretched out ahead of me. Two hours later, with the sun as a beacon pulling me westward, I reached the A470 heading for Dolgellau.

The grey urban landscape of the Midlands had gone, replaced by sharply angled hills sliced apart by insistent silver-black streams. Each dark fold of land, each stretch of wild rock, drew my eye, until I stopped the car, wound down the window and absorbed the silence.

Slowly, I got out, walked across to a rocky outcrop and sat, looking down the valley.

Fifty yards away a buzzard wheeled lazily above a stand of sessile oak in the humid evening sky.

I felt it for the first time then. A sense of having shaken off, if only temporarily, the stench of guilt and failure. I closed my eyes and smiled. Maybe this journey wouldn't be wasted; maybe there was something here, for me.

Christ knows I needed it; needed a balance to pull me back to some kind of normality.

I stayed there for maybe twenty minutes, then climbed back into the car and drove on. Half an hour later I came to the wooden toll bridge just beyond Dolgellau and stopped again, stunned by the riverine landscape.

To my left the Mawddach estuary was as still as glass and the sun was a molten ball burning a red-gold path down the estuary towards the toll bridge and the hamlet of Penmaen-pool.

The mountains on either side of the estuary were covered in forest and the whole reminded me of a sea loch, its beauty and quiet so powerful it sent a chill through me.

I wanted Jenny to see it. I wanted her here, my arm around her; no history, no betrayal, no baggage.

I smiled. There – it had tricked me again, letting me think that all I had to do was forgive and the past would be washed away. I had to let go. Not in anger, but in resignation. What cannot be changed must be endured or at least spared corrosive self-pity.

In the corner of my eye I saw someone approaching from the other side of the bridge.

It was a man around sixty years old. His stride was strong and purposeful and he was dressed in a stained three-quarter-length wax-proofed coat, with a bush hat made from the same material set back on his head. His face was weather-tanned and grimy, but the eyes were shrewd and darted backwards and forwards, missing nothing.

As he reached me, he nodded hello and gave a good-natured smile. I nodded back and then edged the car forward.

I drove on slowly, knowing I was within three miles of the

unit, Ty Hiraeth. Half a mile on, two motorcyclists flashed past me, coming from the opposite direction; their exhilaration at driving the open, winding road easy to understand, though they must have been blind to the wild beauty of the surroundings.

The road ran parallel to the estuary, through coniferous woods that tumbled down to the water's edge. As the trees thinned on the left, I caught glimpses of the huge mass of Cader Idris, the mountain that dominated the southern flank of the Mawddach.

The humidity seemed to be rising and I could feel the sweat running down my back. Thunder flies made the windscreen tacky and I flipped on the washer and blades – only to smear the insect detritus across the remainder of the screen.

I must have taken my attention off the road for barely an instant.

There was a flash of movement and a runner came bursting through the trees on the right. I braked hard and turned the wheel, adrenalin shooting through my body. The car missed him by inches and he stumbled awkwardly.

I held my hands up and shook my head. For a second he stared at me in shock.

'Are you okay?' I called.

There was the melt-smooth mark of burn scarring down the left-hand side of his face, that puckered the skin and pulled at the line of his eye. He seemed agitated and looked from me to something in the distance.

I turned and followed his gaze.

Half a mile away, in the direction of the toll bridge, a tongue of bright orange flame was curling upward. Then I caught the smell of smoke, drifting on the air.

It wasn't the dry scent of woodsmoke, but an acrid smell; like a house fire. I looked at the runner.

'What is it? What's over there?'

He stood still, as though not hearing me. Then, wordless, turned and ran back into the trees.

'Shit!'

I scrambled back into the car and threw a three-point turn, racing back in the direction I had come.

The trees came up fast on the river side of the road and I lost sight of the fire. I was driving too fast and had no choice but to slow down and search for a road or approach that would lead down in the right direction.

Two hundred yards further on I found it: a rough track, slanting off towards the river. Between the trees I could see the increasing glow of the fire and hear the noises of structural disintegration.

Grateful that I had the Shogun, I turned onto the track and immediately had to swerve around a deep rut, wincing as overhanging branches whipped the sides of the vehicle. Thank Christ Alex wasn't there to see the abuse being taken by his favourite toy.

The track came to an end in a clearing close by the river. On the far side of the clearing, a two-storey granite-built house was well alight with flames snaking out of the ground-floor windows and the front door.

Thick black smoke billowed up and sparks swirled in the heat current.

I hit the brakes thirty yards short of the front of the house, grabbed my corduroy barn jacket and ran forward, shouting. The heat was intense, making it impossible to gain entry that way.

I called out again and then walked quickly around to the rear, consciously slowing my speed and steadying my breathing, knowing that if I was to enter the house the worst thing I could do would be to arrive panting.

A black pick-up truck was parked between the trees and in my mind that doubled the chances of the house being occupied.

I tried the rear door, but it was locked. I moved back several feet, then ran forward and booted the lock. The door crashed open, releasing a cloud of thick smoke.

Dropping to my knees, I peered under the smoke into a passageway leading to the bottom of a staircase.

The smoke was heavy.

I couldn't see any indications of small flames within the fume cloud, the tell-tale sign of an impending flash-over, but I was in two minds about going in. On the one hand I was a fireman and on the other I had no equipment and no back-up. If it did flash-over whilst I was in there, I'd be burnt alive.

I hesitated, looking for other options, an edge, anything, and my eye fell on a water-butt next to the rear door.

I pulled off my barn jacket and plunged it into the water, then slipped it on and turned the collar up, pulling the jacket over my head. Then I flattened out and started to crawl in under the smoke band, breathing shallowly. I had my mouth against the floor, where most of the oxygen would be trapped, feeling the fierce heat prickle my skin.

I pulled my hands back into the jacket sleeves.

As I reached the bottom of the stairs I realised that there was a door, about four feet beyond the stairs, that separated the front and the back of the house.

The smoke and heat were getting worse, spiralling towards a simultaneous ignition of the entire passageway. It felt as if I was drowning, the light-headedness of smoke-inhalation was starting to disorientate me and the rising temperature was flooding my brain with panic.

I could feel the heat scorching my back and hear the hollow roaring as the fire ripped through the front of the house.

Somehow I managed to reach the separating door and pull it closed. With my lungs burning and my eyes streaming, I crawled back down the passageway to the rear door.

I emerged on all fours, gulping for air and fighting the urge to vomit. Instinct was screaming at me to stay where I was, but I knew that if there was anyone on the first floor then I was their only chance of getting out alive.

I turned and crawled back to the staircase.

With the separating door closed, shutting off the main fire, and the back door open, the temperature had dropped, reducing the chances of a flash-over and allowing me to get beyond the passage, to the stairs.

The chance of a flash-over wasn't the only danger. I knew that the fire, trapped behind the passageway door, would be eating its way upward, burning away the ceilings and devouring the floors from beneath – and it's a cardinal rule that you never go above the fire.

At the foot of the stairs I started to crawl upward and immediately felt the increase in temperature and thickness of the smoke. I was on the very edge of my limitations, measuring out my chances in seconds.

At that moment I reached the landing and almost immediately touched a body.

I felt along the length of it, grabbed the shoulders and pulled it around so that the head was towards me. I held the collar and started to drag it down the stairs when I saw a flare of light off to my left.

The separating door had just failed and the flames and smoke were pouring back into the passageway. I hurried, knowing that already it would be rising up to the ceiling and mushrooming down again, cutting me off.

The body felt heavy. The smoke was intoxicating me, slowing me down and making my movements clumsy. A surge of panic threatened as I recognised what was happening, but I pushed it away and felt behind me with my feet, trying for the passageway floor.

My leg swung, meeting only air.

Suddenly I slipped, taking the body with me, the extra

weight accelerating the fall and slamming me into the floor at the bottom.

Instinctively I gulped in air and thrashed violently as the smoke invaded my lungs and contorted my body in a savage fit of coughing. I forced myself to exhale and in a frenzied, desperate struggle made for the open doorway, hauling the body behind me.

Outside, I collapsed six feet from the house; unable to give the casualty any help, fixated only with the need to draw my knees into my chest and throw up.

I knew if the casualty was to have any chance at all resuscitation was urgent, but my body wouldn't obey me and stayed in a heap, sucking in air.

Finally, with an act of sheer bloody-mindedness, I wiped at my mouth and eyes and turned him over. Almost at the same time I realised that my arms, my face, my coat – all of me – was soaked in blood.

His throat was cut to the bone.

2

As I stared at the body an eerie sound erupted from inside the house: a whistling, like a scream rising in intensity. Then a sheet of flame curled out of the upper rear windows and attacked the eaves.

The fire was pushing relentlessly into the back of the building and the entrained air from the front was acting like a blowtorch, searing the inside of the building.

I grabbed the corpse and dragged it away from the fierce heat, but I got barely twenty yards before collapsing in a heap. The smoke-inhalation made me feel like a steel band was constricting my chest.

Propped on one arm, I lay there, breathing hard and staring at the victim, noticing only now the extent of his injuries.

There were defensive wounds on his hands and arms and a dark bloody hole in the top of his thigh and another in his right shoulder, but it was the severed throat that fixed my attention.

This wasn't a man stabbed in a fight. This was someone weakened then butchered with clinical precision – perhaps even craft.

The house was a hundred and fifty, maybe two hundred yards from the road and screened by pine woods. No one would have heard the sounds of the struggle, the screams.

I studied his face. He was about thirty years old, with thick dark hair and the complexion of someone who spent a lot of time outdoors. He was fit as well; bulky but muscular.

The clothes also suggested an outside occupation; brown

moleskin trousers and a heavy check shirt worn over a T-shirt. The boots were of good-quality leather.

I didn't have a mobile with me to ring the fire brigade and police. Then I remembered that I'd passed a sign indicating a phone box about a mile back up the road. But then I heard two-tone horns in the distance, coming from the direction of Barmouth.

I'm not sure why I searched the corpse.

Maybe it was a legacy of having been a temporary inquiry agent for Alex McGregor or just plain curiosity. Whatever prompted me, I knew it was unlikely to be appreciated by the police; anything I noted would have to be replaced exactly as it was found.

On his wrist, there was a sophisticated GPS, a Global Positioning System; an advanced navigation aid used by outdoorsmen and the military. The black leather strap was half cut through.

In his back trouser pocket there was a wallet containing a number of business cards and a company ID. The corpse's name was Hugh Jones; a surveyor for the Black River Mining Company. On the back of the business card was one word – *Xingu.*

First the fire brigade arrived and then the police.

I was kept hanging around as the CID were called and my identity checked. The policeman who first arrived was from Dolgellau and he seemed out of his depth, oscillating between nervousness and what I imagine he thought was toughness.

He asked the same questions three times before the CID arrived. Who was I? Where was I staying? Could he see my driver's licence again?

When the CID arrived, it was in the form of a Detective Sergeant John Vaughan, a red-haired man in his mid-thirties, who was switched-on and given to smiling in a disarming manner that made you want to tell him anything he wanted to know.

The constable from Dolgellau hung around, trying to eavesdrop on the questions Vaughan was asking me. I could see in the detective's eyes that he wasn't appreciating it.

Suddenly he turned around. 'Bugger off, Dewi! There's a nice man.'

The constable sniffed and wandered over to talk to the firemen.

'Friend of yours, is he?' I asked.

'Worse – he's my brother-in-law. Look, I can see that you want to get cleaned up and get to Ty Hiraeth so I'll let you go . . . my boss'll want to speak to you, mind – sometime tomorrow if that's convenient?'

'Fine . . . thank you . . .' I was covered in blood and filth and felt weary. I rubbed my eyes and sighed. 'I need a bath and a stiff drink after this lot.'

He smiled. 'How long do you think you'll be staying at Ty Hiraeth?'

'I've no idea . . . a month – maybe two. I'm really not sure.'

'Right, then. Look, Ty Hiraeth is nearby, but the entrance is hard to find. Why don't I show you the way?'

'Thanks, but—'

'Think nothing of it.'

And with that he climbed back in his car and waited for me to turn the Shogun around.

It was late now and starting to get dark; I was grateful for his offer, but couldn't help feeling he was making sure of me.

Ty Hiraeth was less than half a mile away and John Vaughan was right, I wouldn't have found it on my own, but as we came to a halt in the driveway, he got out of his car and I felt a touch of irritation.

'There's no need,' I said as I climbed out of the Shogun and retrieved my case and grip bag from the rear.

'No problem. Can I give you a hand with any of that?'

I shook my head and he rushed ahead to open the door for me. I stopped, put my luggage down and stared at the building.

It was a large granite-built place with high gables and an octagonal tower-like structure at one corner, on the estuary side of the building. Wisteria snaked across the façade and in the gloom it looked like a B-movie haunted house.

He walked back and joined me.

'It's looks better by day.' He laughed. 'The name – Ty Hiraeth – it means Inspiration House. There's great views of the Mawddach from the other side . . . lovely, it is.'

'You've been here before?' It was meant to be ironic, but if he spotted it he didn't let it show.

'Oh yes! Quite a landmark from the other side of the river. It was built a hundred years ago, by a Superintendent of the Mines . . . till he killed himself when the gold ran out.'

'Gold?'

'Of course – the mountains at the back of here are riddled with mines. Some of it used to make royal wedding rings.'

'But there's no gold there now?'

'There is, but not enough for commercial mining. People say that the real bonanza's down there – in the sand and silt of the estuary where it's been washed since the land was formed.'

'Gold.' I yawned, still trying to get my head around the idea.

'And copper.'

He picked up my case and marched forward to the door. I gave a wry smile and followed.

Inside there was a small reception committee waiting. The police had phoned ahead and an attractive dark-haired woman in her early forties was sitting in a small office. Drinking coffee with her was another, older woman, who disappeared when she saw us.

The dark-haired woman stood up. 'Steven Jay, is it? Goodness, what on earth has happened to you?'

'Hello, Julia,' said John Vaughan.

I looked from him to her and then realised why he had been so eager to show me the way. If I judged it right the interest was mainly on his side, but she wasn't panicked by the idea. I caught his eye and gave a flat smile.

'Sorry, Mr Jay – this is Julia Lloyd, the Unit Manager.'

She held out her hand and I held both mine up to show her they weren't in any fit state to shake. She nodded.

'Eve!' she called out.

The older woman came back.

'Mr Jay will be wanting a bath . . . he's in room number seven. Be a love and run it for him.'

She turned back to me, 'Now . . . are you hungry?'

'Starving.'

'Well, the evening meal was at seven, but I could cook you a steak – if you'd like?'

'I don't want to be any trouble . . . a sandwich would be fine.'

'Steak sandwich, then?'

I smiled my appreciation, 'If it's not a problem.'

'It's no trouble. Look, go and have your bath and I'll prepare it.'

I turned to follow Eve up the stairs and John Vaughan stepped forward.

I looked at him directly. 'Problem?'

He shrugged. 'I need your clothes.'

I ate in my room. Like the rest of the house it was wood-panelled, with solid furniture and heavy drapes. From the window there was a view of the night-black river glinting in the moonlight and, beyond, the dark shoulders of Cader Idris.

Opening the window, I stared out into the warm, soft night

and worked out roughly where the house fire had been. The river angled away and I thought I could make out the shape of the land as it fell to the water.

Ty Hiraeth was quiet and the drama of the day seemed unreal. The adrenalin had long since ebbed away and I was left with a feeling of isolation.

It should have been a welcome feeling.

I had come here to escape the turmoil that had shaped my life for the last nine months, but I knew that part of me didn't want to escape it, at least not in its entirety. I had walked away from Jenny. She had returned to me after a six-month affair and I had let her back, because I needed her.

In three weeks, I . . . we, managed to relive the whole fiasco again. We held each other, made love and plans, but still she couldn't let go of him. I believed her when she said she loved me but had wanted him physically. I also believed her when she made a commitment to leave him in the past. She tried, I could see that she tried, but ultimately she'd weakened.

Before she left me for the first time she had lied to me, to cover up what she was doing and when she came back she had lied to herself.

So I walked away. The question was, could I *stay* away?

The night air infiltrated the room and I turned out the light and lay on the bed with my eyes closed; thinking and feeling.

When I left here I would have to be at peace with myself; that was a given. The truth was I had carried on an internal war; ranting at myself that to be with Jenny was to lose self-respect yet knowing that when we were together I felt alive.

I had taken one solid thing from the wreckage of our last interlude; the belief that Jenny needed me as much as I needed her.

To let her have other relationships, licence, would destroy me. Or would it? Was the pain in knowing what she did or in the betrayal? Could I live with her and see it as part, not all? Could I settle for less than the complete woman?

Other people did it. People had affairs that went on for years; never possessing, just . . . borrowing. Blanking out the other partner, being pragmatic. Was that a real option? Or did madness lie that way?

There were still times when I ached for her but was that just physical need? Maybe I could find some peace of mind here, some detachment. Then perhaps I could go and find her, knowing what the game was, knowing what was required.

First I had to get my head right. I had been through months of turmoil with Jenny and then Alex McGregor, my best friend, had offered me a job as an inquiry agent. Alex knew that when Jenny left me I had big money troubles, mainly through financing Jenny's business, a business bought out by her lover shortly before Jenny left me for him.

So when Alex had offered me a part-time job investigating a series of fires with the strong smell of fraud I was interested but sceptical that I could do it. I was a fireman, not a copper.

But then Alex showed me a photograph of the main suspect with Jenny's lover and I leapt at the chance to put him away.

The investigation backfired on me. I was beaten senseless and left for dead. My Leading Firefighter, Sandy Richards, was killed and Jenny and I crashed and burned yet again.

The stress had been crushing. I had bouts of explosive temper, chillingly real nightmares and woke crying tears of frustration and grief. It had all merged into the same thing. Jenny, Sandy Richards's death, my very existence, became a blur of unfocused pain and regret.

I became distracted and questioned and requestioned my fire-ground decisions on the day Sandy Richards died to the point when I could no longer think straight. I was in denial about how badly it had ripped me up and told myself that all I needed was a couple of nights' sound sleep and one less drama in my life.

Others knew better.

What finally decided me on Ty Hiraeth was Bob Grant. He was an Assistant Divisional Officer that I knew and trusted. He taken the time to come and see me, despite the fact that technically I was still under suspension.

'There's a place in Wales, Steve. It's new, but the buzz is that it's good. Go there. Go there and, if nothing else, rest. Switch your mind off for a couple of months.'

Then Chris Adamou, the union rep, weighed in. 'If we can prove stress it might get you off the hook, Steve.' Next in line was John Blane, my Sub Officer. Others followed. People were queuing up to tell me. That was the hardest part. I knew it made sense, but going was an admission that I wasn't functioning right and that in itself can flush your professional credibility straight down the toilet. Damned if you go, damned if you don't.

My inner philosopher settled the issue. 'When your Karma's fucked, back up and see the obvious.'

I drifted off, letting the coming nightmare devour me.

It always started in the same place; I was running through the alleyway at the back of the Heathway shops, screaming instructions at firefighters who ignored me and ran past. Sandy Richards went by and I tried to grab him, to make him listen to me, but he was like vapour passing through my hands.

Then I was standing in the yard at the back of the shop when a deep rumble came from the core of the building, turning my legs dead with fear.

Silence.

From nowhere, firefighters appeared all around me, their faces set in accusation. I could neither speak nor hear them; some pointed fingers, others turned their backs.

The emergency crew entered the building on their way to rescue Sandy Richards and Wayne Bennett.

Minutes ticked by and somehow I found myself at the back of the yard, isolated. I tried to get back to where I had been, by the rear door where Sandy and Wayne had entered, but I couldn't push past the firefighters.

Then the emergency crew emerged, dragging a body behind them. I went frantic; pushing, pulling, shoving, fighting with all my strength, forcing a way through.

Up until that point, the nightmare had been the same as always, but now it changed.

The emergency crew laid Sandy on the ground and stood back. As I went forward and lifted him, his head fell back; the throat had been cut to the bone.

I woke up gasping for breath.

A pool of moonlight was spilling across the floor, throwing shadows against the walls. I was shivering. The temperature had dropped and the muted sounds of the river were carrying into the room.

The irony of the day's events at the house fire merging with my guilt about Sandy wasn't lost on me. So bizarre was the connection, so perverse, it actually helped. It showed me that I was looking to blame myself: that whether I was culpable or not, another process was attacking me emotionally; so that I drew guilt to myself, like an addict needing a hit.

I rolled off the bed and shut the window then undressed and got into bed.

At first I didn't want to close my eyes, for no matter what detachment waking logic brought, the prospect of revisiting the nightmare unnerved me.

I lay there, half asleep, trying to silence my ticking conscience.

I remember a change in the pattern of light in the room, like a shadow passing over the moon. Sometime later, sleep closed over me.

3

I had set the alarm for seven, intending to jog through the grounds and down to the river before breakfast. But when the beeping woke me I still felt tired from my interrupted sleep and turned over instead.

An hour later, better for the extra, I climbed from the bed and looked out of the window over the mist-shrouded Mawddach and lower slopes of the estuary. All the signs pointed to another hot, sultry day.

I opened the window, breathed the clear, uncontaminated air and smiled.

If demons had to be confronted, if I had to cast out the past, then this was the place to do it. If nothing else, I promised myself, I would take time out to walk the wooded, rocky hills and read some Steinbeck. In the evenings I would find a pub somewhere and drink red wine until sentiment and alcohol mellowed the pain.

Balance, rhythm and rest; I would reset my life-clock.

The sound of running feet crunching the gravel path came from the direction of the river. The mist blanketed the runners until they were fifty yards away. When they came into view they were running at full sprint, racing each other. They pulled up directly below my window.

I stood back, so that I could just about see them.

One was a woman, in her thirties, with blond short cut hair

and an athletic build. The other was the scarfaced runner I'd seen the previous evening.

They stood with their hands on their hips, breathing hard and talking in low voices. At one point I thought she smiled at him. He was turned away from me so I couldn't see his expression, but he reached out and touched her on the shoulder. It was innocuous enough, but I felt that ownership was implied.

I tried to see his face more clearly, but they walked from my view, around the side of the house. A dozen questions occurred, but if he was staying at Ty Hiraeth then they could wait; for the time being hunger was giving me a different imperative.

I showered, changed into chinos and a navy T-shirt and made my way downstairs.

'Good morning.'

I turned to see Julia Lloyd standing behind me.

'Morning.'

'Did you sleep well?'

'Yes, thank you.'

'Breakfast is ready whenever you are. I'll tell Eve you're down. Dining room's through there.' She indicated a door at the end of the hall. 'Eddie's in there, Eddie Marlowe. The other lads are still in bed.' She smiled. 'I believe they went into Dolgellau for a few drinks last night.'

I walked down the hallway and opened the door. The dining room was a long oak-panelled affair with lead-glazed windows overlooking the river. On the far bank the mist was lifting and rolling through the treetops, like gun-smoke. Beneath it, the metal-sheen waters of the Mawddach were still.

Sitting by the window was a pale man in his early forties, about the same height and build as me. There was an air of sadness about him, but he smiled when he saw me and beckoned me over.

As I reached his table he got up and held his hand out.

'Eddie Marlowe,' he said in a broad accent. 'Greater Manchester.'

'Steve Jay,' I replied. 'London.'

'Sit down, Steve. Eve will be in to take your order any minute. She doesn't let the grass grow.'

We both sat.

'How long have you been here?'

'Five weeks. Seems longer, though,' he sighed.

'How you finding it?'

'Awful.' He grinned. 'Your first day here?'

'I arrived last night.'

'First day's always a bit strange, but the staff are good at making you feel welcome. Elizabeth Rhys-Davies is the main therapist. She's a psychologist, but nice, knows her stuff.'

'What are you here for?' I said without thinking.

He looked me straight in the eye. 'I'm mad.' Then he grinned again.

'Sorry, Eddie, didn't mean to pry.'

'Don't worry about it.' He looked out the window. 'It's lovely here. Bit of a change from where I come from.'

'Me too.'

'When that mist clears the view's champion.'

'I saw some of it as I drove down yesterday,' I said.

'Oh, I'd have thought it would have been dark when you arrived?'

'I got delayed. There was a house on fire down the road.'

'That was you, was it? We heard the appliances go by and could see the smoke. Was it much?'

I studied him, 'It was a fatal.'

'Oh, that's a shame.'

I didn't want to mention the murder, not till I'd spoken to the police.

'They've been busy, the local lads,' he said. 'The weather's produced a series of forest fires. Some of 'em quite biggish, like. Never fought anything more than a bit of grass, me. How about you?'

I shook my head. 'The odd undergrowth fire in the summer, but not forest. There's not much of it in London.'

He grinned. 'Aye, 'spect you're right.'

Eve, the older woman from the previous night, appeared from the kitchen and took my order. Then she returned with the coffee, and Eddie, who had already eaten, poured for us both. We both stared out the window, silent for the moment. It was Eddie who spoke first.

'Grief,' he said quietly, 'that's why I'm here. We lost our little girl. Run over, she was, just before her ninth birthday. Four months ago yesterday. The wife coped better than me. Well, they do, women, don't they? Have to keep going 'cos of the others. Me, I fell apart.'

'I'm sorry, Eddie.'

'Aye. She were a great little lass. We were best friends.' He sighed.

We fell silent again.

I hadn't planned to tell people, other than the therapists, why I was here, but Eddie's obvious grief beckoned a response.

'I lost my leading firefighter, Sandy Richards; a backdraught got him. I think it was my fault.'

Eddie looked at me. 'Thank you,' he said quietly. 'Life's a bugger, ain't it?'

I changed the subject. 'Who else is staying here?'

'You're the sixth. There's Alby Hutton from the West Midlands Brigade. Keeps himself to himself, does Alby. Not sure what his problem is, but he's nervy, like. Then there's Paul Rider from London and Mick Parker from Essex. In their twenties,' he said wistfully, 'and they're as mad as frogs! They're out drinking most nights. I've no idea what's wrong with them, though both have had bad injuries at one stage.'

'You said I was the sixth?'

He paused, 'Aye. There's another lad, Jamie. Well spoken. Don't know his last name. He were a soldier in Bosnia. Got a nasty burn scar down the side of his face.'

'A soldier?'

'Aye.'

'I thought we'd be all firefighters?'

'He keeps himself to himself as well. Always running, he is. Something disturbing about him.'

'Go on.'

'Nothing I could put my finger on, but you know when people give you the willies . . . well he does me.'

'How long's he been here?'

'Don't know, but before me.' He got up, 'Look, I'll leave you to your breakfast. I've got Elizabeth at half-nine; first appointment of the day. I'll catch you later.'

I took my time over breakfast. None of the other residents showed. A while later Julia Lloyd appeared in the dining-room doorway.

'The police are here to see you, Steve. They're waiting in reception.'

I frowned. I hadn't expected them back first thing in the morning and felt vaguely uneasy that they had shown up quite so early.

Julia came over to the table. 'You had your first appointment with Elizabeth at eleven . . . I'll try and rearrange it for this afternoon.' She handed me a form. 'Just fill this in and take it with you.'

John Vaughan was waiting in reception with a man he introduced as his boss, Detective Inspector Pritchard. I wasn't taken. If John Vaughan had struck me on our first meeting as clever and laid-back, then Pritchard appeared the opposite.

He was polite and businesslike, but spoke a little too quickly for a man at ease with himself.

'I've had a word with Julia and she said we could use the library for our chat, Mr Jay, if that's all right with you?' said John Vaughan.

'Fine. I've no idea where the library is, though.'

'It's this way,' he said, and took the lead.

The library was on the ground floor with the same wide views across the Mawddach as the dining room, but with a better view of the garden.

I sat down on an antique leather sofa and the two policemen sat opposite on separate armchairs. They unbuttoned their jackets and I settled back, trying to recall the exact sequence of the previous day's drama. Had I known what was going through their minds I might have been more wary.

'I wonder if you could take us through the events of yesterday, Mr Jay? In your own words just relate what you saw and the actions you carried out,' said DI Pritchard.

I went through it all again, exactly as I had the previous evening with John Vaughan. Neither of them interrupted me, but John Vaughan made notes. When I'd finished they exchanged looks. Then Pritchard began asking questions.

'You told Detective Sergeant Vaughan last night that you'd never been to this part of Wales before?'

'Yes, that's right.'

'And your sole reason for coming here is to receive treatment at Ty Hiraeth?'

'Yes.'

'Why?'

'Pardon?'

Pritchard leaned forward. 'Why are you here, Mr Jay? What's wrong with you?'

I don't know why the question or its tone surprised me. It's not unknown for the police to try to unbalance people they are interviewing. Perhaps it was my sensitivity at even being in a place like Ty Hiraeth or the lack of sensitivity in the question itself. Either way I didn't like it. I'd done nothing wrong.

I looked at John Vaughan, who seemed to shift in his seat.

'It's very personal,' I said guardedly.

'Is there any reason why you can't tell me?' Pritchard asked directly.

I took my time answering.

Since Sandy's death I'd begun losing my temper for the smallest of reasons. What would normally make me merely raise an eyebrow was tending to trigger overreaction and I'd taken to inserting pauses in my conversation whenever I felt it happening.

I looked at John Vaughan again.

Finally I said, 'I lost a member of my watch in a fire. My Leading Firefighter. It's not an easy thing to deal with and I'm here to get help with that.'

'The Dagenham Heathway fire?'

I went still.

I shouldn't have been surprised that they knew. In any investigation, but especially murders, the witnesses come under a fair degree of scrutiny. One phone call to London would have given them a heap of information on me.

My face and name had been splashed all over the papers in the wake of the fraud case and the police, in the shape of Detective Sergeant Menzies, a cynical bastard who confirmed the stereotype, hadn't been too pleased with my role of inquiry agent for Alex and Andrew McGregor's loss-adjustment firm.

At the mention of the Heathway fire all my barriers went up.

'Yes.'

Pritchard nodded and looked at John Vaughan. 'It's been a long night for us, Mr Jay. We ran a check on you with the

Metropolitan Police and information just came pouring out. It seems you were nearly charged with withholding information from them. Tell us about that.'

I shook my head dismissively.

'That was an empty threat by an empty-headed copper.' I paused to let my words sink in. 'I told the police everything that was relevant to the case.'

He studied his hands. 'According to our colleagues in London, you blundered your way through a murder investigation and ended up nearly getting yourself and a young woman killed.'

I tried a longer pause. 'What does this have to do with yesterday?'

'I don't know – yet. What I want to know from the start is whether you are acting in any capacity other than as a patient at Ty Hiraeth.'

'Any other capacity?'

'Yes, you know, Mr Jay: are you acting as an inquiry agent on anyone's behalf?'

I shook my head. 'No.'

'You're sure about that?'

'Yes.'

'Then why did you have the dead man's business card in the pocket of your trousers?'

I shrugged. 'I must have picked it up at the scene. Look, I've come here to rest – and to receive some help with getting over the death of my leading firefighter.'

'Yes, you've already said that. What I want from you, Mr Jay, is an assurance that you won't be playing the inquiry agent down here.'

'Inquiring into what? I came across a house fire and I did what any other firefighter in the world would have done. Was that wrong?'

'Are you saying that you have no idea about the background to the fire and the murder?'

I closed my eyes and breathed out heavily.

'I have no idea what you're talking about. Look, in London I helped a friend out and paid more than the full price for doing it. I have no intention of ever repeating the experience. Is that clear enough for you?'

The vibe off him said no. He had his teeth in and was determined not to let go.

'That 4 × 4 you're driving, Mr Jay, the Shogun – is it yours?'

'You ask the question so presumably you know it's not.'

'It belongs to Alex McGregor, doesn't it?'

'So? The insurance covers any other driver. What's the problem?' My voice was flat.

'The same Alex McGregor that you were working for as an inquiry agent?'

'Oh, for Christ's sake!'

'No need to lose your temper, Mr Jay. I have a murder to investigate here. I don't need complications.'

'I'm not a complication – if that's what you mean?'

'I hope so,' he said quietly. But tension still framed his body.

I'd become an expert at reading stress in people: the most minute of signs reveal themselves in all manner of ways and Pritchard had several of the key markers.

The mirror had been my teacher and it doesn't lie.

As I studied him I went from irritation to intrigue. Something heavy was eating him up.

'Tell me what happened as you approached the point where you first saw the fire, Mr Jay. Did you pass any other vehicles?'

'Nothing that I can recall.'

'No one driving too fast the other way or anything like that?'

'I passed two motorcyclists, but that was a good two miles before I saw the fire.'

Pritchard looked at John Vaughan as if to say *Now we're getting somewhere*.

'How long did it take you to cover those couple of miles?'

I shrugged, 'Three or four minutes at most.'

'And the fire was well developed . . . when you saw it?' put in John Vaughan.

'Yes.'

'Was there anything suspicious about the motorcyclists?' asked Pritchard.

'They were travelling fast, but that was all – no more than you'd expect from bikers on a clear road.'

'What were they dressed like?'

I thought back. 'Dark clothing. Motorcycle leathers and black crash helmets. Nothing distinctive.'

Pritchard shook his head. 'Well, I'd say leathers were distinctive – in the heat we've been having.'

His voice trailed away, as though he was considering his own words.

'Leathers are worn for more than warmth, they're protection,' I offered.

He shook his head again. It was like talking to a brick wall.

'What else did you notice about these bikers, Mr Jay?'

'That was it: dark clothing and driving fast.'

'No registration numbers?'

I shrugged. 'I had no reason to note them.'

'So you didn't see anything else, then?' he persisted.

I flicked my gaze towards John Vaughan and the runner flashed through my mind. Despite what I'd just said about not having an agenda, my curiosity was aroused, not least by Pritchard. For the moment, I decided not to say anything more.

'If I think of something I'll contact you.'

Pritchard nodded. 'We may need to talk to you further.'

His mobile phone ringing interrupted him.

'Excuse me.'

He went outside the room and closed the door after him.

I looked at John Vaughan. 'Am I supposed to have done something wrong?'

'Wrong?'

'Your boss doesn't seem to like me.'

He was about to say something when Pritchard stuck his head around the door.

'John, I've got to go over to the crime scene. Can you finish off here?'

'Of course, guv.'

'Join me when you're done.'

'Right you are, guv.'

With Pritchard gone, John Vaughan seemed to relax more.

'You were starting to tell me why your boss has a problem with me?'

'Not with you – as such.' He pushed his hair out of his eyes.

'Who, then?'

He paused, then shrugged. 'He's worried that people will think that we can't handle the investigations. Being a rural police force.'

'Investigations?'

'It's complex . . .' His voice trailed away.

'So tell me.'

'What happened yesterday is not a one-off crime. There've been other incidents.'

'Such as?'

He smiled. 'You sound like an inquiry agent.'

'I nearly died myself back at that house. I'm entitled at least to know why.'

He paused, but his eyes held mine, like he was satisfying some hidden protocol. Then he smiled, almost shyly. 'You'll learn it from somebody else if I don't tell you. It's the talk of every pub from here to Aberystwyth.'

I folded my arms and laid back deeper into the sofa.

'The man that was murdered yesterday was working for a mining company. He was part of a team that are surveying the estuary – for gold.'

'And?'

'And for the last two months we've had a series of attacks on the surveying team. Gear stolen, a truck burnt out, two of the team beaten up one night so bad that one of them might lose the sight of an eye.'

'Why?'

Vaughan took a deep breath. 'No one wants the estuary touched. But it goes deeper, see. The survey's stirred up the past.'

'The past?'

He nodded. 'Back in the seventies and eighties we had a campaign of arson carried out against second homes bought up by outsiders and used for weekends and a few weeks in the summer – barely two months of the year.'

'That rings a faint bell.'

'It should do,' he said. 'It went on for years and was covered in all the national newspapers at one time or another. At first the arson didn't stop people buying and it got so local families couldn't afford accommodation because the house prices had gone through the roof.'

'I see. And who was starting these fires?'

'Groups of radicals – the Welsh Defence Force, Meibion Glyndwr . . .'

'The who?'

'The Sons of Glendower.' He paused and studied me. 'They're named after a medieval nobleman who tried to make Wales an independent kingdom . . . as it once was.' He waved a hand dismissively. 'These radicals were trying to make a point, see. Between them they set fire to dozens of holiday homes.'

'Okay, but what does that have to do with yesterday's murder?'

Vaughan stood up and gazed out of the window. 'That estuary out there is the most beautiful thing. You should see it in autumn, when the colours on the hillsides change. Rare beauty.'

'And the mining will change that?'

'That's what people believe.'

'What about the environmental laws? I'd have thought a place like this was protected.'

He sat down again and leaned forward. 'In theory.'

'But not in practice?'

'As I said, that's what people believe.'

'You said something just now. Something about the arson not stopping people buying at first . . . what *did* stop them?'

He got up again and looked out the window. Then he turned and looked directly at me.

'Back in the eighties there was a radical group that was very shadowy. They were more extreme than the others.'

'More extreme than the arsonists?'

'Yes. This group was thought to be small; impossible to infiltrate. They weren't satisfied with burning just the holiday homes – they set fire to them when they were occupied.'

'Anybody killed?'

'No . . . at least, not at first. People suffered burns and smoke-inhalation, but that was it. Then a man from London, with a second home near Ganllwyd, was killed.'

'When was all this?'

'Two years ago. Since then it's been quiet.'

'Till now?'

'Yes.'

'You've lost me. Are you saying that there's a connection with these previous arson cases?'

He went back to the window and looked out across the estuary once more. I saw the same tension in him then that I'd seen earlier in Pritchard.

'Do yourself a big favour, Mr Jay. Have your treatment – and go home.'

4

When John Vaughan left I found Julia, who told me that she'd rearranged my appointment with the therapist Elizabeth Rhys-Davies for half-two.

I went upstairs and unpacked my bags. It seemed the last act of acceptance that I was here.

Then I lay down and closed my eyes for a bit.

Tiredness had been a feature of my stress and had a tendency to hit me without warning, but I felt that this wave was due mainly to the previous day's journey.

Recurrent thoughts of Jenny were also a feature of these periods of fatigue, hitting me at my lowest. I would examine everything that had happened between us; her affair, the nightmare that followed and particularly our brief reconciliation.

At this distance honesty was easier.

I had taken her back not because I wanted her, but because I *needed* her. Whatever her faults, she could connect with me on a deeper level than any woman I'd known.

But she used it.

She could make me want her with just a look. She had a way of moving, of standing, the sexual and the sensual entwined, so that you were irresistibly drawn. She manipulated by reward; play the game and she was yours.

Each passing day without her made the situation clearer; it hurt to have her enter your life, but the exit wound was massive, fatal.

When she'd left me I lost the plot. Such was my anger I could barely sleep. Then came her return and I was desperate to keep her, so desperate that I made mistakes. I gave her too much too quickly and between my need of her and her . . . wanting of me, the mistakes of the past were reborn.

I had wanted contrition and faithfulness. She had wanted me, but was drawn to him. Well, now I knew. She wasn't going to change. The question was could I?

The alternative was to live life without her. To never again feel her nakedness against me, to never wake with her curled into my body. And it felt too soon for that.

I'd been hurt, but I wasn't finished.

There might be other ways, other options. What if I went back and fucked my way to freedom? What if I revisited the centre and then withdrew at my own pace? Could I take back what she had stolen from me and creep away?

I'd always hated it when she was calculating and told myself I could never be the same, but I had to do something.

It wasn't a nice thought to know that that was inside me.

Kindness, consideration and harmony were hardly the benchmarks for our relationship. But Jenny's sins were more character flaws worked through with guile than cold, dispassionate logic.

On balance, I knew I wasn't capable of seeing through such a plan. Simply because I still loved her. Hurt caused by anger was one thing, cruelty, even if born of necessity, was another.

Accept or walk; that's what it really came down to.

I closed my eyes, imagining her next to me, remembering the feel of her skin, the sound of her voice. And that look. The eye contact that said, 'I want you, don't you want me?'

Because I'd been vulnerable the answer had always been yes. Now I would make myself explore other options, but from strength, not weakness. If I could.

I drifted off and was woken by the telephone ringing. It was

Julia telling me that lunch was ready. I stretched, splashed cold water on my face and then made my way downstairs.

I was the only one in for lunch and sat mentally preparing myself for the first session with Elizabeth Rhys-Davies.

No matter how it was portrayed, to most firefighters the thought of therapy was unwelcome. Privately, if not publicly, there was a stigma attached. I'd seen a number of men who had been going through a crisis, end up for ever marked as someone who'd failed to cope.

Looks were exchanged whenever they entered a room or committed the sin of venturing a viewpoint, unaware that they were no longer entitled to confidence.

So I'd held back for as long as I could, knowing only too well that I was in need of something. Guilt over Sandy was the decider; for it had spread to every other area of my life until I was examining my every fault and giving myself hell in the process.

Getting clear of London, getting rid of the flat and coming out here was a start. I had no idea what the therapy would involve and felt uneasy at the thought of someone, anyone, listening to my life and judging it, much less telling me what I had to do to put it right.

But the big fear was what might emerge.

What if it was all my fault? What if deconstruction meant complete destruction? What if what was left was a husk; a man too afraid to take a chance, too apologetic to stand alone?

That would not happen. I'd rather try and fail than curl into a ball. I needed a release from guilt and a few tools for survival, not a series of socially acceptable litanies – slogans for the defeated.

I'd rather be ailing than dead.

Just before half-two, I met Julia in reception and she took me up the main staircase, along a gallery leading to the western side of the building. With every step I told myself to relax, that nothing could happen unless I allowed it.

On reaching the door Julia gave me a smile of encouragement and I gave myself some stick for joining the sad bastards of life.

She knocked and then stood back to let me pass.

I found myself in a large octagonal room that was part of the tower I'd seen the previous night. The tower joined the building on two sides, revealing panoramic views of the estuary and gardens.

In contrast to the rest of the house, the room was full of light, with bright sunlight pouring through the angled windows. The walls were covered with a dense yellow paper edged by an impressionistic frieze and the varnished floors were covered in heavy Afghan rugs.

Standing at the centre of the room, by a semicircle of armchairs, was the woman I'd seen running before breakfast. She smiled and came over to greet me.

'Welcome to Ty Hiraeth, Steve. I'm Elizabeth Rhys-Davies.'

I shook her hand. 'Good morning, Doctor.'

She smiled again, the same smile that Julia used – the soul-destroying 'Trust me, I'm a friend' smile.

'Sit down, Steve . . . and it's Elizabeth. It's all first names here.'

Sweet Jesus! It's worse than I thought.

If she read anything on me she didn't let it show. For my own part I studied her carefully, and probably not too subtly.

She continued with the welcome speech. 'Myself and Eric, that's Eric Lawrence, the head of the unit, want you to feel that this is a place where you can relax and get the most benefit from the counselling.'

I nodded.

'Would you like some tea or coffee?'

'Coffee would be fine,' I replied.

Elizabeth went over to a small table by the door and brought back a tray with a stainless steel coffee pot and two cups. As she poured the coffee I went back to studying her.

She was good-looking: a healthy, outdoors type with soft green eyes that seemed to take in everything. As she handed me the coffee cup that bloody smile popped up again, like a jack-in-the-box. I found myself smiling back automatically. I would have to watch that, politeness just might be the back door to hell.

'Help yourself to sugar, Steve.' She pushed the bowl towards me. 'I was told by Julia that you had an unfortunate time getting here?'

I paused, not because I was angry but because I was acutely aware that this was an ice-breaking question, where you find yourself talking without quite realising why. The problem with pauses is that they merely delay the inevitable.

'You mean the house fire?' I asked.

'Yes.'

'It was more unfortunate for the occupier.'

'Yes. I believe someone died?'

Pause. 'Yes, they did.'

'Tell me, how are you feeling after the fire?'

'Fine. No ill effects.' I should have left it at that, but that simple question was also the big question – how was I coping?

'You were going to say something, Steve?'

'Only that I'm a firefighter.'

'Okay . . .'

It was her turn to pause. I hadn't meant my statement to sound hostile, but that was the way it came out and in stating the obvious I'd just revealed how edgy I really was. I tried to make amends and only ended up sounding like a total prat.

'I meant that fires are my job . . . so you wouldn't expect problems.'

Given that I was here because of my failure to cope with

Sandy's death that had to be the biggest crock I'd achieved to date. Bone-bloody-stupid and getting worse by the minute.

To her credit, she avoided my eye and scratched at a notepad. A tactful change of direction also helped.

'Have you filled in the form Julia gave you, Steve?'

I nodded and handed it to her. She took a minute to study it and then looked up and smiled.

'No medication, then?'

I shook my head. 'I stopped taking painkillers a few weeks ago.'

'No sleeping pills?'

'No.'

'Nothing for blood pressure?'

'No, nothing.'

She made some notes on the form. 'And when was the last time you saw a doctor?'

'When I discharged myself from hospital.'

She frowned. 'Not since? Not even your GP?'

'No.'

'Any particular reason?'

'I think . . . I think I needed to detach myself from people. And I suspected that a fistful of pills was only going to block out the problems, not deal with them.'

At that she gave a short nod.

'Would you object if I got Eric to give you a medical? Given your history it might be helpful, Steve.'

I shrugged. 'Okay.'

'Good.' She reintroduced the smile on a trial basis. 'Do you know anything about what we offer here in the way of therapy?'

'Not a lot.'

'Right. Well, basically we offer a series of sessions during which we attempt to discover exactly what it was that led to your stress. Then, we examine ways in which you can de-stress and finally we advise on ways in which you can prevent it happening in the future.'

'Sounds good.'

'Maybe, but it calls for you to be honest, Steve – completely open. If you hold back or refuse to discuss the things that have caused problems then there is a limit to what we can do.'

'Fair enough.'

She placed the form down on a small table beside her chair and picked up the notebook again. I could feel it coming and willed myself to relax.

'Okay, Steve, can you tell me why you feel you have to be here?'

Her voice was soft, but not artificially so. It was like two people chatting about a third. Having given me the veiled warning about clamming up, she'd called me out. Talk or walk.

'I think I blundered on the fire-ground. I made a decision to commit two men into a building. There was a backdraught – that's like a low-intensity explosion, it occurs when a room has been starved of oxygen and there is lots of heat present. Someone entering the room causes air to rush in, forcing a rapid ignition.'

She scribbled a note. 'You said "blundered", Steve?'

I tried to catch her eye, to weigh her, to see if I could trust this person with my shame. It wasn't guile I was searching for, but judgement, the judgement of someone with the luxury of never having been on the edge, with only skill and nerve preventing you from losing it.

For a moment we looked at each other, both knowing what was going through my mind, knowing how hard it was to open up.

'There were signs . . . thick smoke, blackened windows, things that should have swayed my judgement.'

'So why didn't they?'

We were at the crunch so quickly I almost gasped.

'There were other factors . . . the windows had gone at the front of the building. To ventilate at the back might have caused a through draught and the fire would have got out of control.'

'If that was so, how did you blunder? You had a choice and made it. What else could you've done?'

'I don't know. I've gone over this a thousand times in my head. I could have – should have – played it safe.'

She made another note. 'Okay, so why didn't you?'

If my previous answer about the house fire sounded weak then this time it was transparent.

'Because we're firefighters. It's what we do.'

More scribbling. 'Could there have been other people in the building? I mean, was there even an outside chance?'

'You can never be a hundred per cent certain.'

'Was this part of your thinking?'

'Yes . . . but—'

'But what?'

I sighed. 'But I would have sent them in anyway. We're firefighters . . . sorry.'

'Don't apologise, Steve, not to me,'

I searched for another way of saying it.

'It goes against the grain to let a building burn . . . not if it can be saved.'

She put down her notepad. 'I'm going to stop there. Tomorrow I want to go straight back to that idea, about what it is that makes firefighters enter a building that's on fire.'

'How does that relate to my ignoring the signs of an impending backdraught?'

'Just think about why you do your job and the risks it poses. We'll talk more tomorrow.'

I got up. 'Is this how it's done? I tell you things and you pose the questions?'

'There's no structure, Steve. No structure and no rules.'

'And this will take away the feelings of guilt that I have? You see, I'm not convinced that it is guilt, I think it might be just sound judgement.'

'You have to give it a chance, Steve.'

I nodded, but more from politeness than belief. She read it in me and sat down again, beckoning me to do the same.

'There are other ways which we feel can help. Running, hillwalking and swimming are all good ways to release endorphins, your body's own morphine, into your system. It gives you a natural high and counters many of the effects of stress and depression. We also offer massage, for the sense of relaxation and well-being that it gives you. We're short on pills and long on nurture.'

'I see,' I said flatly.

Elizabeth smiled. 'We're not faith healers here, Steve. All the treatments we offer have a proven medical effect. My suggestion is that you try them all. Sometimes the causes of the problems that bring people here are very complex and not what they first appear. By going along with the programme you should find that you are able to open up more easily.'

'How long does all this take?'

'It varies. Not everyone has the same problems or to the same degree. Are you married?'

'No.'

'Family?'

'No.'

She paused. 'No one waiting for you back in London?'

I hesitated. 'Not now.'

'Then try not to worry about time. Ty Hiraeth is a wonderful place that has a lot to offer you. Let it do just that.'

The session ended with Elizabeth saying that she would try to arrange for Eric Lawrence to give me a medical sometime the next day. She then told me my next session with her was the following day at ten a.m. and gave me a schedule of when the swimming pool would be open.

'You can arrange a massage session through Julia. Just tell her after breakfast any day.'

'And the walking?'

She smiled. 'Are you a walker?'

'Not serious, but it looks good walking country. I thought I'd give it a try.'

'How about tomorrow morning at ten?'

'Isn't that our appointment?'

She turned her head to one side. 'We can walk and talk.'

'Okay,' I said slowly.

'Have you got walking boots with you, Steve?'

'I thought maybe trainers . . . no?'

She shook her head. 'See Bryn Thomas – you should find him in reception at this time of day. We keep a stock of boots, waterproofs and day-sacks for residents.'

I paused. Whatever I'd expected from Ty Hiraeth, this wasn't it.

Elizabeth smiled me away. 'See you at ten tomorrow, Steve.'

I closed the door behind me and breathed out. So much for staying in control. Either she was good or I was nearer the surface than I realised.

Downstairs I searched around until I found Bryn Thomas in the dining room. He was looking across to the far side of the river, to a growing cloud of smoke rising up from the thickly forested bank.

He looked at me and nodded hello. 'Looks nasty, I'd say.'

'How far does that forest go?' I asked.

He sucked his teeth. 'Too far.'

Bryn Thomas was a thickset, red-faced guy in his late fifties with habitually amused eyes. He told me that he was an ex-firefighter from Barmouth, who served as odd-job man and general helper around the place.

'So you've fought fires like that, then?'

'I have,' he said, 'but I'd say that this is the worst year for some time. The lads'll be earning their keep.'

I stared across the water. The red glow of flame flared spasmodically in the thick white smoke.

'Can they not lift from the river?'

He tilted his head to one side and sucked at his teeth. 'Yes, they can lift, but moving hose about on the hillside is another matter altogether.'

'Steep?'

'Steep and rocky. The fire can move a lot faster than a man in there.' He turned away from the window to face me.

'My name's Steve,' I said, 'Steve Jay. Elizabeth said I should see you about walking boots.'

Bryn held his hands out as if to grasp me. 'Ah, boots, is it? Well, we have a fine selection, mind. Follow me.' He led me back to the reception desk and retrieved a notepad and a pen from beneath it. 'Now, would you be wanting any particular size?'

'Nines.'

He nodded. 'Nines with one pair of socks or two? Normal to wear two pairs when walking – saves blisters, you see.'

'So tens, then?' I asked hesitantly.

He shook his head. 'Depends how thick the socks are, really. Now, will you be wearing proper walking socks or something else?'

'I shall need proper walking socks?'

'Oh yes!'

'I don't have any.'

He gave a nod and waited for me.

'So I'd need to buy some, wouldn't I?' I said slowly.

'That you would, boyo.'

I looked at the floor. 'Would you by any chance know where I could buy some?'

He leant forward on the reception desk. 'Yes.'

'I'm listening,' I said.

'Well, let me see, I could get you some when I go in to Dolgellau in a hour's time and leave them here for you when you come down for dinner. Now, it's normal to have inner and outer socks. Would you be wanting both?'

'Have I a choice?'

'Not if you're going to avoid blisters.' His grin was infectious.

'Besides socks, what else might I need?'

'Well, the boots at Ty Hiraeth are good, Gore-Tex, very comfortable they are. And you'll not need a day-sack 'cos they have some very fine ones here, but you might need a sunhat.'

'Sunhat?'

'Very strong of late, the sun. Very strong.'

'You'd advise it?'

'I would.'

'How expensive is all this going to be?'

He winked. 'Cheaper than you can buy in the town. My brother owns an outdoors shop and I get good discounts for customers. Now, give me your hat size and we'll work it out.'

Feeling the fleeced tourist, I gave him my size and to my surprise he said not to pay until I'd tried on the socks and hat and was happy with both.

'We'll sort your boot size out when you've got the socks,' he said, 'oh, by the way, Mr Jay, there was a phone call for you earlier.'

'Me?'

'A Mr McGregor. He said he'd phone back later.'

'Thanks.'

'All part of the service, really. We're meant to make you feel at home.'

I shook my head. 'Home's cheaper.'

He laughed. 'I imagine it is.'

5

Between the police interview and the therapy session my day seemed to have been spent on the back foot.

It was inevitable that in the wake of the fatal house fire I would come under scrutiny from the police. But coupled with Elizabeth Rhys-Davies's therapy session it felt like I was being required to justify every area of my life – and I'd taken just about enough.

It was still only a quarter to four and too hot and sticky to hang around inside the house, so I retrieved a book from my room and went in search of somewhere in the grounds where I could stretch out and read.

On my way through reception Julia Lloyd intercepted me. Behind her, hanging back and watching, was a woman in her late twenties. Julia looked worried and when she spoke her voice was low.

'Steve, are you busy at the moment?'

I lifted the hand with the book. 'I was just going find some shade.'

She nodded and turned towards the other woman. 'Steve, I'd like you to meet my sister Anne. Anne, this is Steve Jay.'

Despite myself I stared.

Women who are genuinely beautiful are usually one of three types: those who are at ease with it, those who aren't and those that appear unconscious of it. Anne Lloyd was one of the latter.

She had the same dark brown hair as her sister, but with a

more delicate face and large soulful brown eyes. She was tanned and fit and her shape suggested that she was a swimmer, with shoulders tapering to a small flat stomach and the proportions of curve to size near-perfect.

I put her height at around five six, perhaps a shade taller, and there was grace in the way she moved, making me switch my guess from swimmer to dancer. She was dressed in tight jeans that finished halfway down her calves and a straight-necked red T-shirt, worn without a bra.

'Anne would like a word with you, Steve . . . about the fire yesterday.'

Holding out her hand, Anne Lloyd said hello in a southern middle-class accent that held the merest trace of a Welsh lilt. Her hand was soft and delicate, but her grip was firm and those soulful brown eyes seemed to bore right into me, as though she were searching for something.

There was a definite presence to her, vulnerability and strength in equal measures and much as I was loath to answer any more questions, whoever asked them, I agreed, providing it was kept short.

'Thank you, Steve. Would you like to use the lounge, Anne?' said Julia.

Anne Lloyd shook her head. 'Where were you heading when we stopped you, Mr Jay?'

'The garden,' I replied.

She inclined her head, as if to say, 'Okay, let's go.'

Just before we left her, I caught a look of concern in Julia's eyes and although Anne Lloyd didn't react, I thought I detected some tension between the sisters and the impression that it somehow centred on me. Intrigued, I let myself be led out into the gardens.

Outside, the afternoon sun was fierce and a heat haze made the gravel pathway dance as we walked away from the house. A scorching westerly wind moved the treetops and I thought of the firefighters on the other side of the river battling the forest fire, hampered by the wind and broken terrain.

A hundred yards from the house Anne Lloyd stopped under the shelter of a huge oak that lay at the centre of the manicured lawn.

'Here?' she asked.

'Fine.'

We sat down opposite each other and I looked about; the gardens were empty, the only sound coming from the wind as it moved through the treetops.

'Well, if you wanted a quiet word then this has to be the spot. What exactly is this all about?'

Anne Lloyd studied me. A lot of people had done that lately, as though weighing their suspicion against their need.

'Julia tells me that it was you that tried to rescue Hugh Jones from the house last night, Mr Jay. Was it?'

'Yes, it was – and it's Steve.'

The eyes swept over me, ignoring the appeal for informality. 'People are talking . . .' She caught her breath and turned away. When she turned back she looked tense. 'There are rumours, some are saying that Hugh was murdered.'

'You knew him?' I asked.

'Yes.'

I inclined my head, for her to elaborate, but she made me ask.

'Was he a relative? Friend?'

'He was a local. Everyone knows everyone around here.'

There was something in her voice or maybe she just spoke a little too quickly; either way I noted it.

'Okay, he's just a local – so your interest is what, exactly?'

'Julia says that you are an inquiry agent.'

I looked at the ground and shook my head. What was it with the people around here? I didn't need this, I really didn't.

'Then Julia's wrong. I'm a firefighter. No, that's not strictly true either, at the moment I'm a resident undergoing therapy. Now if that's all you've brought me out here to say . . .' I stood up to go.

'Wait! Please.'

I turned away and looked over the river. The fire was spreading eastward before the wind, and insistent red flames were infiltrating the trees. They'd be running now, sweating and cursing, trying to outflank it, forcing the fire towards the river, the natural firebreak.

That's what I would have done.

I may not have fought a forest fire, but I knew a little of the basics. As with all fires you analyse it, look for its options, its natural line of spread. Ultimately you have three options: surround it and kill it, deny it oxygen or deny it fuel.

Here the third option applied: drive it towards the river and you gave it nothing to burn.

It hit me suddenly that I was still suspended, with a good chance of never being in charge of a fire again. The realisation produced a hollow ache in my stomach. My life may have moved on before I was ready.

Everyone has something at which they excel or at least hit their natural rhythm. With me it was firefighting. It gave my life shape, purpose.

For all my faults I functioned best on the fire-ground; it was my natural habitat. I'd made mistakes and occasionally I'd second-guessed a fire and had had to backtrack, but I saw that as positive, the required flexibility to get the job done.

In Sandy's case I could have – should have – anticipated what happened, but I made the best call I could. I knew that deep within me. But I also knew that sometimes your best call isn't enough.

In weaker moments, down days, when the doubt was eating me alive, the internal interrogation would start; the self-examination that was never satisfied and couldn't be switched off.

And always it came down to the same unanswerable question: did I make my best call – or was I simply unable to face the truth?

'Mr Jay? Mr Jay?'

Anne Lloyd's voice shook me free of my introspection. I looked at her, not quite sure what she'd said.

'Sorry?'

'Are you all right, Mr Jay?'

I sighed. 'That's a matter of opinion.'

'What?'

'Never mind. What were you saying?'

'Julia said that the police interviewed you this morning.'

'Yes – yes, they did.'

'Can I ask you to tell me what it was that they were interested in?'

Was the world going mad or was it me?

'No, I can't. Look, Miss Lloyd, I came here for some rest – d'you understand?' I couldn't keep all the anger from my voice. 'Last night I happened on a house that was alight and did what any other firefighter would do in the same circumstances. That's it, the whole story. I have no agendas, no interest, and absolutely no involvement in whatever has been going on around here. Now I really do think our conversation has come to an end.'

'I think it was my fault,' she said quietly.

'Sorry?'

'Hugh Jones was supposed to meet me last night. He had some information for me.'

I was my own worst enemy. 'Information about what?'

Her eyes locked on to mine. 'Why would Julia say you were an inquiry agent?'

I sighed. 'Look . . .'

She gave a tight smile. 'Anne.'

I nodded and breathed out audibly, trying to control my

response, knowing that she couldn't be aware of the strain I'd been under.

'Anne, you seem a nice person, so I will tell you the most important thing I told the police. I'm not an inquiry agent.'

'But—'

'I did a favour for a friend. It was a one-off and I still carry the scars, literally. I have no intention of repeating the experience, because the price of my involvement was to end up here. And I don't want to be here, not really. I want to be back at my fire station, doing what I do best.'

The answer seemed to shake her. She just sat there, staring at me as though I'd let her down. It made me feel uncomfortable and guilty. I took a deep breath and exhaled slowly.

'You seem to want something from me. I can't imagine what that might be, but whatever it is I can't give it to you, truly.'

My words hung in the air and should have brought the conversation to a conclusion. Anne Lloyd had other ideas.

'I want to hire you, Mr Jay.'

And there it was. The rock that had so nearly broken me had just rolled back into view.

'Did you hear anything of what I said?'

'I'll pay you the going rate.'

I held my hands up. 'Stop. Please.'

'I'm sorry.' She stood up. 'I'm frightened, Mr Jay. So frightened that I'd approach a stranger on the off chance he could help me . . . I didn't mean to cause you distress. I'd be obliged if you didn't mention this to anybody. Especially about Julia telling me you were an inquiry agent.'

She turned and started walking away. My anger melted as guilt put in its regular post-conversational appearance. Anger can wreck your life in an instant, love can destroy it without you knowing, but guilt has stamina. It can't kill, but it'll gently fuck you until common sense is warped beyond recovery.

I sighed. 'Wait.'

She stopped and slowly turned around.

'I'll listen,' I said flatly.

'Listen?'

'That's what you want, isn't it?'

For a moment she said nothing, just stood there, with an expression somewhere between reservation and accusation, then wandered back. We both sat down again. The air was thick with heat, making my shirt stick to my back. She took out a handkerchief and dabbed at her neck; her slender neck.

'I'll be blunt with you, Anne. I don't think I can help. I'll listen, but I'm not for hire.'

'I see. So what would be the point of telling you?'

I shrugged as if to say that was my point. 'I'll give you my best advice.'

I hated that term. It was one of the new Brigade concepts that burrowed into memos and figured in the language of Brigade apparatchiks and rising-star officers who wanted to be seen to be 'on message'. The second I heard it I would mentally dive overboard and yet here I was, using the same bloody inanity.

She seemed to be deciding what to do. For my part curiosity was gradually starting to kick in, if only because in looking for a place to de-stress and sort my life out I seemed to have landed on an anthill.

'It's hard to know where to begin.' She took another deep breath. 'I'm part of an environmental watch group. We're a bit like Greenpeace, except that we deal only with Wales.'

'Does this group have a name?'

'Eco-watch.'

I nodded, 'Okay. What does Eco-watch do?'

She pushed her hair back off her face. 'Pretty much what you'd expect, really. We monitor pollution and intrusive use of the earth, sky and sea.'

'And what do you do when you find it?'

For a second I thought she was going to look away. Instead she nodded, acknowledging the fact that the question was loaded.

'We take direct action.'

'Like burning second homes?'

'I've never burnt down anybody's home.'

'But you know a few that might, is that it?'

The heat was making me irritable, but I was also trying to get her to reveal herself. It wasn't that I thought she'd lie so much as being aware that only a fool would be completely open with a stranger.

'*I* would never do it.'

'Okay, *you* would never do it. Do you approve of those that do?'

'I understand their motives.'

I crossed my arms and looked over her shoulder to the river bank in the distance. The fire was getting away from them. The wind had changed direction, driving the fire south of the river. The speed at which the fire spread was educational. Even from where I was I could see how dangerous conditions had become. Make a mistake in that terrain and you were in serious trouble.

'So how far do you go? What exactly does "direct action" mean?'

'Anything that protects the environment, but doesn't hurt people.'

'That's a lot of licence.'

The brown-eyes became hard. 'The earth is only pristine once, Steve. Abuse it and we'll lose it for ever.'

'By that you mean the Black River Mining Company?'

She gave a brief humourless smile. 'What do you know of them?'

'Only that Hugh Jones worked for them and someone's been causing them grief.'

'The Black River Mining Company is a part of OPMA.'

'You say that like I should know what that is.'

'Everyone should know what it is. OPMA is short for the Oil, Pharmaceutical and Mining Agency. It's a multinational with a gross national product in excess of Mexico's.'

'And you don't like multinationals?'

'It's not a question of like or dislike. OPMA intends to conduct mining operations here.'

'How? Aren't there environmental laws against that sort of thing?'

'John Joshua Roth, the head of OPMA, has been very clever. There isn't much in the way of work around here, apart from tourism, which is seasonal. There's agriculture, forestry and of course some fishing, but that's it.'

'So?'

'OPMA have done a deal. In exchange for mining rights they'll build a huge technology park and IT research centre near to Aberystwyth.'

'I see.'

'And just to make the whole thing watertight they intend to build low-cost housing, like a modern estate village.'

'Clever. And what's a little gold against that? Is that what you're saying?'

I expected her to come straight back at me. Something along the line that John Vaughan took, about the estuary being beautiful. I was wrong.

'Gold has got nothing to do with what's happening around here, Steve. The dredging for gold is a blind; an attempt to draw the hostility of the locals. The real deal is copper. OPMA intend to conduct opencast mining on a scale that would kill this land for the next two hundred years.'

6

Even through the fog of my preoccupations I could appreciate the significance of what Anne Lloyd had said. The very term 'opencast mining' had a tendency to send environmentalists ballistic.

Emotive terms such as 'rape' and 'ravage' were regularly used to decry and label it in attempts to turn the mining companies into pariahs.

Like everybody else I'd seen television footage of wild, natural landscape torn open and despoiled, with mineral veins ripped from the earth leaving spoil heaps to poison the land and watercourses.

If Anne Lloyd was right then what OPMA intended to do was the political equivalent of kicking over an ants' nest and sooner or later every type of eco-warrior, from tree-huggers to tree-muggers, would make a beeline for this part of Mid-Wales. Throw in the possible link to murder and a natural villain in the shape of a multinational and things could get out of control very quickly.

Did Pritchard know about the opencast mining? Was that why he was nervous?

'How do you know about this?' I asked her.

She crossed her legs and leaned forward, her elbows on her knees. 'Hugh Jones told me. Last night he was meant to meet me and hand over proof.'

'And now he's dead?'

'Yes.'

'So go tell the police what you told me.'

'I can't.'

'Why?'

'Was Hugh Jones murdered?'

I couldn't see any point in denying it. Within twenty-four hours the police would almost certainly release the news, if only to appeal for witnesses.

'Yes, he was.'

She looked down. 'Then other people are in danger.'

'Including yourself?'

'Yes.'

'Why?'

'According to Hugh Jones, J. J. Roth will go to any lengths to protect OPMA's investment. A huge amount of money has been spent making sure the right people have been "persuaded" to allow this. Believe me, the IT centre, technology park and estate village are just cleverly disguised backhanders; politically acceptable bribes.'

'But if Hugh Jones worked for them why would he tell you?'

'Isn't it obvious?' she put in quickly.

I scratched the back of my neck. '*None* of this is obvious. Hugh Jones was a surveyor working for a mining company. Of all people he could hardly be surprised by what he was doing – and OPMA must realise that once opencast mining begins in earnest then everyone will know. The most they could do is buy some time.'

'That's why I want to hire you. You see, if they knew that Hugh Jones was about to hand over proof, then there's something in it that frightens them. Also, they might know it was me to whom Hugh Jones was handing over the proof. I want you to find out what it is they're frightened of, because if they think I know then I'll be next.'

'My advice is the same: go to the police, Anne. Tell them everything.'

She gave a small bitter laugh and shook her head. 'Multinationals aren't just large and complex businesses, Steve. They have clout, huge political clout. They can bankrupt governments, suborn judiciaries and destroy anything that blocks them. They use the law, they break the law, they bribe key players and frame the ones that won't give way. They—'

'Okay, okay, I hear you.'

The more impassioned her argument, the softer her voice became. I was listening hard, but studying her as well: her mouth, her eyes, the sweep of her neck, the rhythmic movement beneath the red T-shirt.

Slowly, imperceptibly, my detached analysis of what I was hearing was being undermined by the switching on of another, more powerful mechanism.

Her eyes were bright with conviction, 'Have you any idea, Steve, how much of this stuff goes on in the Third World? The price paid by the indigenous peoples and their environment? The multinationals simply buy off the politicians and then do what they like.'

I scratched my head. 'I don't see the link. What works in the Third World doesn't necessarily work here, Anne.'

She cupped her chin in her hands and gave a small sigh. 'You think British politicians don't take backhanders? You don't think governments bend in the financial wind? Who's being naive, Steve? J.J. Roth is treated like a head of state.'

'By our government?'

'By all governments.'

'Then what chance do you have?'

'Wrong question Steve – what *choice* do I have?'

I looked over to the forest fire on the far bank. It had spread. The flames were moving south and east rapidly; there had to be twenty hectares of forest alight. What would I do now if I were in charge? What factors could I bring to bear besides more sweat and legwork? Make a firebreak? With what? Could you get heavy plant in there to cut a way through?

Bryn said it was steep and rocky so my guess was that it would be down to the firefighters going where machines couldn't, enduring the hot, back-breaking work for hour on hour in temperatures that could melt tarmac. Steep and rocky: I could only imagine.

When I switched my attention back to her she had leant sideways on one hand, the T-shirt sloping off one shoulder.

'Everything you say may be true, Anne, and I wish I could help you. But I can't. I wouldn't be any use. I'm not a professional inquiry agent – as I said, I'm a firefighter. You need someone with skills that I simply don't have.'

'I don't—'

'Ring around – Cardiff, Swansea, somewhere in the Midlands, maybe – and get a reputable inquiry agency with skilled people.'

'You won't do it?'

'I can't.'

'Your final word?'

'Yes.'

I was about to stand up when I heard a sound behind me and turned quickly. Thirty yards off to my right, just beyond the edge of the tree line, a solitary figure stood watching. I shielded my eyes against the sunlight and tried to make out the face.

'It's Bonny,' she said.

'Who?'

'Bonny.'

She raised an arm and waved. The figure waved back and then I recognised him as the old man I'd seen crossing the wooden toll bridge the previous evening. We watched him for a moment. He didn't move, but carried on watching us.

Anne got up and walked over to him.

They spoke for several minutes and I noticed that he kept looking over her shoulder at me. It seemed a serious conversation and he was doing most of the talking. Then he turned and strode off into the forest. Anne came back.

'Who's Bonny?' I asked.

'A local character. He's been panning for gold in these hills for years. He shouldn't be here, but he comes and goes as he pleases.' She smiled. 'He's been threatened with a trespass action and even shot at by some of the farmers, but he says he owns the land and has a right to come and go as he pleases.'

'You called him Bonny?'

'Short for bonanza. He reckons there's another big gold strike waiting to be found in these hills and he pans the rivers looking for it. He's usually up around the Glas Glyn, plaguing the life out of the Williams brothers who have a small mine up there.' She laughed. 'He's taken a shine to me.'

'I'm sorry I can't be of use Anne, really.'

She nodded and stood up. 'So am I. I may take your advice about finding a reputable inquiry agency.'

'Do that. Come on, I'll walk you to the house.'

We walked slowly back and I tried to make conversation, but it seemed trite and artificial after everything that had been said. I stopped at one point, when a flare of red from the forest fire caught my eye. Anne Lloyd followed my gaze.

'You want to be there?'

I nodded. 'They look like they could use some help.'

'It's artificial, you know.'

'Pardon?'

'The forest. They grow the trees like corn or wheat. It may look nice from a distance, but the trees are conifers, not native hardwoods.'

'You object to forestry?'

'I object to greed at the cost of the land.'

We walked on again until we came to the house. She turned

and shook my hand, which felt rather formal and strange. Then she took out a pad and wrote in it, before tearing out the page and handing it to me.

'This is my address and phone number . . . should you change your mind about helping me.'

I glanced at the page and then surfed an impulse. 'Look, this seems a little weird, I know, but I don't know anybody here – I don't suppose you'd fancy a drink one night?'

She almost didn't react – perhaps a softening of the eyes – but either way she deflected me effortlessly.

'It might be wise for me keep a low profile for a while. Whoever killed Hugh Jones is still out there.'

She must have thought I was a prize twat. There was murder, ecological heresy and Christ knows what else going on in her life and my response was to parade my hormones. Sometimes I despair of me.

She said that she was going to speak to Julia, so I said goodbye and left her at the house entrance before wandering back to where we'd been sitting previously.

I sat with my back resting on the oak and opened my book, a Steinbeck omnibus, only to immediately close it again. Something caught my eye; the forest fire had got away from them and was building into something awesome. They were in trouble.

Rural fire brigades used volunteers for forest fires, the scale inevitably meant that it was beyond the capability of any local-authority brigade to field sufficient personnel, so Forestry Commission workers, the army, even civilians, pitched in under the direction of firefighters.

An idea started to form that had all the hallmarks of a truly stupid decision; it was made on impulse, it was totally against the logic by which I was supposed to be living and serious physical injury could not be ruled out.

Perfect.

I congratulated myself on being a plank.

Although I knew that I shouldn't get involved, I also knew that I would, the second the idea popped into my head. Whether I went or not would not, could not, affect the overall outcome, but they needed help and the truth was I needed to be there.

I ran back to the house and found Bryn Thomas. He was in the dining room, looking out of the widow.

'Bryn!'

He turned.

'How can I get to the other side of the river without taking my Shogun?'

The smile on his face was humourless, 'They're losing it, aren't they?'

'Big time. I want to go and help – will they be using volunteers?'

He nodded. 'Bound to be, fire like that.'

'So how will I get there?'

He glanced at his watch. 'It's very quiet here at this time of day . . . I could take you in the Land Rover, but if anyone found out, mind—'

'Not from me.'

He turned back to the fire and smiled. 'Come on, then.'

7

Bryn Thomas loaned me a set of overalls and sorted me a pair of walking boots. We changed quickly and avoided passing Julia and Anne Lloyd in the reception area by going out through the French windows in the dining room.

As we climbed into his Land Rover Bryn tapped me on the shoulder.

'If Julia or anyone else asks later we just went to take a look, okay?'

'Fair enough. How far would you say it is?'

'Five miles or thereabouts. We'll head for Abergwynant, if we can get through. That's where they'll be organising from, but there's forest on either side of the road and they may have pulled back to Penmaenpool.'

'You know the people in charge of this, Bryn?'

'I phoned the station at Barmouth and got one of the wives, it's Divisional Officer Davy Morgan. I was his Leading Fireman when he first came in the job and he became a Station Officer before I made Sub. Clever he is and with a way about him. He'll be a Chief Officer one day – though I dare say this brigade's not big enough for his talents and he'll be headhunted by one of the metropolitan brigades sooner or later.'

Bryn gunned the Land Rover and I flicked a glance at the speedometer. He was fluctuating between sixty and seventy, not an ideal speed on a road with hidden bends and the stroboscopic effect of the sun between the trees. I suppressed a nervous smile but couldn't stop myself mentally pushing the brake into the floor.

I saw him take his eyes from the road to the cloud of white-grey smoke; it seemed to be following the line of the river again. He reacted by driving even faster. I would have screamed, but I don't think my body would have caught my voice up.

The road opened out and Bryn took full advantage of it by forcing the last bit of speed from the whining engine and nodding in appreciation at the result. I realised then that his driving style owed nothing to the fire and was instead sheer habit.

About a quarter of a mile away I could see that the traffic was backing up across the bridge and sightseers were choking the roads on the far bank. The Land Rover slowed and came to a halt as we connected with the back of the queue.

Bryn hit the horn and flashed the headlights; he obviously hadn't quite made the adjustment to retirement yet. Heads turned and we attracted one or two old-fashioned looks, but no one moved out the way.

I knew what he was going to do before he did it, but it didn't stop me wincing. The driver-side window was wound down and Bryn stuck his head out.

The stream of invective was loud and inventive, enough to make the heads disappear, but it didn't get us an inch forward. Finally a policeman walked over and, recognising Bryn, created a route through for us.

'I thought he might nick us,' I breathed.

Bryn looked genuinely surprised. 'Why?'

The policeman walked slowly along the bridge, speaking to the drivers. Gradually the jam cleared and we were moving.

Once across, Bryn turned right on to the narrow riverside lane below the road and brought the Land Rover to a halt in front of a picturesque white seventeenth-century hotel.

A narrow riverside road ran past the front of the hotel and the Control Unit was parked in a small car park to the side of the building. A mixture of fire brigade, police and army officers were in conversation around a map laid on the bonnet of a staff car.

Behind them, a platoon of soldiers, with six-foot-long beaters, was just setting off down the road towards the pall of smoke. Passing them from the opposite direction was a stream of exhausted-looking firefighters, their faces blackened and sweat-streaked.

Tables with drinks and sandwiches had been set up beyond the Control Unit and a ragged queue of beat men stood noiselessly waiting their turn. The absence of banter wasn't a good sign.

'It's quite an operation, Bryn. How many men d'you think are involved?'

He shook his head, 'Hard to say – two hundred, two-fifty maybe.'

'How do they organise that?'

'A third fighting the fire, another third resting and the rest held back in reserve. It's important to rest and rotate the crews regularly. Exhausted men make mistakes.' Now let's see if we can get on to the Control Unit and find out what's going on.'

I followed him as he strode towards the red and white vehicle. When we reached it a Station Officer stepped forward to block our path. Bryn just smiled and said that the Incident Commander had asked for him. The man looked unsure, but Bryn practically pushed past and we climbed the steps.

Inside was a group of black-faced fire officers, being de-briefed in Welsh by a Divisional Officer in his late twenties. He looked up as we entered and gave a tired grin.

'Be with you in a minute, Bryn,' he said, switching to English.

A map was pinned up on the wall and various areas were

marked off. One of the areas was shown in red hatching, a small area by the river and just east of a stream. Bryn edged forward and peered at it before nodding slowly. He crossed his arms and shrugged, as though we shared a common understanding.

The debriefing was conducted in short order and within minutes the fire officers filed off the back of the Control Unit.

Then the young divisional officer turned to Bryn.

'Good to see you, Bryn, man. I needn't ask what brings you here.'

'Good to see you, Davy – pity it's not under better circumstances.'

The young divisional officer glanced at the map. 'Well, it's not good at the moment, mind. Between the wind and the land it's damn hard work.'

'Davy, I'd like you to meet a friend of mine, Station Officer Steve Jay, from London. Steve, this is Divisional Officer Davy Morgan.'

We shook hands.

'We've come to help if you can use us, Davy,' said Bryn.

Davy nodded. 'Let me show you.' He pointed to the main shaded area on the map. 'This is where we've been fighting the fire all day.'

'Coed-y-Garth,' put in Bryn.

'Yes. It's being driven by the bloody wind. We've concentrated on keeping it away from the Garth-Angharad Hospital, using the A493 as a firebreak and pushing it towards the river. Unfortunately, this afternoon the wind changed direction and picked up strength. The fire leapt the road just to the west of the hospital, so we had to stop what we were doing and concentrate our efforts there.'

'And what about this area here?' asked Bryn, pointing at the smaller red-shaded area.

'My original plan was to keep the fire between the road and

the river and use the Gwynant brook as the cut-off point. The forest is quite narrow there and it seemed the logical place to try to stop it once and for all.'

'But the wind changed,' said Bryn.

Davy Morgan nodded. 'It leapt the brook. There's conifers running right across the ridge there and my latest information is that it's there that the situation is deteriorating.'

'We saw it across the river – that's really why we're here.' Bryn squinted at the map. 'It's mainly hardwood in the lower part of the forest, though. That'll slow it down.'

Morgan looked doubtful. 'Hardwood, yes, but there's no end of undergrowth and it's dry as tinder. With both a well-developed fire and the strong wind there's the possibility it'll get away from us completely.'

I thought his assessment was short. To my admittedly unspecialist eye it looked out of control already, but I said nothing and watched Bryn.

'Are you lifting from the Gwynant Brook?'

'Yes, Bryn, and several of the little lakes and even on from the Mawddach. But the terrain's so bloody rocky and high that lateral travel by men with hoses is almost impossible.'

'And you'll need water up on the top of the hills – beaters won't touch it.'

'Yes.'

You could hear the frustration in his voice.

'So what's the plan now?' asked Bryn.

'Same as three hours ago. Try to surround it with hose and beaters to force it between the river and the Abergwynant brook. If we don't get a handle on it soon it's going to threaten the Abergwynant Hotel and the hospital itself.' He pointed to the map again. 'With the wind driving it and it'll probably leap the road again here!'

He pointed to a spot on the map, just east of the hamlet of Abergwynant.

'What can we do to help, Davy?'

'I've just sent a body of soldiers with beaters down to the brook with orders to follow the brook south to the forest and try and drive the fire towards the river. That's where I've got most of my people. If you could catch the soldiers up and organise them I'd be very grateful, Bryn. Speak to their officer.'

'Can Steve help?'

'Yes, I'm short on experienced officers – we've a few on holiday and two Sub Officers and three firefighters have been injured fighting forest fires earlier this month.'

'We're your men, Davy.'

We all shook hands again. Davy Morgan handed Bryn a sketch map and indicated the areas where we were to be deployed. Bryn asked a few questions and then Morgan showed us to the door of the Control Unit.

Outside a group of fresh fire officers were waiting to enter.

'See Station Officer Griffith for radios, Bryn, one for both you and Steve.' He pointed to the Station Officer who had previously blocked our path. 'Stay in touch and play it safe.'

Bryn Thomas spoke to Griffith and arranged for the radios and a lift in an army lorry down to the fire.

After a wait of ten minutes while the lorry was loaded, we climbed in and sat on a heap of hose and beaters. The lorry started up and drove westwards along the A493. Bryn shouted above the noise of the vehicle as we fought to keep our balance.

'He's not happy, Davy Morgan. I can tell. He's been fighting forest fires for weeks now, but he's just told me that this is by far the worst. The only good thing about it is that it's near a road and they can get people in.'

Out the rear of the lorry we saw lines men of filing back towards Penmaenpool. They looked whipped and I wondered how long it took them to get to that state. Bryn nodded to one or two of them and they raised arms in reply.

I could smell the smoke strongly now and see the thin smog of its advance. Bryn was absorbed in the sketch map and at one point peered around the end of the lorry canvas. When he turned back he saw me watching him and cocked his head to one side.

'Have you ever fought a forest fire before, Steve?'

'No.'

He leaned forward. 'You'll need to keep your wits about you. Wind direction is crucial, mind. Look around you constantly. Never take the fire for granted. There's no more dangerous place to be than a forest fire.'

'I'll keep it in mind, Bryn.'

He sat beside me and put the map between us.

'We'll split the platoon into two and take half each. Keep them under control at all times. Each man must be able to see the next two men to him on either side. You must keep in touch with the ends of your line.'

'Got that.'

'And we need to get some hose of our own . . . plan'll be to beat out the worst and damp down as we go. Leave nothing behind that might flare up again!'

'You're the boss.'

'Anything too fierce, Steve, and we stand back and let the branch-men soak it before we go forward.'

The lorry slowed where the brook ran beneath the road and we turned down a narrow track towards the Abergwynant Farm. We stopped at a small humpback bridge that spanned the brook.

There were more vehicles here, including a Carmichael Land Rover fitted with a two-delivery pump mounted at the front and several four-wheel-drive multi-purpose units. In London, several of the peripheral stations would give their eye teeth for appliances like these.

I jumped down from the lorry and looked around.

Two hundred yards away I could see the fire racing between the trees and the smoke moving through the sharp hills of Coed-y-Garth and the Abergwynant Woods. Silently I wondered how anybody could fight fire in such an uncompromising tract of land.

A Sub Officer, part of the Forward Control, came over. As he and Bryn talked in Welsh I took the opportunity to walk a little way along the track to where two bulldozers were standing idle.

Dozens of men in army fatigues were lying and sitting on the ground, shattered, their faces betraying their thoughts. Two soldiers were moving among the exhausted men, handing out bottles of water.

Fires, all fires, have a feeling, a rhythm, a direction; when it's going wrong you can taste it.

This fire was winning.

'Steve!' Bryn called me back. 'Steve, when the soldiers get here we're to follow the brook down to the river and relieve another group of soldiers already down there. They're up on the hillside to the right there.' He pointed to the foreground. 'See those buildings over there?'

'Yes.'

'Well, we have to prevent the fire from reaching them.'

I looked at the Sub Officer. 'What about those bulldozers? Can't you cut a firebreak with them?'

He shook his head. 'No drivers.'

'No one?'

His face was impassive, but his voice was tired, irritated almost, like he'd been answering the same question all day.

'The original drivers are bushed. They've been at it for five hours and need a break. Anyway, it's too steep on the hillside for the 'dozers and it's on the top where the fire is moving now.'

Bryn looked back up the road. 'That platoon of soldiers

can't be far behind us. As soon as they get here we'll push on down.'

They came into view a few minutes later, led by a young second lieutenant. They all looked fresh, boyish, except for the sergeant, who looked solid and purposeful. We found out later that they were recruits from a depot in Shropshire that were up here on exercise.

Bryn had a short discussion with the lieutenant and it was agreed that once we were deployed the platoon sergeant would go with Bryn and half the platoon and the other half plus the lieutenant would go with me. The Sub Officer was keen to push us forward and hovered, making the point.

Bryn took the lead, walking briskly, and we all set off down the track running parallel to the brook. In several places, the stream had been dammed and lightweight pumps with suction hose were lifting from the man-made pools.

From each pump, twin lines of hose snaked off towards the woods. Every now and again we passed a hose that had been split by a dividing breeching, turning one length of hose into two. They didn't lack for water; it was access that was causing the problems – that and the wind.

In front, about a hundred yards away, was the forest edge. The tree-covered hillside rose sharply and bright red and orange flames were spreading rapidly.

The smoke was thicker here; you could taste it and feel it in your eyes. It swirled in the air, torn between heat currents and the wind, sending showers of sparks skyward. It was a creepy feeling; the hot wind on your face and the smell of burning triggering deep animal instincts.

This was not a fire that you could hold in your eye.

It *felt* elemental; a force gathering strength from the wind by consuming the forest. It was beyond my experience, my skills.

Bryn stopped and called the lieutenant, the sergeant and myself together and spread the sketch map out on the ground.

'We'll keep our backs to the brook and work our way eastward, behind the fire. Apparently it's burning on both sides of the brook, so we all need to stay sharp.' He paused to look from the lieutenant to the sergeant. 'We'll move into the woods to the east of the brook and relieve a group of soldiers and firemen there.'

At that moment a group of firefighters and volunteers came into view along the edge of the stream, carrying shovels and beaters. They were filthy and when they saw us, headed across to meet up.

Bryn shielded his eyes from the sun.

'It's John Williams.'

John Williams was a big man with shoulders like a heavy-weight's and a hard look to the eyes. He walked quickly, like a man who had spent his life in the hills. The rest of the group struggled to keep up.

'What's happening on the other side of that hill then, lads?'

'Not good,' said Williams. 'That wind's been pushing it along the riverside for hours and if anything it's getting stronger. The fire's in the treetops and it'll be moving faster now.'

'How long have you been here?' asked Bryn.

'Just after midday. All we've managed to do is chase it up and down those bloody hills!'

'Dylan not with you?'

Williams turned and looked back to where his group had emerged from the trees.

'He's gone back. There's a group of soldiers working their way east . . . more of a hindrance than a help. Dylan's gone to warn them to watch out. They've left pockets of fire behind them.' He shook his head. 'Bloody danger to themselves, so they are.'

Bryn chuckled and Williams looked beyond to the group of soldiers we'd brought with us.

'This is Steve Jay, John. He's a firefighter, a real one, from London,' said Bryn.

Williams studied me. 'Is there much forest in London then, Steve?'

'Waltham Forest,' I replied, with a straight face.

He tilted his head. 'That right?' He turned back to Bryn. 'So what job you been given, Bryn?'

'Davy Morgan said to relieve those soldiers and chase it east.'

'Well, you'll know your own mind, Bryn, but I wouldn't go on the other side of that hill and that's a fact. Let it burn toward you. You don't want to get stuck on one of those hills with the fire moving around like it is. It's getting bloody dangerous, so it is.'

'Anyone else down there?'

John Williams looked down. 'Just that bunch of soldiers, Bryn. There are people on the track by the river, though, and that's the safest place to be. They've all the water they need from the river and a good escape route.'

At that moment another man emerged from the forest.

'It's Dylan,' said Bryn.

Dylan Williams came running up to us, panting. He was as big as his brother and, if anything, looked even harder.

'Can't find them, John. God knows where they bloody are! Someone's got to bring them back else they'll get themselves in trouble.'

'We'll find them, lads,' said Bryn. 'Go back and get some rest. There's tea and food at the toll bridge. You've earned it.'

There was another shake of the hands all round and then they continued on up to the road. I turned to Bryn.

'What's wrong?'

He shook his head. 'If they say it's dangerous then it is. I'm wondering whether to go on. Or to send our group back and go and find those soldiers myself.'

He didn't ask me – it wasn't necessary.

'I'll come with you if you go. You can't wander around on you own.'

He looked at me hard, then at the soldiers. 'Two men would be exposed. Help me keep them together, Steve. We're going in to get those soldiers and then we'll all come out together.'

8

Bryn looked at the sketch map again.

'I think we should go in the way John Williams and his group came out. We'll try and reach the Mawddach Way, where the brook meets the river. If John says it's safe there, then that'll be our rally point in case we get separated. From there we'll spread out back down the track and move east to find the soldiers.'

The lieutenant and the sergeant exchanged looks, but said nothing. We were all in Bryn's hands and from where I stood he looked equal to the task. It didn't escape me that I'd taken a back seat in the decision-making. Was that self-protection in the aftermath of Sandy's death or was I merely bowing to Bryn's local knowledge?

We set off, walking quickly, and the brook took us between two fire-scarred hills. The trees quickly closed in, coming down to the far bank of the stream and to the edge of the track on our side; ash and dust swirled around us and the acrid woodsmoke sliced my eyes.

I could hear the fire up on the hill now, crackling and whistling as the wind fanned the flames. Bryn stopped and pointed off to our right. As I peered through the trees I could see flame.

It was hard to make out how big an area was involved, but the trees and undergrowth were well alight and burning away from us to the east. Bryn told everyone to stay where they were and motioned me forward with him.

We walked fifty or sixty yards further down the track and then waded across the brook. On the other side the ground was scorched and the trees fire-damaged. The fire had passed this way, but had been beaten out, leaving glowing embers everywhere.

There was no flame and I realised that Bryn had crossed the brook to make sure it was safe behind us before moving up into the hills where the fire now raged.

He moved quickly and I fought to stay with him. We covered a hundred, maybe two hundred yards over the rocky hillside thick with fire-blackened coniferous trees that reared up sixty feet into the sky.

Here it was still; only the wind raking the treetops disturbed the unreal quiet.

Thin tendrils of smoke curled upward from the ground, unmolested by the air currents far above them and there was a heavy, cloying smell of burnt wood, so strong it seemed to settle on you.

Bryn looked up and pointed at the treetops. 'Passed through here less than thirty minutes ago.'

'I haven't seen any fire this side of the brook, Bryn.'

He nodded. 'No. Let's get back to those soldiers.'

If anything, he went back faster and I gritted my teeth, determined to suffer in silence rather than ask him to slow. I was sweating hard and got the feeling he was testing me, seeing what the townie had in his legs. If he'd asked I could have told him: nothing.

I was at Ty Hiraeth to convalesce. It was barely two months since I'd been run off the road and I was still trying to get back to some kind of fitness of body as well as mind.

Eventually we reached the brook and rejoined the soldiers on the forest track. They looked pleased to see us, but the sergeant exchanged looks with the officer again; I had the feeling that he didn't have as much faith in Bryn as I did.

If Bryn noticed he didn't show it. He called the group together and gave them a quick briefing.

'That side of the brook is clear of fire. When we start our search we'll begin here. We'll spread out and move into the woods on this side. I want you all to be able to see at least two men on either side of you. Lose sight of two men and you're to call out. The line will stop and either Steve or I will come back along the side to re-establish the link. Have you got that?'

They nodded and Bryn set off rapidly down the track alongside the stream. The trees closed in tighter and overhead the leaf canopies joined from both sides of the stream.

The track split, one path leading away from the stream and upwards into the forest. Bryn walked past the branch-off, though he pointed to draw everyone's attention to it. A quarter of a mile further on the trees opened out and the stream changed direction, leaving a pool in the angle formed by the track and its new course. Between the trees we saw an embankment and on the other side was the Mawddach River.

As we climbed the embankment we looked eastwards.

In the distance, about a quarter of a mile away, was a ragged line of firefighters spread out in pairs and aiming jets into the forest. Smoke was blowing above them from the crown fire on the ridge, but where they were the undergrowth was alight as well and they looked like they had their hands full.

Bryn contacted them by radio and told them who we were and that we were going back down the forest track before going up onto the ridge looking for the soldiers.

The reply that came back was short and sharp – 'Do it quick and then get the hell out of it.'

'Have you had any contact with them by radio?' asked Bryn.

'Nothing,' came the reply.

Bryn now looked doubtful.

'What d'you think?' I asked.

'I was hoping we could reach them by radio from this side

and then we wouldn't have to go in after them.' He stared up at the ridge fire and his eyes narrowed. 'Steve, I've changed my mind. The soldiers will remain here. I'm going to go back to that track that leads up to the ridge and do a quick search. If we all go it'll be more dangerous.'

'You said safety in numbers, Bryn.'

He nodded slowly. 'Look at it, Steve. That's now a fully developed crown fire and it's up there on the ridge with the wind driving it. It will be moving fast. There's no way a group this size could move quickly and stay in contact with itself.'

'So what's the plan? You and me?'

'You don't have to come, Steve,' he said.

'Yes, I do.'

The soldiers had been following the conversation and were visibly relieved when they realised the change of plan. Bryn handed his radio to the lieutenant and told him that we would make contact every five minutes. Then he led the way back down the embankment onto the forest track.

If he moved fast before he really turned it on now. At times I broke into a trot to keep up. We reached the track that led up onto the ridge and Bryn stopped.

'Stay close, Steve,' he breathed. 'There's no telling what we'll meet up there. If I say run, then run – and don't stop till we reach the river embankment.'

The track climbed steeply on the burnt hillside and everywhere small fires were burning through the under-growth. I kept glancing up into the canopy, but couldn't see any evidence that there had been a crown fire on this part of the hill. Then smoke started to drift across the track. It was streaky at first, but the higher we climbed the thicker it got.

We reached a point in the track where it went over a small brow and cut back on itself. The wind was stronger here. Bryn stopped and pointed. Fifty yards away, travelling at an angle away from us, was a fully developed crown and undergrowth fire.

Bryn cupped his hands to his mouth and called out. Nothing.

'Where the hell are those bloody soldiers?' he rasped.

'What now?'

We looked all around but could see no one. We were safe where we were, providing the wind didn't change direction.

'We can't get any nearer to the fire. We're taking too many chances as it is. We'll search parallel to it. If that fire changes direction we go left, towards the river.'

We went slower now, conscious of the fire and senses alert to any change in the wind. The track took us in a long loop down the hill towards the river but then cut in sharply towards the path of the fire.

The fire disappeared from view as we went down into dead ground, but sparks began falling on the track and smoke followed them. I started coughing and called out to Bryn to stop.

'We're too near.'

'We'll try to find another way,' he replied.

Suddenly, as we came out of the dead ground, three soldiers came running down the track towards us, yelling. Two of them were supporting a third who had bad burns to his arms and face.

Bryn got them all down into the dead ground and looked at the soldier's burns.

'Is this all of you?' he said as he applied burn-gel bandages to the soldier's arms and face.

One of the soldiers shook his head. 'Twenty of us in all. We got split up when the fire changed direction. There were seven of us in the group that was on this side of the fire. The others must be back there. We'd put the fire out and moved right up on to the ridge, but then the wind just took it and suddenly there was fire all around us.'

'Can you make it back down the track?' asked Bryn.

'Yes.'

'Right then, follow the track until you come to a hairpin bend. It leads down towards the stream.'

The soldier nodded. 'I think I know where you mean.'

'Right then, stay there till we come back for you,' Bryn instructed him.

The soldier looked alarmed. 'Where are you going?'

'To look for the rest of your mates. Now get moving.'

As the soldiers set off down the track, Bryn and I left the track and took a course that took us parallel to the fire again. That was when the wind changed.

In disbelief I saw the fire swirl around the treetops like a whirlwind then go back on itself.

There was a roaring noise and a red tongue chased across the trees behind us, faster than a man could run. In the trees directly above, the fire ripped through the canopy, showering burning debris down on us and igniting the undergrowth.

In seconds it seemed the whole forest had caught alight.

Bryn's face drained, 'Move, Steve, move!'

He pulled me away from the fire in the only direction left to us and we ran flat out with the hollow roaring of the fire in our ears.

We covered the ground fast, but I'd totally lost direction.

Suddenly the wind changed and smoke enveloped us. I was coughing and wiping at my eyes. I felt Bryn's hand grab my arm and pull hard. I stumbled and managed to keep my feet, but the noise of the fire was coming closer.

Fire seemed to be on all sides of us and I could feel the smoke tightening my lungs as I fought to breathe. It was getting to me now. The smoke, the proximity of flames and the blind, flat-out running were clawing at my self-control. Christ knows what was going through Bryn's mind.

Flames and smoke weren't the only problems. The radiated

heat was hitting us and proving more of a hazard than direct burning.

For a brief moment the wind blew the smoke clear and we could see that the ground in front rose steeply. But there was no other way we could go. Then the smoke closed in again.

We held on to each other like drowning men and started to climb.

Bryn was pulling me to the left and instinctively I realised what he was doing. If the fire reached the bottom of the slope, it would travel uphill faster than we could run. We would have to get out of its path or it would overtake us and burn us alive.

We were practically bent double as we scrambled upward. Sweat ran down into my eyes and mouth and my legs felt dead with fatigue. I wasn't sure how long I could keep up the pace.

Every time we tried to traverse to the left to get out of the fire's path, self-preservation stopped us and made sure we concentrated on the more immediate aim of staying ahead of the fire.

Sparks rained down on us as the fire gained ground and I pushed myself to the limit. My pulse pounded in my ears and my lungs ached from the combined effects of exertion and smoke-inhalation, but fear overrode the pain and drove me on.

Bryn was worse than me now. I could see his face was bright red and his breathing laboured. I was now the one pulling him – and he was a dead weight.

Up ahead I could see a wall of rock blocking our way.

'Go left, Bryn,' I gasped.

We lurched to the left, aware that every foot of sideways travel allowed the fire to gain on us. The rock wall seemed to run the width of the hill and I scanned it for a way through, a gap, an easy place to climb, anything.

Ten yards from it I saw a break to the right. It would take us nearer to the fire, but there was no other choice. I dragged

Bryn towards it and immediately felt the difference in radiated heat.

At first he fought me and then realised what I was doing.

The gap was a steep crack running up the rock to the top of the wall, about seven metres long.

As we reached it I went forward and started to climb. Bryn was behind me but moving slower and I reached back and pulled him. The heat was unbearable as we'd virtually stopped moving forward and were instead going vertical.

The radiated heat on my back felt like the fire was about to claim me. I swarmed up the rock, not thinking, not allowing the possibility of failure. Then the crack opened out and we were feet from the top of the wall.

Bryn cried out and I turned, grabbed his collar and hauled him bodily upwards. We lunged for the top and reached it, rolling over the edge and away from the fire.

The top of the wall was also the top of the hill and we stood up some twenty feet back from the edge, looking down on the fire we'd cheated.

Below, stretching down the hillside, the whole forest seemed to be on fire. Fiery eddies danced across the treetops as the swirling heat currents sent the fire backwards and forwards.

Nothing, no one, could survive down there. If the soldiers were in there they were beyond the help of man.

As the fire reached the bottom of the rock wall we turned and started down the other side of the hill. It would hold back the fire, but wouldn't stop it creeping around the edges, which meant that we would have to still move quickly. At least from our vantage point we could pick a good route down.

I started to negotiate the steep escarpment when Bryn stopped me.

'Let me try the radio. Someone by the river must be able to hear us up here.'

Clouds of white smoke were rolling over the top of the hill

and fine wood-ash rained down. I wasn't happy with stopping and it showed in my face.

Bryn nodded. 'Okay, we'll walk fast as we do it.'

I handed him my radio.

It took thirty minutes of hard walking and running to work our way down to the river. Several times we tried to go north towards it, but each time the fire closed in and we had to put more distance between the flame front and ourselves before we could risk a change of direction.

Bryn looked in trouble at one point and I poured the remainder of the water down his throat and over his face. He was strong, but we were being pushed to the limit and the age difference was starting to show.

Eventually we got through on the radio to a group of firefighters working down by the river. They talked us through a route that brought us down to a point called Pant-y-cra. From there we contacted Davy Morgan at Penmaenpool and brought him up to speed with what had happened. He informed us that other soldiers had emerged from the forest and had told the Forward Control about the flash fire.

Somehow they'd made it back to the A493. They'd suffered worse than us, with nearly half their group suffering burns or injuries, including one with a broken leg. Two were missing, believed dead.

As no one had been able to raise Bryn and me it was assumed that we'd been caught up in the flash fire. Rescue crews had been assembled and had gone in search of us. They found the three soldiers that we'd sent back to the track and brought them out.

John and Dylan Williams had led a party down to the flash fire from the Abergwynant end and had tried to force their way through. But by then the fire was too well developed.

The flash fire had caused havoc with a number of other

crews getting into difficulty. The order had come from Pen-maenpool that all crews were to be withdrawn immediately. The new idea was to protect property only and let the fire have the forest.

The effects of dehydration and exhaustion hit the pair of us once we were out of the forest. The firefighters who'd met us at Pant-y-cra sat us down, poured water over our heads and backs to cool us down and then gave us rehydration fluid and mint cake as a source of instant energy.

We were shaken and drained by the experience, but most of our injuries were minor: cuts and scratches and dozens of tiny spark burns. We'd come close and knew it.

The mint cake kicked in after about twenty minutes and Bryn and I walked back to Penmaenpool along the Mawddach footpath in virtual silence.

As we came in sight of the toll bridge Bryn took me to one side.

'I'm sorry, Steve, that was my fault.'

'You didn't have a choice, Bryn.'

'Either way I'm sorry.'

He turned and looked towards the forest. It was then that I noticed for the first time that his right hand was burnt. Bryn seemed inured to the pain, but there was something in his face; anger or deep reflection. Either way, his face was set hard and he glared at the fire in the distance.

9

We got back to Ty Hiraeth around eight and were met by Julia and Anne Lloyd. Julia looked furious.

'Why, Bryn?' she asked simply.

'We went to have a look.'

'Dressed like that?'

Bryn shrugged.

She turned to me. 'Steve?'

Bryn and I were in the wrong; me because I was a patient and should be on rest and recovery and Bryn because it went against the whole ethos of the place to have staff putting patients at risk.

There was nothing we could say that excused us, but I wasn't a schoolboy found out of bed at midnight and had no intention of offering explanations for what we'd done. I said that I was tired, dirty and in need of a bath.

Julia looked furious and Anne avoided my gaze.

Bryn was on a different hook and walking away might cost him his job, so he stood there and took the shit as I walked up the staircase to my room.

Julia was just starting to tear into Bryn when I called over my shoulder.

'If you are as concerned as you sound then I suggest you get his hand looked at properly. That army medic at Penmaenpool looked more barber than surgeon.'

Julia stopped and Bryn seized the moment and held up his hand. She immediately went to him and over her shoulder Bryn shot me a wink.

Inside my room I pulled off my boots and clothes and lurched into the shower. As the water ran over me the dozens of minute spark burns on my arms and neck stung like hell. I wanted to ignore them, but burn blisters can turn septic very quickly. I swore and dried myself gingerly before ringing downstairs.

It was Anne who picked up the phone.

'Have they got any acroflavin . . . some kind of burns ointment?'

'I'll bring it up,' she said.

A few minutes later there was a knock at the door. I opened it, still wrapped in bath towels. Anne stood there with a first-aid box, looking unsure.

'Come in.'

'You're sure you don't want me to leave it and go?'

'Please,' I said softly and stepped back from the door.

She came in and stood awkwardly in the centre of the room. I closed the door and then indicated the spark burns that dappled my arms and neck.

'Would you like me to dress those for you?'

I nodded.

I sat on the edge of the bed and she inspected the burn blisters carefully. She was slow and gentle and it felt strange, almost intimate. Neither of us spoke. I knew that I should be the one to bridge the gap and started with a muted apology.

'I'm sorry if I came across as rude downstairs, but the last thing I need right now is a lecture.'

She inclined her head. 'You may not have meant to, but you've put Julia in a very awkward spot. If she doesn't report this to Eric Lawrence then she could get in trouble and if she does, then Bryn will and he can't afford to lose his job.'

'I see.'

Her stillness told me that I didn't see.

'Jobs are very scarce around here, Steve, and the chances of Bryn finding one anywhere as good as this are remote.'

'Will she report him?'

'I'm not sure. She can't afford to lose her job, either.'

I was about to say 'I see' again, but bit it back and said instead, 'How do the burns look?'

'It's not too bad, but painful under a hot shower, I imagine.'

'It's the ones on the back of my neck that hurt,' I replied.

Anne dabbed at the blisters on my arms with a cream and applied dressings to the back of my neck. All the time I could feel she wanted to say more but was holding back because of my earlier reaction. I let her finish the burns treatment and then invited her to sit.

She chose a chair near the window and sat with her legs crossed and her hands together just below her chin, regarding me with a cat's eye.

'You look like you could use a drink.'

I smiled. 'If I had the energy I'd be in a pub in Dolgellau right now.'

'I can get Julia to send some Scotch up – if it's Scotch you want?'

'Scotch'll do fine.'

She went over to the phone and rang down to reception. I went into the bathroom and slipped on the bathrobe that the centre provided. I caught sight of myself in the mirror and stopped. The dabs of cream on my face made me look ridiculous and the surgical tape holding the neck dressings in place completed the clown make-up.

'Perfect, Stevie boy – your ability to shape-shift into the complete prat never ceases to amaze me,' I murmured.

As I emerged from the bathroom there was a knock at the door. Anne opened it and Julia came in with a decanter of Scotch and two glasses on a tray. She laid it down on the small table at the centre of the room and paused.

I took the cue.

'You must have been concerned, Julia . . . I'm sorry, I genuinely never meant to put you or Bryn in a spot.'

A little of the stiffness in her body disappeared and she clasped her hands in front of her.

'We'll discuss it in the morning, Steve, with Elizabeth.'

She went out and closed the door behind her.

I looked at Anne. 'Elizabeth?'

'Better than Eric Lawrence – she's doing you a favour.'

'Right.'

She regarded with that cat's eye again; a blend of curiosity and wariness that made me vaguely uneasy. Something came off of her that was hard to pin down; an intelligence, for sure, but also a hardness that was at odds with the grace and sensuality of her body language.

I was looking a little too hard and she was aware of it. She was looking too, but I had no idea why.

Leaning forward, she poured two glasses of whisky and held up one to me.

'Thank you.' I took the glass and lay down on the bed, propping myself up with pillows. She sat down in the armchair facing me and raised her glass. I raised my glass in return and then sipped the straw-coloured malt, nodding my appreciation of it.

I would have relaxed more, but I felt that she was building towards something. I decided to let her control the pace and just observe how she got to it. She couldn't control my answer so where was the harm?

'You both got burnt today – how dangerous was it?' she asked.

'Dangerous enough.'

There was a suggestion of a smile; an ironic and subtle resentment.

'Are you a danger junkie?'

'No. At least, I don't think so.'

The look said she wasn't so sure. 'So why did you go today?'

I was about to say 'Because I'm a fireman'. But I'd already kicked the arse out of that one in the therapy session so I shrugged and said, 'Force of habit.' She swirled the whisky in her glass and took a sip.

'That was the sixth serious forest fire around here in the last few weeks.'

'Oh?'

'That's a lot of fires, Steve.'

'It is.'

She placed her words carefully, like pieces of mosaic, and watched their effect on me. 'Fires are sometimes a protest, but they can also be a beacon, a cry for help.'

So that's why she was here: she was going to take another run at me. Did I say resentment? I sighed and drew my knees into my body.

'Two soldiers died today, Anne. If you've information you should go and—'

'—See the police. They know, Steve.'

A thought went from my mind to my mouth without clearance.

'Is this linked to what happened to Hugh Jones?'

'Six fires, all deliberate and all in areas where OPMA are test-drilling. What's your guess?'

She was inviting me to speculate, trying to trigger my curiosity. I'd rushed in once and that was enough. *Slowly, Stevie: listen, consider, answer.*

'You're in the protest business, you tell me.'

'I'm an environmentalist, Steve.'

'Same thing . . . if you're in mining. Outwardly an environmentalist is trying to preserve the world, but the world has changed. It isn't a question of protecting the world, but of agitating to turn the clock back.'

She leaned forward. 'And you're in favour of that view?'

'Me? No.'

For the first time I saw some humour in her eyes. She gave a small nod of acknowledgement. There was hope for her yet. I smiled and raised my glass again and she replied with a smile that said perhaps for the first time we'd connected.

'I need help, Steve. *Your* help.'

That'll teach me. I walked right into that. 'We've done this already, Anne. I'm not an inquiry agent.'

She stared down at her glass.

'Tell me how you got involved before.'

'As an inquiry agent?'

'Yes.'

I didn't want the conversation to go this way, so I kept it short and turned it into a dead end.

'A friend asked me. The case turned out to be linked to me personally and I got sucked in. I haven't stopped regretting it; major mistake from start to finish.'

Her head tilted to one side. 'A woman?'

I took a gulp of the malt. 'Yes.'

She lowered her voice. 'And you're still dealing with the fall-out.'

'Oh yes.'

There was a nod of recognition. 'Where is she now?'

'I don't know.'

'So it's at an end?'

'Probably.' Where was she going with this?

'Probably?'

'Very probably.'

'Your choice?'

'At first glance.'

As she considered that we looked across the room at each other in silence.

Perhaps she was repositioning the offer, looking for a way to get me to accept. For my part the conversation had become ambiguous. Had we just discussed me or me as an inquiry agent? It crossed my mind that to take on the investigation would mean lots of contact with her and that meant opportunities to close the gap.

It didn't feel predatory. It felt necessary. I needed someone, because I'd never felt so vulnerable, so isolated and alone.

Jesus, that was pathetic! Steve Jay, firefighter and inquiry agent – very cheap – a screw a day – no case too small.

I should have a business card done.

'So, you got hurt and are still hurting. But this won't be like that, Steve.'

Here we go again. Was I reading this wrong or was there a deal being struck here?

'Oh?'

'I really do need to know what Hugh Jones found out. There's nothing connected to you, nothing emotional.'

So I was wrong, then.

'It was more than that, Anne. People got seriously injured. Some died.' I shifted and sat upright, pushing the pillows behind me to support my back. 'I learnt that to go messing around in other people's lives can be very nasty. People have secrets and they fight to protect them. OPMA is, as you said yourself, very powerful.'

'And very greedy . . . Have you any idea of the lengths they are prepared to go in order to make a profit? In South America—'

'That's your fight, not mine.'

We were back to staring silently at each other again.

She should have given up at that point, but something kept her in the chair. I knew in that instant that she was cleverer than me and – more – that she sensed my vulnerability.

'Then do a one-off job for me, Steve. No investigation – just go and pick something up.'

'What?'

'Hugh Jones's laptop.'

I didn't ask why. I didn't want to know. 'Where is it?'

'London – St Katharine's dock.'

'Can't you go and pick it up?'

'I don't think it's wise for me to travel alone too far at the moment. I think I'm being watched.'

'By who?'

'I don't know.'

Fear is the hardest thing to fake. Here it was soft, understated and therefore as real as it gets, but did I want part of it?

'I don't know. It'd be like getting involved through the back door.'

'I need that laptop and I'm prepared to pay.'

'Then get a proper inquiry agent.'

She shook her head. 'What did you get paid before?'

I sighed; with every question I answered I was slowly buying into the idea. 'Two hundred a day plus expenses and bonuses.'

'I'll pay you five hundred as a one-off fee. Just drive down, pick up the laptop and bring it back. That's a twelve-hour round trip. I'll pay for your petrol, of course.'

'That's not the issue.'

'Tell me what is?'

I shook my head. 'What kind of place did Hugh Jones have?'

'I don't know. I have the address, that's all.'

'So how would I get in? Breaking and entering is not my style.'

'No need, Steve. He gave me a key.'

'Oh?'

'You're suspicious.'

'I wonder why.'

It was Anne's turn to pause.

'You asked me before about my connection to Hugh Jones.' She looked down. 'I didn't want to get into it, but he had a thing for me.'

'He hoped – or was it returned?'

'He hoped. There was never going to be anything between us.'

'But you have a key?'

'Yes. He gave it to me on our last meeting. He said that if anything happened to him I should go there and retrieve his laptop.'

'Aren't the files protected by a password?'

She went still. 'Yes.'

I nodded. 'And he gave you that as well?'

She inclined her head, but said nothing.

There was a softness about her now. If I'd been watching the whole encounter from the side I might have felt more able to reach a conclusion, but I felt, knew, I was being sucked in, but to resist meant to reject, that much I understood.

'A one-off job?'

She smiled.

I got up off the bed and topped up my glass before offering the bottle to her. She shook her head and stood up.

'When you get the laptop, Steve, bring it straight over to me.'

'If I do this when do you want it by?'

'Go tomorrow.'

I shook my head. 'I've only just got here, Anne. It's going to look very strange if I disappear off to London two days after I've arrived.'

Something swept across her face; either panic or desperation. The more I sensed the strength in her the more I wondered what it was that took her to the edge.

'Please?'

I gave in. 'I'll have to make some arrangements.'

'Don't tell anyone.'

'Not even Julia?'

'Especially not Julia. What have you got on tomorrow?'

'An appointment with Elizabeth and maybe a medical with Eric Lawrence.'

'Okay. Go at the first opportunity.'

'You said bring it straight over. Even if there are no hitches, Anne, London is a ten- to twelve-hour round trip and then I have to find the place and retrieve the laptop. It could be the early hours of the morning before I get back.'

'Straight to me . . . I need this from you, Steve. Help me, please.'

Anne went shortly afterwards and left me alone with the Scotch and some heavy thinking.

It had crossed my mind to maybe go back to London at the weekend anyway and the driving didn't faze me, so a slight change of timetable and a detour to pick up the laptop wasn't that much of a problem. What troubled me was that I was working against myself. Julia's attempted admonishment wasn't lost on me and it didn't take a genius to realise that so far, whatever my stated aims, I'd done anything but chill out. If I was going to do this I needed to be straight with myself. I topped my glass up and set myself a few ground rules.

One, no more fires. Two, go to therapy and stop fighting the process. Three, get the laptop, take the money and leave it at that.

The fly in the burns ointment was Anne herself.

Whatever had happened between Jenny and me had left a vast hole in my life. She was a powerful presence and losing her meant losing my gravity. Deep down I knew that the only practical solution was to replace her. Otherwise my life would be spent looking back over my shoulder.

It would be nice to think that I could manage to rebuild my life alone and, when ready, look for someone to share it with. But life doesn't fit into neat packages of old and new, at least my life doesn't. I have a tendency to obsess over Jenny and a distraction was needed, unless I was to repeat the mistakes of the past.

Anne was beautiful, intelligent and deep. In my condition I would have settled for a lot less, but here was the real thing: a woman of worth. And if I was any judge at all, there wasn't a man anywhere near her.

10

Sunday, 5 July

The one big Scotch nightcap turned into two and two into three; I slept like the dead.

I awoke around seven-thirty in the same position I'd gone to sleep in. Overall I felt fine, but slightly sluggish. I rose, washed and dressed, reapplied the burns ointment and made my way down to breakfast early.

The only one in the dining room was Eddie Marlowe and his smile of greeting skidded to a halt when he saw the blisters and dressings.

'I was about to say good morning . . . what happened to you?'

'Got a bit too close to that forest fire yesterday, Eddie.'

'Deary me!'

'Yes, "deary me" just about covers it.'

'Are you going to tell me the whole story?'

'Best not to. Bryn is in trouble with the management for taking me and apparently it might cost him his job. So the less people know or ask, the better for all concerned.'

He nodded slowly. 'People *will* ask, though . . . with the ointment and everything.'

'Does it notice?'

He grinned. 'I knew yesterday that you'd be the cause of excitement round here. Not the type to sit quietly and take the tablets.'

'Eddie, I intended to, I really did, but I seem to have life's bungee rope tied to my arse.'

'Well, you would, being you.'

'And what's that?'

He paused. 'You're a catalyst.'

'Go on.'

'You make things happen or are drawn towards them.'

'Reckless?'

'No,' he said slowly. 'I imagine you love the fire-ground, though.'

I smiled, 'I feel at home there.'

'Yes, yes, I can see that. Got to be kind to yourself occasionally as well, though. Still, 'spect you know that.'

There was a gentleness and genuine concern for others about Eddie. It came off him in a way that made me reflect on my own view of the world. I knew that if I'd suffered the intense grief and sense of helplessness that he had then it would have spilled out as anger – as had my guilt about Sandy.

His quiet forbearance was a lesson in dignity.

'I wonder where Eve's got to?' I said, looking around.

'Seems very slow this morning. 'Spect she'll appear soon enough.'

A few minutes later the door from the kitchen swung open and Eve came over with a menu. She stopped a few feet short of the table.

'What happened to you?'

'Fell off my bicycle,' I answered, nudging Eddie under the table.

She frowned, then tutted good-humouredly before taking our breakfast order and disappearing back into the kitchen.

'She'll find out, Steve. Likes a good gossip, does Eve.'

'If she mentions it to the wrong person Bryn will end up in it.'

'Oh, she won't find out anything from me. Not that I know anything, like.'

Eve brought the coffee and as soon as she left I told Eddie that Julia Lloyd was going to tell Elizabeth about the forest fire.

'Better than Eric Lawrence,' he said.

'That's what Anne Lloyd said.'

His eyes sparkled. 'Well, she's right; bit dry is Dr Eric, make a very good mortician.'

'Where is everybody else, Eddie?' I laughed.

'No one really bothers coming down for breakfast. Alby Hutton has his on a tray in his room. Paul Rider and Mick Parker get sloshed every night and don't show till their first appointments. Jamie always runs with Elizabeth first thing.'

'So you eat breakfast alone every morning?'

He gave a wan smile. 'I don't sleep too well, so I get up early and read the papers in the lounge first thing, then come through at eight. Eve sometimes sits and has coffee with me; nice woman, Eve.'

'Well, I seem to be waking early, so give me a knock when you're ready and we'll have breakfast together.'

He gave a sly grin, not unlike a child invited to a party. 'You're on.'

As we were finishing breakfast Julia appeared and said that Elizabeth wanted to see me straight after eating. I said fine and went back to talking to Eddie, but she stayed where she was.

'You had a man ring several times yesterday,' she said, meaning I wasn't there to receive the call. 'He said his name was Alex McGregor.'

Shit! I'd intended to phone Alex back after Bryn had told me he'd called yesterday. I thanked her, told Eddie that I'd catch him later and went up to my room to ring Alex.

I rang him and there was no reply. I let it ring for a few minutes and then rang off, relieved. Now was not the time to talk to Alex. He'd be bound to ask, half-jokingly, if his Shogun was still in one piece and I would be obliged to tell him about the damage to the paintwork.

Later, after it had been polished or 'T-cut' out, would be best and if it turned out well then maybe I wouldn't have to tell him at all.

At nine sharp I made my way to the counselling room and knocked on the door.

'Come in.'

Inside Elizabeth was sitting on a long sofa, dressed in a black tracksuit and trainers. Her face was neutral enough and the words were spoken evenly, but there was an air of business about her.

'Sit down, please, Steve.'

I sat opposite her in an armchair and waited.

'What happened yesterday?' she began.

I went into my now habitual routine of pause, think, reply. I think she spotted it right off.

'I wanted to see the forest fire up close and asked Bryn to run me across the river.'

Her head tilted to one side, as though to get a better look at me. 'How did you both come to get burnt?'

'Wind changed direction.'

She considered that and gave a short nod. 'Julia said that the pair of you were dressed for more than sightseeing.'

I agreed. 'Fires are dirty places and you wouldn't want to go there in anything decent.'

She gave a half-smile, but there was little humour in it. 'You're fencing with me, Steve.'

'You seem angry.'

She shook her head, 'Disappointed, as much by what you've just said as anything.'

That was a fair one, but I was loath to open out too quickly because I couldn't be sure what was going to happen to Bryn. I was careful to keep my tone and volume in tune with hers.

'It was a fierce fire and dangerous. They needed help and I find it hard to turn away when firefighters need help.'

Elizabeth took her time over that, whether to allow me to regret my explanation and amend it or to consider her own response I couldn't tell. In the event she merely spoke the truth and planted it in front of me like a roadblock.

'You need help, Steve . . . that's why you're here.'

I should have left it there, but like a man with two legs thrust through the same trouser leg, I was doggedly committed to an act of stupidity and bare-arsed to boot.

'What happened yesterday wasn't connected to my being here, Elizabeth.'

She blinked. 'You're sure about that, are you?'

'Pretty much.'

That was when I thought she would lose it. Slowly she folded her arms and looked down at my case notes on her lap.

Perhaps glancing at them caused her to think that maybe I wasn't being awkward, just judging things badly. Or maybe it underlined our respective roles. Either way, she sighed and looked up.

'You can't keep doing this to yourself, Steve. You can't keep acting on impulse.'

'Instinct,' I put in unnecessarily.

'You can label it anyway you want. But everything you do here affects the chances of you regaining your health.'

I exhaled slowly. 'Is this now a therapy session or still about yesterday?'

'I'm not the enemy, Steve, just someone trying to help.'

She was right, of course, and I must have looked a prat to her: macho, bloody-minded and damaging myself in the process. Trouble was, I knew Bryn and I had made a difference at the forest fire, if only by guiding the three soldiers away from danger. Nevertheless, it was time to drop the barriers a fraction and accept that from her viewpoint the whole incident must have looked an exercise in attempted self-destruction.

'I'm sorry Elizabeth. Yesterday shouldn't have happened and I know what it must look . . . sound like,' I corrected myself. 'It won't happen again.'

At that she sat up straight. It was pound-of-flesh time. 'It can't happen again. Otherwise I'll recommend that you leave the unit.'

I shrugged in resignation and then nodded.

'What'll happen about Bryn?'

'I've told him to take two weeks leave . . . unpaid.'

'I see.'

'You think I'm being unfair?'

I did. 'It's not for me to say.'

'No, it's not. If Eric Lawrence found out he'd sack Bryn on the spot.'

'So the leave's to keep Bryn out of sight?'

'Exactly.'

'He really did just run me you know. It was my idea.'

At that she said nothing and I felt transparent. I tried to read her, but the therapist face was on and it just shone straight back at me. She must have heard every self-justifying excuse a patient can throw up and had perfected the art of sitting still and letting the words run slowly, but inevitably, aground.

However, I'd apologised and it was time to alter course.

'Is the walking therapy session still on at ten?'

'No. You're having a medical with Eric Lawrence at half-eleven and I'm running Bryn to hospital in ten minutes.'

'I see.'

'He can't drive with that hand, so someone has to do it.'

'Okay, point made.'

'I hope so.'

There followed an uneasy silence until she said, 'How are your injuries?'

'Minor.'

She looked sceptical. 'I'll have Julia re-dress your neck after Eric's seen you. If he asks you how you came to be burnt tell him something plausible. And whatever you do, don't mention fire-fighting.'

'Okay.'

She got up to leave.

'Elizabeth?'

'Yes?'

'Thank you.'

I left Ty Hiraeth just after one.

The medical with Eric Lawrence took longer than I expected. He was very thorough and quite shrewd, picking up on several old injuries that were long since healed and nigh-on invisible.

He asked about the burns and I said that I'd got too close to a bonfire. If he disbelieved me he didn't show it. All in all, he didn't seem a bad sort and told me to come and see him if I had trouble sleeping or anything particular was bothering me.

Eddie was right, though; I'd never seen a face so ripe for morbid employment.

I left a written note for Eve that I wouldn't be back for dinner and slipped out without being seen.

London was between five and six hours away, depending on the traffic. I only stopped once, for coffee and petrol at a service station on the M6. It occurred to me that I should ring Alex again, but the last thing I wanted was to explain the dramas of the past forty-eight hours and the fact that I was going back to London so soon.

He'd want to meet up.

Over the last couple of months he'd become very protective of me: probably as a result of watching stress strangle the joy from my life.

Alex was my best friend and friends came no better. He was a hardbitten Glaswegian who had once been my Sub Officer, before being pensioned off with a due-to-service injury to his back, sustained while rescuing a man from a collapsed trench.

Nowadays, he made his living as a partner in a loss-adjustment business owned by his cousin Andrew.

It had been Alex that had got me involved in inquiry work, partly because he knew of the crippling money problems that had followed in the wake of Jenny's shop going under.

I had a substantial sun of money coming as a result of the investigative work I'd done, but it hinged on the outcome of a successful conviction of the people involved and the insurance company getting their money back. That looked odds-on. So in theory things had improved financially, but in reality I was still on a hook that bit deeper every day. And court cases can take months.

Part of the reason for giving up the flat was that I could no longer afford to keep it going. The plan was to move in with Alex after Ty Hiraeth; something that was a growing cause of embarrassment to me.

Anne Lloyd's five hundred would at least enable me to pay some rent in advance on another flat; somewhere cheaper and smaller. Not that the last place was big.

So my reasons for getting involved in further investigation work were pressing and complicated. It didn't help that the agreement to act the part of courier for the laptop felt like the start of a particularly greasy slope.

Then, of course, there was Anne herself.

Jenny and I had a sexual history that had burnt her so deeply into my psyche that instinctively I still slept with my body shaped to receive her. I wasn't sure I could or would want to connect with anyone else in that way again.

But Anne had her own gravity and I felt its pull.

11

St Katharine's Dock is an example of how the past can meet the present without both suffering.

At first glance, turning docks into a marina by converting old warehouses and throwing in some sharp new apartments might not seem the most original conversion, But the combination of brick and water worked well and drew the professional and tourist alike.

It was the kind of place beloved by advertising agencies and used to push everything from bottled cocktails to bottled blondes.

It looked and felt stylish.

I know we hadn't met under the best of circumstances, but somehow Hugh Jones didn't strike me as one of the smart set. It wasn't a question of money: I didn't know what mining surveyors earned – probably good wedge – but it struck me that he'd have stood out here like the bollocks on a bulldog.

Hugh Jones's apartment faced south over the marina in the East Dock and enjoyed the kind of security you'd expect in such a place; uniformed guard, secure underground parking, subtle, but effective CCTV cameras.

Getting in without being challenged was not going to be easy and I decided to stroll around for a while and mull it over. There was a warm softness to the early evening and I joined the tourists and sightseers in a waterside inn opposite the apartment block.

Had it been a weekday the inn would have been banged out

with office workers; this was the perfect place to wind down after nine hours at the coalface, but in the afterglow of a perfect summer Sunday it had a holiday feel, so I treated myself to a beer and sat gazing at the water lapping the stone quay.

It felt strange. I was in London, but detached from my normal life.

But was that so strange? I'd probably been detached from 'my normal life' ever since Jenny had walked out on me for the first time. And so much had occurred since then that finding my way back was probably never going to happen.

So was this feeling one of being out of synch or getting used to a new existence after sloughing the old?

Elements of this new life, though, were strikingly familiar. It was typical of the old me to find myself near a crisis and loitering on its edges hoping to catch the wind. Eddie Marlowe's shrewd observation that I craved drama or at least was the catalyst for it rang true and when you coupled that to Elizabeth's assertion that I acted on impulse, was it any mystery that my life was being played out the way it was?

Was I doomed to repeat the past merely in a new guise or could I make real changes, better choices?

For a moment I considered walking away from the courier job. I barely knew Anne Lloyd and although the five hundred was useful, I was hardly going to end up on the street. A little honesty was called for. A little owning up to the real reason I was supping beer about to retrieve a suspect laptop from a dead man's apartment.

Anne herself was my primary reason for getting involved. The money was self-justification.

She had been aware of me watching her; appraising her, but she hadn't backed off. Perhaps I was being gullible and she was only using my interest to get me to fetch the laptop. It wouldn't be the first time I'd been used by a woman, but the candle flame couldn't hurt if I knew of its dangers, could it?

I finished my beer, strolled across the bridge and walked past the apartment block.

I saw the security guard sitting behind a desk watching a bank of CCTV cameras. He was middle-aged and had the look of ex-military about him. That posed problems, but also suggested a possibility.

I walked back directly in front of the entrance, beneath the high white canopy, and began looking at the ground. At one point I went up to the front door, opened it and peered at the marble floor inside.

The guard got to his feet, about to challenge me, when I distractedly turned my back towards him and walked out again, still looking at the floor.

I stopped outside and shook my head, then started the performance all over again, but this time walking further into the entrance hall.

'Can I help you, sir? Sir? Can I help you at all?' asked the guard, appearing alongside me.

'Pardon?'

'Are you looking for something? Can I help you?' he said slowly.

'My key!' I said and walked away from him towards the lift, still staring at the floor.

Caught between courtesy and professionalism, he compromised by helping me search.

'Are you a resident, sir?'

'Good lord, no!'

'Then I'm—'

'I'm a friend of Hugh Jones. He loaned me his apartment – third floor – and I've dropped the bloody key somewhere.' I stopped as though an idea had just occurred to me. 'I don't suppose you keep spare keys behind there, do you?' I said, going up to the desk and peering over it.

His face tightened.

'I'm sorry, sir, you can't go behind there. We keep spare keys for emergencies, but they're kept secure in a safe and we can only use them with the express permission of the apartment holder. There's no way I could let you have it, I'm afraid.'

His voice was apologetic, but firm.

I nodded and turned away, searching again; he followed, as concerned as me now.

'There!' I pointed.

'What?'

I rushed forward and pointed down by the litter bin next to the lift. As I reached the bin I stood between it and the guard and palmed the key.

'Got it!' I smiled.

The guard smiled back and nodded, relieved that he wasn't going to be put in a situation where he'd have to refuse a request for the spare key.

'Must have dropped it when I pulled out my car keys.'

I thanked the guard for his help and pressed the lift button. He hovered, a question forming on his lips, but he became distracted by a man and a woman coming through the entrance and asking directions to St Katharine's Way. As he dealt with them the lift arrived. I got in and pressed the button for the third floor.

I emerged from the lift into a thickly carpeted hallway.

There were only four apartments to the floor and I quickly found the door to Jones's apartment. I'd brought a pair of driving gloves with me and I slipped them on before entering.

Before giving the details of how to find the place, Anne had said that Hugh Jones lived alone, so the chances of there being a problem with company were zero. But that's what they'd said at Pearl Harbor.

The apartment was a two-bedroomed affair, with good-quality furniture, a Bulthaup kitchen complete with granite worktops and a bathroom with ceramic walls and floor.

In many respects it was the classic bachelor pad. Understated colours, the polished timber flooring divided up by thick rugs and the generally muted decor spoke loudly of 'male alone'.

To confirm that, there were lots of boys' toys, from the wide-screen TV and DVD player to the state-of-the-art stack system and concealed spotlighting.

I'd have been happy to live there.

The whole place was spotless, with a faint smell of polish, so a maid seemed on the cards. But on a Sunday evening the chances of her turning up were slim to none. That said, it didn't make sense to hang around.

I searched the whole place systematically, careful to replace things as I moved them. It took me less than fifteen minutes to confirm that there was no laptop.

It crossed my mind to ring Anne. But I didn't want to use the apartment phone and I didn't fancy going out to use a phone box only to have to try and bluff the security guard a second time.

I searched again, this time checking even the most obscure possibilities, and still drew a blank.

The beer was starting to work its way through me and I took a leak in the bathroom. As I stood over the toilet bowl, my eye fell on a stainless steel inspection panel on the back wall next to it.

One of the heads of the securing screws was slightly damaged, as though someone had opened it with the wrong-sized screwdriver or a knife.

I bent over and examined the panel. There was minute damage to another screw, though you had to look very close to see it.

I checked my pocket. The smallest coin I had was a twopence piece. Its edge was too thick to go into the screw groove so I went out into the kitchen and searched the cutlery drawer for a suitable knife. Several looked promising so I took them back to the bathroom and began to remove the screws.

The damaged ones were not surprisingly the hardest to undo. But eventually they came out and I removed the panel.

Behind it was a small cavity, used to gain access to a water valve. The recess was just about big enough to hold a laptop and sitting just inside the concrete box was a set of keys. I lifted them out and examined each in turn. They were neither front-door nor car keys and there was a leather fob attached, with 'SH' in metal lettering.

I clipped them onto my keyring and pocketed them before replacing the panel and taking the knives back to the kitchen.

Just as I closed the cutlery drawer I heard a sound and froze.

The door of the kitchen was half open and I could see a lean, hard-faced man. He was wearing an open-necked shirt, casual jacket and trousers and heavy lace-up shoes. At first he didn't see me and I used the few seconds I had to check that his hands were empty and that he was alone.

He was looking around and moving very slowly, but there was nothing nervous or shifty about him, just an air of animal sharpness; the sleekness of someone physically fit and close to violence.

I felt a prickling down my back and my mouth went dry.

At one time I would have put that down to fear, but fighting in the ring had revealed these sensations to be an adrenalin dump: the body's preparation for fight – or flight. The trouble was that fear is so similar that unless you're sharp and training hard, the 'dump' can turn your legs to noodles and wreck your heart rate.

I kept very still and concentrated on controlling my breathing.

He saw me.

His gaze swept over me without visible reaction; it was almost as if I wasn't there. Then he smiled; not a gesture of warmth, but equally not an expression of malice. It was more a recognition, a threat appraisal that told him what he wanted to know. He had sensed my uneasiness and had read it as weakness.

Logic said do nothing and switch him off, but something more primitive wanted him to know that there would be a price.

Neither of us moved.

The seconds went by without words. Then I took a couple of steps nearer to the kitchen door and he moved back, throwing a look over his shoulder towards the front apartment entrance.

He looked like he was going to exit, so I moved forward again, out of the kitchen into the lounge.

Mistake.

I felt a sudden explosive blow hit me in the left kidney and an arm tightened around my neck until I thought my head would burst. Struggling to maintain my feet I ripped at the arm, knowing I had seconds before I lost consciousness. The unseen attacker was pulling me backwards with a fierce strength and the intruder I'd first seen came rushing over and punched me violently in the lower abdomen.

I ignored the pain and stabbed my fingers over my shoulder, trying to gouge the eyes of the unseen strangler then kicked out with my right foot, catching the intruder in front on the inside of the thigh, missing his groin by an inch.

Another punch slammed into me below the belt.

I wanted to vomit, scream, breathe, but the strangler was preventing all of these. Instinct made me lash out, but the arm tightened irresistibly around my neck and coordination deserted me. The last thing I was aware of was a buzzing in my ears.

★ ★ ★

When I came to I was lying on my side, facing the wall with my hands stripped of the gloves and bound behind my back. My feet and my mouth had been gaffer-taped. My jacket was pulled down over my upper arms and the pockets were turned out; the keys and my wallet, its contents scattered by my head.

I lay still and tried to work out the state of play. I had a dull persistent ache in my lower abdomen and my neck felt like someone had jumped on it. I rolled over slowly, listening hard.

On the good side, I reasoned, I'd woken up; on the bad, they were still here.

I could see them in the bathroom. They had taken the panel off and the intruder I had seen was examining the concrete recess. He looked at the other one, who had his back to me and shook his head. Then he saw me watching.

He came running over and kicked me in the stomach so hard it folded me in half. As I heaved and fought the urge to vomit he straddled me, wrenched my head back and gaffer-taped my eyes. Blind, dumb and bound there was nothing I could do as two more kicks thudded into me.

I heard the other intruder approach and tensed myself for more blows. But instead they stood over me for a few minutes and then I thought I heard them leave the apartment.

For a quarter of an hour I stayed where I was, straining my ears to be sure that they'd actually gone. When I was certain I tried to wriggle free.

I fought the tape binding and it bit into my wrists. As I tore and twisted in vain, skin came off and I could feel my fingers thicken as they swelled; still the tape refused to give. I took a minute for my breathing to steady, then strained my whole body against the binding – only to succeed in banging my head against the wall.

Bastards!

Wet with sweat and my body shaking from exertion, I finally got one hand free and ripped the gaffer tape from my eyes.

I lay there on the verge of passing out, feeling the sweat stinging my burn blisters and willing myself to remember every feature I could about the one I saw. But the one thing that preoccupied me, that crossed the anger and disturbed me, was the fact that, from the moment they had entered the apartment until they left, they had been totally silent.

12

I gathered up the keys and the contents of my wallet.

My fire brigade ID had been removed from the zip pocket inside the wallet and thrown to one side, presumably to let me know that they'd had a good look.

It was already playing on my mind that they had been coldly detached throughout. Even the kicking I was given when caught watching them was measured; deterrence equal to the perceived crime.

I had meant nothing to them, a minor problem dealt with by the minimum of fuss and it thoroughly pissed me off.

The problem now was deciding what to do.

A six-hour drive back to Wales empty-handed wasn't attractive. I wanted a bath, a stiff drink and somewhere to lick my wounds. That meant Alex.

His house was in Upminster, the best part of an hour from St Katharine's Dock. I decided not to ring him and invite a whole lot of unwanted questions while I was still trying to get my head around what had happened; the drive would give me thinking time.

Alex lived alone in a large detached house in a smart, semi-affluent neighbourhood. His wife Margaret had died a few years ago and although he hid it well I knew he still felt the ache of her loss.

As a couple they were complete opposites: she, a clever accountant with pretty eyes and a style about her, him, a rawboned, hardbitten ex-fireman with a moral code that wasn't so much pure as fair.

When he had been my Sub Officer he was the rock on which the watch had rested. No one took liberties with Alex and most liked him, but he was choosy about his friends and I counted myself lucky that we were close.

We shared a love of boxing and he had been the one who had virtually forced me into training again to take my mind off Jenny. His non-sentimental approach to supporting me and wise words throughout my problems, especially when Sandy died, deepened our friendship and allowed me to trust him completely; probably the only person I ever had.

By the time I turned into the drive I'd decided to tell him everything. I knocked on the door and waited. Alex appeared and his face broke into a quizzical smile.

'Stevie? What in the name . . . come in, come in.'

He stood aside and I entered the hallway.

'Go through, you know the way.'

We went into the lounge and he took a good look at me. His head shook with amused wonder and he sat me down with a Scotch before pouring himself one and sitting opposite me.

'Tell me,' he said simply.

I gave him everything and received constant interruptions for clarification. In turn he smiled, frowned and laughed, but when I got to the part about Hugh Jones's apartment he went quiet.

'They sound professionals, Stevie.'

'But professional what?'

Alex shook his head. 'Is that all of it?'

'No.'

His face looked guarded as he picked up on my tone. 'Does it involve the Shogun?' he said intuitively.

I nodded, 'Scratches . . . I think they'll polish out.'

He closed his eyes and hissed out air. 'You might just be the maddest bastard I've ever met. You left Friday . . . it's only Sunday night!'

'Feels longer.'

'Aye, I'll bet it does. What are you going to do now?'

'I was hoping you'd give a little unbiased advice.'

He leaned back in the armchair. 'Lie down in a darkened room, don't talk to strange women and buy into the treatment you're supposed to be getting the benefit of,' he purred.

'I've fucked up?'

He laughed out loud. 'That's one way of putting it.'

'So walk away, put it down to experience?'

'That's what a sane man would do.' He smiled. 'She's a looker, then, this Anne Lloyd?'

'Oh yes.'

'Can you separate the woman from her troubles?'

'Doubt it.' I took a sip of the Scotch and let it trickle down my throat slowly.

'Ah, Stevie boy, you sound like your hormones are ruling your head.'

'That not sound then?' I grinned.

'No, it isn't. When did you last eat?'

'About half three . . . motorway service station.'

'Hungry, then?'

I nodded.

'I'll phone for a Chinese . . . there's a good one in the high street . . . they deliver.'

Alex made the phone call and I reflected on how bizarre my tale must have sounded to him. Forty-eight hours ago I'd left to get some much-needed rest and treatment and here I was now, looking beaten and barbecued with God knows what additional problems following in my wake.

I rubbed the sides of my neck; it didn't feel strong enough to support my head. I was lucky they didn't want to kill me, because, and this was the scary thing, there was nothing I could have done about it. On the plus side the ache in my stomach had stopped.

Alex came and sat down again, then noticed my glass was empty and topped it up. He looked as if a question was forming in his mind.

'Go on, ask it,' I said.

He shrugged. 'Jenny rang me.'

'Oh?'

'Friday night. Did you tell her you were going away?'

'I haven't seen or heard from her since I walked away, Alex.'

'That's what I thought. Spooky, isn't it?'

'What did she want?'

'She'd gone to your flat Friday evening – she must have missed you by hours – wanted to know where she could find you.'

'What did you say?'

'That you had gone away and I didn't know how long for.'

'What did she say to that?'

'That she wanted to speak to you.'

'And?'

'I said I'd tell you if and when you rang.'

'That all?'

'She sounded shocked that you'd moved – panicked, almost.'

'I've nothing to say to her she doesn't already know.'

He smiled and nodded. He had wanted me to cut Jenny out of my life for some time. It was nothing that he'd said, just a look and a surgically placed grunt; she was water, he was rock.

'This new lady in your life . . .'

'She's not in it yet.'

He chuckled. 'Is she a reaction against what happened?'

'Probably.'

'I don't normally give uninvited advice . . .'

'Go on.'

'Whatever you do, take it slowly. You're not going to last at this rate and, all joking aside, Stevie, your health comes before everything.'

'Agreed.'

'What are your immediate plans?'

'Eat, sleep – here, if that's okay – and leave for Wales early tomorrow.'

'Will that plan stand a little more Scotch?'

'Just about.'

We talked well into the night and Alex posed the question of whether Anne knew about the possibility of intruders at Hugh Jones's apartment.

'Is that why she didn't fancy the trip herself?' he asked pointedly.

'Don't know.'

'How confident are you that she's on the level? I mean, have you considered the fact that she might have a criminal record?'

'What?'

'Think about it, Stevie. She gives you the key to a dead man's apartment with instructions to pick up his laptop. That's theft.'

'Hugh Jones gave her the key and told her to take the laptop,' I said defensively.

'How do you know that?'

'How else would she have got the key?'

'If I knew that I might be more confident you hadn't just unwittingly escaped becoming involved in a crime.'

'Well, I have, actually.'

'What?'

'Become involved in a crime.' I held up the keys.

'Aye, I'd forgotten about those. What do they open, exactly?'

'I don't know. I'm hoping she does.'

Alex rubbed his face with his hands. 'Stevie, I'm going to make a suggestion here.'

'More advice?'

'A suggestion.'

'Go on.'

'Write down for me all that you know about this woman.'

'Anne Lloyd.'

'Aye. Write it all down and I'll see if I can get Roley Benson to check her out. You never know.'

Roley Benson was an ex-detective with a severe drink problem. He'd done some work for Alex on the same job that I'd become involved in. He'd once been a clever and experienced copper, but drink had destroyed his career. That said, he was still a useful contact and Alex had a point.

'I'm going to say no, Alex. I hear what you say, but there's no need. I intend to give Anne Lloyd the keys and then back off – well, back off in terms of doing work for her.'

He looked doubtful. 'Are you sure?'

'Certain.'

Around one in the morning we turned in.

I set the alarm for five and left the house without waking Alex. There was nothing on the road and I put my foot down, hoping to do the journey in less than five hours.

Progress was good until Birmingham, where I made the mistake of stopping for a quick breakfast and petrol. It's amazing how half an hour can change the rate of traffic and I paid for the error when I hit the back of a massive queue.

There was no escaping the slow lines of heavy lorries as the traffic crawled through a five-mile stretch of coned contraflow. It put the best part of an hour on the journey.

I hadn't wanted to be back later than, say, ten or eleven. I didn't have an appointment in the morning, but all the same, questions might be asked if I didn't appear until midday. Even that was starting to look in doubt and I sat fuming as I listened to the radio weathergirl forecasting another day in the low thirties with an expectation of more to follow.

It was past midday when I reached the bridge at Penmaenpool. There was still a small fire brigade presence in the form of a Carmichael Land Rover and a group of fire-fighters milling around aimlessly next to the riverside hotel.

On the far side of the bridge I halted and gazed down the estuary. Isolated wisps of dark smoke were still curling lazily upwards against the stark blue of the sky, evidence that stubborn pockets of fire held on in the jangle of rock and vegetation on the southern edge.

It would take days criss-crossing the hard terrain with beaters – or a heavy thunderstorm – to extinguish all of them and with the major drama past there would be little joy in it for those whose task it was to damp down.

The sight of the firefighters reminded me of Bryn and I made a mental note to ask Julia how he was mending as soon as I got to Ty Hiraeth. I intended to visit him. It crossed my mind briefly that he might have known Hugh Jones. But I'd meant what I'd said to Alex, I was done with mysteries – every time I stuck my nose in I lost a bit more skin.

As I swung into the drive I passed Eddie and Elizabeth walking in the direction of the woods backing Ty Hiraeth. I raised my hand in hello and Eddie smiled. Elizabeth gave a half-smile, which left me wondering whether I was still in the shit for the forest fire or had found new areas of irritation for her.

If asked, I had originally intended to say I got up early went for a long drive, but in that moment a touch of my own irritation kicked in. I had no need to account for anything.

I found Julia in the kitchen, talking to Eve.

Both women stopped talking as soon as I came in and Eve glanced at Julia before excusing herself. Julia waited till Eve was out of earshot.

'Hello, Steve. We've been worrying about you. Your bed wasn't slept in last night.'

'That's true.'

There was a heavy pause that was laden with disapproval and when she spoke it seeped into her voice.

'Normally I wouldn't pry, but being so soon after our last discussion I thought . . .'

'Ask Anne.'

She hesitated. 'Did . . . were you with her?'

I gave her a look. 'I'm here for therapy, Julia, and although I appreciate everyone's concern I'm an adult and entitled to some privacy.'

She didn't colour, but I'd obviously embarrassed her. I moved the conversation in a different direction.

'Do I have a session with Elizabeth this afternoon?'

'Yes. Yes, at four.'

I nodded. 'Fine. What's the plan for lunch today?

'Eve will lay out a cold table in the dining room around one.'

'Thank you. Oh . . . how's Bryn?'

'I . . . Elizabeth said the burn wasn't too bad and he should be back the week after next.'

'Have you an address for him? I'd like to visit sometime.'

'I'll write it out for you.'

'Great.'

There was an awkward silence.

I stayed where I was until she got the message and moved off in the same direction Eve had taken. Julia was a nice woman and I didn't like making her feel uncomfortable, but equally I didn't want to establish a practice of accounting for my every move, to her or anyone else for that matter. Hopefully, the exchange had put paid to further questions being asked.

I walked out through the dining room and into the reception area just as Jamie, the scarfaced runner, came through the main entrance.

When he saw me he slowed.

He had intense, deep brown eyes that darted quickly and seemed to be constantly searching. There was something else about him, something feral. I could see how he made Eddie uneasy.

I judged his height to be around six foot with a wiry, athletic build and he seemed to lope rather than walk – as if walking was a discipline.

We reached the bottom of the staircase together and I smiled and said hello. He looked straight through me as though I wasn't there.

13

In my room I telephoned Anne but got no reply. I let it ring for a while to see if an answer-phone kicked in, but it didn't. I immediately redialled in case I had rung a wrong number; still nothing.

I didn't have the laptop so there was no point in driving over to Tabor where she lived. Besides, she might well be on her way over to Ty Hiraeth. My stomach rumbled and I glanced at my watch; if I was going to make lunch I had to get my skates on.

Before getting in the shower I took the opportunity to examine myself in the wardrobe mirror. I still felt like I'd been run over by a car, but no matter how hard I looked I couldn't find any evidence of the beating.

Those bastards knew exactly what they were doing.

There was, however, plenty of evidence left over from the forest fire. The smaller burn blisters had turned hard and white and the bruises on my forearms had taken on a mottled appearance, all of which looked awful but were painless. I made sure, though, not to let the hot water hit the back of my neck.

I towelled myself dry carefully and selected something to wear.

The police hadn't returned the clothes I'd come down in and I hadn't brought that much with me plus I seemed to be going through what I had brought a bit too quickly. First opportunity I'd drive into Dolgellau and buy some shirts and an extra pair of chinos or something similar.

I'd just finished dressing when there was a knock at my door. I opened it to find Eddie standing there.

'Are you going to lunch, Steve?'

'Yes. Elizabeth finished with you?'

He smiled. 'Just the hour today. A swift walk and some exercises.'

'Exercises?'

'Mental ones – you know . . . life is a wheel . . . don't get stuck in a rut!'

'You're joking.'

'I am, actually.' He grinned. 'Come on, otherwise the cold table'll get warm.'

As we walked down the stairs he nudged me.

'There's a rumour that you went over the wall last night.'

'I sighed. 'Did Eve have breakfast with you this morning?'

'Yes. How did you know?' He laughed.

'This place is a nightmare, Eddie. You can't scratch yourself without it being known.'

'Well, here's something not everybody knows, Anne Lloyd has been trying to get hold of you all morning. She's rung three times. Eve took the calls and apparently Anne didn't want Julia to know that she'd rung. Strange, that.' He shot me a sideways look. 'You don't take long.'

'Eddie?'

'What?'

'There's a strong rumour that you're inside Eve's drawers . . .'

He nearly fell over. 'Bloody hellfire!'

I nudged him, 'Just joking. Let's eat.'

Over lunch Eddie chatted away. He seemed to have lost some of the melancholy that had surrounded him the first time we'd met and I believe I caught a glimpse of the man before the tragedy had struck. He seemed instinctively kind and gentle and, if it's possible to say it of a man in his early thirties, innocent.

I envied him.

Throughout the meal he tried hard to engage me, but my mind was elsewhere.

As soon as I'd finished eating I told him I had a headache and was going to lie down. He said that all the residents, with the exception of Jamie, were going into Dolgellau that night for a drink and he asked me to join them.

'We all have dinner together here, then go for a few pints. It's nice, you'd enjoy it,' he said hesitantly.

'I am interested, Eddie, but I'll see how my head feels. Can I just show up at dinner?'

He seemed disappointed. 'Of course.'

I left him there and went back up to my room. I tried ringing Anne again, but there was still no reply. If we hadn't managed to connect up by the time my appointment with Elizabeth was over I intended to drive over to Tabor on the off chance she was there but not answering the phone for some reason.

My lie to Eddie was more of a half-truth because the lack of sleep was catching up with me and felt like a clamp around my head. I also suspected that it was, in part, due to the stress fatigue that never quite seemed to leave me. I lay down on the bed and closed my eyes, intending to rest rather than sleep.

The nightmare that ambushed me was horrific and deeply disturbing.

A disjointed series of images brought me once again to the yard at the back of the Heathway and the circle of silent, grim-faced firefighters. I was standing behind them when I heard someone whisper my name. I looked around but couldn't see who had called me. Then I noticed that they had turned and were all looking in the same direction.

I called out and the circle parted to reveal the slumped

figure of Sandy Richards. A sound was coming from his throat – a rasping, as though he was trying to breathe.

'Clear his airway!' I shouted. 'His tongue's in the back of his throat.'

My voice echoed in the confines of the yard, but nobody heard me. Sandy arched his back and the rasping seemed to form into words. I leaned forward and strained to catch them, but his mouth flapped and gaped and the rasp became a wet gurgle, like he was drowning.

I tried to go forward, but my feet wouldn't move. Then the circle closed and once again I was on the outside.

I struggled violently, pulling people aside, screaming at the top of my lungs, all the time getting nearer, but never near enough. Suddenly they parted again and Sandy turned and fixed his gaze on me. I saw the animal fear in his eyes, the awful self-knowledge that he was dying.

His head titled to the right and that sound came again, as though he were sucking air yet trying to talk. His raised a hand and it looked like he was beckoning me.

My body felt impossibly heavy, almost incapable of movement. All I could see was Sandy trying to hold on to life and losing. With a sob of exertion I lunged forward, trying to reach him, but my feet went from under me and I fell heavily on to the cobbled yard.

I couldn't regain my feet and was forced to crawl through the legs of the firefighters as they watched, mute and seemingly dispassionate. Inch by inch I clawed my way forward until I had to stop, exhausted.

His head turned and I pressed my ear against his lips and heard him gasp, 'Help me . . . please!'

I came to and sat bolt upright, sweat soaking me and my body trembling.

'Dear God, what are you doing to yourself?' I whispered.

I sat there with my heart pounding, the image of Sandy

begging me for help unbearable and the horror clinging to me, refusing to release its grip.

I fought it, pushing the guilt away, forcing myself to reject it. It was almost a physical struggle and a series of shudders coursed through me. I recognised then what was happening to me; I was in shock.

Shock – from a crazy fucking dream!

Gradually, the sensations subsided and the rational mind took control, analysing and weighing.

Part of me was consumed with grief, with guilt, but it was more than that. It had become intrinsic, invading my mind and my conscience, bonding and controlling me. It was viral in nature, pernicious in intent and I was forced to accept that it was winning.

'Deal with this, Stevie,' I murmured. 'Deal with it before it destroys you.'

Denied much-needed sleep, but reluctant to close my eyes again, I lay back on the bed with my hands behind my head.

The nightmare had scared me. It was proof, if proof was needed, that I was on the edge; there could be no more excuses now. There was only so much balancing; so much rationalisation I could do before I was forced to admit that the emotional damage was too big to self-heal.

But even now the thought of opening up to Elizabeth, of allowing her unrestricted access to my feelings of guilt and shame, was hard, perhaps impossible.

I don't know how long I lay there weighing and examining, but finally I willed myself to stand up and walked like a drunken man into the bathroom.

Splashing my face with water, I ran my wrists under the cold tap until the flesh turned white and pulpy and my hands stung.

I had to steady myself before attempting to look into the mirror.

'Come on, Stevie,' I whispered. 'Control it.'

I decided to get out of the room, to go outside into the sunlight. I still had over an hour till my appointment with Elizabeth and I didn't want her to see the ghosts in my face.

I found a bench and sat facing the sun with my eyes closed. For maybe fifteen minutes I rested, letting the dazzling sunlight burn off the residue of the swirling, poisonous images and the insect noises of the garden reassert some normality, reality, into my self-induced turmoil.

When the footsteps sounded on the gravel path I kept my eyes shut and hoped that whoever it was would take the hint and keep on walking.

'Hello, Mr Jay.'

I sighed and turned towards the voice. It was John Vaughan.

'Disturbed you, have I?' said the policeman.

'You could say that.'

'Ah well, there's sorry I am.'

He sat down next to me and dabbed at his forehead with a handkerchief as he looked around. 'I don't know how you can sit in the sun like that, not today in this heat.'

'It's the sunlight, not the heat I want.'

He looked at me strangely. 'What have you done to your neck there?'

'Burn blister.'

'Ah, right, the house fire,' he said, unbuttoning his shirt and running the handkerchief around his neck.

'What can I do for you?'

'Well, my boss, Inspector Pritchard, wanted me to speak to you again – in case you've remembered anything else.'

'Did he say when I could have my clothes back?'

'Forensics have them. They work on a different timescale to the rest of humanity,' he grinned.

'So not soon, then?'

'I really don't know. I'll ask, though.'

'Thank you.'

He leaned forward, his elbows on his knees and his hands clasped in front of him.

'Have you remembered anything extra, Mr Jay?'

If for no other reason than the nightmare, I'd told myself that I was not going to get involved in anything else. Now I had a chance to prove that. There was Anne, of course. But I wasn't breaking a confidence, because she wasn't a client as such, was she?

'Yes, there was one thing. It slipped my mind before.'

'And what's that?'

'Just before I saw the house fire a runner came sprinting out of the forest, right in front of me. He looked agitated.'

'James Howard?'

I shrugged.

'Tall, athletic-looking chap with a burn scar on his face?' he indicated on himself.

'That's him.'

Something crossed John Vaughan's face, a confirmation, like I'd passed a test. What had I just told him?

'You knew?'

He smiled. 'Sad about him, isn't it?'

'What is?'

He lifted his head.

'He was an officer in the army, wounded in Bosnia. Had some sort of breakdown due to the injuries he received. Bit of a mystery in some ways, he is.'

'A mystery?'

He took a moment, as if he was thinking through his own ideas.

'Reminds me of Peter O'Toole in *Lawrence of Arabia* – you know, very English, bit mystical . . . driven . . . that's it, driven.' Vaughan looked rueful. 'Not the sort of man you'd want to upset, if you know what I mean?'

'Well, I try to avoid mysteries nowadays. They have a way of getting you hurt.'

He smiled again. 'My boss will be pleased to hear that.'

'Good for him.' I closed my eyes again and turned my face back towards the sun.

He didn't move away and I sighed heavily.

'There was something else,' he said quietly.

'I'm listening.'

'Hugh Jones had a colleague who was working on the survey with him – Russell Evans.' He watched me out of the corner of his eye as he spoke. 'Evans is missing. No one's seen him since the day Jones was murdered.'

'Why tell me?'

'I was wondering if you saw anyone in the vicinity of the house itself?'

'I'd have said.'

A fat bead of sweat formed on his forehead and then ran down to his eyebrow. He dabbed at it and then ran the handkerchief around his neck again.

'He's about your height, maybe a bit smaller, with a thin face.' He gestured with his hand. 'And a lot of blond hair tied back in a ponytail.'

'I've not seen anyone like that.'

'If you do—'

I cut him short. 'Then I'll let you know.'

His eyes caught and held mine. 'Are you sleeping well, Mr Jay?'

'Why?'

'You look . . . tired.'

'Do I?'

'Ty Hiraeth okay?'

'Fine.'

'Food? Facilities? That sort of thing?'

'No problems.'

He looked thoughtful. 'Must be something else, then.'

I said nothing while he stood up and looked around him. 'Well, I'll be going now . . . leave you to enjoy the sunshine.'

I watched him walk back towards the house. The questions had been a blind. I had no doubt that it was me he'd come to see, rather than any answers I might yield.

Why?

14

At four, I met Elizabeth and like John Vaughan, she was quick to spot the distress signals. At first she didn't say much, but suggested we walk the route she had taken earlier with Eddie Marlowe and led me towards the woods at the back of Ty Hiraeth.

A stiff gust of wind rippled the tree line as we approached, bringing with it the smell of burning from the southern side of the estuary. I turned and looked across at the ragged, isolated columns of smoke and I wondered if they'd found the bodies of the soldiers yet.

Then we entered the woods.

The broad path followed a stream up the hillside and passed some of the old mine shafts that riddled the slopes. Elizabeth walked quickly and in the heavy afternoon heat the sweat ran freely down my back.

Seeing I was struggling she slowed and waited for me to catch up.

'You should see this stream in the spring, Steve. Right now the lack of rainfall and summer heat have reduced it to a fraction of its normal size.'

I watched the water splashing over the rocks and stones as it tumbled down the hillside. The sound and the sight of the running water acted like a balm to my nerves, which was perhaps the intention. We started walking again and she let me set the pace. Between the lack of sleep and being jerked awake by the nightmare I was walking on borrowed legs and losing the will to hide it.

'How are you sleeping, Steve?'

'How does it look?'

'You seem tired,' she said.

'I am.' I paused and gave the decision one last thought, 'I've been getting nightmares.'

She looked at me carefully. 'About the Heathway fire?'

'Yes.'

She didn't comment at first, just threw me the occasional sideways glance. I could feel her searching for the right words, the right tone, matching her decisions against what she read in my face.

'How long have you been having them?'

'Soon after it happened.'

'Not straight away, then?'

'No. Two to three weeks after.'

'After Sandy died?'

After Jenny and I split, I thought with sudden intuition. 'Yes, after Sandy.'

'Frequent nightmares?'

'Every night . . . sometimes during the day if I nap.'

Elizabeth stopped walking. 'Today?'

I nodded. 'After lunch. The worst yet.'

'Tell me— Can you tell me about them?' she corrected herself.

I started slowly, building to the most recent. She listened intently, never interrupting, but as I described the last nightmare lines of concern began to shape her face. When I'd finished it was obvious that, therapist or not, she had been affected by what she'd heard.

'Did you tell Eric Lawrence about these experiences?'

I thought 'experiences' was an odd choice of word.

'No,' I breathed.

At that she gave a single nod and we walked on in silence. The sunlight broke through the canopy in places and streaked the forest floor with fingers of gold. Above us the wind continued to come in gusts, moving the treetops in fits of violent rustling and producing dry, cracking sounds from the branches.

Despite the talk of nightmares, the walk was having the desired effect. The trees seemed to draw some of the tension from me and the simple act of walking somehow countered the feelings of desperation; the slow release of endorphins, maybe.

Eventually we reached a clearing by the stream edge and Elizabeth sat down and invited me to do the same. I sat with my back to a pine tree, facing her.

'Have you told anyone else about these nightmares?'

'No.'

'I'm the first? The only one?' she confirmed.

'Yes.'

'Thank you for trusting me. It couldn't have been easy.'

She talked me through her ideas on guilt, about how it seemed to pick up on latent insecurities and reinforce them. She also asked me if I had had any experiences prior to the Heathway that had troubled me.

Again Jenny popped into my head and momentarily I hovered on the brink of telling her, but then rejected it. I was in enough trouble without pulling the one strand that would unravel my life.

I needed to deal with the issues around Sandy's death. I needed to focus on the nightmares, on separating reality from shadows. Which wasn't going to be easy.

Where did stress end and everyday trials and tribulations begin? And what about character? What about obsessive personalities? When did my determination to achieve something or hang on to Jenny, for that matter, become obsessive?

No. The nightmares were about Heathway, Sandy's death and my operational decisions. The labyrinthine sexual politics of my life with Jenny could not be a subject for deconstruction.

Focus; deal with the guilt.

Elizabeth broadened the subject of blame and the effects it could have. The logic of her answers was what I wanted to hear, but she was astute enough to keep it impersonal and therefore kept me engaged and actively responding.

Every now and again she probed and, wary as I was, little by little she drew things out of me and hinted that there was more going on internally than perhaps I was aware or prepared to admit.

I had no doubt that she was reading as much in the gaps of our conversation as the substance. Every now and again the green eyes would sweep over me, gathering God knows what clues.

I felt a sense of relief at having discussed the nightmares and believed that I could now grant Elizabeth some trust. The hour slipped by so fast that I was almost sorry when it came to an end. As we walked back to the house she said she would ask Eric Lawrence to prescribe sleeping tablets.

'Thank you for today, Steve. It was valuable, a turning point.'

'But?'

She smiled. 'But you have got to *want* to release the grip you have on blame. Because you *feel* guilty doesn't make you so. The nightmares are fears played out while your mind and body are passive, not rational judgements, not truth.'

'Feels like truth.'

She stood up and brushed dried grass from her tracksuit.

'Is this where you bring Eddie?' I asked.

She turned and pointed, 'Further up the hill.'

'The better we get, the further we go?' I grinned.

'Something like that. Sometimes we just walk along the hill.'

There wasn't so much as a feather of irony in her voice or judgement in her face. She was good, really good.

As we emerged from the wood I noticed that the wind had

died and the sticky oppressive heat had closed in. Elizabeth said it was often like that: the proximity of the sea and the mountains created their own mercurial weather systems – fickle as people.

Back at Ty Hiraeth, Eve was waiting for me.

'Anne Lloyd rang about ten minutes ago. I told her that you were having an appointment and to ring back around half-five.'

'Thank you, Eve.'

It was twenty past five now. I said that I'd be in my room and to put the call straight through to me when it came. The phone rang at half-five dead and I immediately picked up the agitation in Anne Lloyd's voice.

'Where have you been, Steve? I've been trying to get hold of you all day.'

'Well, you've got me now, but unfortunately I haven't got—'

She interrupted me. 'Just meet me in an hour.'

'Where?'

'There's a roadside diner next to the turn-off for Dol-gun on the A470. Do you know where I mean?'

'I'll find it. What's wrong, Anne?'

'When I see you.' She put the phone down.

I looked up the Dol-gun road junction on the map and it was fifteen, maybe twenty minutes away. That left me forty minutes to remind myself that Anne Lloyd owed me petrol money, plus a little something for the trouble and that I now owed her nothing.

But I was attracted.

The one problem with that is, swimming alongside someone in the middle of a whirlpool and trying to tread water at the same time was unrealistic. That left two courses of action. One, help them to get out of the water. Or two, go down with them.

Seventy-two hours ago I'd have argued that I needed rest rather than therapy. Now I knew different. The signs weren't good and I had to protect myself. I wanted Anne, but if I couldn't pull her away from the edge I would give advice one last time and then withdraw.

I kept repeating this to myself as I drove the Shogun to the Dol-gun road junction.

As I pulled into the car park I saw Anne sitting in a silver Ford Cougar next to the exit, with the driver window half open. I parked alongside, she opened the passenger-side door and I climbed in.

She was pale and although outwardly in control she looked like she had been badly shaken up. There was also a heavy, stale smell of cigarettes in the car and a half-empty box of Marlboros on the console next to a blue plastic lighter.

'What happened, Anne?'

'Two intruders broke into my cottage around three this morning.'

'*Two* intruders?'

She nodded. 'I saw one clearly and caught the movement of another as they fled.'

'Are you okay? They didn't hurt you?'

'No.' Her right hand trembled slightly as she spoke.

I thought she was going to add something, but instead she drew a Marlboro from the pack and inserted it in the corner of her mouth. With the same hand she flipped open the lighter and played the flame around the end of the cigarette, then inhaled a lungful of the blue pungent smoke and blew it from the corner of her mouth.

The inconsistency made me smile. Here was a vegetarian environmentalist, with all the life-path that implied, racing towards lung cancer with an elegant abandonment.

But, then again, there was little that could be called stereotypical about Anne Lloyd.

'Tell me what they were wearing, exactly.'

She drew slowly on the cigarette, her face almost hard for an instant – hard, but also intensely feminine.

'The one I saw was wearing black motorcycle gear. He kept the visor down so I didn't get a look at his face.'

'Did he speak?'

She shook her head. 'No.'

'Okay, take me through what happened from the moment you became aware of them.'

Again she drew on the cigarette, but then, as a concession, changed hands and held it vertically, letting the smoke spiral out of the driver-side window.

'I was waiting up for your call and fell asleep in a chair. A noise woke me and I saw him standing about six feet away.'

'What did you do?'

'He went for me, but I kicked him in the knee and ran into the bedroom. He followed me and I stabbed him in the arm with this.'

Reaching across me, she opened the glove compartment to reveal a hatpin, about six inches long.

'It was lucky you had that handy.'

'I live alone, Steve.'

I held a hand up and shook my head to show I hadn't meant anything by it. She searched my face and closed her eyes for a second. I made a mental note not to push.

'So you stabbed him in the arm. What happened next?'

'I tried to kick him between the legs, but he turned away and I stabbed him in the thigh, quite deep. I couldn't get the hatpin out. I think it struck the bone.'

'Jesus, Anne!'

A tight smile flickered, but there was too much fear for her to sustain it.

'After a struggle I managed to push him as far as the

bedroom door and that was when I saw the other one – just a glimpse – by the front door.'

'And he was wearing what?'

'Black motorcycle gear, like the other one.'

'Were they tall, short?'

'Tall.'

'Both of them?'

'I think so. Not small, I'm sure of that. I'm sorry, Steve, it happened very fast.'

And there it was again; that mixture of toughness and vulnerability.

Her beauty and sensuality were what struck you initially. But up close, seeing the intelligence, the alertness, you gained a different perspective and somewhere out there was a man with a limp who now shared my opinion.

'Don't apologise. Finish your story, Anne.'

'Where was I?'

'You'd got to the part where you were pushing him out of the bedroom door . . .'

She paused to think and then took up the story again.

'He'd grabbed my throat and I managed to get hold of the end of the hatpin – it was still in his leg – and I wrenched it as hard as I could. He screamed and hit me across the side of the head. As I went backwards the hatpin came out and he tried to grab me again, but I dug him in the hand and shoved him away, out of the bedroom.'

'Go on.'

'I locked the bedroom door and tried to phone the police, but the phone was dead. They must have ripped the wires out. I heard them drive away so I gave them ten minutes. Then got in my car and drove.'

'To Julia's?'

'No.'

'Why not?' I asked softly.

'I don't know . . . I wasn't thinking straight.'

For the first time an element of doubt entered my mind. It wasn't what she said, it was the uncertainty. Up until then she'd been very positive about everything. Now it was suddenly vague.

'What do you think they were after, Anne?'

'The laptop.'

'How did they know you might have the laptop?'

She paused and went to draw on the cigarette yet again. I must have pulled a face, because she stared at me for a moment and then threw the half-smoked Marlboro out of the window. She mouthed 'Sorry', but I shook my head and repeated my question.

'I don't know,' she said, 'maybe they found out something . . . maybe they tortured Hugh Jones before he died.'

I thought of the stab wounds in Jones's shoulder and thigh. I'd read them as attempts to weaken him, before his throat was cut, but they might have easily been signs of torture.

'Didn't Hugh Jones give you any idea what was in the laptop?'

'No.'

'So he gave you the key to his apartment and the password to access the computer?'

'Yes.' Anne reached for another cigarette and my eyes followed her hand. She stopped.

'But he didn't give you any idea as to what it was you were supposed to see?'

'Not directly. Only that it was connected to J. J. Roth.'

'J. J. Roth?'

'Yes.'

'You never mentioned him in connection with the laptop before.'

Maybe some of the doubt crept into my voice or maybe it was her sensitivity. Either way, she didn't like it.

'I didn't say anything about anything.' Her eyes were bright and this time she took a cigarette from the pack and lit it.

I held up my hands. 'Okay – I'm not the enemy here.'

She considered that and when she spoke again her voice was softer.

'Hugh Jones said that he was in fear of his life and if anything should happen to him I should retrieve the laptop. He gave me the key to his apartment and told me it was in St Katharine's Dock in London. That's it. The whole story.'

I nodded to send the right signal. 'So where did you go after you left your cottage?'

'I drove, Steve, as far and as fast as I could. They killed Hugh Jones – and I think I'm next.'

15

'Why are you still here, Anne? What's keeping you?'

'I . . .'

'Leave – take a flat in London, Manchester, anywhere. Just get away, because if what you say is true then they'll be back.'

She shook her head slowly. 'I can't leave, Steve.'

'You mean you won't.'

'Okay, won't. Those bastards from OPMA are trying to frighten me.'

'Frighten you or kill you? Which is it?'

'Both, either – does it matter?'

'I'd say so, yes.'

Again she searched my face. 'It would matter to you?'

'I think so.'

Her eyes became moist and she turned away.

The urge to reach out and put an arm around her shoulders was strong, but I didn't trust my own motives; vulnerable women and overactive hormones in the confines of a car have a history. I peeled away, from instinct.

'I didn't get the laptop.'

She turned back. 'Oh.'

'I searched the place from top to bottom. All I found was these.' I pulled out the keys.

She stared at them for a moment. 'What do they open?'

'I was hoping you'd know.'

She reached out a hand and examined the keys then handed them back.

'I've no idea.'

'They were concealed behind a valve-inspection plate in Jones's bathroom.'

She took them again and fingered the metal lettering. 'Nothing with them? No clue as to what they fit?'

'Not that I could see.'

'You searched everywhere?'

'Twice.'

She offered the keys back to me, but I declined to take them.

'They're of no use to me,' I said evenly.

She got it in one. 'I can't convince you?'

'No.'

Anne covered her face with her hands and sighed. I nearly told her about the intruders in the apartment, but something made me hold back. Maybe it was a test of my own resolution not to become involved any more or maybe because I felt she hadn't been totally open with me. Either way, I kept it to myself.

We sat in silence for a few minutes until she looked at me again.

'The laptop . . .' she began.

'What about it?'

'Maybe it's in a locker somewhere.'

'Maybe. But where?'

Her eyes locked on to mine. In her face I could see fear, determination and calculation. I had no idea what she saw in mine.

'It's decision time, Anne. I'll go back to your cottage with you and you can collect some things and go to Julia. My long-term advice remains the same: get out of Wales. Disappear for a while. There must be other people to take on the fight with OPMA.'

'Not so easy, Steve.'

She went quiet and again I got the feeling that I was way

behind the game. But that was just fine because as far as I was concerned the game had stopped.

'Are you alright to drive?'

She nodded, then suddenly reached out a hand and touched my cheek. I jumped; it was as though an electric shock had gone through me.

Jenny used to touch my face like that when I put up barriers between us, when I backed away from the power she exerted. She'd sense my wariness and reach out to claim me. It always worked, always forced me acknowledge her as a woman with a different set of rules and a different intention. It would be a mistake to assume that was what was happening here with Anne, yet the timing was perfect.

'Are you okay, Steve?'

'Fine. Bit tired, that's all.'

She looked at me, concern written on her face.

'Thank you for what you've done, Steve. I'm sorry if you had a wasted journey to London.'

'I still get paid?'

'Of course.'

'Then it wasn't wasted.' I smiled. 'Time to go, eh?'

I got out of the car and climbed back into the Shogun. Anne reversed and swung the Ford in a tight arc before straightening it up and leading the way out of the exit onto the A470.

We drove for just over a mile and then she turned off on to a B road towards Tabor. We came to a T-junction and she turned right. A quarter of a mile later she swung into a concealed driveway and stopped alongside a squat stone cottage.

I pulled up just behind her and climbed from the Shogun. Anne had got out of her car and was standing beside it, apprehensive.

The sun was low in the early evening sky, casting long shadows from the trees bordering the property, and the air was heavy and still, laden with the scent of roses. Normally it would have seemed idyllic. But its isolation, the shadows and Anne's uneasiness lent it an oppressive atmosphere, a deadness.

'Are you up to this?' I asked.

She hesitated. 'Yes.'

'Did you lock it before you left?'

Her face was pale. 'I can't remember.'

'Wait here.'

I went forward and tried the door. It was unlocked.

The cottage was old, with stone walls three feet thick and heavy, crude timber strutting. The door was low and I had to bend to go through. Inside was a small passage that led directly to the base of a flight of stairs. To the left was an open door that revealed a living area and to the right was an oak door that I opened.

Behind it was a small library room.

The walls were covered in bookshelves crammed tight with books and journals. In one corner was a computer surrounded by CDs, floppies and scattered sheets of A4. I closed the door and went into the living area.

A coffee table was over on its side and cup lay smashed on the floor next to a sticky brown stain. An armchair, presumably the one Anne had been sleeping in, was leaning at an angle against the wall.

Leading off from the room was the kitchen, complete with a cast-iron cooking range and enough copper pans and tied bundles of herbs to convince me that she was serious about food.

Then I searched the bedroom.

It held a large double bed and a suite of typically solid Welsh furniture. Next to the bed was a low chest of drawers and on the chest was a silver photo frame containing the image of a man in his early forties. I picked it up and examined it. He had a strong face with shoulder-length hair and a warm, thoughtful smile.

I put it back and continued my search.

In the far corner of the bedroom was another door; the bathroom. It contained a cottage bath, the old type that you sit in, like a tub. The one concession to modernity was a shower cubicle. I closed the door and went back to the living room.

The decoration throughout the cottage was what you might expect: print-fabric curtains and furniture covers, timber floors, rugs and strategically placed lamps to give the lighting a muted, cosy effect.

All this may have been unoriginal but it was completely authentic.

The style, the function, could have been seen in an artificial form across the breadth of the country maybe fifteen, twenty years ago. But after the fashion had moved on the strictly functional style had survived in the place where it had originated.

I matched what I was seeing against Anne.

In many respects the place reflected her character, yet I felt that there were parts of her not revealed in the cottage; that there was compromise, a studied choice. What had been left out?

The only place I hadn't searched was upstairs.

As I climbed the wooden staircase I heard a sound behind me. I turned to see Anne standing just inside the doorway. I held a hand up to stop her coming in and continued up the stairs.

At the top was a small door. I opened it and went inside to a storage room that ran the length of the cottage. It was crammed full of trunks and tea chests, with a battered sofa against the gable end wall.

I closed the door and went back down to Anne.

'There's no one here. I've looked everywhere.'

She closed her eyes in relief and I took her by the shoulders.

'Call the police. There might be enough blood from the hatpin or drops of it on the carpet to get a DNA test done.'

'No.'

'No?'

'No police.' She was firm and to ask why was to buy back in.

'Get your stuff together and we'll go.'

'No.'

'Anne!'

'They're not going to drive me out of my home.'

'And if they come back? Tonight?'

Anne looked into my face. 'Stay here.'

'What?'

'Tonight. Stay here.'

I opened my mouth, but the situation was so ambiguous I didn't dare speak. Was she asking me to protect her? Or was there more?

She tilted her head to one side. 'Please.'

There was a definite energy then; that electricity that tells you to cross the line, to take a chance. But I couldn't. I held back, not wanting to take advantage of someone driven through fear to ask for help and not wanting to mistake my need for her desire.

'I need to be here,' she said softly, 'and I can't be alone.'

I let go of her.

'Okay.'

She leant forward and kissed my cheek in thanks; dragging the ambiguity back over the line.

'Julia pulled me about the unused bed last night.'

'What did you say?' she breathed.

'I told her to speak to you.'

There was the merest hint of humour in her eyes. 'Did you?'

And there it was all over again, that charge. Was she playing with me?

'I need a bath, then I'll make us something to eat. Would you like a drink?'

I probably looked like I could use one. 'Please.'

'I've Scotch, brandy . . .' She paused. 'And I've got some good Australian red, but perhaps we can save that for the meal.'

'Scotch, then.'

She nodded and went over to a dresser and opened a cupboard at the bottom. She took out the red wine first and pulled the cork before setting it down on one of the shelves. Next she took out the Scotch and two heavy tumblers. Pouring a healthy measure into each she handed me one and then pulled the armchair upright.

'Sit.'

I did as I was told and she handed me the Scotch. Then she pulled down a flap on the dresser to reveal a record deck.

'I keep promising myself a more modern system, but I've lots of vinyl and the music's too good to waste. Do you like Mahalia Jackson?'

'Who?'

'Black gospel singer, died quite a while ago . . . no?'

'Never heard of her. I like Aretha Franklin.'

She smiled in approval. 'Mahalia's the best . . . her voice does it for me. Close your eyes and listen.'

She went into the bedroom and left me to the music.

At first I wondered what the hell she'd put on. When she'd said 'gospel' I thought it would be in the gospel/soul crossover mould, like early Aretha Franklin, but these were hymns. As I listened, a growing sense of awe overtook me as the most amazing sound I'd ever heard issued from the record deck.

Hymn after hymn rippled through me, moving me almost to tears. The emotion, the utter honesty of the voice, shook me and when she sang 'The house I live in' I shook my head; how ironic the words now sounded.

When the album stopped I felt as though I had meditated. I was calmer, more at peace with myself, than I'd known in months, perhaps years. I didn't want to analyse what had happened, I just wanted the feeling to go on and on.

'Steve!' Anne's voice broke into my thoughts.

'Yes?'

'Bring my drink through, please.'

I looked over and saw the Scotch beside the record deck. I fetched it and took it to the door of the bedroom.

'Anne?' I called out.

'In here.'

I pushed the door open. The room was empty, but the door to the bathroom was ajar. Slowly I walked to the door, deliberately dragging a foot; I wanted no misunderstandings.

I knocked on the bathroom door.

'Come in.'

Anne was in the bath, with the water up to her shoulders.

There was nothing to see, except perhaps the smallest of indentations at the top of her breasts, but the obvious intimacy was enough. Her smile was enigmatic, neither come nor go and she was totally relaxed. Whatever frightened her in life, it wasn't men.

I was very aware of her looking at me, reading my reactions, but I was in neutral. If she'd stood up I would have remained in neutral and if she'd screamed I would have again remained in neutral, because if this was going to go anywhere it would be at her bidding, her pace.

She raised an arm out of the water and I gave her the tumbler.

'Thank you.'

I sat on a stool opposite her and lifted my glass. 'Bottoms up.'

The smallest of smiles creased her eyes and she took a sip of the Scotch.

'She's good, isn't she?'

'Extraordinary voice.'

'My mother used to play her endlessly on Sunday afternoons. She never went to church. I think it was meant to be some kind of compensation.'

'It does have power.'

She smiled. 'What do you believe in, Steve?'

'A little less each year.'

'A Zen Buddhist would like that, reducing.'

'And what do you believe in? Besides the planet.'

She closed her eyes, 'In people . . . some people . . . and the ability to reinvent ourselves, to take charge of our lives, to change them . . . for the better.'

'And winds of change . . . things that you can't control, but affect your life . . . what of them?'

She thought about that. 'Listen to your heart, to the things that matter to you.'

'Responsibilities?'

There was a look, almost a smile, but not a smile of humour. She was remembering something. There were other things as well, things deep and personal. She gave a small, dismissive shake of the head.

'More often than not we choose those too, Steve. We just don't admit it.'

She moved and the water swirled and curled around her. She really was beautiful.

'So we're responsible for what happens to us?'

'Usually. Can't control everything, but always have the choice to change.'

'And what about what's happening to you now . . . this break-in, Hugh Jones's death?'

'Karma.' It was said like she was trying to convince herself.

'You can't plead choice and fatalism in one breath, Anne.'

'Karma isn't fate, it's a life-path. Even living is a choice.'

That stopped my glass halfway to my mouth. If she meant the words to shock me she couldn't have done a better job.

'Is that why you're staying here and not at Julia's?'

'No.'

'Then why?'

'She's like you: she wants me to leave Wales.'

'What if I choose to leave, now?'

Her head tilted again. 'You won't.'

'Sure of that, are you?'

'Aren't you?'

16

Anne sipped at her Scotch and, seeing that the glass was nearly empty, swirled it around and finished it before handing it to me.

'Could you pass me that towel behind you?'

'Sure.'

It was beginning to feel very strange – intimate, but with blurred rules. I had a sense that she wasn't manipulating, but reaching, slowly, trying to decide.

'Put some more music on if you like,' she called out.

'Mahalia Jackson again?'

'Something different. You choose.'

I placed her tumbler on the dresser and flipped through the album collection expecting more Dylan than Domingo. But, again, she surprised me. There was more opera than any other kind of music. I found a compilation album and selected Elisabeth Schwarzkopf and Jeannine Collard singing the 'Barcarolle' from the *Tales of Hoffman*. As the music seeped beyond the living room Anne called out.

'Good choice!'

I sat down in the armchair and let the lilting sound wash over me.

She had collated mood music. I'd have guessed that the whole collection had been selected to produce particular atmospheres, release certain feelings. This was a person so in touch with her emotions, so close to knowing herself, that she could accurately reflect it in her home and her possessions.

Perhaps that was the strength I'd been sensing from our first meeting?

And yet there was still something else; something missing from the picture.

When the music ended I got up and went through the collection again. Although mainly opera, there was some contemporary.

I came across some Hall and Oates and felt a smile of irony spread across my face; Jenny had always liked their music, always danced on hearing the white rock/white soul fusions.

Perhaps that's why it felt strange. Jenny was far from out of my system that even being here raised questions of guilt and belonging. Under the circumstances, time and distance, that was illogical, but emotion and logic rarely share the same shoes.

I put the album to one side.

Anne appeared at the bedroom door, wrapped in a large bath towel with another wound around her head. She went over to the dresser and poured herself another Scotch.

'Can't decide?'

'You decide,' I said.

She flipped quickly through the records and settled on some Eurhythmics. Then held up the bottle.

'Top you up?'

I held up my glass and she walked over and poured the Scotch. I noticed then that she had a circular scar on the right side of her chest. She caught me looking at it.

'Car accident . . . some years ago,' she explained.

'I didn't mean to stare.'

She spoke softly. 'You've been staring from the minute you arrived.'

'Have I?'

She nodded slowly. 'Thank you for staying.'

I shrugged. 'You're isolated here.'

'Very.'

'Deliberately so?'

'Of course.'

'You've always lived here on your own?'

'Always,' she paused, 'ah . . . the bedroom?'

'I couldn't help noticing it when I looked around.'

She walked back over to the dresser and replaced the bottle, speaking over her shoulder at me.

'He never lived here.'

'Past tense?'

She turned and looked at me directly. 'Yes.'

I said nothing, but she read the silence.

'So what am I doing with a photograph next to my bed? Remembering, Steve.' She closed the dresser and again spoke without looking around. 'I'll get dressed and cook us dinner.'

She disappeared back into the bedroom, leaving me wondering whether I'd just blundered into something intensely private or had inadvertently slipped back into an inquiry agent mode without realising. Perhaps it amounted to the same thing either way.

I would have to watch that.

Five minutes later she emerged, dressed in black leather trousers and a black silk blouse. She wore them spectacularly well. Between her graceful way of moving and elegant, simple dressing I couldn't help thinking that I was seeing the other side of her, the 'something else' that wasn't fully revealed.

The cottage and the environmentalism were one thing, this, the sophistication, was another. There was a duality here: two people residing within one and not completely reconciled, as though she was aspiring to something that wasn't instinctively her.

Who are you, Anne Lloyd? Why the schism?

She beckoned me to follow her into the kitchen.

'Do you cook?'

I laughed. 'If I have to.'

'No one to do it for you?' she asked as she opened the fridge.

I'd started the personal questions so I could hardly refuse an answer.

'Not any more.'

'Were you married?' She took out a large fish that I didn't recognise and held it up. I nodded.

'Lived together,' I said, leaning against the wall.

'Long time? Short time?'

'I asked for this, didn't I?'

'You don't have to answer.'

She said it almost playfully. Beautiful and intelligent and each effortlessly achieved. *Any man would want you, Anne Lloyd.*

'Five years,' I said.

'Oh, long time.'

'Felt a long time.'

She stopped. 'No photographs around the place, then?'

'No *place* any more.'

'It happened or you chose?'

I laughed. 'This a test?'

'No, a question.'

I nodded slowly, accepting the logic of her earlier argument. 'Yes, I chose.'

'But it feels like you had no choice?'

'Something like that.'

She nodded, took down a large pan and poured a little oil into it. Then selected some herbs and chopped them finely.

'Garlic?'

'Fine,' I replied.

I watched as she prepared the fish, quickly, almost professionally so.

'You can pour me a glass of wine if you like.'

She opened a head-height cupboard, took two wine glasses

from it and set them down on a large wooden table at the far
end of the kitchen.

The ritual of cooking and the opening of the wine felt as
intimate as talking to her while she'd been in the bath and all
the time I was matching my thinking against what I felt. *Switch
off, Stevie. What happens, happens.*

Plates were produced as she worked around me.

Every now and again she'd smile and ask me to do some-
thing small or ask me about Ty Hiraeth. Did I like it there?
What did I make of Eric Lawrence and Elizabeth Rhys-
Davies? Twice I mentioned fire-fighting and twice she let it lie.

When it was ready – the fish, the salad, the home-made
bread and the wine – we sat down.

'It looks good,' I said.

Anne filled the glasses and said, 'Salut.'

The fish was good, really good, and every once in a while I
caught her watching me. I smiled and told her what I thought
of the food and she responded by topping up the glasses and
pushing the bread towards me.

When we'd finished we took the remainder of the wine into
the living room and made ourselves comfortable in the two
large armchairs.

'Can we talk about your trip to London?' she asked.

'Sure.'

'I got the impression that there was something you left out.'

'Why do you say that?'

'Just a feeling.'

'You were shaken up by what happened last night . . . it
didn't seem too clever to add to it.'

She considered that. 'Tell me now, please.'

I took a sip of the wine and looked at her carefully. 'While I
was in Hugh Jones's apartment two men broke in and beat me
up. I was left tied hand and foot.'

The colour drained from her face.

'What time was this?'

'Early evening.'

For a moment she didn't speak, but it didn't take a genius to work out where she was going to end up so I saved her the trouble.

'They had time to get back here for three in the morning. It could have been your two intruders.'

'The laptop?'

'The laptop,' I agreed.

'Which was why you asked me how tall they were?'

I inclined my head.

She propped her head in the fork of her hand and sighed.

'You asked,' I said.

'I did. Thank you for telling me. At least I now know that they weren't trying to kill me.'

'How do you make that out?'

'Well, they had the opportunity to kill *you*. But they didn't.'

'I don't know anything, Anne.'

'They didn't know that. No, if they didn't intend to kill you, then it was the laptop. It had to be.'

'*If* they're the same two men,' I put in.

'Who else could it be?'

'Well, I wouldn't know that, would I?'

She went quiet at that.

I had to admit I was curious, but reminded myself that to ask questions was to row myself back in and that was no longer possible.

'If I could find what those keys were for, would you try again for me?'

'No.' My voice was flat.

'Even if I might be in danger?'

'You have options, Anne. You don't have to be in danger. Okay, I accept that you're committed to stopping OPMA. But, as you said, we make choices.'

'It's not that easy, Steve. They might not let it go at that.'

'Why?'

She sighed and fell silent again.

I put down my drink and waited.

Her hands came up, 'Okay, I owe you, but I'm not going to tell you. It's better for you that I don't.'

'Your choice.'

For a minute, maybe longer, we stared at each other. I sensed fear, stubbornness, but above all a feeling that she was protecting something, someone. I had no right to the information; I was refusing to become involved, but I did feel protective no matter how illogical that seemed.

She closed her eyes and sighed. 'Have you ever heard of a drug called Pheladone?'

'No. Is this connected to the laptop?'

'I don't know.'

'I risked my arse for you, Anne.'

'I can't tell you what I don't know, all right! Look, it's not you they want.'

'You?'

'Me and the laptop – one's no good without the other.'

'Jesus Christ, Anne, how many more times? Go to the police!'

'That's not possible, Steve.' She was very still.

'Going to the police means exposing yourself, doesn't it?'

She nodded. 'And others.'

'Which leaves you where?'

Her face became hard, like I'd seen it in the car.

'Which leaves me with little choice . . . I'm not going to back off.'

When a woman as intelligent and strong-minded as Anne Lloyd commits herself to a cause, then she has to be taken seriously. But, as she knew, multinationals are super-predators:

they deal with opposition groups in all forms regularly, and have a track record of winning.

You don't beat them. At best you can mobilise public opinion and force the government of the day to take account of that, but that's all. Occasionally, somewhere, an environmental group wins, but it's rare and it's dangerous.

The exchange had changed the atmosphere in the room and I was annoyed with myself. Anne seemed on edge and, with the wine finished, went back to drinking Scotch.

I decided that the drink had played a part in my letting the conversation run into a cul-de-sac and decided to stop while I could still make the decision.

She tried to lighten the mood, but it was artificial, forced, and she was pouring bigger Scotches each time. I knew she was trying too hard when she brought up the fire brigade. As I watched she became tearful and started to slur, before slowly slipping into sleep. I managed to catch her glass before it hit the floor.

I left her in the armchair and explored the kitchen for coffee.

There was a full pot, already made, to one side of the cooking range. I poured myself a cup and wandered back into the living room. Apart from Anne's muted breathing the cottage was eerily quiet so I sat and drank the coffee, watching her sleep, aware once again of just how intimate that was.

After a while I got up and wandered outside to the driveway. It was around half-nine but still warm, with the light of the day edging the mountains and the evening air heady with rose scent.

The edginess that I had sensed on arrival now seemed fanciful. Instead, the cottage and its setting were revealed as perfect, replete; a place of solitude.

I could live here; escape to a new life.

Lost in thought, something caught my eye and I turned and smiled. It was a bat, hunting insects; then another and another.

They flew by like stroboscopic birds; their flight erratic, bewildering, and I felt a sudden wave of elation.

As a child I'd loved nature with the passion of someone brought up in a city. The trees, mountains, woods and sea that I'd yearned for were all here. Doubtless the locals would add – no work, but this was a place to live, to stay in balance, away from the rasp that passed for modern urban existence.

It wasn't hard to see why someone would want to protect it, why they'd fight to keep it whole. Too much was being given to industry, to greed, for along with our inheritance we were selling our soul.

I stayed there, feeling the warm breeze on my face and watching the light gradually fade from the horizon as the night seeped across the landscape to claim the mountains and the sea.

The breeze picked up and I thought I heard a sound from inside so I went back into the cottage.

Anne was still sleeping; leaning to one side in the chair. She looked . . . magical; the anxiety and fear that had haunted her earlier had gone, leaving a creature so lovely, so beguiling, it made me stand and stare.

I thought of the framed photograph from the bedroom. Why would someone leave a woman like this? What had happened between them to leave her with a memory precious enough to sustain?

It was a redundant question. Even if I knew it would mean little for we all harm each other in the end; we just find differing ways to do it.

I thought of waking her, but instead picked her up, immediately aware of the heavy perfume and softness of her body against me; there was nothing beneath the blouse. Carefully, I carried her through to the bedroom and laid her down on the bed.

As I turned her on her side to make sure she didn't swallow

her tongue two buttons popped open and her left breast tumbled from the silk.

I stepped back. 'Sweet Jesus!'

I stood dead still for what seemed an age then reached out, pulled the silk from beneath the breast and covered her. Her breathing changed and I thought for a moment she would wake, but she merely moved in her sleep and her breathing resumed its rhythm.

Moving as quietly as I could, I backed out of the room and closed the door behind me.

There was a small sofa against one wall in the living room and I turned off all but one of the table lamps and made myself as comfortable as I could. I dozed fitfully at first, the sofa offering me no chance to stretch out and relieve the cramp in my legs. Eventually fatigue and drink won out and I drifted off.

I woke once and settled down again. It was then that the nightmare claimed me and, if anything, it was even more horrific than the last.

It followed the usual pattern of stark images and faceless firefighters, but then confronted me with the scorched and blackened face of Sandy screaming uncontrollably; writhing in agony from the horrific burns.

I screamed out, but no one would help me. I was holding him in my arms, telling him to hang on and trying to get him to keep his head back, when he reached out and touched my face.

I sat bolt upright, hearing myself cry out.

A pair of hands seized my head and pulled me close. I wanted to struggle, but then caught Anne's perfume as I tried to choke off the sobbing.

'It's all right . . . it's just a dream,' she said softly.

My body was shaking uncontrollably and a spasm of anger, of shame, chased its way down my spine.

'I've got you . . . relax . . . I've got you,' she said, pulling me tighter.

As I regained control the shaking stopped and she released her grip. I looked up at her; she was wearing only the blouse. I stood up and began to speak, but she put her hand across my mouth, then removed it and kissed me.

The sensation of her against me was incredible; the silk of the blouse was tissue thin.

I returned her kiss, sliding my hands up to her waist, and in return felt her press against me. Cupping her face in my hands, I kissed her eyes, her throat and then her mouth. She pulled at my belt, releasing it, letting my trousers fall to the floor. I stepped out of them and her hand found me.

I could smell her then, her arousal.

The feel of her, the combination of perfume and her, made me tingle as though someone had run ice along my spine.

She took my hand and led me towards the bedroom, stopping halfway to turn and kiss me again. Inside, beside the bed, she slipped the shirt from my shoulders and slid my boxer shorts down until she was kneeling before me.

'Close your eyes,' she breathed.

I closed them and felt her tongue trace along the underside of me, before she enveloped me whole. My whole body was alive as her hands held and her lips and tongue worked slowly, delicately, producing shudders that swept my body in repeated waves.

Slowly, subtly, she caressed and licked, bringing me near, very near, until she stopped and I took her shoulders and drew her to her feet. I opened the blouse and held her breasts as my tongue found hers. She was so soft, so silken beneath my hands, so beautiful.

I laid her down upon the bed and found her with my tongue. She arched her back and held my head as she pushed against me and a small cry, almost a sob, escaped her. I tried to match my movements to her breathing, responding to the subtle vibrations that rippled through her, bringing her near, but controlling it, as she had me.

Then I entered her and she groaned and moved beneath me.

Each time she was near I withdrew and kissed her and each time I felt myself near I stopped and looked into her eyes. The feeling of being inside her was so good, so wondrous; I wanted it to go on and on.

She gasped and moved suddenly and I knew she was there; only then did I release, holding her so tight I had to let go for fear of hurting her.

When, finally, we were still, I held her in my arms and for an instant and to my shame, I looked for Jenny in her eyes.

17

We made love throughout the night and held each other in between.

The one lapse of thinking about Jenny was balanced by a feeling that Anne was also compensating for pain and hurt. Perhaps that's why we didn't talk, perhaps that's why we just held and kissed, letting the physical sensations hold the past at bay.

As the night wore on, for me, at least, the ghosts vanished.

Anne was so alive, so sensual, that no memory could subvert her. The woman in her was so strong it demanded all my attention, all my thoughts and feelings. I became so wrapped up in the fierce emotion, so immersed in her that the night slipped by unregulated by hours and minutes, shaped only by periods of furious lovemaking.

She'd hang her arms around my neck and nuzzle me into her breasts and I would come alive again, would need to be inside her, possessing her, losing myself in the intensity of our lovemaking.

I don't remember falling asleep, but the bright morning light streaming through the window woke me.

I lay there, the scent of her, the scent of her perfume, clinging to my body; still able to feel the sensation of her breasts pressed against me.

The sounds of Anne in the kitchen carried and then the light slapping sound of her footsteps on the stone-flagged floor announced her return. The bedroom door opened and she stood there naked, her head tilted characteristically to one side. There was a cup in each hand.

'Morning.'

The smile on her face sent a shiver through me and for a moment I said nothing, just stared at her, marvelling at her unselfconsciousness.

'Come back to bed,' I said.

Her smile became a tease. 'Coffee?'

'Here.' I threw back the duvet and she walked over, placing the coffee cups on the bedside dresser.

She knelt on the bed and I took her hands and kissed the palms of each in turn, then each breast and finally her lips. She threw her head back and laughed; a sound so musical, so deliciously feminine I felt myself become aroused again.

She saw the way I looked at her and she reached for me, clutching me tightly.

Something changed then.

I had the feeling that she needed to hold me, as if for an instant she'd become uncertain. Then she released me and slipped under the duvet, moulding herself against the side of me, her head resting on my chest.

'When did you last make love to someone, Steve?'

The question caught me off guard and I turned to face her; she was deadly serious.

I thought for a minute, 'A couple of months, getting on for three. Why?'

'Not that long, then?'

I didn't know what she wanted, where she was going with this, so I spoke what I felt.

'Time doesn't always show the size of the gulf. Three months seems an age.'

She snuggled into my chest again.

'For me it's been longer . . . much longer . . . yet seems only the other day.'

'I don't know what to say.'

'Say nothing,' she whispered, 'just hold me.'

She lay there for a while and then suddenly turned, reached up and kissed me passionately. I don't know what I'd done, but it evidently had been the right thing. We kissed again and then she settled back down.

I'd have been content to stay there the rest of the day, but I had to show my face at Ty Hiraeth.

'Do you know that it's nearly nine?' she said.

'Your sister will know that my bed's not been slept in again.'

'To hell with her. It's about time she stopped fighting herself and took John Vaughan to bed.'

'Ah, that's the way of it?'

She gave that delicious little laugh again. 'He's had the hots for her for years.'

'Doesn't she fancy him?'

'She fancies him like mad, but she's too straight.'

'Straight?'

She leant up on one elbow. 'I forgot, you don't know all the local gossip, do you? He's married.'

'I see.'

'I don't. He wants her, she wants him and life's short.'

I thought of Jenny. She'd have phrased it differently, but the viewpoint was the same, except perhaps Anne was more open.

'We're back to choices . . .'

A shadow passing across the window cut me short and Anne spun, her eyes wide.

I mouthed at her to stay still and slid from the bed. The shadow swept across the window again and I quickly pulled on my boxer shorts and walked towards the bedroom door, careful not to make any noise.

Although the curtains were closed in the bedroom the living-room ones were merely pulled halfway, allowing anyone outside to look in. Peering around the edge of the bedroom door, I saw my trousers in front of the sofa, where they'd fallen and retrieved them, then walked quietly out into the passage-way.

Suddenly there was a heavy knock on the door.

'Anne! Anne . . . it's me, Bonny.'

Anne appeared behind me, the duvet wrapped around her. I shrugged, to say 'What d'you want to do?'

She nodded and I opened the door, my foot planted six inches behind it.

I'd seen him on the bridge and at the back of Ty Hiraeth, but up close I saw for the first time just how big he was and his extraordinary mass of curly silver-grey hair and dark, pene-trating eyes. It was the sort of face that might appear on a tobacco tin or in an advert for country ales.

He was wearing the same waxed three-quarter-length coat that I'd seen on the toll bridge and carried a heavy hiking stick about four feet long.

My first instinct was to smile, but he had a presence, a weight to him that suggested more than the bucolic geniality of the surface.

He leant forward, peering through the gap in the doorway.

'I'm sorry to call if it's inconvenient, only I chanced by yesterday afternoon and your door was wide open . . . thought something had happened to you, Anne.'

'Come in, Bonny.'

He hesitated and stared at the duvet.

Anne laughed, 'I'll put some clothes on . . . Bonny, this is Steve Jay. Steve, meet Bonny.'

I stood back and pulled the door fully open. He came in and pumped my hand; the grip was firm to the point of pain and I nodded to him.

He walked in, almost filling the cramped passage, and turned into the living room as though he knew his way about. I followed him through and he stopped in the centre of the room, his eyes coming to rest on my discarded shirt and shoes by the sofa.

Anne came out of the bedroom with a blue silk dressing gown on that hid little. She scooped up my shirt and shoes and threw them to me with a mischievous smile. Bonny took all this in and beamed at Anne like a randy uncle.

'Coffee, Bonny?' she asked.

'That's very good of you . . . three sugars and black, please?'

Anne disappeared into the kitchen and I put my shirt on and started to button it up. He waited, trying to catch my eye.

'You're up the house, then?' His head went back, waiting for the answer.

'The house – ah – Ty Hiraeth?' I said. 'Yes.'

'Lovely place, lovely. Not long been there, then?'

'Last Friday.'

'Oh, Friday. You'd have seen the forest fire?'

He was looking around the living room the whole time. Nosy came nowhere close.

'Yes, terrible.'

I didn't mention being there or what had happened to Bryn Thomas. He turned to look in the direction of the kitchen.

'Known Anne long, have you?' His eyes met mine.

'Not long.'

'Ah,' he said, as though breathing out.

Four straight questions on the trot made me sit down and busy myself with putting my shoes and socks on, avoiding his eyes and the opportunity for him to ask any more. Thankfully, Anne appeared with his coffee and sat next to me.

'They found another of those trucks, Anne,' he said.

She frowned. 'Where exactly?'

'Middle of the Coed-y-Garth.'

'Wasn't that where the fire was the other day?' I asked.

I looked at Anne and she exchanged looks with Bonny. He

nodded, as if agreeing to an unasked question. Anne paused, then explained.

'Every time there's been a forest fire it's because of a mining survey, Steve. The trucks and equipment are burnt and then they set fire to the forest, to make the point.'

'I think the bodies of those young soldiers do that only too well, don't you?'

Bonny leant forward. 'Most people around here would agree with you. But some – a few – don't, see?'

'The fires are wrong, Bonny,' put in Anne.

'Desperation it is,' he said.

'You're a gold prospector yourself, aren't you?' I said.

He sighed and his mouth turned down at the edges. 'I pan for gold. I work the rivers and the streams where nature has washed the gold from the land. I don't kill wildlife and poison the land.'

I shook my head and looked at Anne. 'Kill the wildlife?'

'Tell him, Bonny,' she said.

He loosened his coat and scratched under his arm. 'When they mine the hills they get water in the shafts – collects naturally by percolating through the hillside, see. Then they have to pump it out and all the mineral layers that they've cut through, like iron – especially iron – leech out into the rivers and turn them a rust colour. Poisons the fish and everything else.'

'You're part of the movement, then, Bonny?' I asked.

He shook his head. 'I'm Welsh, born and bred,' he said firmly. Then added, 'I don't belong to anything much, but like most around here I've had enough.'

'I see. So these forest fires are meant to drive the mining company away?'

He shrugged and smiled at Anne. 'Wouldn't know, but people are angry, yes. I'd say some are even angry enough to start fires.'

There's a history of people around here starting fires when things don't go their way, isn't there?'

He nodded glumly and Anne went still. Something passed between them, something unspoken yet instantly understood by both.

She placed a hand on my forearm. 'We left our coffees in the bedroom. I'll make us some fresh.'

As Anne disappeared Bonny started to ask questions again. I decided to make him work for it and kept the answers short, leaving him little place to go.

'You're a fireman, then?'

'Firefighter – we're all politically correct nowadays.'

He looked puzzled and then a slow smile spread across his face.

'Firefighter . . . is that so?'

'They insist,' I explained.

'Where're you from?'

'London.'

He nodded as though it confirmed things for him.

'I was there once.'

'Travel broadens the mind.'

He gave a sly smile and held his finger up, not that it stopped him.

'Are you going to be here long, Steven?'

No one had called me 'Steven' since baptism.

'Don't know . . . hopefully a few weeks . . . might try panning for gold.'

He grinned. 'Not that easy.'

'I bet.'

Anne came back with two fresh cups of coffee and sat down next to me again. I must admit it was good feeling her against my arm. I looked at her and she gave me a smile that made Bonny's departure seem desirable. I'm sure he saw it too, but he didn't budge.

He suddenly frowned. 'D'you know, Anne, I've come here to check that you were all right and I haven't asked you how you are.'

'I'm fine, Bonny.'

'Are you sure, now?'

'Yes, really. I left my door open when I went out, that's all.'

'Good, good. I hope you don't mind only I looked inside. Saw the chair overturned and thought something nasty had happened,' he continued.

'An accident,' she lied, 'tearing around to get out the door.'

'Right. Didn't hurt yourself at all?'

He seemed to be spinning things out. Anne deliberately took hold of my arm and leant into me and at last he stood up, but still held his ground, reluctant to go.

'Was there something else, Bonny?' asked Anne.

He sighed. 'Well, it might be nothing, but I saw that strange fella from Ty Hiraeth, hanging around when I found your door open.'

'Hanging around?' She queried

'Seemed to be. He was in running gear and when he saw me he bent over, like he was out of breath. But I think he was waiting.'

'Waiting for what?'

'I thought maybe you'd know.'

She shook her head.

'Bit of an odd customer, that fella . . . right, I'll be going then. Thanks for the coffee, Anne.'

'You're welcome.'

Anne showed him out. When she came back she was grinning like mad.

'He's unbelievable,' I said.

'Ask you a lot of questions, did he?'

'Didn't stop and there's no point in hinting, is there?'

She burst out laughing. 'None whatsoever. He's a one-off, is Bonny. King of the mountain.'

'How d'you come to know him?'

She paused. 'I made a point of it. He knows everyone and everything around here. There's a lot more going on behind the eyes than there first seems with Bonny.'

I took hold of her. 'I've got to be making a move as well, but I'd like a shower before I go.'

'Not staying for breakfast?'

'Can't.'

Her face was serious, 'Come to dinner, then – tonight.'

18

I stayed for breakfast in the end and eventually got back to Ty Hiraeth after eleven, only to walk straight into Julia.

'You've an appointment with Elizabeth in fifteen minutes,' she said, with the suggestion of a sniff. 'I was told to tell you to wear walking boots.'

Great. That's all I needed.

'Nothing like a walk in the hills to clear your head.' She gave a thin smile.

'My head's clear,' I said flatly.

She paused. 'You're married, aren't you, Steve?'

'No.'

Her head tilted to one side, like Anne's. 'Live with someone, then.'

'Do I?'

Her mouth opened, but I turned on my heel and walked up the stairs, feeling her eyes boring into me. I bumped into Eddie Marlowe at the top and he grinned at me.

'Just back?'

'What's your guess?'

'It's always an adventure with you isn't it?'

'If only you knew, Eddie,' I smiled back.

'Don't suppose you're up for a drink tonight?'

I winked. 'Dinner with Anne.' I glanced down the stairs. 'Don't mention it to anyone, especially Eve.'

'I'm pleased for you . . . the both of you.'

'We will have that beer, Eddie, but at the moment . . .'

'I understand. Breakfast was quiet again this morning.'

I shook my head, 'Breakfast was perfect. Listen, I've got Elizabeth in fifteen minutes and I've got to change – knackered before we even start.'

'I've no sympathy for you, none whatsoever.'

'Cheers, mate.'

The session with Elizabeth followed much the same pattern as before, except I felt stronger and able to open up more easily. As we sweated our way up the hill I told her about Jenny – everything – and I didn't regret it.

We stopped at one point and caught our breath; me more than her.

That's when she hit me with the link from Sandy to Jenny.

Her theory was that in some way my feelings of guilt over Sandy were triggered by my failure to control events. That it had hit a panic button deep inside me, the same panic button that Jenny had pressed by leaving me. In both I had been reduced to a spectator, involved, but unable to influence the outcome.

My instinct was to dismiss the idea, but under her cool gaze I bit the rejection back. Then, at the end of the session, she said something that at first deeply irritated and then later intrigued me.

'There's something trapped inside you, Steve, something that's been there a long time. It ticks away and governs your reactions, rules your life.'

The weeks that followed were special.

I walked the hills by day, sometimes with Elizabeth and sometimes on my own and the nights I spent with Anne, drinking wine, making love and listening to the astonishing Mahalia Jackson.

The word joy was not one I tended to use about myself, or my life, but that's what I felt then. Towards the end of the first week the blindingly obvious once again tapped me on the shoulder; I was falling in love.

Occasionally the outside world impinged on my new life; a faint column of smoke on the horizon where a forest fire raged, or the sight of a police car at the turn-off for Hugh Jones's house, which was still a crime scene. But these I was determined to make echoes.

The one sour note was Pritchard. He turned up on a couple of occasions without John Vaughan and spoke to Jamie Howard, but took the trouble to make sure that I knew he was about.

There was something about him that triggered an irrational anger in me and I think it showed in my face.

But I had other things to distract me.

One day Anne and I went skinny-dipping in Llyn Cwm-Mynach, a secluded lake in the mountains. We took a picnic and a bottle of Shiraz and lay naked, letting the sun dry us before making love.

We talked and laughed, but there were also silences; periods when to be together seemed enough.

That Saturday, I arrived back at Ty Hiraeth after spending the night with Anne and was told by Elizabeth to meet her outside, ready for walking, at eleven sharp.

When I emerged from the house Elizabeth was sitting in the Land Rover.

'Climb in!'

'Where are we headed?' I asked.

'Craig-yr-Aderyn.'

'Where?'

'Bird Rock . . . feeling fit?'

'Is it high?'

'Not too far.'

Like Bryn she drove insanely fast.

London traffic creates chancers, thinkers and the hopelessly lost; the open roads of Wales seemed to produce potential orthopaedic cases in transit. It was just as that thought entered my head that a fully laden gravel lorry tried to overtake us on a bend and Elizabeth had to hit the brakes to let him through before he hit another lorry head-on.

She glanced at him as he went by and made a dismissive hissing sound.

At Cross Foxes we turned onto the A487 (T) and shortly after reached a rugged U-shaped glacial valley that dropped steeply down to Tal-y-llyn Lake. My eyes were everywhere and a smile never left my face, for this was untamed land of crag and water and the high dark green shoulders of mountains.

At the hamlet of Abergynolwyn we took the narrow twisting road to the wild Dysynni valley, emerging just beyond the Pont Ystumanner Bridge into the neck of the valley itself.

Further on I saw a sheer rock face erupt from the valley floor. It drew the eye and sent a shiver through me. I looked at Elizabeth and she just smiled and nodded before bringing the Land Rover to a halt at the side of the road.

We got out and stared up at the rock.

'Not high?' I queried.

'Two hundred and fifty-eight metres, but it rises from sea level, that's what makes it seem so big.'

'It *is* big!'

She looked at me. 'Ready?'

'For what, exactly?'

'I've something to show you,' she said seriously. 'Stay with me.'

She went over the stile like it wasn't there and set off at a fast clip. I'd been getting fitter with each walk and the nights spent in Anne's arms had seen me sleep better than for months. Now was as good a time as any and I was determined to match her.

Within ten minutes I was wet with sweat and Elizabeth had

opened out a fifty-yard lead. I started to get a second wind and increased the pace, but the footpath was steep and getting steeper all the time. Every now and again she'd turn and smile in a very untherapeutic way and I'd pretend not to notice.

Twenty minutes in and I was breathing hard and feeling it in the thighs and calves whilst she seemed to have the constitution of a Sherpa – and no pity.

The path took us in a loop so that behind us the blue-green bulk of Cader Idris dominated the skyline. I paused for breath at one point and ran the back of my hand across my face. Everywhere I looked was forest and mountain, with only a few farms hugging the road in the valley.

Further on she waited for me, below a particularly sharp rise. As I reached her she pointed into the sky and I saw the black shapes of birds wheeling and diving in the thermals.

'There!'

I squinted against the bright sunlight. 'What are they?'

'Cormorants.'

She was smiling, waiting for me to get it.

'Is that why we're here?' I said finally.

'Yes. Come on.'

With that she started climbing quickly again and I swore softly and tried to keep pace. Cormorants?

Ten minutes later I made it to the top. Elizabeth was waiting with her back to me and her hands on her hips. As I approached her I realised that she was on the very edge of the cliff face.

The warm wind was blowing strongly and as I stood alongside her I tried not to look down. I wasn't nervous of heights, but it was a sheer drop and the feeling of exposure was acute.

'Magnificent, isn't it?'

'Pretty good,' I agreed, planting my feet.

She sat down, her legs over the edge. 'I don't come here often enough.'

'So why today? And don't say cormorants.'

She looked up at me. 'But that's exactly why we're here.'

'I'm listening.'

She patted the rock edge. 'Sit down.'

I sat and waited.

'Last time we spoke, Steve, you told me about Jenny, about how she cheated on you and how you let her back only to watch her cheat again.'

'I don't know that she cheated a second time,' I corrected her. 'In fact, I don't believe she did, although I had no way of knowing. It was just that she was finding too many excuses to see him. I was frightened – I wasn't going to go through all that again.'

She nodded. 'Either way, you felt out of control and decided to take back control by pushing her out of your life.'

'Yes, I suppose so.'

'And when Sandy was injured, again you couldn't control what was happening.'

I shook my head. 'You said this before, Elizabeth, but I'm not convinced it's connected.'

'Okay. Let's leave that for now. Instead, I want you to tell me about how it was for you as a child.'

'Why?' I asked guardedly.

'Because I've been reading your notes.'

'Bad potty training, you mean?'

'I'm serious, Steve. Tell me, please.'

I sighed and phrased the words carefully, letting the facts speak for themselves.

'My mother was an alcoholic. When I was young—'

'How young?'

'Five . . . maybe six . . .'

'Continue.'

'When I was five she was hospitalised.'

'Why?'

'She was a drunk . . . used to be on binges for days on end. My father, what I remember of him, was a bastard, pure and simple. He didn't give a damn about me. When she went into the hospital he left. I was fostered and never saw either of them again.'

'I'm sorry.'

'Long time ago. I survived.'

'Can you speak about this? I mean, even now – can you talk about everything that happened . . . without anger?'

I smiled tightly, 'Talk yes, without anger? Not so sure.' I paused, 'Anger's like grief . . . it diminishes, but never quite leaves you. That's what a therapist would say . . . isn't it?'

She didn't answer me, but instead gently asked questions about my childhood and particularly my teenage years. What were my foster-parents like? Did I make friends easily? Did I have girlfriends? And – the killer – did I want children?

I answered truthfully, but flippancy and sarcasm crept in once or twice. I didn't faze her and even I realised why I was doing it. The process hurt. It dredged up a lot of shit and made me uncomfortable.

But I found my answers got longer, like she'd breached a barrier, letting the words flood through. When, abruptly, the questions stopped and she went quiet, I felt open, vulnerable.

I'd just told her things I didn't even like thinking about, but I also felt relief. When she spoke again her voice was soft.

'I'd like you to hear me out, Steve.'

'Go ahead.'

'I think you have an ingrained dread of things being out of your control. You blame yourself whenever things go wrong in your life and you cannot stop them from happening. I believe that your experiences as a child tore away any real sense of security and that you still blame yourself for what happened.'

I worked hard not to dismiss that. 'Maybe.'

'When Jenny left you the insecurity of your childhood erupted. Then, when you'd made some adjustment to her going, when you found that anger kept the pain at bay, she came back and threw your life into turmoil. To let her back you had to let go of the anger, only to get hurt again.'

'Go on.'

'Think about it, you gave her a chance and she let you down and then your anger was redirected against yourself.'

I nodded. 'I was angry for being mug enough to take her back.'

'Perhaps you didn't have as much choice as you thought, Steve. You needed her, needed to be her lover again. Then doubt crept in and you leapt for the only control mechanism available, reject her before she rejected you. Finally, there was the disaster with Sandy and whether you knew it or not you were in no shape to deal with the consequences. Result; the nightmares and intense feelings of guilt. Guilt is what's ticking away inside you, Steve; the automatic assumption that you are to blame.'

There was truth in that and this was a time for truth.

I gave a short nod of recognition. 'And the cormorants?'

She looked down the valley towards the dark blue of Cardigan Bay.

'What we're sitting on is a sea cliff, Steve. Nine hundred years ago the sea receded, but the cormorants stayed. They won't leave. They're tied to this rock and they won't accept that the sea has gone.'

I looked up at the birds again.

She continued, 'In many ways that's like you, Steve. You're tied to your childhood insecurity, to your guilt, refusing to leave it, but you *have* to leave it because Jenny, Sandy, everything, is viewed from the presumption that you are to blame, that you were in control or should have been in control. But that's impossible. None of us control our lives to that degree. You have to relinquish the past, Steve. You have to let go – if you're to have any future.'

We got back to Ty Hiraeth mid-afternoon and I decided to get cleaned up and pay Bryn Thomas a much overdue visit.

He lived in Barmouth, at the very mouth of the estuary, a cramped tumble of a town with houses hugging the mountain on one side and overlooking the sea on the other. It had seen better times and the views as I walked to his house alternated between seascapes of power and beauty to oppidan quaintness and, at times, scruffiness.

I loved it.

Above me gulls banked and dipped, their ragged, indignant cries slicing the air, announcing their presence.

Below them, the streets held knots of outsiders, tourists, bringing their annual lifeline of money, that enabled so many of the locals to eke out a living across the twelve months.

Bryn's house lay back from the sea, at the end of a narrow, steep lane lined with tiny two-up, two-down houses with flaky, salt-dried paintwork. I knocked at the door and an old woman answered it, her face a smaller version of Bryn's own.

'Hello, I'm Steve Jay. From Ty Hiraeth?'

At the mention of the house the old woman stepped back and looked me up and down, puzzled and slightly anxious.

'I'm a fireman,' I offered.

At that her face broke into a broad grin and she beckoned me inside.

The street door took you straight into the tiny living room. It was ten by eight feet at most and through a doorway on the far wall I could see the even smaller kitchen.

Bryn sat at a table in the centre of the room, bent over a map that had pencilled grid lines drawn on it. Some of the squares were cross-hatched. He looked up as I came in and for a moment looked concerned before folding the map over.

'Steve . . . good to see you.'

He got to his feet and folded the map over again, placing it on an armchair behind him.

'How are you, Bryn?'

'Fine. Still not allowed back to work, mind.'

'It's been over two weeks, hasn't it?'

'Two weeks today. Back Monday, least that's my understanding.'

He looked concerned again and raised his eyebrows.

'Have you spoken to Elizabeth?' I asked.

'Yes.'

'And?'

He motioned for me to sit down at the table.

'She's still annoyed . . . I can tell.'

'But your job's secure?'

'I think so.'

I looked at the map on the armchair. 'Thinking of doing a spot of walking?'

At that the old girl came in again and asked me if I wanted a cup of tea.

'Yes, please.'

'And cake?'

'Please.'

She leant forward. 'Our Bryn's being doing a lot of walking. Needs to build his strength up. Been off work sick, haven't you, dear?'

Bryn nodded as he caught my eye and grinned, embarrassed.

'Mum looks after me,' he explained.

'So I see.'

As the old girl disappeared into the kitchen I asked him where he'd been walking.

'Here and there. Nothing serious.'

'Can I see?' I looked at the map.

He hesitated, but then reached behind him and picked up the map. He opened it out on the table. He looked away as I studied the map, then got up and went out to the kitchen.

I recognised the area immediately. It was a large-scale map of the Abergwynant woods where Bryn and I had narrowly escaped the forest fire. There was an arrow drawn in that at first I couldn't make out the purpose of. Then I realised, it was showing the direction of the wind on the day.

Bryn and his mother came in with the tea and cake and placed it on the table. I folded up the map to create more space.

His mother went out to the kitchen again and Bryn sat down. He was definitely uneasy.

'Is this where you've been walking?'

'Yes.'

'I can think of nicer spots than a burnt-out wood, Bryn.'

'I went up to chat to some of the lads when they were still damping down.'

I nodded. 'What are the grid squares for?'

He looked down and smiled. 'Trying to work out where the crown fire started.'

'Why?'

'Crown fires are rare.'

'What did you find out?'

'Nothing. I found one of the bodies of those young soldiers, though. He was the last of them, poor bugger.'

'Someone told me that they found a Black River Mining Company vehicle burnt out in the Coed-y-Garth. They said that's where the fire started.'

'Yes, I heard that as well,' he said, 'but it doesn't explain how it got in the tree-tops.'

'Is that important?'

His mouth turned down at the edges, 'Don't know. Anyway, enough of the gloom, how you've been? Is the treatment working?'

'Seems to be.'

'Well, you're looking happy enough.'

I agreed. 'Very happy.'

'Good, good.'

We chatted for a while and when I said I had to be getting back Bryn said he'd walk me back to the car. He seemed to know everybody we passed. Some waved, others called out, always they smiled. He left me at the car park entrance and shook my hand.

I'd never see him alive again.

19

I drove back to Ty Hiraeth and read in the garden for an hour or so.

The late-afternoon sun etched the Cader massif with a sharp, yellow-gold light that was reflected in the surface of the estuary waters.

I had got into the habit of arriving over at Anne's around seven in the evening and she'd make dinner for eight. I hadn't spoken to her all day; that was deliberate. I wanted to keep the evening fresh, special. Now, I wanted to be there and decided to drive over early and surprise her.

It must have been just before six when I pulled up in her drive. Her car wasn't there. More in hope than expectation I knocked at the door. Nothing.

I climbed back into the Shogun and turned the radio on, settling back to wait.

An hour went by, but she didn't show.

I started to get worried the nearer eight it got. I got out and walked to where the drive met the road and looked up and down. The road was quiet, still. Even the birdsong had stopped.

When eight came and went I started to invent excuses for her; a flat tyre, engine trouble or simply delayed somewhere talking, but I didn't believe it. I thought of the motorcyclists, but pushed the idea away.

I left the Shogun in the drive, in case she turned up and walked back to the T-junction, where there was a phone box. I rang Ty Hiraeth in case she'd rung and left a message. Eve answered. She said that there had been no calls for me and that Julia had finished work at six.

I walked back to the cottage.

In all I waited till half-ten, then reluctantly drove back slowly to Ty Hiraeth. I checked with Eve and she said the same as before; no one had phoned. I said that I'd be in my room and would accept any calls irrespective of the hour.

I couldn't read, because I couldn't concentrate and I wouldn't drink in case I had to suddenly drive somewhere. I hoped, really hoped, that she'd broken down on an isolated road and would ring for me to fetch her.

I must have fallen asleep in the early hours and woke only as dawn entered through the open curtains. I stripped off my clothes and climbed into bed, knowing nothing could be done until Julia came into work. She was on the morning rota and wasn't due in until nine when Eve went off duty.

Eddie Marlowe woke me when he knocked on the door to see if I was going to have breakfast.

'I saw your car outside and— Is everything all right? You look like you haven't slept.'

'I haven't.'

'Oh? Something wrong?'

'I don't know. Look, give me five minutes and I'll be down, Eddie.'

He looked uncertain. 'Okay.'

I had a quick wash and shave and told myself that there was no need to panic, but the face in the mirror wasn't buying it. I decided to have breakfast and ask Julia, when she turned up, if she knew anything and if not, then drive over to the cottage again and wait. No matter how long.

Therapy could go hang for one day.

In the event Julia knew nothing, but she didn't seem alarmed. I told her my plans for the day and said I would ring in every hour. She wasn't impressed and said that Anne was someone who tended to be spontaneous. I shouldn't read anything into the fact she'd disappeared; it wasn't unusual.

She said the last bit with more than a touch of reproach, as though I was getting the run-around from Anne and deserved it. I think my look was reply enough.

I was back at the cottage before ten and waited till early afternoon. Every time I rang Ty Hiraeth Julia answered and simply said no calls. She also said Elizabeth wasn't too impressed by my late cancellation of a session.

I couldn't think what to do.

Anne didn't have a mobile, at least, not one that I knew about and during our conversations she'd never mentioned friends, although it was hard to believe she didn't have any. I decided to go back to Ty Hiraeth and see if Julia was prepared to give me some addresses.

My worry was starting to turn into fear.

When I arrived back I went into reception and sought out Julia.

'Anne's rung.'

'What? When? What did she say?'

She paused, 'She said that she had to go away for a while and to tell you that she was sorry.'

'Sorry? That's it? Sorry?'

'That's all she said.'

I looked for triumph in her eyes, but if anything there was pity; like she'd known it all along. A feeling of utter emptiness overwhelmed me and I stood there, like an idiot, waiting for her to say something else.

'You'll have to excuse me, Steve. There are the dinners to prepare.'

That night I crept slowly, but relentlessly inside a bottle. I had no idea how much Scotch I put away, but it wasn't enough. Oblivion evaded me. I couldn't sleep, couldn't switch off and all the time I could hear Elizabeth's voice in my head telling me how I couldn't control everything in my life. Well, that was just fine, because I would have settled for controlling just one of them.

In the days that followed I missed every therapy session and avoided Elizabeth. Twice I drove over to the cottage and convinced myself that I should break in and find the letter Anne would have surely left me, but each time managed to stop myself. How pathetic would it have been to break in and find nothing?

A week to the day after Anne disappeared Elizabeth approached me in the garden.

'How are you?'

I smiled. 'Fine. Couldn't be better.'

'Okay. Want to talk about it?'

'No.'

'No – or too frightened to?'

I glared at her.

'That was harsh, sorry.'

'No more than the truth, but I really don't have an interest in talking. Now if you'll leave me—'

'Have you given up therapy?'

I laughed out loud. 'It's given *me* up.'

'Come on, Steve. You're tougher than that.'

I shook my head. 'Not any more, I'm not. You'd be wasting your time. Can't win them all, Elizabeth. Some of us are just totally fucked up. Beyond help.'

'You're going back?'

I nodded, 'Tomorrow.'

'You've not dealt with your problems, Steve. It's still all in there.'

'Best place for it.'

'If you leave now . . .'

I closed my eyes and my head slumped forward in a classic

shutting-out gesture; to the therapist in her it must have seemed like shouting. She watched silently, letting me work my way through it, allowing the knee to unjerk.

I sighed long and heavily and willed myself to be more polite, more honest.

'Look, for what it's worth I've accepted what you've said about the connection to my childhood. But knowing isn't solving. At least now, thanks to you, I can understand what happened. You've every right to be satisfied.'

'See me before you go tomorrow. Please?'

'I'll be going early, just after breakfast.'

'I'll come and find you.'

I said my goodbyes to Eddie, thanked Elizabeth, but could only bring myself to nod towards Julia. Which was unfair because she'd never done less than her job and she was good at it, but the resentment bubbling away inside me wouldn't allow more.

I stopped at the toll bridge and looked down the estuary for what I told myself was the last time. It had only been four weeks, but this place had touched me, had created a space inside me that would be reflected on for many years to come.

I climbed back into the Shogun and wound down the window.

If anything, the day was hotter than any previously and the river shimmered beneath the sun's glare. Sooner or later the weather pattern would have to break in a thunderstorm and with it, wash away any traces of my footprints.

In a moment of weakness I turned off of the A470 towards Tabor.

I knew she wasn't there, but the child in me had to be sure. *Nice one, Stevie*, I counselled myself, *not so much putting your fingers in the holes of the hand as the holes in your head*. Why settle for mere greasepaint when you can be the complete fucking clown?

I pulled into the driveway and stopped, with the engine still running.

It felt pathetic and in a surge of humiliation and regret I turned the Shogun around intending to drive away, but the child was in the ascendant. I switched off the engine and got out.

Twice I knocked and waited. Twice I felt emptiness, the hunger of failure.

I got back into the Shogun and shook my head.

Enough, Stevie, enough. She's gone. Accept it!

I thought it all through then and heard Elizabeth's voice in my head. She'd wanted me to stay, to deal with the demons, but she had given me a starting point and some tools to rework my life, so that I would go back to London, not whole, but functional, not healed, but rested, with breath enough to start over.

I drove away, resisting the urge to look in the rear-view mirror.

I was done with looking back. I had to count myself lucky for knowing Anne, for being allowed into her life. Not everything in life is permanent, in fact, nothing is. I was better for having met her, for having held her, for possessing the time and the person, if only briefly.

That was gone and this had to be a fresh start.

I drove fast and with the radio turned up too loud; station-hopping and unable to settle for a type of music or suffer the inane gibbering of the DJs.

By the time I reached the M25 the radio was turned off and the gnawing ache in my stomach had returned.

I reached Alex's house around five and he came out to greet me.

'Stevie boy, you're back!'

'No, I'm still on the M25 between South Mimms and the M11, Alex.'

'That's what I've missed, sarcasm as conversation. D'you want to carry your bags in yourself?'

'What d'you think?'

He grinned. 'I see the therapy has worked. Shall I prepare your padded cell for you now, sir, or will you have a cocktail in the lounge first?'

I threw a holdall at him. 'I'd like a cocktail . . . in a pint glass.'

'Now you're talking. There's a good boozer over Horndon way. I've taken to drinking there of late.'

'Horndon?'

'Aye.'

Later that night we went to Horndon by cab and got rat-faced. It was while we were on our sixth pint that he broke the news.

'I took the liberty of getting the company solicitors to write to the Brigade on your behalf. Michael Sheldon has been charged with the Stratford job. That means his complaint to the Brigade about you is invalid, it has to be seen as prejudiced.'

'So?'

'I've had it in writing, they're going to lift your suspension.'

'When?'

'I rang Bob Grant, he reckons you'll get the letter this week.'

I was numb.

'You're certain about this?'

He nodded. 'Bob Grant says that as soon as it's official he'll contact the Occupational Therapy Unit and get you fixed up with a medical . . . hopefully a cancellation. You could be back at work before you know it.'

I racked my brains. When were Blue Watch on again? I took my wallet out and hunted through it for my rota card. Blue Watch would be on their first day duty Tuesday. Even if Bob Grant worked miracles I wouldn't be able to return to work before the shift after that, Wednesday, the 12th August.

If the suspension was lifted? If I got a medical?

'You've gone quiet, Stevie boy.'

'Thank you, Alex.'

'You're not going to go sentimental on me, now, are you?'

'It's been tough, mate, I don't mind admitting it.'

'Aye, well, drink up. I didn't bring you out here to listen to your blubbering. Scotch?'

'Scotch'll do nicely.'

'Oh . . . I meant to tell you, Jenny's rung again.'

'So?'

'Fair enough, Stevie, fair enough.'

20

Walking back into Wells Lane Fire Station after three months was like being stripped naked.

Being suspended from duty marks you out, but that wasn't the whole story. Everybody knew about the therapy unit and many thought that the reason I'd been suspended was connected to Sandy's death. They were wrong, but truth is always the first casualty of absence.

Despite Elizabeth's sessions, away from Ty Hiraeth I was slipping back into old ways, which, in fairness, she'd warned me would happen if I didn't stay. The guilt had crept back into view, which I reasoned was triggered by Anne leaving; the stress of returning to work did the rest.

The expressions that greeted me as I crossed the yard ranged from stunned surprise to barely concealed wariness and it took an act of will not to climb back into my car and drive away. I loved my job, but it's intensely parochial. Stay away from the pack too long and you're an outsider, people sniff the air and read your body language; you might have changed, might have busted out of the box to which you'd been assigned.

I'd arrived early, twenty past eight, so none of my own watch were on duty yet. The first reactions didn't bode well, so I put on a front, smiling and nodding, sometimes to the backs of heads as people turned away. I hoped my own watch would be different, but if the reactions of the white watch were anything to go by I was about to experience the first frost of August.

I walked through the station to the Station Officer's locker room and was brought up short by an unfamiliar face; a tall thin guy with green eyes and cropped red hair.

'Mornin',' he said. 'Tim Maynard.'

I held out my hand. 'Steve Jay.'

I thought I detected the smallest of hesitations before he took my hand and his smile seemed to fall away.

'Are you the new Station Officer on the white watch? I asked.

He turned and went back to sorting though his locker.

'No. I'm the temporary on the blue . . .' He blinked. 'Your watch,' he corrected himself.

'Where's John Blane? Why isn't he acting up?'

He shrugged. 'Perhaps he didn't want it. I've been here for three months. Are you coming back light duty?'

'No.' I studied his face. 'I'm back to full duty as of today.'

He went still and disappointment shaped his face.

'I see.'

'You weren't told?'

He looked at the floor. 'No.'

'Then give staff a ring at nine.'

I didn't intend to say it harshly, but there was an edge to my voice. He nodded, closed his locker and went out the room; another friend I'd made in short order.

The tannoy announced that there was a phone call for one of the guys on the white watch and I heard laughter echoing from the stairwell; some joke being played out to the maximum audience. Then I heard the sound of the two-tones being tested on one of the appliances; that would be one of my watch and I wondered who it was.

I opened my locker.

Everything was how I'd left it on the night I had been suspended. Sandy Richards' task book, his promotion-pro-gression log, was on the centre shelf, still waiting to be marked. I touched it and a sense of shame swept over me.

Elizabeth had warned me that I might suffer relapses. She called it 'the process of transference'. A barrier I had to go through before I could move on.

For months my life had been on hold, waiting just for this moment. But so much had happened in the months I'd been away it seemed like I'd never return. Then I got the phone call and suddenly I was an operational Station Officer again.

Now all I had to do was cope.

Just before nine o'clock, Dave Chase, one of my watch's senior hands, peered around the door.

'You're back, guv!'

I smiled. 'Looks like it.'

'No one told us.' He beamed.

'I only found out a couple of days ago, Dave.'

'Full duty?'

'Suspension lifted last Wednesday, had a medical Monday. I'm back for real.'

'The lads'll be pleased.'

'I don't think Tim Maynard was.'

He looked over his shoulder and then turned back to smile.

'He's all right, Tim, bit new and keen. He's been through what you might call a learning curve in the time he's been here, but the one you have to meet is our new Leading Fireman – a total plank! Have I got stories for you.'

I grinned. Dave Chase was a subversive by nature, with a sharp wit and the fractured smile of an anarchist.

'That bad, eh?'

Dave nodded fiercely. 'His name's Gerry Mudd. The lads call him 'Barking Mudd'. He *is* spectacularly incompetent and is rapidly acquiring the status of legend. It's been total entertainment from the moment he arrived.' He paused, his voice quieter. 'It's good to have you back, guv.'

'Cheers, Dave. I needed to hear that. Have we got a replacement for Wayne yet?'

'Brian Tyler. He came from Southern Command. Quiet chap, bit deep. His main vice is 'Blackwall Tunnel Vision'.

'Eh?'

'All he thinks about is going home!'

I grinned.

'Are we having roll-call, guv?'

'Yes.'

'I'll let the lads know.'

As the door closed I shook my head. I felt strange. On the one hand the sights, the sounds were so familiar and on the other it felt so distant, as if a membrane had grown between me and what I'd once known so well.

If I'd silently hoped for a homecoming then the reality looked like burning that illusion away. The terms of reference had changed and I had to change too. Patience was never my first instinct; now it would have to be.

The watch had been my anchor and I had to reclaim that, earlier rather than later. With luck I could slowly regain my confidence, rebuild my career. I would take things gently; slowly reabsorb rank and responsibilities.

The watch would also have its needs. When new faces come onto a watch there's a ripple effect. Alliances are formed and re-formed. Old tensions disappear and new ones creep above the horizon.

Top of the list of priorities was a talk with John Blane. As a popular and experienced Sub Officer I was surprised to find that he hadn't acted up to Station Officer in my absence. My gut feeling was that something had happened to prevent him.

As the nine o'clock bells rang I walked into the muster bay to roll-call and saw the watch lined up. John Blane called them to attention, but they just turned and walked straight over to me. The two new men, Gerry Mudd and Brian Tyler, hung back.

There were smiles and shouts of 'Nice one' but there were looks of uncertainty as well. Tom Reed, the oldest man on the watch, and Jim McClane were on leave, but everybody else was there.

It felt good and I choked back the emotion.

'Forget roll-call. Just do your Breathing Apparatus sets and then we'll do this properly in the mess,' I said.

I caught John's eye and motioned him into the office. Harry Wildsmith, one of my most trusted hands and arguably the shrewdest, gave me a slow nod and a grin that spoke volumes.

Once inside the office I closed the door.

John Blane was a big man with subtle ways and gentle insights into life that belied his appearance. He had been as steady as a rock for me throughout the three years that he'd been my Sub Officer, but the man before me now was different. Concern had replaced humour in his eyes and he looked worn out.

'How are you, John?'

'Better for seeing you, guv. The watch have missed you.'

'I've missed them. In fact, until last week I was reconciling myself to never coming back.'

'What happened?'

'It turns out that the bloke that made the complaint about me has finally been charged with arson. Alex McGregor got a solicitor to write a stiff letter to the Legal Section at Brigade HQ reminding them that I was instrumental in the arrest. Under the circumstances the Brigade declined to press disciplinary charges.'

'I should think so, too.'

'Apparently there was a body of opinion that I should still face some kind of reprimand, but when Alex threatened to spread it across every newspaper in the country, they backed off.'

'Because you saved that woman?'

'Yes.'

'And Wales?' He hesitated. 'Are you fully fit now?'

'Wales! You wouldn't believe me if I told you, John. I'm a bloody lightning conductor for trouble.'

'Trouble? You were supposed to be going there for a rest . . . and counselling.' He said the last word softly, as if it might give offence.

'Well, I got plenty of counselling, but not much rest.'

'Are you better?'

'Better than I was. They told me that I had to let the past go, move on. Trouble is, it feels like desertion.'

'I know,' agreed John.

His large face was pale.

'Is that why you didn't act up?' I asked.

He hesitated before answering, then nodded slowly.

'I saw what it did to you, guv. I never want to go through that. I've heard people, people who were nowhere near that fire-ground, criticise and condemn you. And the worst of it is that the rumours have become the conventional wisdom. The consensus is that we screwed up big time; as officers, as a watch.'

The bitterness in his voice took me off guard.

All the time I'd been focused on what Sandy's death had done to me. Now the reality of what the watch had been through in my absence sank in.

'I can't tell you how tough things have been. Dave Chase is waiting to hear if he's going to face disciplinary charges.'

'Dave? For what?'

John sighed. 'He went out-duty a couple of weeks ago and some idiot made a crack about you.'

'Go on.'

'Dave slammed the bloke up against a wall. The officer in charge was a temporary, but quite a sound lad by all accounts.

He took them into the office and read the riot act to the pair of them and was prepared to let it go at that.'

'And?'

'Out of courtesy he decided to inform the duty Assistant Divisional Officer. Thank God it was Bob Grant.'

'Is that not the end of it, then?'

'Not entirely. Bob sat on it, but the next day the duty DO was Charnley.'

'Don't tell me, let me guess. He got wind of it and wants to push it.'

'In a word, yes.'

'I'll see what can be done, though I doubt it'll be much if it's gone up the road. Other than that, how are things on the watch?' I asked.

'Morale's taken a nosedive since Sandy. Wayne Bennett came up the station on the last tour of duty. He stayed for tea break, but when he left it was as if the wind had been taken out of their sails. It's a hard thing to see a young man like that made an amputee.'

He fell silent and we both looked at each other.

If I'd returned looking to the watch for strength then now I knew that they also looked to me. There were unresolved issues and half-truths strewn around like broken glass and situations such as the one involving Dave Chase were only too likely to occur again.

I had to find a way to change that.

'Give me five minutes, John, and I'll see everybody in the mess.'

As he closed the door I sat down in my office chair and sighed.

What to say and how to say it? It seemed all I'd done lately was talk to therapists, doctors and patients. Now I had to find words for my own people. I had to show that I knew where they were and how they felt.

Watches are the greatest observers of human nature that I know. Bluff and they smell it. Lie and they'll never forgive you. They are composed of individuals, but at moments of weakness they can act like a herd, panicking and kicking out.

You don't stop a herd by standing in front of it; you have to join and gradually take the lead, steering them from the front. Anything else is doomed to fail.

Trust yourself, Stevie, because if you don't no one else will.

With that thought I got up and walked through to the mess. As I appeared in the doorway John called for quiet and all faces turned towards me.

'First things first, just so that you know it for certain, my suspension has been lifted and the Occupational Health Unit say I'm fit for duty.'

'Good one, guv,' said Mike Scott.

I smiled, then said softly, 'I've missed this place, I've missed you. It is good to see you all again.'

There was silence at that and I saw John smile his approval. I looked around the table and knew that they were waiting for something from me. I hoped that what I had to say would capture them.

'A lot has happened in the last three months – to me, to you. I hear that people don't rate us any more, that we're suddenly no good at our jobs. Well, that's rubbish. I may well have made a mistake at the Heathway fire. I may be in part responsible, but the decision I made was based on what I knew, what I could see and my experience. No one is more cut up than me about what happened to Sandy and Wayne, but that doesn't reflect on you.' I turned towards John. 'Any of you.'

'It was a hard call, guv. There was no right and no wrong. We know that,' said Doug Russell.

'Cheers, Doug. We can't stop people from thinking and saying what they want, but we have to ignore that and show them that we're not buying it. The alternative is to curl up into a ball and surrender.' I glanced around the table, gauging their reactions. 'From now on we think, speak and act as a watch. We close ranks against those that criticise us and treat them with the contempt they deserve.'

Harry Wildsmith looked at Dave Chase, 'Silent contempt, then, guv?'

Dave Chase looked down at the table.

'Yes, Harry. However tempting it might be to deal with it differently.' I paused to let my words sink in. 'I've served with a number of watches and without question you're the best of them. Don't let what happened destroy that. Remember, there're good people out there who know the truth. We have to do our jobs and let the message spread. It can't be forced or faked. It'll take time, but it starts here, now, from the minute we get up from this table—'

A low-pitched boom followed by a deep rumble shook the windows and doors, cutting me short.

Everyone looked shocked and for a few moments no one spoke.

'John,' I said quietly, 'ring Control and find out what the hell that was.'

A minute later the bells crashed down.

21

John's voice over the tannoy.

'Explosion and fire, A12 Gants Hill Pump and Pump Ladder.'

There was a scramble as everybody made for the machines, leaving cups of tea half drunk and chairs scattered in their wake.

Gants Hill wasn't our ground, it was Ilford's, but very close to the border; a good five minutes on the bell. At this time of the morning traffic would be heavy and already the seconds were counting down, narrowing options before we'd even arrived.

As we reached the appliance bay a second, smaller boom, rattled the station and stopped everyone in their tracks.

'What is that?' breathed Dave Chase.

'Whatever it is, it don't sound healthy!' shouted back Harry Wildsmith.

You could feel the tension. There were no attempts at banter, the incident foreplay that frequently ricocheted around the rear cab. Instead, the crew were pulling on their fire-fighting gear in concentrated silence.

I lowered my side window and called across to John.

'Make sure you pull up well short of the job – and park with your back to it.'

He nodded. I didn't have to spell it out. Bomb Procedure was one of the most frequently read of all operational notes. A thousand possibilities raced through my mind; was it a bomb? What were the chances that it was something else? I hoped, really hoped, for gas. Either would be a nightmare, but bombs don't always come in singles.

I needed to kick-start my mind into gear.

If it was a bomb, how many casualties would there be? Would it entail a building collapse – the single most dangerous type of incident you could face? If so, what was the scale? What type of building – offices, school, factory, leisure centre? It was morning, so the population of each was potentially high, perhaps slightly less for a leisure centre.

Jesus, not a school!

Ideas and fears tripped over themselves as I struggled to push three months in the wilderness to one side.

I had wanted time; two, maybe three weeks of gentle re-entry. I needed to adjust, to remember, to get switched on; to lose some rust. It wasn't a case of not knowing what to do, but of thinking fast enough.

Trust yourself! See what there is to see; Look, Prioritise, Act.

As we pulled out of Wells Lane onto Chadwell Heath High Road I had the first glimpse of what we were to face; a huge column of smoke was rising up in the distance, swelling and darkening against the morning sky.

'They're calling us up, guv,' said Harry Wildsmith, nodding towards the radio.

I turned the volume up and gave my call sign.

The Control Room Operator related the stark information. 'M2Fe, multiple calls being received, F41 Dagenham's Pump and F38 Romford's Pump Ladder are attending as additional, further traffic, over.'

'Foxtrot 801, received, go ahead with further traffic, over,' I replied.

'M2Fe, we are receiving reports of a massive building collapse following a series of explosions, F39 and F446 attending, over.'

F39 was Hornchurch's Assistant Divisional Officer, Bob Grant; a sound head, a good firefighter and a man to trust when it was all turning pear-shaped.

The call sign, F446, was East Ham's Fire and Rescue Unit, a heavy-rescue vehicle carrying five hands.

Harry pushed the appliance to the limit, racing westwards along the A12, swerving and braking, angling between the surly traffic. We went through as the lights at Newbury Park were changing, missing a cyclist by inches.

I nearly told Harry to slow down, but held back, knowing how good he was and how sluggish I'd become. There was nothing I could say that he hadn't already thought of or acted on. Overreacting was a bigger sin than under-reacting – people see and note it – it destroys collective confidence.

'Can you believe that?' asked Harry.

I switched my eyes back to the horizon where the ominous black funnel was growing and spreading, magnified by the fact that we were getting nearer with every passing second. The traffic had stopped now. Drivers were climbing out of cars, staring in bewilderment at the erupting smoke on the crenellated horizon.

A quarter of a mile from the incident we started to see tangible signs of the explosion. Debris littered the road and windows were blown in down whole sides of buildings. Two hundred yards out we were forced to swerve around a huge chunk of concrete lying in the middle of the road.

I could smell it now; the thick odour of dust and smoke and the acrid smell of burning, yet I could see no flashing lights, no ambulances and no police. We were the first in attendance.

Trust yourself!

'Here!' I ordered Harry to stop the machine. Automatically, he swung her round and did a three-point turn, keeping the back of the machine towards the incident, giving the crew cabs the maximum shielding in the event of another explosion.

I clambered from the Pump Ladder and raced forward, circling around several cars that were on fire and stopping less than fifty metres from the shattered building.

Behind the smoke and dust cloud it was hard to see anything.

A woman appeared through the smoke; her clothes her hair, were on fire. She was speaking, asking for help, in a voice so normal, so free of panic and pain she could only have been in the deepest shock.

Two firefighters immediately went to her and laid her down, beating out the flames.

To my left was a fire-blackened torso and next to that something I couldn't recognise. Something small.

A gust of wind pulled at the curtain of smoke and dust until it suddenly parted and I gazed at the huge shattered building.

It reared up, fourteen storeys high; the entire left-hand side of the building gone, clawed away, leaving a gaping hole through the centre of the remainder.

Ten storeys up, on one edge of the hole, suspended by reinforcing rods and twisted through fantastic angles, were two vast slabs of fractured concrete. Between them, they must have comprised the entire floor area of that side of the building.

Mangled, twisted, dented, buckled, hollowed out and burnt; the fabric of the building – the concrete, steel and glass – had been torn apart in a split second of white-hot violence.

I froze.

It might have been seconds, it might have been minutes, but I stood rooted, trying to get my head around the heart-stopping enormity of what had happened.

And then, with cruel perspective, directly in front of me on the edge of the rubble field, something was moving, a convulsive, griddled form, raw, with life enough to die.

Think!

I turned and ran back towards the machines.

The men of both machines were coming towards me, carrying first-aid kits, shovels and pickaxes, crowbars and spades. I stopped them all and ordered them back to the machines where John was organising the crews in unloading equipment.

'Stop! I want everybody here now!'

They hesitated, stealing looks over their shoulders, torn between instinct and instruction.

'Now, please!'

They grouped around me, silently. The two new men, Gerry Mudd and Brian Tyler, glanced at John Blane, looking for reassurance. They'd heard the stories.

I kept my voice calm, hoping they couldn't see the agitation that was striving to take control of me, turning my brittle confidence into shards of doubt.

'Casualties will have to wait . . . I need to carry out an assessment of what we're facing. You are to ignore anyone asking for help. I repeat . . . anyone . . . have you got that?'

I could see the consternation in their faces, it went against the grain not to immediately help, but I knew that if we were to maximise the chance of life for the majority, individuals would have to suffer.

'John, I want you to take Doug Russell and carry out a complete reconnaissance of the rubble field. I want to know how many live casualties, how many trapped, what dangers are immediately a threat, electricity cables, fractured gas mains, chances of further collapse . . . anything and everything.' I turned to the new Leading Firefighter, Gerry Mudd. 'Gerry, I want you to take Mike Scott to do the same with the part of the building that's still standing.'

'Do we gain access to the upper floors if we can get in, guv?' asked Gerry Mudd.

'No! Carry out your assessment from ground level and ensure the safety of yourself and Mike at all times . . . I don't want us becoming casualties as well.' I looked at John and then back to Gerry Mudd. 'Keep your wits about you, look up as well as around and especially watch where you put your feet. I want you back here in under five minutes . . . go!'

As they ran off I turned back and spoke to Martin McClane, a lean, experienced hand who was one of the quiet, do-your-job school of firemen.

'Martin, there's a serious fire in the rubble field . . . if it isn't controlled it will cook anyone remaining alive. Take two blokes and get a spray to work on it. Keep it moving and shield any obvious casualties you see.' I looked at Dave Chase. 'Dave, I want you to supply their jet. Watch the amount of water they use. I don't want any buried casualties being drowned.'

That left me, Harry Wildsmith and the new hand, Brian Tyler. I told Brian Tyler to set up the Incident Command Wallet and then gave Harry a list of messages to send.

'Harry, from me, "Make Pumps twelve, two Fire and Rescue Units and two Ariel Ladder Platforms required, further traffic . . . half the attendance to assemble at the A12 junction of Bee Hive Lane and half to assemble at Gants Hill roundabout where they will be met. This excludes F41 Dagenham's Pump and F38 Romford's Pump Ladder." Read it back to me, Harry.'

He scribbled the message down and repeated it.

I nodded, 'Then, as an informative, from me, "A block of offices of fourteen floors, seventy-five by thirty metres—"'

'Excuse me, guv – I stood by at Ilford a short while ago and we visited this building . . . it's got a basement and two sub-basements used as garages. I think it's called the OPMA Tower.'

Jesus! I turned to look at the building, but the smoke had enveloped it again, keeping its surprises, its ambushes, hidden.

'Right, a block of offices of fourteen floors and three basement levels, seventy-five by thirty metres, fifty per cent destroyed by explosion, twenty per cent of remainder alight . . . further traffic . . . Initiate Major Incident Procedure.'

'That all, guv?' asked Harry.

'No. Send those first, then, from me, "Electrical and gas apparatus involved, request the urgent attendance of both the electrical and gas authorities." Then, request the urgent attendance of the Borough Surveyor . . .' I stopped, 'you were going to say something, Harry?'

He gave a grim smile. 'Welcome back, guv.'

'Somewhere, in a previous life, I really pissed someone off, didn't I, Harry?'

He nodded. 'It's the only rational explanation.' And with that he ran off.

An incident this large, this complex, is an escalating series of priorities. You deal with what seems to be important only to have something bigger and nastier climb out the woodwork.

And that was what Dave Chase came running back to me with.

'Guv, you've got to come and see this.'

He led me to the edge of the rubble pile. The wind had been building, clearing the smoke and fanning the flames or at least that's what it first looked like.

Dave pointed to the right-hand side of the rubble pile.

'We can't risk extinguishing the flames, guv. They're being fed by gas below the top of the rubble. If we knock them out we'll have free gas escaping . . .'

'But if we don't then anybody trapped is going to fry?' I reasoned aloud.

'What do you want us to do, guv?'

I didn't know what to do. No one had ever taught me what to do about collapsed buildings. There was no operational note, no training and the only guidance came from the manual of firemanship; all two paragraphs of it.

Improvisation was all very well, but this wasn't a place to try and get lucky.

That was the moment that Gerry Mudd came pounding over.

'Guv – there are two huge slabs of concrete flooring hanging over the rubble pile. We need to cordon off the area directly below them to stop any rescues being attempted in the area . . . And there's more. The weight of the concrete is threatening to tear the slabs free at any time. The noises coming from the reinforcing rods aren't good.'

I looked from the escaping gas flames up to the hanging slabs.

'Dave,' I said quietly, 'use a spray on the flames . . . the source of the escaping gas is below the surface and it's very unlikely that you'll knock out the flame where it meets the gas, but you might be able to minimise the damage the flames are causing . . . got me?'

'Fair enough, guv.'

I turned to Gerry Mudd. 'Gerry, see Brian Tyler and get him to use traffi-tape to cordon off the area below the slabs. Then he's to cordon off the entire rubble field and finally cordon off the area.'

'On his own?'

'He'll have to do his best – we all will. Have you finished your recce of the building?'

'No, guv.'

'Tell Brian quickly and then do what I asked you to do. I want as full an estimate of what we have as possible – not parts of it.'

'Sorry, guv.'

'It's not a problem . . . just get a move on, Gerry.'

22

I turned back to the broken building, trying to shape some kind of plan.

The first consideration, a reconnaissance, was obvious, so was the next, shutting off the gas, electricity and the water. The first two of which posed hidden dangers for the fire-fighters and surviving casualties, whereas the water would run to the lowest point, flooding the basements and drowning anyone down there.

By requesting the attendance of the utilities authorities I had covered those risks, but until they arrived searching the rubble field would be extremely dicey.

Think!

I started to note the main features of the structure, trying to see where the dangers lay and trying to keep the nagging fear of a secondary explosion under control.

The reinforcing rods holding the two massive hanging slabs of concrete groaned and protested under the outrageous weight. Pipework and cabling hung from every floor and sheets of paper floated down from the shattered, gaping floors.

The rubble field itself was a haphazard mound of concrete slabs lying in uneven layers, with jagged pieces as big as a house rearing up like a broken jigsaw. Beneath them, between them, crushed by them, were God knows how many people. Some would still be alive; lying in the dark, frightened and in pain, praying we'd get them out while the thick, pungent smoke percolated through the cracks in the debris to fill the voids and suffocate them.

The sound of two-tones in the distance announced the approach of the reinforcing appliances, putting pressure on me to come up with a cogent plan, something holistic but flexible that didn't extend the crews beyond their skills.

The wind strengthened and changed direction, blowing the smoke across the rubble field. I saw Rod Brody and Martin McClane trying to move back, dragging the hose with them, but the smoke moved too fast and they were enveloped.

I went forward, the acrid smoke stinging my eyes and making me choke. I took in a great lungful of the fumes and stumbled, losing my feet and falling heavily onto my shoulder. I swore, rolled away and scrambled to my feet, coughing and blinded.

A pair of hands grabbed me by the injured shoulder and pulled violently.

I cried out as I was half dragged, half lifted across the rubble and out of the smoke. In fresh air I couldn't open my eyes, they were stinging that much, but I heard a voice and recognised it.

'You all right, guv?'

Harry.

'Rod and Martin were forward of me, Harry. They'll be in trouble if we don't get them out of there.'

I rubbed fiercely at my eyelids, making my eyes water more, but diluting the irritants. I managed to get one eye open and continued to massage the other one.

At that moment the wind swirled again and most of the smoke was swept away, revealing the figures of Rod Brody and Martin McClane stumbling towards us.

'Keep going straight, watch your footing!' Harry yelled.

At that moment Rod went down and took Martin with him.

'Shit!'

As one, Harry and I went forward, scrambling over the

debris on the edge of the rubble field. We reached them and pulled them upright and then away from the smoke. All four of us, bent double and half blinded, scrambled to safety.

When we were in fresh air, I asked them if they were all right.

'Just, guv,' said Rod, between coughing and wheezing.

Martin nodded, wiping the soot from his face. 'Guv.'

At that moment John Blane and Doug Russell came running back from their reconnaissance. John looked from one to the other of us.

'Everyone okay?'

'Almost. What did you find out?' I asked.

He looked grim. 'There's bodies everywhere, guv. And we heard people calling out. There's also the very real possibility of a secondary collapse. There are some massive chunks of concrete suspended directly over the rubble. It wouldn't take much for them to snap the reinforcing rods holding them and in this wind that's only a question of time.'

Now what!

I took a minute to think. It was a nightmare. Even keeping the fire in the rubble under control would require breathing-apparatus sets. I couldn't risk exposing men like that again.

'John, we're going to have to use BA sets for all work around the rubble field. That's means a massive BA operation, until those fires are under control. Harry, get on the radio . . . from me, make pumps twenty.'

That decided me.

'John, I want all oncoming crews held back. I want no freelance rescues, no penetration of that rubble field until we have enough BA sets and resources in place.'

'Right.'

'I want you to collate all information that we have gleaned from the recces. Then I want three crews with sprays to try and get that fire under control. Dave Chase reckons it's coming from gas beneath the rubble, so go carefully. Measured amounts of water. I want each crew under the control of a junior officer and a safety officer with each crew. There's too much smoke at present to site safety officers where they can see much, so we'll go for individual crew safety. Understand?'

'Clear, guv.'

As John took the others with him back to the appliances to get breathing apparatus I saw Gerry Mudd and Mike Scott coming in a looping run, skirting the smoke that was now moving backwards and forwards, buffeted by the gusting wind and influenced by the irregular shape of the fractured building.

Gerry Mudd was red-faced and panting when they reached me. Mike looked worried.

'Tell me.'

'You won't believe it guv . . .' he turned and pointed at the remaining upright portion of the building '– there's virtually nothing holding that up! There's a rectangular hole . . . probably thirty foot by fifteen running through the centre of the building . . .'

'The lift shaft?'

He nodded. 'That's where the break is. Anything beyond that point is down . . . it's as though whatever did this came up through the shaft and split the fucker wide open.'

'And this is where the standing part finishes?' I said, pointing so that he could correct me.

He turned to the building, 'Yes, guv. There's bodies all around the shaft hole . . . I think some of them are still alive . . . we need to get crews in there fast—'

'They'll have to wait, Gerry. The only way we can work in this is in BA. The plan for now is to control the fires in the rubble field and kill some of this smoke.'

Doubt swept his face.

'I hear what you say, Gerry, and I want to conduct a surface search, remove any obvious casualties, but I'm not going to commit men blindly. We'll help no one by getting injured ourselves.'

He looked at Mike Scott. Mike nodded slowly, clearly unhappy but accepting the logic.

'Get yourselves over to John and help him.'

'Yes, guv,' they chorused.

With the bare bones of a plan I now applied myself to the practicalities of carrying it out. If men in BA were to search, then they needed a safe path into and out of the rubble field. From the path they could search outwards.

I knew also that I had to sectorise the incident ground, divide it up into three or four parts with an officer in charge of each sector answering directly to the Incident Commander.

I didn't have the firefighters or officers to do that at that moment, but I could lay the foundations of effective command and control by roughing out the sectors and feeding the officers and firefighters into the allotted areas as they arrived.

The potential for the job to turn to rat shit was only too obvious.

By making pumps twenty I had started a process; specialist appliances, control units, senior officers, would all be mobilised and at Brigade Headquarters, Command Support Centre would already be monitoring the job.

There is a problem with major incidents; if a job develops slowly, then the reinforcing appliances and manpower can be absorbed gradually and used to good effect, but if it kicks off big, then the world and his wife arrive *en masse* and the bewildering changes of command can throw the whole process into chaos.

There is a belief that the bigger the job, the more rank required to handle it, despite the fact that senior officers spend most of their time in an office, an emotional light year from operational command and control.

As each successive senior officer assumes command the

process of handing over becomes like a relay race, each officer knowing less about the incident confronting him than his predecessor.

There was nothing I could do about that, except try and grab it by the scruff of the neck and set it on the right road. If I got the chance.

I walked back to the Pump Ladder and told Harry Wild-smith to tell control that the Pump Ladder was now the Incident Control Pump.

'Bob Grant's just booked in attendance, guv,' replied Harry.

I looked around.

Bob was walking slowly down the centre of the road, taking in the incident. He had his tell-tale smile in place, that if you didn't know him you could mistake for amusement.

He saw me and raised his hand; he might have been meeting someone in the High Street. When he reached me he patted me on the shoulder.

'Hello, Steve.'

'Bob.' I nodded.

'Tell me what you can.'

I gave him a run-through of what I knew and had done. He said he was taking command immediately.

'I want you to take sector one, Steve – that'll be the entire front of the building. I think you're right about getting that fire under control, but I want the surface search to go in more or less immediately. The jet crews can be paired up with the search teams and protect them.'

'And safety officers?'

'We'll go with your idea of a safety officer per crew until we've got the fire under control. Have you asked for the Borough Surveyor?'

'Yes.'

'Good. I'm not too happy about the state of the bit that's still upright.'

'Fair enough Bob.'

'We're in luck.'

'We are?'

He nodded. 'Yanny is in charge of East Ham's FRU. They were coming back from a road traffic accident at Poplar, I heard them being called up on the radio. Should be here in about twenty minutes.'

Yanny was Johannes Van Der Waal, a South African fire-fighter who had joined the London Fire Brigade two years ago and became an instant celebrity. He was a clever, experienced and powerful character who had served in overseas rescue missions to earthquake zones while with the South African fire service. He was the nearest thing we had to an urban search-and-rescue specialist in the entire brigade.

Over the next half-hour men and machines arrived and were deployed or held in reserve, waiting to be allocated a task. I had a thermal-image camera do a sweep of the rubble field and it revealed live casualties among the debris.

The first BA searches, three teams of two, recovered six bodies. I eventually got five two-man teams working. But that was the limit if I was going to be able to control safety in the sector.

The one positive thing was that with water being applied the fire in the rubble field reduced in ferocity and the smoke died down, allowing a clearer view of operations.

At one point there was a small secondary collapse as broken concrete fell from the upper floors, narrowly missing a BA team. Shortly after that we recovered our first live casualty, a man with horrific crush injuries.

The minute that Yanny arrived he sought out Bob, who pointed him in my direction.

Yanny was big, not just tall, but wide. He went about seventeen stone and was as fit as they come with hard eyes softened only by a boyish grin. He had a confidence that made him a natural leader.

'Morning, boss.'

'Morning, Yanny.'

'Sorry we took our time, we couldn't get through the traffic. The entire area is jammed solid.'

'You're here now and we need you.'

'You've found yourself a good one and no mistake.' His clipped accent made people's heads turn.

'Maybe too good for us.'

'Is it a bomb?'

'We don't know yet, Yanny, but it's looking that way.'

'Who's in charge at the minute?'

'Charnley. He's acting up as Senior Divisional Officer.'

He scowled. 'SDO? That prick?'

'That prick, Yanny.'

'God help us. Look, boss, I've been sent to help you.'

'Well, as you can see, we're still searching the surface for casualties. I've no idea what we plan to do after that.'

He shook his head. 'You've got to tunnel in or remove debris. Removing's safer for us, but more dangerous for them. If you use heavy machinery there's almost certain to be secondary collapses from the vibration. On the other hand, tunnelling, breeching, cutting and shoring will put us at risk – and the boys haven't been trained in the proper techniques. They're game enough, but this is a serious business.'

I told him everything that John Blane and Gerry Mudd had told me.

'What do you think we should do next, Yanny?'

He scanned the rubble field and shattered, standing remains. I saw his eyes settle on the two massive slabs of concrete overhanging the lift shaft. A low hissing sound came from his lips and his arms crossed in front of him.

'I'd say get the Borough Surveyor to take a look at those slabs first. Try to keep your boys away from there.'

'Will you stay with me and advise me, Yanny?'

'Love to, boss. It's better that I keep my boys fresh. If we have to go in there I want everyone sharp.'

Fifteen minutes later Bob Grant informed me that he was replacing me as Sector Commander and asked me to stay as Assistant and continue organising the surface search.

I lost track of time after that. More and more men and equipment were deployed, and equal amounts held in marshalling areas and equipment dumps. The ambulances were being kept close to the casualty clearing area, but so far there hadn't been many survivors.

The only subject of discussion was, what do we do when all the obvious casualties had been cleared?

It was another hour before the surface teams had been withdrawn. At that point Bob called Yanny and me over for a discussion.

'What's the best way forward, Yanny?'

Yanny took a moment. 'You need to shore up the upright section of the building.'

Bob shook his head. 'I've been told that that's not possible for twenty-four to forty-eight hours.'

The big South African's face clouded over. 'We're a fire brigade . . . we should have the capability to shore it ourselves.'

'Well, we haven't. What else do we need?'

'Dog teams, if you can get them.'

'Police dogs?' queried Bob.

'They'd be no use here, boss. You need proper urban search-and-rescue dog teams. Can't we get on to CSC and ask what they've got on file?'

Bob looked sceptical. 'I'll ask, but I wouldn't hold your breath.'

Yanny looked at me and I shrugged.

'Then while they're finding out, we have to do listening

searches. Battersea's FRU is here and they've got Trapped Person Locators and a snake-eye fibre-optic viewer.'

'Let's do that,' said Bob.

I went with Yanny and heard him brief his men. They listened closely and followed his directions to the letter, setting up the Trapped Person Locator on the edge of the rubble field.

The cry for quiet went up, once, twice, three times, until an eerie silence settled over the building and surrounding streets. Yanny put the headphones on and closed his eyes for a few minutes. Then he opened them and motioned one of his men forward.

A Leading Firefighter from the FRU went up to the edge of the rubble field and climbed up to the middle of the layered concrete.

'Baton!' shouted Yanny.

The Leading Firefighter struck the nearest concrete slab with a hammer and Yanny closed his eyes again. Next to him, another firefighter wore a second set of headphones. Yanny coached him as the man listened.

'Don't look at the screen on the apparatus. Close your eyes and trust your ears!'

The firefighter held a thumb up.

Three times they went through the same routine; each time the microphones were moved along the concrete without result. Minutes of utter silence crept by, with only the sound of the wind cutting the edge of the building disturbing the stillness.

Then a police helicopter came over low, the sound of its rotors thrown out like sonic impulses. Yanny ripped his headphones off and ordered everyone to stay where they were. He motioned Bob and I to follow him and led us to the Control Unit, about a hundred yards away, which was filled with senior officers, including Charnley.

'Gentlemen,' he shouted, 'I'm trying to listen to the sounds of people in the rubble. Can any of you tell me why I'm having to shut out the noise of that bloody helicopter in order to do that?'

Faces looked at each other, but no one answered him. He filled the door of the Control Unit.

He sighed deeply. 'Can I respectfully suggest that one of you finds out who is flying that bloody thing and get him to go away? Then I would be really grateful if the man in charge here could use his influence to get a no-fly zone in place over this incident ground. Thank you!'

With that he turned on his heel and marched back to the rubble field with Bob and I following.

Bob looked at me. 'Would you argue with him?'

'No way.'

'Me neither.'

Back at the rubble field Yanny chose another area and set about organising another electronic search pattern. Almost immediately they picked up the sound of someone tapping. Yanny organised selected debris removal and uncovered a void four feet down. Inside were two women – bloody and bruised, but alive. They were quickly removed by a medical team and Yanny's people went back to their TPL sweep.

The cordons that we had set up initially had been moved back further and only authorised personnel were allowed inside the inner cordon. Rows of police, ambulance paramedics and waiting firefighters gathered between the inner and outer cordons and it was these who had to be quietened whenever an electronic search was in progress.

It became almost comical. Yanny would stand up to shout for quiet and before he opened his mouth the onlookers fell silent. Bob Grant looked at me and nodded approvingly.

I watched Yanny go through his routine time after time, never losing patience and seeming to affect those around him

with his presence. At one point, while he was being relieved on
the headphones by another firefighter, I asked him what he
was doing in those minutes of quiet before he called for the
baton to strike.

He pulled me to one side, away from the others.

'You have to build up a sound map. Buildings have
noises . . . rubble settling, water running . . . girders and
timber straining beneath the weight. You have to listen to
that, so that when the baton strikes the concrete and
someone in there taps back, you can differentiate between
the two.'

'Okay. But I got the feeling you were doing something else,
something more.'

He grinned. 'I may make a search specialist out of you, boss,
you've got eyes.'

I shook my head. 'Wasn't anything I saw. Just a feeling.'

A huge arm settled around my shoulders and his voice
dropped to almost a whisper, his Afrikaans accent becoming
thicker.

'I'll tell you something – back home we have people called
Bushmen. They're magnificent hunters and the nearest thing
to primitive man alive today. Their skill is extraordinary.
When they track through the bush after game, they put their
fingers in the spoor – the tracks of their prey – and think
themselves inside the mind of the creature.' He paused,
finding the right words. 'They know that they and the animal
are part of a whole, part of one pattern.'

'Go on.'

'When I listen on the headphones, I try to put myself inside
the trapped casualty – do you understand?'

'I do Yanny, but I'd be careful who you tell that to.'

He burst out laughing. 'You might be right, boss.'

For over an hour Yanny and his men extended the search
pattern. The rest of us stood silently watching, but strangely it

wasn't boring, it was hypnotic. You felt as though you were listening for the casualties as well, tuning in.

Whenever there was a cough or someone merely walked, heads turned towards the isolated and seemingly magnified sound. For we were linked now, by remaining silent we were contributing.

At one point I noticed that Charnley had left the Control Unit and was standing thirty yards behind us.

As the microphones were moved further and further into the rubble field we all became aware of how perilously close to the hanging slabs the search area had gone. We had even tuned into these, our heads turning at any difference in the creaking from the reinforcing rods.

And then we went silent again and Yanny closed his eyes.

'Baton!'

The Leading Firefighter struck the nearest concrete slab three times and withdrew to the front of the rubble field. Suddenly Yanny's arm shot up, closely followed by the other headphone operator.

Yanny looked at the other man. 'I got something then.'

The other man nodded firmly. 'Definitely!'

Yanny called for the Leading Firefighter to go forward to shift one of the microphones. The man held up his hand to indicate that he understood and walked forward to the edge of the lift shaft. He planted the microphone and then looked up.

He was directly beneath the hanging slabs.

Again the hammer struck and both Yanny's and the other headphone operator's right arms shot up.

Yanny turned and looked at me. 'There's someone under there, boss, no question.'

I looked at Bob Grant.

'Two men only,' he said.

I nodded. 'Yanny and me?'

Bob now turned and looked at Charnley. Charnley walked forward.

'Don't stay there longer than you have to, Steve,' he said.

'Guv.'

Yanny picked up the snake-eye fibre-optic viewer and we went forward, picking our way carefully, avoiding the slabs' probable landing site should they fall, but when we reached the microphones there was no avoiding the danger zone.

The lift shaft was full of debris and thick wedges of concrete overhung the shaft itself, which reached down to the bottom-most basement, some fifty feet below.

Yanny got down on his belly and slid forward. I followed him.

At the nearest shaft edge were some laminated-timber sheets and smaller rubble. Yanny and I lifted some and scraped away what we could. We uncovered a hole, about a foot long and six inches deep. He handed me the snake-eye and I slid the end inside the hole.

I moved it slowly from side to side, while Yanny watched the small viewing screen at the other end.

'Bend it, boss!

I pulled on the cable that rang along the shaft and the probe bent through an angle of ninety degrees.

'To your left – steady, boss. There!'

'What is it, Yanny?'

'Something moving down there. Help me widen the hole.'

We carefully removed more of the rubble until the hole was wide enough for a man to crawl through. I undid my torch from its shoulder holder and slid head first into the hole, while Yanny held my waist.

The torch beam lit the interior, revealing a huge fissure through the rubble, right on the edge of the lift shaft. I shone the torch directly down, but couldn't see anything except a mass of concrete and steel.

Then, suddenly, eight feet below to one side, I saw a movement. I angled the torch and the beam lit up the face of a woman buried up to her shoulders.

It was Anne.

23

She was leaning out over the edge.

The fissure ran from the top at an angle so that it merged with the shattered lift shaft wall and then plunged forty feet to the lowest basement. There was water down there. I could hear it rushing as it escaped a main. Left unchecked, it could undermine the rubble and create dangerous voids, leading to a cave-in.

Above were heavy concrete slabs and twisted steel joists.

One stood out.

It was two feet deep and nine inches across; a massive steel beam, running the length of the fissure and pinning the concrete slabs beneath it.

Wisps of smoke curled in my torch beam as they seeped from the rubble, slowly invading the void. So far the smoke was insubstantial, barely enough to irritate my eyes, but its presence meant that the fire was eating its way towards her.

I felt Yanny tug my waist and I edged backwards out of the hole.

'What can you see, boss?'

'It's a woman. She's buried up to her chest, and her head and one arm are hanging out over a fissure.'

'Conscious?'

'I shone the torch in her face, but her eyes didn't open. I think she's in a stupor.'

He took the torch from me. 'I'll take a look.'

Yanny flattened his body and inched into the hole, head first. 'Hold my legs,' he called out.

I sat down with my legs astride and gathered his huge calves under my armpits, leaning back to take the weight. If he slipped I had a feeling I would be dragged straight through the hole after him.

Minutes ticked by and I was straining to hold him. Each time he moved or twisted I braced myself, digging my heels in and gripping his legs tighter.

'Pull me back,' he shouted finally.

I pulled steadily as he came out of the hole on his hands. When he had emerged, he sat facing me, his back resting against the edge of a slab.

'Two chances, boss, one slim, one dangerous.'

'The slim one?'

He sighed. 'Get some heavy plant as near to the edge of the rubble field as we can, preferably on it. Then start trying to lift some of this.'

'That's the slim chance?'

'Yes.'

'Why?'

'Not good. Did you see that big joist?'

I nodded.

'The weight in that thing means that you'd need a big crane and I mean big and it would have to be stationed directly above the spot, but that's not possible because that fissure means that the rubble could buckle beneath the weight and the crane would end up at the bottom of the lift shaft. Plus it would have to work directly beneath the widow-makers.'

'Widow-makers?'

He pointed above his head, 'The hanging slabs.'

'Right. And the dangerous option is what, Yanny?'

Scepticism lined his face and his shook his head slowly as if trying to accept his own reasoning.

'My Fire and Rescue Unit crew working in teams of two. We'd need to go down and see if it's possible to dig away the rubble around her, putting in props as we go . . . then try and prise her free or, if that wasn't possible, we might try the slice pack.'

The slice pack was a small thermic lance worn as a back-pack. It worked by blowing oxygen through a tube over stainless steel rods and igniting it. The lance burned at temperatures around six thousand degrees centigrade, hotter than the surface of the sun and would cut through concrete, stone, steel, anything.

But you couldn't use it near a casualty.

He watched me to see if I had taken in everything he said. For my part I tried to take each element and weigh it on its merits; there was nothing to be gained by emotionalising the dangers and relating back to my feelings for Anne.

'Is there any more?'

'If she's trapped for more than an hour and has crush injuries . . .'

He didn't have to spell it out. He knew what I knew, what every firefighter knew, that someone suffering crush injuries for more than a hour couldn't be released without being intubated because toxins from the damaged tissue would be released once the weight was removed and result in massive renal failure.

'Anything else, Yanny?'

'We'd have to be suspended on lines, couldn't risk falling into the fissure and that means that if anything happened there would be no way of getting the men on lines out of the fissure quickly. Also, she's going to need a face mask connected to an air line soon. I don't like the look of that smoke.'

'Put percentages on it, Yanny . . . the first option.'

'Less than fifty percent, much less.'

'And the second?'

He paused, then gave a shrug of his massive shoulders.

'With luck? Fifty-fifty.'

'Only one option then, really.'

'I think so, boss.'

I didn't mention to Yanny I knew Anne. The last thing I needed was anyone suggesting that I shouldn't take part in the rescue because I was too close to the casualty.

If Anne was to stand any chance, then I wanted to be involved, influencing the decisions that her life would depend on.

Strange; I felt no fear about making decisions, no residual hesitation. I just wanted the best chance for her and I trusted myself to be detached.

There were, however, questions lurking on the periphery; how far would I risk men's lives to rescue Anne? If it came to it and things got too dangerous for the crews, could I leave her there? Could I abandon her?

Yet there was no way I could back off this; it was out of the question. If it became that close then I had to make sure that it was my arse on the line and no one else's.

The wind picked up again and the hanging slabs creaked on the reinforcing rods above us. Smoke once again started to seep from below, emerging as viscous black-grey fumes.

Yanny looked up. 'Let's move away from here, eh?'

We scrambled over the rubble field, back to the road where Bob Grant and Maurice Charnley waited.

The shock passed and I started to wonder what the hell Anne was doing under the OPMA building. And if it was a bomb that had brought this down, what were the chances of a coincidence that she just happened to be there when it went off?

I wouldn't, couldn't, believe that she was involved, but that was emotion and the facts put her eight feet under the concrete.

As soon as we cleared the rubble field Bob Grant grabbed me.

'Steve?'

I deferred to Yanny, who took them through his appraisal of the situation. Charnley listened intently, then looked at me.

'Did you see any other casualties down there?'

'No, guv.'

'Could there be?' asked Bob.

'It's possible.'

Charnley looked at Bob and then back to me. 'But not that you could confirm?'

'No, guv.'

He went quiet and pulled Bob to one side. Yanny's face seemed to confirm my own fears. I didn't trust Charnley and said so to Yanny.

'He's the wrong man for this – he's a politician, not a leader.'

Yanny crossed his arms, 'Maybe that works for her. If he leaves her there and the press find out they'll skin him, boss. I think he'll have to make a try for her.'

'Hope you're right.'

Charnley and Bob came back and their faces looked set. It was Charnley who spoke and he put his question directly to Yanny.

'What's the smallest number of people required to attempt extracting the woman?'

The big man paused, 'Two down the fissure at any one time; three directly above ground controlling the lines and providing a radio link. Two additional as emergency crew.'

'What about the smoke?' Bob pointed over my shoulder and we all turned to survey the rubble field. With the jet crews withdrawn the smoke was getting thicker by the minute.

'We'll use breathing apparatus – and for her we'll connect an airline to a facemask. The emergency crew will also have to have BA,' I replied.

'And crews with jets, Steve,' put in Bob, 'You'll have to control the fires with men down there.'

Charnley's face was impassive. 'So, we have a minimum of seven as rescue and safety and at least one two-man crew providing a covering jet?'

'Yes,' said Yanny.

'For one woman?'

I fought to control the tension in my voice. 'Leave her down there then, guv?'

Charnley looked down, his voice almost a whisper. 'It's not what I want to do, but I have to weight the risks, Steve. You want me to put nine firefighters in danger, with what you admit is a high possibility of failure. I'm not sure I'm prepared to do that.'

Bob intervened, to offset the brewing row.

'Steve, get two jet crews in breathing apparatus to protect the area around the fissure. Put a safety officer with them and keep them away from those hanging slabs.'

I paused for a fraction to let Charnley know he wasn't off the hook.

'Right.'

As I organised the jet crews Charnley went into conversation with Bob Grant again. Five minutes later, with the jet crews deployed, Yanny breathed into my ear.

'If he doesn't make up his mind soon, then either she'll be dead or the opportunity to get to her will be lost.'

'The smoke?'

He shook his head. 'I didn't want to say too much, but the rubble is moving.'

'What?'

'It happens with all building collapses. The building will try to settle until it's stable. The fissure is the weak link and the weight, especially from that big steel above it, will push out the fissure wall. We don't have long if there's to be any chance.'

I nodded towards Charnley. 'You didn't tell him that?'

'Would you?'

We stood and waited for Charnley to make his decision. I didn't like the man and with good reason, but logic was on his side; nine men at risk for one casualty wasn't an equation, it was a gamble.

Yanny tapped my shoulder and pointed. I turned to follow his gaze. On the edge of the outer cordon there was a commotion. Police were struggling to push back several television camera crews who were in the process of setting up.

Yanny grinned. 'That'll be the decider, you see.'

'Let's go see Charnley.'

We walked back again and Charnley and Bob Grant met us halfway.

Charnley shook his head.

'Steve, I don't think I can authorise a rescue attempt. However, I'm prepared to allow a crane to set up on the edge of the rubble and a limited number of people to service the crane and have the concrete and joists pulled out by chain.'

'It won't work, boss.'

Bob Grant put in, 'If we can pull some of that debris off the casualty we might be able to reach her with a maximum of two firefighters loading the chains at any time.'

Yanny looked him directly in the eye.

'You've a crane here? Now?'

Charnley went still, uncomfortable, 'There's one on its way. Should be here in about an hour.'

Yanny nodded and pointed out the television crews.

'Well, whatever we do, it's being recorded for posterity. If they get wind of the fact that there is a live casualty down there and we intend to do nothing, then serious questions will be asked, boss.'

'We *are* doing something. We've sent for a crane.'

'Boss, an hour might see that woman die . . . I believe there's a compromise.'

Bob edged in to hear.

Yanny chose his words carefully and watched their effect.

'We can use the hour to attempt my plan. If the situation deteriorates then we pull out. If the crane arrives before we've reached her, then we'll pull out and if she dies before we can free her, we'll pull out. It leans to safety and gives her the best chance.'

Charnley turned to see the television crews. It seemed every eye on the incident ground was trained on our group and our eyes were on Charnley.

He stared down again and took his time; whether it was consideration or hesitation was hard to say, but his left foot tapped on the ground, betraying his inner debate. When he glanced up he looked far from comfortable.

'Very well, Yanny, but I'll brief the crews myself.'

'Thank you, boss.'

24

Yanny brought his crew together and Charnley gave them a broad outline of what was being proposed. They listened and then ignored Charnley and aimed their questions at Yanny.

There were five men on the Fire and Rescue Unit, which included Yanny, so four more were needed. After some intense discussion I agreed it with Charnley and Bob Grant that I would be involved with the initial descent into the fissure with Yanny to carry out a close reconnaissance of the situation.

I spoke to Bob Grant and he agreed to use my crews for the extra men and Dave Chase, Mike Scott and Martin McClane volunteered. Further discussion led to two additional people being added to the nine proposed; Ilford's Station Officer, Stuart Docherty, as Sector Commander in control of the team on the surface of the rubble field and John Blane as Safety Officer.

The first thing John did was to make sure that the evacuation signal of six whistle blasts was re-emphasised to everyone.

The rescue team finalised, lowering lines, BA sets, a resuscitator, jacks, acrow props, the slice pack and a range of other equipment was brought together in an equipment pool on the road, in line with our approach on to the rubble field.

Yanny and I rigged in Breathing Apparatus and rescue harnesses and Mike Scott was appointed BA entry control operator. Then, with a final check that everyone knew the plan, we picked up the gear and made our way towards the fissure opening.

Two jet crews, besides the one that was to protect us, were working the rubble field with spray, white steam erupting whenever they hit a hotspot.

'It's cooking in there, boss. We're going to have to be very careful how we move,' said Yanny.

It took two trips to ferry all the gear over to the hole above the fissure and once it was all there, Yanny briefed Dave Chase and Martin McClane to monitor the lines.

The wind picked up again and dust and smoke swirled around the rubble field. The hole that led to the fissure needed to be enlarged and the slice pack was used to carve through the concrete and steel until a hole three feet by four had been cut.

A jet crew cooled the edges to prevent the lines being burnt.

With Anne eight feet below it was safe, but care had to be taken to ensure no off-cuts fell down the fissure. The creaking of the hanging slabs concentrated minds and everyone was edgy as they worked in virtual silence.

Last checks were made and Yanny and I started up our BA sets and the lowering lines were connected to the harnesses. I had the comms set, a BA set adapted to take a radio and earpiece, so I did a radio check with Mike Scott and told Yanny I was ready.

'I'll lead,' he said and started to edge himself into the opening.

Although our first entry was only a reconnaissance, we still carried a lot of equipment, including hand-held wolf lights, crowbar and a first aid kit. Yanny had opted for the wolf lights because they had no trailing cables that might foul our lowering lines or BA sets; the trade-off was that they weren't a patch on halogen lights.

As Yanny climbed down to where Anne was trapped I waited for his shout. When it came I bent down and slipped through the opening into the confines of the fissure, careful not to snag the airline attached to the facemask.

The enlarged opening gave more light than before, but away from the opening it was still gloomy. I aimed my wolf light down the fissure at Yanny and he gave me the thumbs-up.

I started to climb down as the line was paid out behind me. The lines had already been tied off at twenty feet, which allowed for the distance to the opening, the eight feet down to Anne and another four feet with which to manoeuvre. The idea being that if either of us slipped and fell we'd drop a few feet at most.

The fissure was an irregular chasm that ran at an angle down to the shattered wall of the lift shaft. Inside it, the settlement noises of the rubble were magnified. There were other sounds as well; the rushing of the broken main far below us and the crackling of the fire as it ate its way through the wreckage.

There were plenty of foot and handholds, but much of the rubble on the face of the fissure was loose and gave way when touched. Twice I shouted out 'Stand from under!' as I dislodged debris with my feet.

Although only eight feet down it seemed much more as I was forced to move slowly beneath the weight of the gear I was carrying. At one point I stopped and shone the wolf light straight down, past Yanny.

The beam fell on the half-naked body of a man, his clothes ripped from him by the force of the explosion and his face set in death's astonishment. Next to him was a burnt androgynised torso.

Beyond the bodies the beam faded, leaving me to guess at the extent of the shaft.

'Boss! Are you all right, boss?' shouted Yanny.

I held my thumb up again and continued on down. As I reached him Yanny pointed out a small ledge of concrete on which he was balanced and he guided my feet towards it.

We had to speak above the noise of the exhaling valves and our own panting to hear each other clearly and when we did the sounds echoed into the depths. With the yawning shaft beneath us and the heat and confinement it felt tomblike, dead; not the place to be if you suffered from claustrophobia.

We positioned ourselves either side of Anne and for the first time I got a good look at her.

Amazingly, her face was untouched, except for a dusty, blood-streaked smear down one side. Balancing on the ledge, I took her head in my hands. It felt so light, so fragile, that I was scared to let it go. She murmured and her eyes flickered, but didn't open.

A wave of emotion hit me and I forced it away. This was not a place to lose focus.

Yanny fixed the facemask on her and tightened the straps; the demand valve on the mask popped as she inhaled and then settled into rhythmic breathing.

I looked for some way to rest her head and searched around. I found a small piece of sheet timber and wedged it under her back then pulled my spare flash hood from my tunic pocket and folded it into a small bundle, enough to act as a buffer between her head and the timber. Next we turned our attention to what was trapping her.

The rubble around her shoulders and chest was loose and as I shielded her head Yanny scooped some of it away, then used the crowbar to prise out several chunks of concrete from between the two slabs that held her fast.

I listened to the sound of his exhaling valve as he sweated and strained in the cramped conditions. After about ten minutes we swapped places, Yanny acting as a shield while I dug around her.

It was desperately hard working the rubble whilst balancing on the ledge and wearing BA. Every movement seemed an effort in the hot, cramped and gloomy environment. I was running with sweat and could feel my pulse hammering in my ears as I levered at the debris wedged between the upper and lower slabs.

I stole a glance at my BA gauge and realised I'd gone through half my air in fifteen minutes. I willed myself to slow down and worked more methodically, but it was still hard going.

When I couldn't remove any more debris, I leaned back and shone the wolf light into the cavity. She was pinned fast at the waist, with her lower trunk and legs pinched between the concrete.

'Could we get a jack in there and try and lift the top slab, Yanny?' I shouted. He bent his knees until his face was level with mine and peered into the gap.

'I doubt it.'

'Airbags, then?'

'Too much weight.'

'What do you think, then?'

He pulled his head out and stood up. I followed him.

'She's held fast by this.' He smacked the top slab with his hand, 'It doesn't look good.'

'I know it doesn't, but what do we do?'

'Steady, boss.'

He tapped me on the shoulder and I nodded, acknowledging that I was letting it get to me. For the first time it hit me that we might not get her out and the effort of suppressing the panic found my throat.

There had to be a way!

'Do we pull out and wait for the crane, then?'

'No. Start to pull this about and the whole thing will crumble into the shaft.'

'Tell me we're not going to abandon her, Yanny.'

He paused. 'There is a way . . . but we need to go back to the surface and discuss it.'

Mike Scott's voice sounded in my earpiece.

'Entry control officer to Foxtrot 443, over.'

'Go ahead, Mike,' I replied.

'I'd like a gauge reading and Station Officer Docherty wants to know what's happening.'

I related Yanny's gauge readings and mine and told Mike that we were coming out to brief Stuart Docherty. Then Yanny pulled twice on the line and started to climb back to the opening.

Alone with Anne, the feelings I'd been keeping at bay claimed me. I held her head and turned so that I was to the side of her.

There was no way I could kiss her and in a firefighting tunic and harness there was no way I could hold her so that there was any sensation, so I did the only thing left to me, I took off a glove and held her hand.

She immediately stopped breathing and for a moment I'd thought I'd lost her, but I placed two fingers on her carotid artery and felt her pulse beat against me. Then she shuddered and the demand valve popped again and I heard the inrush of air.

I closed my eyes.

'Don't die,' I whispered. 'Choose life!'

I didn't want to leave her. That was a common reaction of rescuers with trapped casualties, but the only way to free her was to go out, reassess and re-quip then come back.

A sharp tug on the line diverted my attention and I answered it with two tugs. Carefully, I checked to make sure the flash hood was under her head and gave her hand a final squeeze then started back up the fissure wall.

It was harder than the descent and my legs started to shake from the combined effects of heat, wearing a BA set and carrying so much gear.

I could see faces at the opening, but the sweat was running

into my eyes and my breathing was all over the place, so I concentrated on moving steadily and safely. The line holding me was pulled in gradually, ready to take the weight should I fall.

Near the opening I could hear the wind had got stronger and was making a whistling noise as it swept across the hole, sending dust and small pieces of debris down on top of me.

I ignored the distractions and kept focused, but I was feeling exhausted, which I put down to the stress of the situation as much as the physical strain.

At the top, I lay half in and half out the opening, gasping like a beached fish until two sets of hands grabbed me and pulled me through the hole and to my feet, but my legs buckled and they sat me down again.

Someone pulled off my helmet and facemask and water was poured over my head. I took a couple of deep breaths and came up onto one knee. Immediately hands grabbed me and I was lifted and supported.

As I stood upright I realised then just how strong the wind had become. Dust and smoke were being blown across the rubble field and fine particles of concrete stung as they were whipped against hands and faces.

Yanny appeared and stood in front of me, grinning

'You all right, boss?'

'Hits you when you come out.'

He patted my shoulder. 'Let's get clear of here and talk on the road.'

He shot a look at Stuart Docherty, who nodded. Everybody grabbed something and Dave Chase took my BA set off me and carried it. We retreated back to the road with the gusting wind snatching at us.

Charnley and Bob Grant came over and asked me for an assessment.

'Doesn't look good, guv.' I turned to Yanny, 'Tell them.'

The big South African laid out the problems we'd encoun-
tered and how Anne was wedged between the two massive
slabs of concrete.

'But there is a way to get her out, boss.'

'I'm listening,' said Charnley.

Yanny looked around at everyone, 'She's free from just
below the hips up . . .'

There was silence as everyone took in the implications and I
felt fear run through me.

'A surgical team? Is that what you are suggesting, Yanny?'
asked Bob Grant.

Yanny shook his head.

'I don't think you could get a surgical team down there to
work in those conditions . . . it's tight and hot, very hot.'

'So what are you saying?' asked Charnley.

Yanny crossed his arms and his voice was soft, so that we
had to strain to hear it above the wind.

'Use the slice pack to cut through her legs – it will seal the
wounds as it goes, but she'd have to be anaesthetised.'

The full impact of his words stunned me and drained the
remaining strength from my body. My mouth opened to
speak, but behind me there was a loud crack and we all turned
and looked upwards.

One of the reinforcing rods holding the hanging slabs had
snapped and the other was making a noise that was halfway
between a cracking and a screaming sound. The wind gusted
again and the final rods broke and the slabs crashed down onto
the lift shaft area with a massive thump that shook the ground.

A huge cloud of dust erupted and then the entire rubble
field around the shaft sank and disappeared into a huge hole.
Everyone except me was rooted to the spot.

My fatigue vanished and I ran forward to the edge of the
hole. The shaft, the fissure and the slabs, were all gone, leaving
a huge gaping hole that was fifty feet deep.

25

The slabs had not only taken the lift shaft and fissure, they had smashed through to the triple-level basement below the rubble field so that a third of the entire site had effectively dropped three storeys.

Anne was dead.

Nothing could have survived the massive secondary collapse.

I stood alone on the edge of the rubble field, trying to accept the evidence of my own eyes and rejecting the seductive fantasy that she could be down there, in a survival void, breathing.

Prayer had no meaning in my life. Wishes were for children, hopes for the weak. I had always kicked against my fate, refused the balm of acceptance, of acquiescence. Submission was a cancer long ago rejected by a child not allowed to give the responsibility for his security over to a parent.

Damaged? Yes. Reactive? Hopelessly so, but always, always, a realist.

Yet I felt . . . punished.

Dust and smoke rose from the depths and there was an unnatural silence across the incident ground as people struggled to take in the enormity of what had happened.

Yanny appeared alongside me. Then John and Bob Grant. No one spoke. Ironically it was Charnley who snapped out of it first; *the bonus of superficiality*, I thought unkindly.

He ordered all crews to withdraw to the edge of the inner

cordon and a roll-call taken to ascertain that no one was missing.

Miraculously, no firefighters had been killed or injured, the jet crews having withdrawn with the rescue crew.

It was John Blane who spoke the thought that was coursing through all our minds.

'What now?'

Charnley coughed and we all looked at him.

'Now we wait. For the Borough Surveyor and the crane. Unless there are surface survivors that we've missed, then no more rescues are to be attempted.'

So we waited.

Several times Yanny asked permission to carry out Trapped Person Locator searches and every time Charnley shook his head.

Around midday, just after the crane arrived, the Chief Officer visited the scene.

The press went into overdrive on catching sight of him and we watched from afar as he approached them and talked long and earnestly on a subject he knew nothing about.

Yanny stood with his arms folded, making sucking noises, and his crew shared the same subversive grin.

I couldn't shake the numbness that had enveloped me after the secondary collapse. A process of self-protection had detached me from the yawning black hole that hovered just beyond immediate thought and feeling. I was thankful, the crash would come, but the further away the better.

It was early afternoon before the crane was offered up to the rubble field.

The plan was no-plan.

We were to work from the edges, removing debris piecemeal in a way that provided maximum safety for firefighters and little else.

Yanny talked his way into acting as liaison between the

crane and the Incident Commander. Gradually, assisted by the vacuum of knowledge and skill, he took control of operations and organised the debris removal and even managed to talk Charnley into the occasional Trapped Person Locator search, but the building was now a sarcophagus, unwilling to yield up any, but the dead.

I was still numb, disconnected, when we were relieved at three o'clock.

We'd been there for the best part of six hours, but apart from the vivid images on arrival and the entry into the fissure, the only thing I could fix on was the collapse of the slabs.

Just as we were about to leave the incident ground, more heavy plant arrived and Yanny's FRU crew were relieved as well, effectively ending any pressure to resume TPL searches.

Yanny came and found me before he left.

'You all right, boss? You went a bit quiet back there.'

'It got to me . . . the woman trapped in the fissure.'

He nodded. 'You bonded with her – it happens with casualties, boss.'

'Yes, it does.'

'If you want to talk about this at any time . . .'

'Thank you.'

There was an awkward silence and I could see in his eyes that he was genuinely concerned; I must have looked like shit. I rubbed my face with my hands and then for some reason shook his hand.

'Take care, now,' he said and then walked back to the Fire and Rescue Unit.

I climbed aboard my appliance and told Harry Wildsmith to take us home.

None of us spoke on the way back to Wells Lane Fire Station, but I caught Harry giving me some sideways glances.

Back at the station we got cleaned up and spent the rest of

the afternoon in front of the television, channel-hopping to watch the rolling news coverage on satellite.

Image after image flashed onto the screen, with every aspect of the devastated building shown. Once or twice it was possible to make out individual firefighters, and at one point the camera picked up on Yanny, Bob Grant, Charnley and myself as we discussed the situation after the reconnaissance in the fissure.

The next images were the slow-motion collapse of the hanging slabs.

In the bottom right-hand corner of the screen you could see our heads turn and then the camera panned to the slabs; the cameraman alerted by our reaction.

When the first set of reinforcing rods snapped, the slabs swung through an arc and twisted. The second set of rods parted as the slabs reached the highest point of their movement.

The collapse of the basements under the rubble was equally dramatic, as though a huge fist had smashed down, caving in the entire area around the lift shaft. A helicopter-mounted camera gave a perfect view of the crater-shaped hole; so much for Yanny's suggested exclusion zone.

We watched it again and again – in slow motion, in freeze-frame, in real time – as a talking face speculated on the chances of anyone remaining alive under the rubble.

Instant experts appeared and debated the possible causes.

The word 'bomb' was tossed around and heads nodded wisely, despite there being no announcement from the police. Gas was also discussed, but it wasn't as sexy as a bomb and was glossed over.

That's when they got to speculate as to why.

They homed in on the fact that it was OPMA's head-quarters and then shot from the lip: it was a political statement, an attempt to strike at the heart of OPMA's operations; it was blind luck. The theories piled up, unfettered by fact or feasibility.

OPMA was described as controversial and its head, J.J. Roth, acknowledged as a figure attracting his share of enemies – as most powerful figures do.

A self-made man who had started work as a junior pharmacist, he'd dragged himself up to command one of the largest, most powerful multinationals in the world and much was made of his shrewd, ruthless business deals and of how he dealt with heads of state rather than other business chiefs.

Then they showed a clip of him shaking hands with a South-East Asian President and I was struck by how tall he was.

A close-up revealed him to have steel-grey hair and sharp features with dark, almost black eyes; the type of face a feature writer might describe as aquiline and what a firefighter would call shifty.

The piece finished by saying that he was presently in London.

I left the watch in front of the television and went and sat in my room, expecting the reality of Anne's death to hit now that the adrenalin had subsided. It didn't.

At six o'clock I went off duty and shook my head at the offer of a drink from John and Harry. I needed to talk calmly about the idea that was shaping in my head and the only person I could trust with it was Alex.

The drive to his house took under half an hour and I found him in front of the television.

'Stevie! Were you there?'

He pointed at the screen and I nodded.

'Jesus! Some first day back, eh? I bet that—'

He stopped, 'What is it?'

When I'd returned from Wales I hadn't said much about Anne. He'd asked, but I'd shrugged it off. I didn't want to go into it because her disappearance had hurt and, if I was truthful, had left me feeling foolish.

Now I told him everything.

He didn't interrupt me, but there was something in his eyes. When I got to the part where I found her in the fissure he swore gently in amazement, but it was only when I related the fact that the slabs had hit the rubble directly above her did he comment.

'You'll go to the police, naturally?'

'No.'

'No?'

I paused. 'You're the only person besides me that knows she's down there, Alex. If she was involved in the bombing of that building I want to find out why.'

'This is serious shit, Stevie. You can't go fucking around with terrorism, the police will cut your nuts off.'

I clasped my hands and looked at the floor.

'There's a chance . . . one . . . two per cent . . . that she's alive and I won't do anything until her body is recovered or she's brought out. Either way, until they find and identify her I've got time and I intend to use that time.'

'Stevie man . . . I can understand your feelings, but you mustn't get involved with this. You've been back one day . . . three weeks ago you'd have given anything to get your job back – well, you've managed it, but this . . . this will backfire horribly, I know it. And there'll be no saving you.'

'I don't give a fuck,' I said softly.

He got up and went over to the drinks cabinet and poured two large Scotches. He gave me one and sat down opposite. I hadn't eaten all day and my stomach kicked against the neat spirit.

'You know, the very fact that you haven't told the police already could be viewed as withholding evidence. Have you any idea of the powers of arrest and detention the police enjoy when terrorism is involved? Or the penalties? If she had a hand . . .'

'That's just it, Alex. I don't believe she could have.'

'Why? Because you slept with her?'

I glared at him.

'I mean it, Stevie. You know nothing about this woman, nothing.'

'I know enough.'

The words sounded hollow even to me and Alex wasn't buying any of it.

He sat back in his chair and nestled the drink on his lap. I avoided his eyes because I was afraid of what I might see in them. After a silence that stretched on for several minutes he cleared his throat and I looked up.

'What?'

'How long do you think it will take for them to find and recover her body?'

'I've no idea . . . a few days . . . a week . . . I really don't know, Alex.'

'I want your promise that until her body is recovered you won't go off half-cock. No running off to Wales and terrorising the locals. Just sit still and see what comes out of this.'

I spoke softly, trying to rein in my frustration, 'I've got some time until she is found and identified. We're the only people who know that she's dead.'

'That certain, is it?'

'I can't believe she's involved.'

'It's a hell of a coincidence if she isn't. Wait, Stevie.'

'I can't do that.'

'Scared that the truth might surface?'

'I *want* the truth.'

'You've a tour of duty to complete, Stevie, another day duty and two nights. I want you to promise me you'll do nothing until after then.'

'Why?'

He got that look in his eye again. 'Promise me.'

I exhaled slowly. 'Until I finish my night duty.'

26

The next day I got up early and watched the seven o'clock news bulletin over several cups of coffee, but most of what they had was the previous day's clips of film and rehashed opinions.

Alex offered to cook me breakfast, but I passed and wolfed down a couple of bowls of cereal and plenty of thick, heavily buttered toast; I'd been caught out the previous day and wanted to make sure I had plenty of fuel in the tank.

I drove into work early and tried to get some more information on what had happened overnight, but although the Pump Ladder had been on relief down at the collapsed OPMA building no one seemed to know very much. They'd been employed shifting rubble in a chain and briefings had been perfunctory.

Several bodies had been recovered in the night and I wondered if Anne was amongst them. Apparently a temporary morgue had been set up in a school near Beehive Lane.

The only other bit of useful information I gleaned was that they were bringing in a Super Crane later that day, because none of the cranes used so far had been man enough for the job.

There was a buzz on roll-call at nine and I noted the difference the last twenty-four hours had made in terms of confidence; we were a watch again.

At ten past nine the bells went down and the Pump Ladder was ordered as immediate relief to the OPMA building – to the surprise of no one.

Dave Chase opened up the 'nutty', the watch canteen, and we all stocked up on bars of chocolate and crisps while the mess manager, Mike Scott, made two flasks of coffee. Then we set off.

On arrival, along with the other relief crews we were divided up into crews who would work immediately and those who would be stood by, waiting to give the working crews a rest.

The tension and drama of the previous day had been replaced by an air of limbo. No one was really sure whether the situation was still technically live, that is whether we were still searching actively for casualties or whether the job was now merely recovery of bodies.

My guess was that it was recovery, but no one had the balls to tell the Press. It wasn't the time factor; people had remained alive for up to two weeks under buildings, it was the scale of the secondary collapse. It was almost impossible to conceive of anybody surviving it.

As we were one of those crews stood by I took the opportunity to wander over to the temporary morgue.

I found a policeman there who was helping to run it and I explained that I might know someone who worked in the place and asked if I could view the recovered bodies. He was happy to oblige and told me that so far none of the bodies had left the temporary morgue because of the fears that it was a terrorist incident and the Anti-Terrorist Branch wanted all the bodies kept together so that they could be identified and eliminated from inquiries.

He then took me around each body in turn. Anne wasn't amongst them.

I strolled back to the waiting area and sat drinking coffee with the lads.

The relief was four hours in all and we were to rotate every hour with the other crews. When it was our turn to work we gathered together with our rota crews and received a briefing that consisted of pointing out the safety officers, reiterating the evacuation signal of six whistle blasts and reminding people to keep their personal protective clothing on while within the inner cordon.

Of rescue work or the overall strategy, we heard nothing and questions were answered with shrugs.

One Station Officer, from a Western Command Station, a dry man with wit underlining his every word, tried hard to get more information, but his questions only seemed to irritate the young Assistant Divisional Officer, 'probably', as Harry remarked, 'because he was clueless himself.'

Work was slow, as we constantly had to wait while a crane was loaded up or jet crews damped down the fires still burning in the rubble field. In the four hours we were there only one body, a boy in his late teens, was recovered.

Once or twice I found myself on the edge of the crater, staring down, trying to connect with the reality of Anne's death.

To imagine her lifeless and grey was impossibly hard. Our affair had been so intense, so vital and my own needs so strong, that to accept her death was to sever the past and that I wasn't ready to do.

Just after one o'clock we were relieved by Romford's Pump Ladder and drove back to Wells Lane for a late lunch.

In the bizarre routine that is brigade life we went out on hydrant testing in the afternoon, as though it were a normal day. It's one of the things that an outsider can't get a handle on; you go to a tragedy or a disaster and then go back to the office work or equipment testing or fire-safety inspections, any of which might be curtailed by another fire or road accident.

Your mind does the same gearshifts; on the way back from the OPMA building the discussion had been about fishing tackle.

When we got back from hydrants it was twenty to four and

the Pump's crew were sitting in the mess, drinking tea. They looked up as we came in.

'There's been a couple of firefighters hurt at the OPMA building,' said John Blane.

'Badly?' I asked.

'One's snapped his ankle and the other's got cuts and bruises.'

'How did that happen?'

'They were recovering a body and as they crossed the rubble field one of them fell over and took the others with him.'

'That'll please Yanny, he was having a go yesterday about none of us having received training on moving across a rubble field.'

'Alex rang for you, guv,' said Dave Chase, 'he wants you to ring him. There's a note on your desk.'

I poured myself a cup of tea and took it through to my office. Dave's scribbled note said 'ring me, urgent, Alex.'

I dialled the number and Alex answered straight away.

'Is there a problem, Alex?'

'Not a problem as such. Have you been down there today, Stevie?'

'This morning. They were bringing in heavier plant when we left.'

'Rescue phase over, then?'

'Looks that way,' I breathed.

'Nothing out of the ordinary?'

'No.'

'Well, don't hang around at six.'

'Why?'

'We've a guest for dinner.'

I arrived at Alex's around half-six and he went all enigmatic on me. Try as I might to get him to open up, he just gave a tight grin and sang to himself as he prepared the dinner. So I gave up trying to get a response and settled for beer and the news.

Just before eight there was a knock on the door. Before I could move Alex called out that he'd get it.

I was hooked, but there was no way I was going to let the bastard see it so I stayed where I was and prepared myself for anything. As soon as I saw the visitor I realised that I'd been ambushed. It was Roley Benson.

Roley was a large, battered-faced man with world-weary eyes. I'd never seen him completely sober, but just then he seemed pretty close.

'Evenin', Steve,' he said, with a smile.

'Roley,' I nodded.

'Let me take your coat Roley, sit down, sit down. Drink?' Fussed Alex.

'Have you got a tonic water?' Roley asked.

Alex stopped. 'Tonic?'

'I've given up the drink . . . I've been on the wagon now for over two months.'

'Good man, good man,' beamed Alex.

'What brought this on, Roley?' I asked.

The big ex-copper looked from Alex to me, embarrassed, 'Carol Carver.'

Alex looked rueful and I acknowledged the breathtaking logic of it.

Carol Carver was the widow of Peter Carver, a CID man stabbed to death in an abortive drugs raid. Roley, his partner, had been drunk at the time and had frozen when the drugs dealer turned on Peter Carver. As Carver lay dying, Roley somehow managed to overpower the dealer, sustaining a stab wound himself in the process.

The police, mindful of the potential bad publicity, had overlooked Roley being drunk and awarded him a commendation after which Roley was quietly pensioned off.

He responded to this by drinking himself into oblivion.

After the funeral, Carol Carver had taken it upon herself to be Roley's housekeeper. It wasn't that she didn't know he was drunk when her husband was killed, but rather, being a Christian, she'd forgiven him.

Now it seemed she'd shamed him off the drink.

'You're not an item, are you, Roley?' teased Alex.

The big man wrung his hands and there was a pregnant pause.

'We've been out to tea.'

'Tea!' blurted out Alex, tactlessly, 'fucking tea!'

Roley looked torn between embarrassment and irritation.

'Something wrong with that?'

Alex shot me a look and I shrugged to say that he was on his own. If he was going to dig himself into a hole I didn't see why I should be buried as well.

'Well . . . that's good very good,' said Alex with a crude attempt at recovery.

'Well, get the man his tonic water, Alex,' I said, chipping in to worsen his discomfort.

Alex's eyes narrowed, but he was at such a disadvantage he was forced to swallow it and went out to the kitchen.

'And how are you Steve?' said Roley, with an affected air of normality.

'Couldn't be worse, seeing as you ask. Why are you here?'

He paused, 'Alex invited me.'

'Why did he invite you?'

Alex appeared in the doorway. 'Leave him alone till we've eaten.'

I glared at him again, but he ignored me and gave Roley his tonic water before disappearing back into the kitchen.

'Alex says you've been away on holiday,' began Roley.

'He lied. I was at a therapy centre for dysfunctional firemen.'

'Oh.'

'Do you miss the drink?'

He raised his eyebrows, 'All the time.'

'Life's a fucker, ain't it?'

'All the time.'

Alex brought the food in; grilled steaks with organic mushrooms, mange tout and 'Potatoes Anna'. Not subtle, but then again, neither were we.

As we ate I kept my anxiety under control and went along with whatever Alex's plan was. Roley looked like a different character sober, not the snarling, bad-tempered neo-drop-out that I'd seen three months ago. He seemed to be trying to turn his life around and Carol Carver was obviously helping him do that.

Meanwhile, as he sipped his tonic water, Alex and I quaffed claret without a trace of conscience.

For dessert Alex had prepared ice cream with amaretti macaroons. Roley said little unless spoken to, so Alex and I kept up a stream of questions as though we were carrying out interviews for the parish council.

When the coffee was produced Alex turned to me. I half expected what he had to say, but it didn't make me any less nervous.

'Stevie,' he began, 'shortly after you told me about St Katharine's Dock I contacted Roley and asked him to find out if Anne Lloyd showed up on any police files.'

'That was good of you.'

'Don't be angry, I was concerned.'

I looked at Roley, 'Isn't it an offence to obtain data from police files? Or am I being naive here?'

'Steady, Stevie,' said Alex, 'If this is anybody's fault it's mine.'

I could feel the anger rising. 'Can't leave things alone, can you?'

'Let's just hear what Roley has to say, eh?'

'What, like you don't know already?'

Alex was impassive. 'Actually, no, I don't.'

At that I shut up and Alex nodded to Roley.

'When Alex contacted me, Steve, I was reluctant to do this. But when he told me that you might be in danger I put wheels in motion.'

Nice one, Stevie, slag off a man whose only crime is to help you. I should give lessons.

Roley continued, 'I got hold of a friend of mine, one of the few who still talk to me, and asked him to run a check on Anne Lloyd.'

'And?'

He paused and looked at Alex. 'There's nothing in criminal records on Anne Lloyd.'

I breathed a silent sigh of relief.

'So it was a waste of time, then?'

'Not quite.'

'Go on,' said Alex.

Roley drummed his fingers on the table. 'How did you come to meet Anne Lloyd, Steve?'

'She asked me to help her find out some information.'

'On what, exactly?'

I paused. 'It was to do with a multinational firm.'

'Was it OPMA?'

I went still. 'Yes.'

'I see.'

'What is it, Roley?' asked Alex.

'You have to keep this to yourself, both of you. If this got out . . .'

'Just tell us, Roley,' I said softly.

'Anne Lloyd didn't show up on criminal records anywhere, but my friend did manage to trace her. She was shot in an incident eighteen months ago . . . whilst in the line of duty . . .'

'*What?*'

'Anne Lloyd was a policewoman. A detective sergeant.'

'Was – you said "was" Roley.'

He cleared his throat. 'She took a bullet in the body, and it came out of the side, just below the armpit, apparently. She was lucky to live. Shortly after, for reasons that my friend can't find out, she retired as an alternative to dismissal.'

'That doesn't make sense!'

'I can only tell you what I know.'

27

I fired questions at Roley, but he had little information to add.

The reason he had asked about OPMA was that the investigation Anne had been involved with was in some way connected to them. After that his friend had drawn a blank. Before Roley left I made him promise to dig deeper.

Alex and I sat drinking until the early hours of the morning. I think he suspected that I might just jump in the Shogun and head for Wales and he wanted me too drunk for that to be an option. On one level he was right, but I was under no illusions as to how serious a situation it was and I wanted my targets clearly identified before I went after them.

That Anne had been holding things back didn't surprise me, but one thought in particular was starting to burn a hole in me.

The next morning I was awake early with a thick head and a thousand possibilities racing through my brain. I was due on my first night duty at six, which left me most of the day to come up with a plan.

It was ironic, I'd fought not to become involved in the conflict between OPMA and the environmentalists, but now Anne was dead, when she was beyond help, I was going to do just that.

I got up, pulled on a tracksuit and went downstairs.

Over coffee I sat with a pen and paper, making notes and going over everything that had happened from the moment I'd arrived in Wales. When I'd finished I don't think I had two things that showed a link.

There was obviously a history here that was still being acted out and I was starting in the middle of the maze, so I had to pick a route and see what turned up. My first aim would be to find out what had happened in between her disappearing and the bomb incident at the OPMA building.

For that I needed more information, but from whom?

Julia.

If anyone knew about Anne it was her sister. There had been tension between them, but why? And how does a police-woman graduate to environmental agitator?

I looked at the clock. It was ten to eight and if I knew one thing for certain it was that Eddie Marlowe would be having breakfast.

I picked up the phone and dialled Ty Hiraeth. Eve answered and I asked for Eddie without saying who I was. There was a pause while she went and fetched him.

'Hello, Eddie Marlowe speaking, who is this?'

'Eddie, it's me, Steve. Am I disturbing your breakfast?'

There was a pause on the end of the line.

'No, no – I've just finished. Steve . . . how are you?'

'Fine, Eddie. Look, something's come up and I might need your help.'

'Sailing close to the wind again, eh?'

'This is serious stuff, Eddie. Is Julia there?'

'She was until about seven last night. She's due in at nine today.'

'I want to know if the police contact Julia.'

'Why?'

'It's better I don't say, just note it, but tell nobody and I want to know if anything out of the ordinary happens.'

'Well, funny you say that 'cos something odd *has* happened.'

'Go on.'

'Bryn Thomas has disappeared.'

I got a sick feeling in my gut. 'What d'you mean, disappeared?'

'Well, apparently a couple of days ago he went out walking and never returned. His mother rang here about midnight on the day he went, worried out of her wits. She thought he might have called in here. Eve said she were crying and all sorts.'

'How are the police taking his disappearance, Eddie?'

'Well, there's been appeals on the local radio, but the police have got their hands full, what with the forest fires and all. People are saying that perhaps he's had a bit of a breakdown and wandered off.'

'Bryn? Never. Look, Eddie, I'm coming up to Wales either tomorrow or more probably the day after – and it won't be a social call. I'd like to meet up with you, but it has to be discreet. Do you know where Abergynolwyn is?'

'Just beyond the Tal-y-llyn lake?'

'That's the one. There's an inn there, Castell Coch, I'm going to try and book in there for a few days, but no one and I mean no one must know, Eddie.'

'I don't know it, but Abergynolwyn is just a village, I can find it easy enough and don't worry, I won't tell a soul.'

'Right, when I arrive there, I'll ring and tell you when to meet me. Have you got a pen with you?'

There was another pause and I heard him fumbling.

'Go ahead.'

I gave him Alex's phone number and told him to ring me the instant anything happened.

'Bye, Eddie, see you in a couple of days.'

I put the phone down.

Alex appeared in the living room doorway, 'Are you using my phone again?'

'Only to ring the Sydney talking clock – you deserve no less after pulling that stunt with Roley Benson.'

He smiled. 'But then you wouldn't have known that Anne was once a policewoman.'

'True.'

'When are you going back to Wales?'

'Who said I am?'

He raised his eyebrows, 'You did last night, with every studied silence.'

'You don't approve?'

'Since when did my approval come into it?'

It was my turn to smile. 'Look, I'm going to have a shower then I'd like to borrow your computer for a couple of hours.'

'Researching OPMA?'

'You're a witch.'

'And you, Stevie, are sometimes a little too obvious for your own good. Shall I cook breakfast?'

'Throw in sex and I'll marry you.'

'Not tempting.'

In the shower I started to think about Bryn Thomas. What had happened?

I knew about breakdowns; I'd been living on the edge of one since Sandy died and the signs and symptoms tended to show whether you wanted them to or not. Bryn was a hundred per cent; the vibe off him was free of interference.

So where was he?

Over breakfast I talked to Alex about it and he agreed it didn't look good.

'You're going to have to watch out for yourself, Stevie, the attrition rate is climbing.'

'You think he's dead?'

'Don't you?'

'I don't know . . . maybe.'

He stopped eating and punched the air with his fork, as though interrupting his own thought. 'Aye, and I have to ask the question, why are you going to Wales anyway? Anne's dead . . . probably, so who are you doing this for?'

'Me.'

He put down his knife and fork and clasped his hands together, before resting them on the table.

'You had an affair, Stevie. All right, it was good, but brief. A few weeks in which you met and slept with a gorgeous woman, but you owe her nothing. Nothing at all.'

'You sound worried.'

His face changed, 'Don't go all flippant on me, Stevie. I know you too well. You'll go haring up to Wales creating God knows what kind of mayhem and risking your neck, for what? A sense of being noble?'

My anger flashed and subsided in an instant. Alex watched me, knowing the arc of reaction.

I smiled. 'If you know me so well, why try and talk me out of it?'

He picked up his knife and fork again. 'Oh, I'm not trying. I just want you to be clear in your own head as to why you are risking your future after only just getting it back.'

'For me, Alex. For her, for sanity, for the craic. Quite simply because I have to do it. So accept it and help me, please.'

He sighed. 'There are names for people like you . . . long medical ones.'

After breakfast I logged on to the Internet and tried to find OPMA. I got the Ohio Petroleum Marketing Agency, the Oregon Petroleum Marketing Agency and a thousand variations on the same, but no OPMA that mattered.

I typed out Oil, Pharmaceutical and Mining Agency in full and thousands of hits came up. I tried advanced searches and keyword searches, but nothing seemed to pin down their operations in Wales.

Then I tried the Black River Mining Company and got over fifteen hundred hits. One was an official business site and the rest were general sites given over to worldwide mining as a whole or to environmental groups campaigning against mercury pollution in the Amazon. They did all agree, however, that the Black River Mining Company was named after a river.

Then I tried J.J. Roth.

The amount of data on the man was phenomenal.

Newspaper reports, magazine articles, committee hearings in America, Europe and Asia, there was simply too much of it to wade through. By midday I'd had enough and called it a day.

As soon as I got off the Internet the phone rang and I picked it up. It was a recorded message, from Jenny.

'Hello, Alex, it's me, Jenny. Look, I know you probably don't want to get involved, but I really do want to speak to Steve. Could I ask you to contact him and give him my new mobile number, please?'

It was strange to hear her voice again and it caught me off guard. I hesitated for a moment, but only a moment, then pressed the '3' key and wiped the message.

I went into work early, around five, having watched most of the hourly news bulletins. I was itching to get back to the OPMA site and intended to ring Control and volunteer our Pump Ladder as the first relief after the six o'clock change of shift.

It seemed the Super Crane had been making inroads to the crater area and the smaller plant had nibbled effectively at the edges of the rubble throughout the day, but the thing that had caught my ear on the four o'clock bulletin was the speculation that they were going to try to lift the hanging slabs from the base of the crater around eight o'clock that night.

Mark Kinch, the green watch commander, was filling in an accident report for one of his watch who had twisted an ankle on the rubble field earlier that day. He held a hand up as I came into the office.

'Hi, Mark.'

He swivelled on the chair. 'Steve, you had a phone call earlier today, a woman. She didn't leave her name. I told her that you'd be on duty at six.'

'Cheers, Mark.'

'How does it feel to be back?'

A number of people in the office went still.

I looked around and made sure I caught their eyes, 'It feels good, especially when people put themselves out to make you feel welcome.'

Mark grinned, 'Rumours, mate . . . never let a good one interfere with the truth.'

Just after six the orderings for the reliefs came through. Someone had taken the decision to drop from four to three hours reliefs earlier that day, due to the harsh working conditions. I studied the teleprinter sheet, we had not made first relief, but were instead allocated the nine pm to twelve slot.

There was no guarantee that when the slabs were lifted Anne would be found or that the attempt to lift them would occur before the nine o'clock relief, it was just that I was getting twitchy.

The three hours dragged by and we had an early dinner, knowing that by the time we got back to Wells Lane it would be well after midnight.

At twenty past eight we left the station.

Mike Scott was driving and he queried us leaving so early.

'It'll give the crew we relieve a chance to eat dinner at a sensible hour,' I explained.

He looked at me as if to say, 'come again!' and I pretended not to notice.

It was still light and the heat of the day was oozing from the concrete. We drove with the windows open, watching the sun turn blood red on the horizon and the sky become streaked with orange.

The nearer we got to the OPMA site, the greater the damage to the buildings flanking the A12. No traffic, except emergency vehicles, was allowed past Gants Hill roundabout and as we came off the roundabout we had to stop while the police opened the outer cordon.

We booked into the control unit and were told to report to Sector One, at the front of the rubble field.

The Super Crane dominated the incident ground, dwarfing the other plant and we stood for a moment and watched it.

'Impressive, isn't it, guv?' said Mike Scott.

I nodded and Gerry Mudd appeared alongside me.

'I wonder what they'll find when they lift those slabs?'

'Bodies,' I breathed.

'No one alive, then, guv?'

'No, Gerry. At least, I don't think so.'

'Makes you wonder at the minds of the people who do this sort of thing – fanatics, I suppose.'

Mike Scott gave him an old-fashioned look. 'Well, it wouldn't be anyone normal, would it, you plank!'

I thought of Anne: preparing a meal, swimming in the lake . . . and lying next to me. Normal.

Over the next half-hour we watched as crews changed over and the plant came to a halt, waiting for the new crews to be deployed.

There were a lot of non-emergency workers on scene, from the Borough Surveyor to Health and Safety Executive representatives and all three utilities services workers; there had been a persistent smell of gas throughout the incident despite assurances that the mains had been cut off.

There was also still fire in the rubble field. Smoke seeped from the debris and the night air was heavy with its acrid smell.

I was appointed Safety Officer and given a white tabard to

wear; the rest of my crew became part of a chain passing rubble back to a series of skips which were periodically driven away.

There were more police around now, sifting through the rubble before it was removed from the site.

Scene of Crimes officers and Home Office Forensics people mingled with the firefighters and called things to a halt every now and again as they went in and looked at anything interesting.

As the sky darkened, the harsh glare of the halogen lighting units painted angular shadow across the shattered building. The street lighting having been turned off due to damaged and uprooted lamp-posts.

I was absorbed in watching the scene, keeping switched on to the dangers in order to warn the crews in the event of secondary collapse, when I became aware of a discussion going on at the edge of the crater and then I recognised the big man at the centre of it; Yanny.

Two minutes later the group walked towards me, Yanny leading and a harassed-looking Assistant Divisional Officer trailing behind along with a Health and Safety Executive man and some of the Fire and Rescue Unit crew.

'Boss!' called Yanny as he approached.

I smiled and nodded.

The group gathered around me and before anyone could say anything I held up a hand to quieten them. Then shouted out, 'Rest!'

The crews working in the chain stopped and, on my hand signal, withdrew to the road. When the last man was clear I turned to Yanny.

'Right, go ahead,' I said.

'Boss, I want to run a Trapped Person Locator search at the bottom of the crater before they lift those slabs. Once they take the strain on that crane the slabs will move and kill anyone under there.'

'Right.'

'And I think it's dangerous,' put in the ADO.

There followed two minutes of debate with everyone putting in his two pence's worth. I pointed out that I was only the Safety Officer and the decision was rightly the Sector Commander's and that meant the ADO.

The ADO didn't look happy and I think he wanted me to rule out a search on the grounds of safety. Yanny's eyes pleaded.

'How long will a thorough search take you, Yanny?' I asked.

'Hard to say, boss.'

'Try.'

He crossed his arms. 'Fifteen, maybe twenty minutes.'

I looked at the ADO.

'I'm happy for fifteen minutes, providing that there's the minimum number of personnel involved.'

The Health and Safety Executive man nodded slowly and the ADO became unhappier still.

'It's a tough one, guv,' I said, 'but Yanny's right. It may be the last chance to bring out live casualties.'

He paused, like he was making a decision, but I fancied it was more angst.

'Okay,' he said, finally, 'but if you hear something what will you want to do?'

Yanny looked him straight in the face. 'Whatever it takes to get them out, what would be your plan, boss?'

The ADO coloured and for a moment I thought Yanny had shot himself in the foot. There was a strained silence and then the ADO mumbled for Yanny to 'get on with it'.

I ordered all crews working in my sector withdrawn while the TPL search was carried out. Yanny and the Fire and Rescue Unit crew all went down into the crater and I repositioned myself so that I could see all of them.

The dangers for them were twofold; one, the danger of

secondary collapse from above and two, the danger of cave-in below. Yanny knew this and discussed it with me just before he led the way down. But if it worried him you'd have never guessed by the look on his face.

He was everything so hated by a weak and vacillating management; bright, confident, physically strong, decisive and independent.

He would make Station Officer because of his obvious skills, but I doubted that he'd go farther; they simply wouldn't let him.

Each of the FRU crew wore harnesses with lowering lines attached, against the possibility of a cave-in. It restricted them, but to go without was potentially fatal.

When they were in position at the bottom of the crater, Yanny turned and looked up at me. I shouted for silence, twice, and then held up my hand to indicate that silence was imposed. Yanny saw it, nodded and turned back.

'Baton!'

A crewman went forward and struck the slab about twenty feet in front of Yanny.

If the TPL searches were tense by day, by night, under the stark white of the halogen lamps and with the remains of the OPMA building rearing up over them, they became surreal.

The heavy humid air seemed to cloak everything and made it oppressive. Just standing there I could feel the sweat running down my back.

Below I watched Yanny try several areas with his search patterns, drawing a blank after blank. I could sense his frustration and fancied I could see it in his movement.

I glanced at my watch; they'd been at the bottom of the crater for twelve minutes. The ADO was fidgeting and looking at me. I gave him a nod and held up three fingers.

I allowed more time than was agreed, but after twenty-five minutes the ADO was bordering on a seizure. Reluctantly I called Yanny up on the radio and told him to withdraw.

He looked at his watch and gave a short nod.

When Yanny and the FRU crew had been brought up, the Super Crane was manoeuvred into position and the chains attached to the slabs. Slowly, inch by inch, the slabs were winched up.

When they were above the level of the rubble field the Super Crane swung them away from the crater and we all peered down.

Fifty feet below us I saw her; a doll, broken and bare, stark against the concrete. She was dead, her lower half crushed flat and her eyes wide in death.

I asked permission to be relieved as Safety Officer in order to go down to help and because I'd been involved in the earlier rescue attempt I was given the go-ahead. By the time I got to the bottom of the crater I found Yanny's crew about to put her in a body bag.

I pulled Yanny to one side.

'I want to do it,' I said softly.

'What?' He saw the look on my face.

'Just let me do it.'

'For sure, boss.'

Her face was blue from where she had been crushed and most of her clothes had been torn off. There was no dignity; her body was caked in dust, the humanity squeezed from the form.

As I lifted her there was a jingle and I saw a set of car keys beside her; attached to them were the keys I had retrieved from Hugh Jones's apartment. I picked them up and slipped them into my tunic pocket. Yanny's face became a frown but he didn't question me.

It was then that it hit me and I started to shake.

'Steady, boss . . .' he stopped and looked at me hard, his face changing slowly as it dawned on him. 'You know this woman?'

'Yes,' I whispered. 'Help me, Yanny.'

Together we lifted her and laid her gently in the bag. I zipped it up to her face and Yanny stood back as I paused for one last look. Then I said a silent goodbye, sealed the body bag and tagged it.

28

We got back to the station around half-twelve and because so many of the surrounding stations were being sent on relief to the OPMA building, we found ourselves covering the gaps and going out on fire calls throughout the night.

Nothing was spared us. We endured the whole gamut of 'nothing' shouts that so often formed the backbone of our existence and normally I would have cursed it along with the rest of the crew, except that I was anaesthetised from everything.

Horrific images of Anne's death kept flashing through my mind and I just wanted to close my eyes, and blank out the pain, but the dark kaleidoscope kept turning and try as I might rational thought was only possible in snatches, the one thing that helped was that we were constantly on the go.

The night was so uncomfortably humid that my skin felt like it was crawling. A wet patch formed and grew between my shoulder blades until sweat trickled down my back and soaked the waistband of my trousers. I unzipped my tunic and flapped the edges to cool down.

The hours passed and gradually fatigue overcame every other consideration. When finally we got to bed at half-five in the morning I collapsed and fell into a deep, imageless sleep.

I awoke with the seven o'clock 'wake up' bells and dragged myself from bed, numb with fatigue and my brain settled into neutral.

Before going off duty at nine I rang Eastern Headquarters

Staff and asked to take one day's leave for the second night duty. They said that all Station Officers' leave was taken, but I could ring in at six and 'if they were flush' I could have the leave.

If I didn't get it I'd have to leave for Wales a day later than I'd planned, but the way I felt then it would do me no harm to spend the day in bed catching up on my sleep.

I drove to Upminster on autopilot and didn't see the big Saab slide in behind me at the Hall Lane turn-off.

The first time I became aware that something was wrong was when a Range Rover overtook me and slowed. I braked and tried to drop back to give myself stopping distance, but a glance in the rear-view mirror showed the Saab tight in behind me.

Between them I was forced to slow and then stop.

I gasped as I realised what was happening, but I switched on quickly and had the sense to keep the engine running.

Four men, fit and fast, got out of the front and rear vehicles and ran towards the Shogun. Adrenalin screamed through my system and I locked the doors and hit the road horn, trying to attract attention and put some pressure on them to break off their attack, but the road was empty.

Two took the driver's side and two the passenger's in what looked a practised routine. A face loomed at the driver's window and I recognised it as the bastard who'd roughed me up at St Katharine's Dock.

'Switch the engine off and open the door, Jay . . . open or we'll smash the glass and haul you out of there.'

The urge to stick my foot through the window and break his face was physical, but even when tired I can count so I hit the horn again and kept it pressed.

I had no doubt that if they had wanted me dead the holes would already be in me, but if they planned another beating then I'd be fucked if I was going to go quietly.

'Last chance, Jay.'

I heard a noise and spun. The two on the passenger's side had sprung the lock somehow and had pulled the door half open. That's when I took my chance; I slammed the Shogun into reverse gear and hit the accelerator, smashing into the front of the Saab.

There hadn't been enough room to do too much damage, but it caught them off balance and I sensed the alarm spreading through them.

'Get him!'

There was a flurry of activity and I was aware of someone climbing in the back of the Shogun and another one reaching from the passenger's side. I used the remaining seconds I had to slip into first gear and drive the accelerator to the floor.

There was a tremendous shock and the sounds of distressed metal and glass as the Shogun impacted the rear of the Range Rover. I was thrown forward and the seat belt cut into my chest. The attacker in the front, who was halfway inside, fell out heavily onto the tarmac.

I reversed and turned the wheel hard, but there still wasn't enough room to drive clear.

Suddenly the one behind grabbed my hair and a fist like a brick connected with my jaw. I reeled away and a hand clamped tight across my mouth.

I was restricted by the seat belt and fighting back was difficult, but I saw an eye belonging to the intruder at St Katharine's Dock and dug my thumb into it as hard as I could. I heard a scream of pain and he disappeared.

It was frantic now, swift movements and hard short blows from both sides of me, they were all piling into the Shogun and I had seconds to do as much damage as I could before I went under.

I drove my left elbow backwards between the seats and connected with a body. There was a curse and I followed it up by biting the hand across my mouth to the bone, but it was my last success.

Something heavy and soft hit my temple and blackness claimed me.

I came to in the Range Rover, trussed up and blindfolded with gaffer tape and in the footwell of the rear passenger seats. Two pairs of feet were pressing down on me hard and I heard a voice grunt that I was awake.

My head pounded from the blow that had knocked me out, my body ached in a dozen different places and I could smell blood in my nose, but I had the satisfaction of knowing that, no matter what happened, the bastard from St Katharine's Dock would have cause to remember me.

I had no idea how long I'd been out cold, but now awake I was determined to switch on and make things as awkward for them as I could, whatever it was that they wanted. At one point I rolled to ease the pressure on my shoulder, the one I'd bruised at the OPMA building on the first day and immediately a foot crunched down on my ribs, forcing the air out of me.

There was nothing I could do except lie still and take it, but I made a promise to myself that if anything like a chance presented itself I intended to get away or at the very least inflict some more damage.

My mind was racing and I started to deal with probable outcomes.

It occurred to me that if this was a one-way journey then I'd like to leave a few calling cards; I swiped the blood from my nose into the car trim and broke off some bits of fingernail and pushed them into the footwell carpet. I might never be found, but there was no reason not to leave a little DNA in my wake.

Next I tried to orientate myself.

My guess was that we were on a motorway, because of the

speed and the noise of the traffic outside. M25? M11? I didn't know, but wherever we were going we were moving fast.

I estimated that from the time of being awake until the time we stopped was about half an hour, but half an hour from where? I could feel the vehicle slowing and veering to one side, which I assumed was the turn-off from the motorway.

Then we were moving more slowly, with several short stops that I interpreted as road junctions.

Once it came to a halt I was dragged out, stood up and held on either side. Then there was silence. I thought I was standing on grass and imagined I could hear the wind in the trees. The edge of a wood, maybe?

The sound of a car door slamming was followed by several pairs of feet walking towards me and instinctively I tensed, expecting the pain to start, instead, there was a voice with a harsh Midlands accent.

'I've some questions for you, Jay. If you answer them you'll be free to go.'

'And if I don't?'

There was a pause and I heard someone move behind me.

'That's not really an option.'

'So subtle,' I breathed.

Somehow I just knew that whatever I said I was going to take a kicking.

'How do you know Mark Haig?'

Haig?

'I don't,' I replied.

'Why were you in his apartment?'

'Apartment?'

'St Katharine's Dock.'

'No, you've lost me there.'

I immediately got punched in the kidney and despite myself I cried out.

'What were you looking for?'

I tried to bluff, 'I was waiting.'

There was a pause. 'For who?'

'Haig.'

This time both kidneys got punched and I grunted and arched my back. The second the pain was past its peak I jerked my head violently sideways, to try and butt someone. I missed and for my trouble I was forcibly straightened up and kicked hard in the crotch. I went to my knees with the taste of vomit in my throat.

'Try that again and you'll be beaten so hard you won't recover. Now tell us who you were waiting for?'

I was hunched forward, snatching gulps of air and my body was shaking from the shock, but I was also pissed. So pissed that I would rather take the beating than let them know that I didn't know.

Clever boy, Stevie, that'll show them.

I was pulled to my feet again.

'I told you, Haig.'

Pain came from all sides and I tried to turn away from the punches and kicks, but the men on either side of me kept me upright and available. The beating went on for several minutes and they weren't crude in the way they went about it; kidneys, liver and lungs all received due attention.

It was like they had a copy of *Gray's Anatomy* and were working their way through it.

I swear I could sense when 'Old One-Eye' was at work, it was personal for him and he made sure I felt it in my bones. When they stopped I fell to the ground, convulsing; wet with blood and sweat.

This time a middle-class English accent asked a question. 'Let's move on, shall we? Where is Anne Lloyd?'

They didn't know she was inside the OPMA building . . .

Careful, Stevie, very careful.

I spat blood from my mouth and tried to steady my breathing.

'I don't know.'

There was a pause. 'We've seen you . . . you've been watched for weeks. We know that you are lovers . . . so where is she?'

'I've not seen her in weeks,' I said truthfully.

'Seen maybe, but you work for her so you must have spoken to her on the phone.'

'I've not seen, heard or spoken to her for weeks. We broke up. I came back to London and if you've been watching me like you say then you'd know that.'

'You were at the apartment to steal the laptop—'

'What and you're the police eh?'

He closed in, 'If it's handed back then this stops . . . you understand?'

'I have no idea where is it . . . that's the truth and beating the shit out of me won't change that.'

Maybe it was the way I said it, but the tone changed completely.

'If we were to hire you to . . . recover the laptop, how much would it cost?'

'I don't know where it is – all right?'

'But if you did know . . . if you could . . . find it?' He said softly, 'how much?'

I was about to repeat myself, but the part of my brain dealing with escape suddenly woke up.

'If I could find it – ten grand.'

There was the sound of feet walking away. I stood for several minutes with just the men at back and on either side of me. No one spoke. Then the footsteps returned and something was thrust into my rear trouser pocket.

'There's five hundred pounds there, Jay. Call it inconvenience money. There's also a mobile number. Find that laptop and you get ten grand, screw around and you'll wish you didn't.'

And that was it. I was bundled back into the vehicle.

We didn't use the motorway going back, probably to stop me calculating where we'd been. I estimated we drove for well over an hour. When we finally stopped I was pulled out of the vehicle and the gaffer tape cut from my hands, but the blindfold left in place.

Just to slow me down, one of them dug me in the stomach and as I doubled over I heard the sound of footsteps running away.

When the pain subsided I ripped away the gaffer-tape from my eyes and looked around. I recognised where I was immediately; a disused service station on the A127 about two miles from Hall Lane, where I was ambushed.

I used my handkerchief to wipe some of the blood and mucus that was encrusted on my face and sat down. The fatigue I'd started the day with had re-emerged now that the adrenalin had subsided and all I wanted to do was lie down and sleep, but I had a two-mile walk ahead of me.

I must have sat there for ten minutes, attracting stares from motorists as they passed.

Two miles at good walking pace would normally take forty minutes; it took me well over an hour to limp it and all the time the same question ricocheted around my head; who was Mark Haig?

I had assumed when they grabbed me that it was to do with the OPMA building explosion, but I had been way off the mark. What the hell was going on?

As I neared Hall Lane more prosaic thoughts offered themselves; it occurred to me that the Shogun might not be drivable.

Alex would have a fit.

I limped the last two hundred yards from the A127 anticipating the wreckage.

When I reached the scene I found to my relief that the bull

bars had protected the front of the Shogun; the only obser-
vable damage being to the paintwork. The back of it was a
different story. The rear door was badly dented and a set of
lights on the nearside had been completely taken out.

It was true also that most of the glass in the vehicle was
smashed or cracked, but other than that, I reasoned, Alex had
nothing to complain about.

I opened the driver-side door and found the keys missing,
well, they would be wouldn't they? I had no choice, but to find
a phone box and ring Alex.

'Stevie! Where the hell are you?'

'Hall Lane.'

'What's wrong?'

'Can't say on the phone . . . look, can you come and pick
me up?'

There was a pause, 'What's wrong with the Shogun?'

'I'm two hundred yards from the junction with the
A127.'

'Stevie . . . what happened?'

'Tell you when I see you.' I put the phone down.

Fifteen minutes later Alex pulled up in his BMW.

He looked at me, fixing on the large puffy swelling that had
grown where I'd been knocked unconscious. He gave a short
nod of acknowledgement, then slowly walked around the
Shogun, stopping at the rear.

'Well, that won't polish out, will it?' he said.

'No.'

'So tell me.'

I related what happened and he shook his head. When I had
finished he sighed.

'How bad are your injuries?'

'Feel like I've been run over . . . it could have been much
worse.'

'Aye, well, I won't say I told you so.'

'You just did, Alex.'

He held out his hand. 'The keys?'

'I think they took them.'

The look on his face said it all.

29

Alex drove me back to Upminster and gently pumped me for information. It wasn't that I was reluctant to tell him so much as him being aware of the pain I was experiencing.

Only once did he ask me to let it go. He knew I wouldn't, I knew I couldn't, but we did the question and reply anyway. Deep inside me black resentment was festering.

When we arrived back at his house, he called a recovery service to fetch the Shogun and I took myself upstairs and ran a bath.

I had stiffened up over the last hour and I hoped a soaking followed by some sleep would fix the worst of it, but then other considerations started to occupy me; there was the problem of getting to Wales now that the Shogun was out of commission and asking for the loan of Alex's BMW didn't seem wise.

Alex said he had to call into the office for a meeting and would be back around five. I asked him to wake me if I wasn't up when he got back.

By the time I climbed out of the bath and dried myself it was half-two. I had to be at work at six so the most sleep I was going to get in was two and a half hours; not enough. In the event I didn't get that; a banging on the front door woke me around four.

The knocking was loud and persistent, but I could only move slowly. I slipped on a dressing gown and made my way downstairs, calling out to the knocker that I was coming.

I opened the door and there stood Jenny.

'Hello, Steve . . .'

Karma as a brick wall is my own personal contribution to Buddhist philosophy. It is coupled with my theory of enlightenment by means of continual conflict. Few walk this path, I can barely escape it.

With a large purple swelling on the side of my head, dark rings under my eyes and angled like a man of ninety, I must have looked pretty much the same as when I'd last saw her, three months ago.

She didn't even attempt to disguise her reaction.

'My God! What's happened to you?'

Her hand came up to touch my face and I moved back quicker than I would have thought possible.

'Car accident,' I lied.

She hovered, waiting for me to invite her in. I hesitated. For a minute neither of us spoke, then slowly I opened the door fully and gave a nod.

She stepped inside and waited for me to lead the way.

I took her through to the lounge and I offered to make her coffee, she declined and offered to make me some in return. In the event we sat without it and regarded each other awkwardly.

If I could I would have gone straight upstairs and back to sleep, shutting out this unwelcome and redundant encounter, but we don't always get what we want in this life, do we?

'I've been trying to contact you,' she began.

'Alex said.'

'I've left my phone number.'

'He said that as well.'

She seemed to go pale then she looked down.

'I've missed you, Steve.'

At that I said nothing, but although impassive I watched her closely. We had a history of missing clues in the way we spoke to each other and this wasn't a time to be casual.

Where was Alex when I needed him?

'You've been away?'

I nodded, 'Convalescence.'

'Where?'

'Devon.'

'Oh? Is that a Fire Service Benevolent centre?'

'Sort of.'

If it felt awkward to begin with, it was fast plunging down-hill.

In the past, when we'd quarrelled, when she'd betrayed me even, there was always something in our meetings, a look, a smile, a gesture that connected us. We said, others said, that there would always be something between us. Now, there was just dislocation and forced politeness.

The judging of pace, the weighing of words, the physicality, were finally memories, not feelings.

'Have you missed me? I mean . . . do you miss me?' she said softly.

'I've been ill, Jenny.'

'Sorry, that was wrong of me. It's just that . . .'

'What?'

'I need to know.'

'Need to know what?'

She looked scared, vulnerable. 'If there's a chance . . . for us. I know what you think, but there was nothing between Kris Mayle and me after I came back to you. Surely you see that?'

Despite myself I sighed, 'A lot of things were going on then . . . I'd lost a firefighter . . . I was nearly killed myself . . . it was blurred and painful, very painful. The truth is I don't know what happened.'

'Meaning you don't care what happened.'

At that I said nothing.

Her eyes moistened and her voice was breaking, 'I know that when I came back to you . . .'

I looked away.

'Please . . . Let me say this!'

I nodded slowly.

'. . . When I came back, Steve, you wanted me to say I'm sorry . . . and I did, but not in the way you wanted. I've thought about it and I was wrong . . . very wrong. I allowed my pride to get in the way, but I was hurting too.'

Again I nodded.

She clasped her hands together, composing herself, 'I was wrong to leave you for Kris, I was wrong not to admit it and for not being strong enough to keep away from him.' Her voice became softer still, till it was barely a whisper, 'I've changed, Steve. I realised that the day you got out of that car and walked away from me. I need you . . . love you . . . I always have.'

Irony is the loser's wisdom.

'I don't know what to say, Jen. Three months ago I would have given anything to hear you say that . . .'

'And now?'

I fell silent.

'I see.'

She studied me and suddenly her hand came up to her mouth.

'You've found someone . . . oh God . . . dear God, no . . .'

She stood up quickly and made for the front door. I chased after her and caught her just as she opened it.

'Why now, Jen . . . why, after all this time?'

'Let me go!'

I released her arm. 'I'm sorry . . . my life has . . . changed . . . I've changed. It'll change for you, too . . .'

There was fear and desperation in her voice, 'It won't . . . it can't.'

'Why?'

'Because I'm pregnant!'

30

Alex returned just before six, saw the way I was moving and suggested that I ring work and book sick. That was the last thing I wanted to do, I'd only just got back. We argued about it, but in the event I got my one night's leave granted by Eastern Area Staff so it didn't matter.

Determined to mother me, Alex poured a large therapeutic Scotch and thrust it in my direction before starting to prepare the evening meal. I thanked him and sat in front of the television with the sound turned down, waiting for the seven o'clock news bulletin. We conversed by shouting through the doorway at each other.

That was when I told him about Jenny.

He stopped and came into the lounge, drying his hands on a towel.

'What are you going to do?'

I shook my head, 'No idea.'

'You'll insist on a DNA test?' he said, with wonder in his voice.

'That should piss her off nicely, don't you think?'

'Don't tell me you'll just accept that it's yours . . . Good God, man, I don't mean to judge her, but surely there's a question mark in your mind?'

'I don't intend to do anything – yet.'

He sat down. 'How was it left?'

'She thinks I've got someone else.'

'Shrewd.'

'I wasn't trying to be shrewd, she read it in my face,' I said irritably.

'I meant Jenny, not you!' He got himself a Scotch and sat down again, staring at me.

'What?' I snapped.

He raised his eyebrows. 'You'll come up for it, won't you? I can see it in your big dumb face . . . you'll see her need and forget your own.'

'I've decided nothing . . . look, the last thing I want right now is, Jenny, with or without a baby.'

Yet even as I said it the word 'baby' exploded in my head.

Having been abandoned and then fostered, to walk away from a child that was possibly mine would make me a total hypocrite. Alex had put his finger on it, of course; DNA testing was the logical solution.

'I don't suppose the word "abortion" was mentioned?' he said.

'Jenny? Get real, Alex.'

'Aye, well, it's going to be tricky whatever the pair of you decide.'

'You think we should talk?'

'Now whose turn is it to get real? Of course you've got to talk . . . and get a test.'

'She'll hit the roof . . .'

He got to his feet. 'The dinner'll spoil.'

As he went back into the kitchen I turned my attention back to the television and turned the sound up. The news came on ten minutes later.

I wondered whether there would be further information on the rescue operations at the OPMA building, there was, it was the second item; first was an interview with J.J. Roth.

The interviewer was Justin Archer, a sharp, young journalist who started by laying some innocuous questions before Roth, one of which was the extent of OPMA operations in the Third World.

Roth came across as intelligent and very smooth, but the studio backdrop of a silent newsreel showing the destruction of the OPMA building was a subtle counterpoint to his answers.

They ran it thirty seconds into the interview, just out of Roth's view.

'Mr Roth, only a few days ago your UK headquarters was blown apart by what appears to be a terrorist bomb . . . can I ask you for your reaction to that?'

'Outrage . . . and great sadness. This mindless act has killed many innocent people. I offer my condolences to the families and dependants of the victims and make the promise that OPMA will ensure that their financial needs will be met.'

Archer nodded. 'Why do you think OPMA has been attacked in this way?'

Roth paused. 'I don't know.'

'It has been suggested that eco-terrorism may lie behind the attack, do you think that's possible?' asked Archer.

Roth paused again, 'It would be naive to say that oil and mining operations are not controversial in the present day, but our record on the environment is second to none.'

'So OPMA's power and influence is a positive force?'

'Without question,' replied Roth. 'It is written into OPMA's constitution that we will keep ecological damage to acceptable minimums and provide housing, schools and infrastructure that improve the lives of the people affected by its operations.'

'Such as in Brazil?'

Roth picked some fluff from his immaculate navy suit.

'We have operations in Brazil . . . I'm not sure to what you are referring.'

Archer shuffled his papers and set one down on the top of the pile.

'I was referring to the mining operations started by OPMA in Brazil in the early nineties.'

Roth nodded, 'There had been a number of cases of mercury poisoning in the Amazon in the late eighties and early nineties. It had been caused by *garimpeiros*, artisanal miners trying to extract gold. The methods they used were crude and resulted in mercury entering the watercourse and poisoning the fish, which is a major food source for the indigenous Indians . . . many of whom were showing the classic symptoms of mercury poisoning.'

Archer measured his next question, 'And OPMA did what, exactly?'

'We offered our services to the Brazilian Government to clean up the area . . .'

'In exchange for mining rights for OPMA?' interrupted Archer.

'Yes.'

'Even though the gold miners that were stopped had no other means of income?'

There was no change in Roth's relaxation level and his reply was perfect.

'That may have been the case, initially, but the situation had gotten out of hand. The whole area was virtually lawless. There were thousands of people without even basic health and hygiene and death and illness were a daily occurrence. Plus the fact that the Indians in the region were suffering.'

'So what changes were brought about by OPMA in exchange for the mining rights?'

'The area was de-polluted, a modern hospital was built together with much infrastructure and we became the major employer in the region.'

Archer paused, 'Can I go back to the bombing of OPMA's headquarters . . . do you believe that there is a link to OPMA's mining operations in Mid-Wales?'

Roth looked genuinely surprised. 'I'm not aware that that is a line of investigation being pursued by the police.'

'You were due at the building that morning were you not?'

'I had a meeting there timed for ten o'clock.'

'So in actual fact it can't be ruled out that this was an assassination attempt?'

'I couldn't comment on that.'

'Well, it's simple enough, Mr Roth, you're due at a place and a bomb destroys the building . . . seems too much of a coincidence, wouldn't you say?'

Archer overplayed it in both tone and directness and Roth gave him a look as if to say, 'I beg your pardon.' Then brushed the question off effortlessly.

'I don't want to get into any areas of speculation. I don't believe it would be helpful to the police inquiry.'

'Why did you come to the UK at this time, Mr Roth? Was it due to the problems in your Mid-Wales mining operations?'

'No.'

'Yet it has been said that those mining operations have mobilised the local population against you and there have been several instances of arson. In fact, my information is that the series of large forest fires in the region are a protest at your plans to conduct opencast mining in one of the most beautiful estuaries in the British Isles.'

'What is your question, exactly?' said Roth.

Archer dropped his voice; the tone soft, but telling.

'It's well known that you like to troubleshoot problems yourself, Mr Roth . . . do you believe that the fires could have been a device to get you into the UK, where an attempt might be made on your life?'

For the only time during the interview Roth looked uncomfortable and I got the feeling that the whole interview had been shaped around that one question.

Archer deserved his reputation; it was a very clever ambush.

He used Roth's hesitation to turn back to the camera and word the close.

'Thank you, Mr Roth. That was J.J. Roth, head of the troubled Oil, Pharmaceutical and Mining Agency, a multinational that has recently seen forest fires used to hamper its Welsh operations and a terrorist bomb destroy its UK headquarters. I'm Justin Archer and this is News Online, a simultaneous digital and Web broadcast.'

They cut to a break, but left the camera running live for a few seconds more, enough to catch Roth ripping his microphone off and giving Archer an icy stare.

If that wasn't shown across the world I was no judge.

Alex served up dinner a short while after and tried to get me to discuss Jenny, but my mind was elsewhere. I was thinking of how I was going to get to Wales. Then an idea popped into my head.

'Alex, will you drive me to Wales?'

He stopped eating. 'No.'

'And the BMW is out of the question?'

'Completely.'

'I need to get to Wales, Alex.'

'Hire a car.'

'What will I use for— I have five hundred pounds,' I realised aloud.

'You do? Ah, the guys that kidnapped you? And what do you think they'll do when you don't produce the laptop?'

'They said it was inconvenience money. The laptop came at ten grand, not five hundred.'

He virtually threw down his knife and fork.

'Will you listen to yourself? You haven't the faintest idea of what's going on here, have you?'

'And you do?'

'No. And I want it to stay that way. If you go to Wales, Stevie, you could end up dead on the side of the road, you know that, don't you?'

'It's possible.'

'Then why?'

'We've done this already, because I have to do it.'

He drummed his fingers on the table and I knew he was angry with me. Then he got up and disappeared down the passageway towards his den. When he returned he was holding a mobile phone. He threw it at me.

'That's the same phone I lent you when you worked on the Sheldon inquiry . . . take the BMW – and I want it back without so much as a scratch on it! You're to keep in touch – twice a day. D'you understand?'

'Thanks.'

'Don't thank me, Stevie. Whatever you do, don't thank me.'

Sunday, 16 August

The next morning I woke early and threw some things into a bag, including a torch, camera, flask of coffee and a set of binoculars borrowed from Alex along with Anne's car keys.

I still didn't have any hiking boots and made do with two sets of trainers. Lastly, I placed ten one-pound coins in my barn jacket hip pocket.

Alex got up to see me off, his face full of reservation.

'I'll be back late Wednesday, Alex.'

'You're on days Thursday.'

I nodded. 'If I'm on to something I'll ring Staff for another leave day.'

'Ring every day!'

'I will.'

We shook hands and he promised to check with Roley Benson to see if anything else had come up.

It was half-eight when I set off.

The traffic was light and I made good time. The BMW was

a superb drive and I hit the Cross Foxes junction around half-two. Anne's cottage was less than two miles away.

My plan had been to book into the Castell Coch Inn in Abergynolwyn and phone Eddie Marlowe, but on the way up I'd decided to check out Anne's cottage first. On her car keys, apart from the keys retrieved from Hugh Jones's apartment, was her front-door key.

I turned off half a mile short of the cottage onto a forest track and parked out of sight of the road. There I changed into trainers and made my way through the forest, keeping roughly parallel with the road for a couple of hundred yards. Then I went west on a looping route that would bring me to the rear of the cottage. The woods were thick and strewn with rocks and I was soon sweating in the heavy afternoon heat.

Slowly, the trees thinned and I glimpsed the cottage through them. I was less than fifty yards away.

In the back of my mind was the statement by Bonny that he'd seen Jamie Howard from Ty Hiraeth hanging about, the morning after Anne and I had first made love. If he was around I didn't want to be seen by him or anyone else.

Maybe no one in London knew that Anne had been inside the OPMA building when it blew up, but someone up here had to know and I didn't want them down on me before I could unravel what had happened.

Thirty yards short of the cottage I sat down between some undergrowth and a large rocky outcrop.

I watched the place for half an hour, until convinced there was no one about. Cautiously, I got up and made my way down to the edge of the forest and the wire fence that bordered the garden.

There were no cars in the drive and I couldn't see any movement in the house. I climbed over the fence and made my way along the edge of the garden to the drive. Again I stopped and listened.

Nothing.

Finally I walked quietly up to the door and opened it. I stepped inside and closed the door, listening hard. Nothing.

I searched the place room by room.

The first thing I noticed was that it smelled slightly dusty, but not stale.

In the bedroom I paused; a sensation of emptiness, of aching sadness, settling in my stomach.

I stared at the bed and tried to think back to when it was that we'd last slept together. It was Friday night, 31st July, just over two weeks ago. Anne had disappeared the next day.

The image of her face, just before I closed the body bag, loomed up before me and I sank down, my back propped against the wall.

I decided then to stay the night.

I would go through the cottage meticulously and find anything there was to find. In the morning I would go early and leave everything as I found it. I told myself that it was being professional, but in my heart I knew that I wanted to be here one last time.

Gradually I gained some detachment and went through the bedroom, cupboard by cupboard. Some were almost empty; others were full. The wardrobes also had clothes in them, although there were some gaps. More importantly, there were towels in the bathroom but soaps and shampoos and her lady razor were missing.

Everything in the kitchen was how I'd remembered it; the lounge was the same. Pictures, ornaments . . . records. Would someone intending to plant a bomb and then disappear from view leave her house like this?

Someone intending to go away for a few days, maybe, but it had been twelve days from her disappearance to the OPMA building bomb. I couldn't see that she'd taken enough for twelve days.

I searched the study.

There were books on a range of environmental subjects, journals, magazines and cuttings from newspapers, nothing unexpected; at first.

Then something started to register. The newspapers put me on to it. They were all new, at least, fairly new, so I went back and checked all those that I had come across so far. There was nothing over a year old.

Surely an environmental agitator would keep records, case histories of pollution or articles on ecology?

It was weird.

I took the largest file containing newspaper articles and went back into the lounge. I read them one after the other and made my second discovery; all of the articles were about OPMA.

For a self-proclaimed environmentalist, Anne had a narrow view. Surely there were other transgressors in Wales; factories, fly tippers, farms guilty of slurry run-off, something?

But there wasn't.

When I finished the file I went back and read through another. Again, just articles on OPMA and not all of them Welsh articles.

The third file I went through was different. The newspapers were older; the earliest cutting was four years old. And there was a file within a file. An A4 clear plastic envelope labelled with the word 'Pheladone'. These weren't a year old, or even four years old; they were all early nineteen-nineties.

As I read through the articles it was clear that they referred to the case that the reporter Justin Archer had questioned J.J. Roth about.

They told of how an environmental monitoring group came across a series of small villages deep in the jungle. The group, led by a man called Ruddock, had found many cases of Indians with tremors and ataxic gait – apparently an inability to control their limbs – as well as birth deformities, convulsions and slurred speech, all the results of mercury poisoning.

Among these older files were a series of scientific notes that appeared to be incomplete. They referred to a drug called Pheladone and were written by a man called Mark Haig.

31

The find threw up a dozen new questions, but despite turning the study upside down I found no answers. I folded up the clear plastic file and pocketed it before turning my mind to more practical matters.

If I was going to stay the night then I would have to be careful not to draw attention to myself. That meant not going back to the car or leaving lights on when it got dark.

An exploration of the kitchen revealed some tinned fish and vegetables, but obviously no milk or bread. I ate some of the fish with crispbread and drank black filter coffee. Not great, but it kept the hunger at bay.

I tried to ring Alex on the mobile, but the mountains must have masked the signal. I looked at the landline and decided against it. Sooner or later the police would turn up and I didn't want to flag up that I'd been here.

There was always the telephone box back at the junction, but I ruled it out. Better to stay inside, out of view. As the evening wore on and the cottage was caught in the half-light between night and day, I decided to make use of the enforced idleness and catch up on my sleep.

In the bedroom the heavy curtains stopped anyone looking in unless they went right up against the window, so I felt safe enough to lie on the bed, but out of caution jammed a chair under the door handle. I left my clothes on, but took my shoes off and put them next to the bed.

There was a smell to the bedclothes, a faint residue of her

scent that stirred to life memories. I closed my eyes and slipped into a dreamless sleep.

The noise that woke me was small.

My brain screamed a warning and I stayed dead still; someone was moving in the passageway inside the front door. I glanced at my watch; I'd been asleep just twenty minutes.

The noise was so faint, so difficult to hear that I opened my mouth and turned my head from side to side slowly, trying to tune in. I picked up barely a footfall. There was a silence lasting a minute, maybe more. Then another footfall sounded.

I slid from the bed and walked noiselessly over to the door. Gently I removed the chair before easing the door open. On the other side of the lounge I could see a faint glow around the edge of the door into the passage.

It sounded like one person, but I couldn't be sure.

I stepped through the bedroom door and onto the thick lounge rug, hoping it would cushion my footsteps, but I realised after the first step that I was unlikely to make the passage door in complete silence.

Creep or rush; decide.

I took three quick steps forward, the rug muffling the sound.

The door was still eight feet away and I could see the fluctuations in the glow around the bottom of the door, like someone was using a torch to guide their steps. I took two more steps and listened.

The person on the other side of the door had stopped moving. I rushed forward and pulled open the passage door.

The intruder turned, saw me and reacted by swinging the torch at my head.

I ducked, but it caught me on the shoulder and as I moved to the side he swung a kick at my groin. Twisting away, I took the force of the kick on my thigh then grabbed him by the collar and kicked both his feet out from under him.

He went down hard, but instinctively tried to get to his feet.

Fear kicked in now and I swung a right hook with as much body curve as I could get behind it. The punch caught him flush on the temple and he went down and stayed down.

Turning quickly, I looked back towards the front door; he was on his own.

I spun back and jumped down on top of him, straddling his body and pulling his jacket down over his arms to restrict his movement. He groaned and tried to raise his head so I smashed my elbow into his face and he slumped back.

'Still!' I hissed.

His torch was lying to one side; I retrieved it and shone it into his face.

He was a thin-faced man of about thirty, with cropped blond hair and a scruffy beard. There were deep black rings under his eyes like he hadn't been sleeping well and in the artificial light of the torch he looked ill.

'Who are you?'

There was fear in his eyes, but anger as well. I grabbed his throat with my left hand and held the torch like a club.

'If you don't tell me I'll smash the teeth out of your head. Now what's your name?'

Still he said nothing.

Suddenly he lurched to the left and tried to throw me off. I squeezed his throat hard and brought the torch down across his nose. There was a sharp crack and I knew I'd broken it. Blood flowed freely and he tried to wipe it away, but I raised the torch again.

'Bastard!' he snarled.

'I can be a lot nastier than that.' I pushed the end of the torch against his nose and he jerked his head away. 'Now, who are you and what are you doing here?'

'Fuck off!'

I gave his nose a sharp tap with the butt end of the torch and he kicked out furiously and nearly dislodged me. I reacted by dropping my weight forward so that his throat was crushed and squeezed it till he stopped kicking. Then I brought my face nearer to his.

'Either you tell me who you are or I'll break your skull.'

Again he lurched left and right and I cracked him on the jaw with the torch and then forced it across his throat with both hands. He was a ballsy bastard and continued to struggle until he was gagging and lack of air forced him to stop.

'Right, let's start again. Who are you?'

I took some of the pressure off his throat and he coughed violently. I sensed he was going to struggle again so I twisted around and slammed the torch between his legs.

His body tried to jackknife, but I spread my knees and kept him pinned down.

The blow to the groin took some of the fight out of him. I took my hand off his throat and went through his pockets, starting with his jacket.

His wallet contained several hundred pounds in notes, some odd receipts and a driving licence in the name of Russell Evans – the man who went missing the day Hugh Jones was murdered.

I thought back to the description that John Vaughan had given me. Other than the hair being cropped short it was the same.

'Evans?'

He gave me a look of pure malice.

'You're Russell Evans – you worked with Hugh Jones?'

'Who wants to know?'

'What are you doing here?'

'I've every right to be here . . . and who the hell are you?' He squinted in the half-light and his head came forward. Then he gave a snort. 'You're him, aren't you? You're Jay. Get the hell off me!'

I sat back and allowed him to prop himself up with his elbows behind him.

'You know me? How?'

'How d'you think? Anne.'

There was something about the tone that told me he didn't know she was dead.

'Where is Anne?'

'If she wanted you to know she'd have told you,' he said acidly.

'Fine. I'll call the police, then, shall I?'

At that he went still.

'I'm waiting . . . where is she?'

He blinked. 'Right now I don't know . . . London . . . I think.'

'What would she be doing in London?'

'Ask her when you see her.'

Either he was a good actor or he genuinely had no idea, but that was no reason not to pressurise him.

'You're starting to annoy me, Evans.' I took the mobile out of my pocket and started to dial.

'Wait! Look, I don't know why she went to London – not for sure.'

'Think! Was it to pick up the laptop?'

'What laptop?'

I started to dial again.

'Okay, okay – maybe.'

'Maybe what?'

'I think she went to Hugh Jones's boat, the *Sea Horse*.'

You dumb bastard, Stevie. 'At St Katharine's Dock?'

'Yes.'

'And that's where the laptop is – on the boat?'

He looked deflated, 'I think so . . . Anne thought so.'

'How do you know this?'

'Because I told her where Jones kept the *Sea Horse* – and you supplied her with the keys.'

'When was this? When did you tell her about the boat?'

'Sunday.'

I felt cold. 'Which Sunday?'

He frowned, 'Last Sunday – seven days ago . . .'

Seven days ago?

I doubted Anne then. I don't know why, because nothing had been said about bombs or OPMA, but the feeling that I'd been conned reared up and bit me.

'Did you give her the password for the laptop?'

'No, she already knew it – her and Jones were close . . . you weren't the only one,' he said, with a sneer.

The urge to belt him across the nose with the torch again was tempered by my need of more answers. But I noted it.

I climbed off him and dragged him to his feet. I walked backwards into the lounge and pushed him down on the sofa.

'Why did you go missing after Hugh Jones was murdered?'

'Wouldn't you?'

I shrugged and he shook his head slowly.

'I saw it . . . I came in when they were torturing him. They stuck a knife . . .'

'Who did?'

'The same bastards that have been watching Anne and are looking for me to finish the job.'

I put my hand up to stop him. 'The guy with the burn scar at Ty Hiraeth? James Howard?'

'Yes.'

' "They"? You said *they* were torturing him?'

'There were two of them . . . I'd been out to the survey site and Jones had gone back earlier. I finished up at the site and drove back. I must have been half an hour behind him . . . maybe a little longer, I don't know, but when I got to the house the door was wide open and his black pick-up truck was left with the keys in. I thought something was wrong because we'd been getting a lot of grief from the locals . . . a truck was burnt out . . . tyres slashed . . . general harassment.

Jones wouldn't have left his keys in the ignition . . . you know what I'm saying?'

'Go on.'

'The one with the scar . . . Howard . . . he had Jones around the throat and was throttling him from behind. The other one . . .'

'What did he look like?'

'Hard-faced bastard . . . had a look to him – ex-military, I'd say.'

One-Eye! And it was a fair guess that Howard had been my unseen attacker at the apartment.

'You said torturing him?'

'The hard-faced bastard had a knife in Jones's leg and was twisting it . . . Jones was screaming . . . there was blood everywhere. They saw me and the one with the knife chased me.'

'And?'

'I ran – towards the river – then doubled back to my Land Rover. I couldn't think where to go, so I camped out in the mountains for a couple of days. Then I drove south to a caravan site in the Brecon Beacons. I came here Sunday and Anne hid me in the loft – I've been using it ever since.'

'Why did you come back – if you were scared for your life?'

'Money . . . I ran out ten days ago. Anne loaned me five hundred pounds.'

'Why didn't you use a credit card?'

'And be traced?'

'Slow down . . . how could they trace you? Only the police or a government department could do that . . . I don't believe . . .'

'Certain of that, are you?'

My head spun.

What the hell was going on here?

I took my eye off Evans for a split second and he took his chance. Jumping up, he kicked me full in the face and sent me over the side of the chair. As I tried to rise he followed it up by kneeing me in the ribs.

By the time I'd gathered my wits enough to follow him, he'd disappeared into the night.

32

If one thing was certain, Russell Evans was one very frightened man.

He'd put serious doubts in my mind about Anne, but backing off now would have been weak, there were questions to which I needed answers or I would never have any peace.

Evans thought he was being actively sought and that implied that the cottage was still being watched. Had I been seen? If I had, then they knew that Evans had been and gone and their interest would be in pursuing him, not in harassing me.

I decided to gamble by staying.

I propped a chair under the front-door handle and another behind the bedroom door and tried to get some sleep, but instead lay awake, listening to the building and letting my mind hunt. The one positive thing that I connected with was the need to speak to Julia.

At some time or other I must have slept because the dawn light woke me.

I lay still for a moment and reminded myself just why I was here. My time with Anne had been so special that to walk away was to lay judgement on it. I accepted that what we'd had was intensely physical, but I couldn't believe that someone could give so much of herself yet withhold any semblance of true affection.

I knew what I'd seen in her eyes.

I rolled off the bed and put my shoes on.

There was no point in hanging around so I got up and left

the cottage straight away. I made my way back through the forest to where I'd left the car, checking all the time to see if I was being followed.

It crossed my mind that the car might have been found by either Evans or the people watching the cottage so when I reached it I gave it a swift check over; there was no obvious damage.

I drove towards Abergynolwyn and the Castell Coch Inn. I should have booked in the previous night but I had used a credit card to confirm the booking so I reasoned that, providing I could find someone awake, I should be able to get into my room.

I got there around six.

Castell Coch was a solid two-storey granite building that was also a pub. It didn't look big enough to warrant night staff and no one seemed to be about, so I dozed in the car until seven.

When lights started to come on inside I got my bags from the boot and rang at the front door. The owner, an old, red-faced man, said that guests normally arrived from midday onwards. I told him that I'd broken down in the middle of nowhere the previous evening and had had to wait for a breakdown service.

'Terrible thing, road rage,' he said.

'Pardon?'

'Your face.'

I glanced in the mirror in the hallway. Where I'd been kicked by Evans the cheekbone was grazed and swollen. It was complemented by the bruise on the other side of my face from the Shogun incident.

As I booked in he continued to stare at the bruises, muttering to himself.

The room was small but comfortable and the owner said there was only one other guest.

'Just the two bedrooms there are, so there's no rush for breakfast. Come down when you want.'

I shaved, took a shower, changed my clothes and went straight down to breakfast. I ate like a starved man and drank so much coffee the old boy asked if I'd like another breakfast to go with it.

'Are you serious?' I said.

'No,' he replied and disappeared back into the kitchen.

When I finished I went up to my room and rang Eddie Marlowe.

'Hello, Eddie. I'm here, where I said I'd be.'

'Hello St—'

'Don't say my name, Eddie. I don't want anybody to know I'm here, remember?'

'Right.'

'Is Julia in?'

'Due in a short while . . . nine.'

'Okay . . . have you seen that Jamie . . . James Howard about this morning?'

'Went for his morning run with Elizabeth. He hasn't been about much lately.'

'Right, when Julia comes in tell her to make an excuse and get away to meet me. I'll be waiting for her at Cross Foxes at eleven . . . tell her . . . tell Anne's in trouble.'

'Oh dear.'

'Look Eddie, I'm counting on you. I must see her.'

'Don't worry, I'll tell her.'

'Good man.'

Next I phoned Alex and told him everything.

'So you want me to get Roley Benson to see if he can find out anything on the Mark Haig character?'

'Yes. And while he's at it, I'd love to know if this Russell Evans shows up on file.'

'Hang on, Stevie. Roley hasn't got instant access to this stuff. He's taking chances as it is.'

'Ask him, Alex! This is all starting to smell iffy to me and I want to know everything and anything that might shed some light on what's going down here.'

'Aye, well, I tried to tell you. Is the BMW still in one piece?'

'Yes.'

'Well, that's something, anyway.'

'Early days yet, Alex, give me time.' I rang off.

I arrived at Cross Foxes well before eleven and parked up. I was out of view of the road, but easily seen once you pulled into the car park. I debated whether or not to tell Julia Anne was dead and decided play it by ear.

Whatever happened, I had to get as much information out of her as possible.

Julia pulled up in a VW Polo just after eleven. Looking worried.

I motioned to her to get into my car. If she'd been followed I wanted my foot on the accelerator. As she climbed into the BMW I leant across her and locked the door.

'Precaution,' I said. 'A lot of people seem to feel the need to hit me lately.'

Her mouth opened, 'My God! Your face – what happened to your face?'

'Bitten by a weasel – several, in fact.'

'What?'

'Not important.'

She was pale and tense. 'Where's Anne?'

I chose my words carefully, but I still felt like a snake. 'I was hoping you might know.'

'Eddie said that she was in trouble.'

'Who is Mark Haig, Julia?'

Her mouth opened, but for a minute she didn't speak.

'What's going on, Steve?'

'Tell me about Mark Haig.'

She shook her head, 'I – I can't tell you.'

'Not even if Anne's life was threatened?'

'Oh, my God – where is she? You must tell me.'

'Haig, who is he, Julia?'

'I knew something was happening – I told her not to approach you . . . can't you just . . .'

'I can do nothing until I know about Mark Haig.'

She turned away and looked out of the window; she was shaking. When she turned back there were tears in her eyes.

'If I tell you, will you tell me where Anne is?'

'At this moment I don't know myself, Julia.'

She took a deep breath and dabbed at her eyes with a handkerchief.

'Mark Haig and Anne were lovers. Two years ago Mark was murdered.'

'Two years ago? Where?'

'At Mark's house in Ganllwyd.'

Ganllwyd? Why did that ring a bell? 'What happened?'

'Anne was a policewoman – a detective sergeant. She was part of a team watching Mark . . .'

'Why were they watching him?'

'I don't know. Anne never told me.'

'Go on.'

'Anne was undercover and part of her brief was to get to know Mark better. She got to know him too well and fell in love. One night something happened. Despite asking her a thousand times she would never tell me, but what I do know is that Mark was found dead in his house – he'd been strangled and stabbed and the house had been set on fire. Anne was found naked in the driveway. She'd been shot.'

'Badly?'

'She nearly bled to death.'

'Is it Mark Haig's photo by her bed?'

'Yes. She never stopped loving him – there was no one else

till you came along. She liked you – a lot. I thought you might
be the one to replace Mark.'

'Me and Hugh Jones.' I couldn't keep the peevishness out of
my voice.

'Pardon? Hugh? Anne and Hugh? Never.'

She stared at me.

'According to Russell Evans they were close.'

'You've seen him? Russell Evans?'

'At Anne's cottage last night.'

'You know the police are looking for him?'

'They're not the only ones. Did Anne tell you she was being
watched?'

'No, but the day she came to the house to meet you she was
frightened and wouldn't tell me why.'

'How was Mark Haig linked to Hugh Jones?'

She shrugged. 'They both knew Anne . . . other than that I
can't imagine.'

'Was Mark Haig into boats?'

'I don't know . . . Anne never mentioned it – he could have
been.'

'Why did Anne ask me to act as an inquiry agent for her?'

'I don't know.'

'But it was you who told her I had once been employed as an
inquiry agent. You read it from my file.'

She frowned. 'No. It wasn't me.'

Then who the hell . . . 'Why was Anne forced to resign as an
alternative to dismissal, Julia?'

'I'm not the person to ask that question.'

'Who is?'

'John Vaughan . . . he was part of the same team.'

33

I gave Julia Lloyd my word that if I found out exactly where Anne was I would tell her. I also made her promise not to tell anyone that I was in the area.

As she drove away I gave myself some massive stick.

I've always hated the clever bastards in life who don't so much lie as avoid the plain truth. The senior ranks of my job are populated by their like, people who sell deception as wit and dress self-interest as altruism.

Yet I'd just done that and in circumstances that couldn't be more cruel.

The justification I offered myself was that if I was to find the truth, then I had to be sparing with it. But it still felt a cheap trick.

I made a mental note to put in for promotion on the next round.

There was a more defensible safety element; Mark Haig, Hugh Jones, Anne . . . and the soldiers in the forest, made a grim and growing list, if they were all connected I did not want to join them.

Haig and Jones's murders were two years apart. But the similarities were unmistakable, as was the conclusion that James Howard and One-Eye were the prime suspects, if Russell Evans was to be believed. Anne was the link between Haig and Jones. The soldiers, I decided, were just collateral damage.

And then there was Bryn Thomas.

I left Cross Foxes and headed for Barmouth. The route took me past the entrance to Ty Hiraeth and then on down the estuary road with its stunning views across the sandbanks and the river. It was another hot, clammy day and a thunderstorm threatened.

Parking up near the railway bridge I walked to Bryn's house. The town was packed with people and I walked quickly, avoiding eye contact. I saw no one that I recognised.

I found Bryn's house, knocked on the door and waited, looking up and down the street. After a few minutes I knocked again. This time there was a noise from within, but still no one answered. I got the feeling that the old girl was just on the other side, too frightened to open the door.

'Mrs Thomas,' I said quietly. 'It's me, Bryn's friend . . . the fireman.'

The door opened slightly and the old girl peered around the edge. When she saw me she gave a nervous smile and opened the door fully. As I stepped inside she went past me and looked into the street. Then came in and closed the door.

'I've come to look for Bryn, Mrs Thomas.'

'My Bryn? You've come to find my Bryn?'

Her eyes moistened and she looked like she was going to keel over.

I took her by the shoulders and sat her down in the tiny living room. She grabbed my hand and kissed it and I had to kneel down by her as she refused to let go.

She was trembling.

'Can I make you a cup of tea?' I asked.

'Tea . . . I'll make you a cup of tea . . .'

I held my hand up and spoke slowly. 'No. *I'll* make you a cup of tea, Mrs Thomas.'

The old girl got to her feet and went out to the kitchen and I decided she was either hard of hearing or confused, possibly both. Embarrassed, I followed her.

She placed a kettle on a gas ring, and then turned and smiled nervously.

'Mrs Thomas, I know this is hard, but where exactly did Bryn say he was going when he went missing?'

'You will find him, won't you?' She took my hand again.

'If I— Yes . . . yes, I will find him.'

The look on her face was heart-rending; she was near to breaking down.

I tried again. 'Can you remember where Bryn said he was going when he went missing, Mrs Thomas?'

Her hand came up to her face and her eyes widened then she went past me, through the living room, and climbed the small, cramped staircase.

She was gone a long time and I thought about going. At this rate all I was going to manage was to upset the old girl and whatever my need of the truth it was small measure against what she was going through.

But I stayed where I was.

I heard her coming down the stairs and went through to meet her.

She was carrying some maps and an old haversack. I took them from her and steadied her down the last steps. When she reached the bottom I gave her the maps and haversack back. She shook her head.

'They're for Steve!'

'I'm Steve,' I said, with a smile.

She blinked. 'I know. Bryn said they were for you . . . he said if anything should happen then I was to give these to you and no one else. Now, would you like a cup of tea?'

'I'd love a cup of tea, Mrs Thomas.'

'I'll put the kettle on.'

While she went and made the tea I looked through the maps.

On the first map, the area where Bryn and I had fought the forest fire was marked off. I remembered it from last time I'd called and if I interpreted the hatchings and grids correctly then he'd completed his search of the area. Each square had a date written in it.

One grid square had a double line around it and in the margin he'd written *origin of crown fire*.

The second map covered an area in the Coed-y-Brenin forest. A heavily wooded valley, called Glyn Glas, was marked off, but not cross-hatched. There was a date on it – 12th Aug – the day Eddie Marlowe said Bryn had disappeared.

The old girl brought the tea in and smiled at me. 'You'll find my Bryn now.'

'I'll try, Mrs Thomas . . . I really will.'

We sat and drank the tea and she talked of Bryn; how he was always good to her and how, when his father had died, he'd moved back in with her.

' "I won't leave you, Mum," he'd say,' said the old girl. ' "I'll look after you." ' She paused, lost for a moment. 'He's alive – I know it.'

I nodded and hoped my pessimism didn't show.

After the tea, I opened the haversack. Inside, in a plastic carrier bag, was a battered and scorched petrol can and a small piece of metal that obviously wasn't anything to do with the can.

'Have you shown these to anyone else, Mrs Thomas?'

She shook her head. 'My Bryn said only you. They will help you find him, won't they?'

'Yes,' I lied. 'Yes, they will.'

I left Bryn's mother and drove back along the estuary road, heading for the Coed-y-Brenin Forest and Glyn Glas. The forest was huge. I couldn't put a size on it, but one look at the map told me that it covered many miles and lay across rugged mountain and hillside, split by rivers and streams and peppered with old mine workings; the perfect place to disappear.

It was early afternoon and the sun was high, but clouds were forming and as they passed in front of the sun they sent shadows rippling across the wild landscape.

As I neared the turn-off for the toll bridge I saw two policemen flagging down the traffic. I joined the back of the queue and wound the window down.

I recognised the policeman who approached the car. It was Dewi, the first policeman on scene at Hugh Jones's murder and John Vaughan's brother-in-law.

He nodded, 'Morning, I wonder if I could ask you to take a look at this poster, sir. One of the locals is missing, Bryn Thomas—' He stopped. 'But of course you must know Bryn, being at Ty Hiraeth?'

'Yes,' I said simply.

'Well then, you know that he's missing?'

'Yes.'

'So you won't need one of these, will you?' He held up the A4 poster.

It showed a photo of Bryn and gave a description of his height, weight and the clothes that he'd been wearing when he'd disappeared. It also had the number of the local police station printed along the bottom.

'I will take one, if you don't mind.'

'By all means, sir.'

'I don't suppose you'd do me a favour, would you?' I asked.

'If I can, sir.'

'I'm trying to get hold of your brother-in-law, John Vaughan. He gave me his number, but I can't seem to find it.'

'I'm not allowed to give out his home number. Can I ask you what it's about?'

'The killing of Hugh Jones – I've remembered something more. He said to ring him if I did.'

'Right, well, I can give you his mobile number – or, failing that, I can get in touch with him myself.'

'The mobile number will be fine.'

He wrote it down on the back of the poster and waved me
on.

I drove on down to where the A470 (T) met the estuary
road and turned left, heading for Ganllwyd and the Coed-y-
Brenin. Within a few miles the forest closed in and the high
rock faces and dark conifers hung silently over the valley road.
Even now, in the height of summer, mine seemed to be the
only car on the road.

If the forest looked large on the map, here it was daunting,
the trees stretching out mile after mile across the mountains
and it hit home that even if Bryn were up there he might never
be found.

I reached Ganllwyd and continued on to Pont Cadno,
turning off the A470(T) and slowing to navigate the unfenced
forest road that led upwards into the heart of Glyn Glas.

Below me I could hear the river rushing as it was forced
through the ravine. Every now and again the trees thinned so
that I could glance down at the violent, swirling waters. Two
miles further on the road became impassable to anything other
than a 4 × 4 so I parked in a clearing and continued on foot.

I took Bryn's maps and haversack, a torch, Alex's binoculars and some chocolate that I'd bought in Barmouth; a poor
attempt at a late breakfast.

The shaded area on Bryn's map dated 12 August was still
some distance into the forest and as I walked I took my time so
as to tune in to the surroundings and occasionally sweep the
area with the binoculars.

The track forked; one part crossing the Glas River at a ford
and leading up a steep hillside that twisted through rocky
outcrops and the other continuing on my side of the river. I
doubted that even Bryn's Land Rover could have climbed the
far bank so I kept going straight.

Warning signs started to appear on trees, stating that the

land was private and that hikers should keep to the track as there were hidden mine shafts everywhere.

I saw two hikers on the other side of the river, but that was all. Where were the police? Where were the searchers? They should have been swarming all over the mountain.

The only logic was that the old girl, Mrs Thomas, had not breathed a word to them. Bryn having told her to show the maps only to me, she'd literally done just that. If he'd got into trouble he might well have shut the door behind himself.

The track was becoming more and more overgrown and if Bryn had brought his Land Rover up here then there should have been signs that he'd come through – ferns flattened, twigs snapped, something.

There was nothing – so where was his vehicle?

The further I walked the wilder the land became until I was on the edge of the '12th Aug' square. The track ran along a spur and then downhill, through a river-cut ravine that no 4×4 could have negotiated. I stopped and checked the map.

The ravine was shown as a narrowing of the contour lines that curved and ran down the hill away from the Glas River on the other side of the spur. Beyond the ravine the map showed a small humpback bridge.

Most of the '12th Aug' square lay to the west of the track so I decided to trace the edge of the ravine from above, keeping the drop on my right and searching as I went. The plan, if you could call it that, was to walk the edge of the square that Bryn had marked out and then move inwards a hundred metres and walk the square again. With the first circuit I would be covering about four kilometres and each successive circuit would be eight hundred metres less than the previous circuit.

Timewise that meant something like two hours for the first circuit and a total time of at least twenty hours to conduct even the most cursory search of the square. On my own it was practically futile, but I owed Bryn – and tilting at windmills was about my mark lately.

I had no compass, but enough of the sun came through the canopy for me to use it as a very rough direction-finder, which together with the ravine as a reference was better than nothing. The scope for error was huge.

I set off slowly, keeping parallel to the track along the top of the ravine, and stopped for regular sweeps with the binoculars whenever the forest opened out. The warning signs about mines were more frequent and once or twice I saw shaft entrances in the ravine wall.

Three hours later, away from the ravine edge, I was hot, sweaty and lost.

I knew that the ravine ran the length of the square and was to the east so if I lined up the sun and walked I would hit it sooner or later.

The search pattern idea I'd abandoned an hour before due to continually having to go up and downhill, skirt mine shafts, thick clumps of conifer, and continually cross a fast mountain stream in a rocky gully that ran at an angle to the ravine.

I was on the verge of abandoning the whole idea and making my way back to the car when I stumbled across the stream again and decided to follow it. I could hear the sound of tumbling water nearby and walked towards it. I saw a large pool with a wooden sluice gate that was leaking into the stream.

Twenty metres on, the gully suddenly opened out and the stream plunged into the ravine. Twenty-five metres away, on the stony river bank at the base of the falls, two men were arguing heatedly with a third. It was Russell Evans and the two men giving him a hard time were John and Dylan Williams.

'Keep still!' a voice behind me said quietly. 'Walk backwards from the falls and crouch down where they can't see you.'

I turned to see John Vaughan standing a few yards away. He was dressed in a green cagoule, green walking trousers and a floppy bush hat, with his face and hands blackened.

'Do it, Jay – do it now or they'll see you.'

34

I moved back from the edge and dropped to my knees.

Vaughan put his finger to his lips and motioned me to sit alongside him. From where we sat we could see them, but they would have been hard pushed to see us in the jumble of rock and vegetation.

Behind them I could see an adit – a horizontal mine opening into the hillside – and an array of tools scattered on the ground.

We sat watching, unable to hear above the sound of the cascading water, but picking up on the body language. Evans looked frightened and small alongside the two burly brothers. He cried out when Dylan Williams got behind him and wrapped his arm around his throat, wrenching his head back.

Suddenly John Williams picked up a sledgehammer and thrust the butt end of the shaft into Evans's stomach. I started forward, but Vaughan pushed me back down again.

'Do nothing!' he breathed.

Dylan Williams released his grip and Evans fell heavily to the ground. A look passed between the two brothers and they grabbed Evans and dragged him towards the mine entrance.

'You're going to do nothing?' I whispered.

'Not yet,' Vaughan said evenly. 'I don't think they're going to kill him.'

'And if you're wrong?'

He ignored me.

A few minutes later the brothers dragged Evans back into view and threw him to the ground. Dylan Williams placed his boot on Evans's neck and John Williams bent over him. It didn't take a lip-reader to interpret the short expletives that punctuated the speech.

When Evans was dragged back to his feet he was pale and shaken, with none of fire that had been in him the previous night.

John Williams picked up a crowbar and threw it at Evans who caught it and looked from one brother to the other. Then all three went back into the mine.

When they were out of sight Vaughan turned to me.

'Let's go.'

He led the way back along the river gully, moving fast and confidently. After half a mile or so he stopped and asked me where I'd parked my car. I told him and he looked at the map, took out a compass and nodded.

'Due south,' he said, 'but there's a track that will take us on an easier route.'

'I'm all for easy.'

He set off again, turning away from the gully and heading straight up the hillside without looking back. It was hard going but I stayed with him, the price of which was within minutes I was dripping with sweat and snatching breaths where I could.

Just when I was starting to buckle, we crossed the brow of the hill and stopped. Vaughan took a cloth from his pocket, splashed water over it from a plastic water carrier and started removing the face blacking.

'So what were you doing there?' he said sharply.

'Looking for Bryn Thomas.'

'Bryn?'

'Aren't *you* supposed to be looking for him?'

Vaughan looked back along the way we'd come, 'The uniform boys are searching the area around the Abergwynant woods . . . apparently he'd been seen walking there over the last few weeks. What makes you think he's here?'

I ignored the question. 'If you're not searching for Bryn, what are you doing here?'

'Police work.'

He shrugged as he said it and his face was impassive, but I shook my head.

'On your own? No back-up? No radio? I don't think so.'

He stopped, a thick greasy smear across his face. 'It's *connected* to police work.'

'Connected? Like Anne Lloyd was connected to police work the night she was shot?'

He went still. 'Maybe. Were you up here looking for me?'

'No. Like I said, I was looking for Bryn Thomas.'

He nodded. 'You'd better tell me as we walk.'

I didn't move, 'I'll do better than that – I'll trade you information.'

'Trade?'

'I want to know about Mark Haig.'

He smiled. 'You *have* been busy.'

'Don't tell me you're surprised. You put yourself out to load me.'

'Load you?'

'The day after Hugh Jones was murdered and you came up to Ty Hiraeth with Pritchard . . .'

'Yes?'

'And when Pritchard left to go back to the murder scene, you told me that two years ago a man from London had been killed and his house set on fire at Ganllwyd.'

'You asked about the history of arson cases we'd had,' he said evenly.

'No, that's not quite the way it was. You fed me information about Welsh radical groups . . . arsonists burning second homes.'

'Well?'

'Well, why? I didn't need to know that, but you linked it to

the death at Ganllwyd . . . what you left out was that the dead
man was Mark Haig.'

'What difference would that've made?'

'I don't know – yet. Then you turn up at Ty Hiraeth again –
when was it? sixth of July . . . I think. And for some reason you
sought me out and just started talking about the day Hugh
Jones was murdered?'

'There's an ongoing murder investigation – it's my job to re-
interview witnesses.'

I nodded. 'But you made sure that you slipped in the bit
about Russell Evans – you even gave me a description, enough
for me to recognise him last night, even though he'd cut his
hair short and had grown a beard . . . Why?'

'You saw Evans last night? Where?'

'Anne's cottage. But let's get back to the point: why tell me
anything? Except that you thought you'd use me as a stalking
horse. I was meant to run around, creating a diversion and
beating the bushes for you, and if it all went wrong . . . well,
you and your boss Pritchard already had me marked down as
a troublemaker. So, between you, you saw a good opportunity.
How am I doing?'

He rubbed fiercely at the backs of his hands with the cloth,
absorbed for the moment. When he looked up he was smiling,
but it wasn't humour.

'Right actions – wrong motivation.'

'I'm listening.'

'Not here. Let's get back to your car and you can drop me
back at mine. Then we'll talk.'

He stuffed the cloth into his pocket, took a glance at his
compass and set off again.

For an hour we walked along a small rough track without
seeing a soul. Vaughan didn't talk. I thought back to the day I'd
met him and how laid back he'd been. I wouldn't have thought of
him like that now. Something was eating away at him.

We reached the BMW and he pulled off his cagoule and shirt and wet the cloth again, rubbing his hands and face until all that remained of the blacking was a dark tinge to his skin.

'When you said a track I thought you meant something a bit more substantial than that,' I said.

'Deer track – fallow deer. They stay away from people and only come down into the valley when the weather's bad. If you want to stay away from people it's as good a method as any.'

'Where am I driving you?'

'The other side of Ganllwyd. There's a bridge that leads on to a forest road, follow that for a mile or so and you'll come to another bridge, Pont Wen. Just beyond Pont Wen there's a car park—'

He must have seen the look on my face.

'Just follow the signs to Llanfachreth,' he said.

He put his shirt back on and bundled up the cagoule.

The drive took twenty minutes and Vaughan was silent the whole time. When I pulled into the small Forestry Commission car park his was the only vehicle there; a green Vauxhall Frontera.

'Right, get in my vehicle and we'll talk.'

Did he think I was wired up? I shrugged and we both got out of the BMW and got into the Frontera.

Once we were sitting in it he turned to me and said, 'That's a nice car you've got there.'

'Not mine . . . Alex McGregor's – like the Shogun, only the Shogun's off the road at the moment as a little posse decided to kidnap me and it got damaged in the fracas.'

'Is that how you picked up the bruises?'

'Most of them.'

'You seem to have survived,' he said. 'Why were you kidnapped?'

'They wanted something and needed me to get it.'

'And what was that?'

'My turn to ask questions . . .'

'Go ahead.'

'I want to know about the night Anne was shot . . . everything.'

'Such as?'

'Such as why a team of police were watching Haig in the first place?'

'He was suspected of having stolen something and we wanted to see what he'd do with it.'

'What had he stolen?'

'A laptop computer.'

'From whom?'

'OPMA, the parent company of the Black River Mining Company – Hugh Jones's company. My turn. Who told you about Mark Haig?'

'The people who kidnapped me.'

'And who told you about Anne getting shot?'

'Julia – she said to ask you about it.'

Vaughan gave the same humourless smile I'd seen earlier. 'Where's Anne now?'

'If I told you what would you do with the information?'

He looked at me directly. 'It's not Anne I'm after.'

'Maybe, but what would you do with the information?'

He paused. 'Initially, I'd keep it to myself.'

'And after "initially"?'

'I'm a policeman investigating the murder of Hugh Jones . . .'

'And you think Anne had something to do with it?'

'I think she knew people who might know something.'

'Like who?'

'Like Russell Evans. Where is Anne?'

'If I tell you I'd need to know everything . . . about Haig . . . Hugh Jones, Russell Evans . . . and why I was kidnapped by people looking for the laptop.'

There was a visible reaction. 'The laptop?'

'Yes, the laptop and unless there are two laptops out there I'd like your best guess as to why two years after Haig stole it I'm getting the shit kicked out of me.'

At that he went silent.

When he spoke he seemed more subdued, more tentative.

'Have you any idea who might want to kidnap you? Who the people are?'

'I know one of them – not his name, but what he looks like – and according to Russell Evans it's the same guy he saw sticking a knife in Hugh Jones.'

He closed his eyes. 'Description?'

I described One-Eye and the air seemed to go out of Vaughan. Again he fell silent and for the umpteenth time in my life I was run over by a truism travelling as relentlessly a steamroller.

'You know who he is, don't you?'

'Yes.'

'So?'

'If I tell you, you can never repeat it – any of it.'

I studied him. 'Any of it?'

'Any of it . . . Haig, the laptop . . . any of it. But if I do tell you it will only be in exchange for knowing where Anne is.'

'My word on it.'

35

John Vaughan led the way to his house in Bronaber, half hour's drive north, along the A470(T).

Anne had said he was married and the house showed all the signs of being a family home, but there was no one else around and Vaughan never mentioned where his wife and children were.

He made us coffee and we sat in a small back room, which housed a computer and a fax machine; it fell short of being an office.

I got the feeling that he was in some way embarrassed and was not at ease with the place, as though he lived there, but had not settled to it, in the way that I'd never settled to the flat at Romford.

I almost felt that I had to get him to relax instead of the other way around so I decided to lay it out for him, where I was, what I'd seen and experienced. I went through it all, up to and including my run-in with Russell Evans at Anne's cottage. The only bit I skipped was my attendance at the OPMA building explosion and discovering Anne's body.

I finished by restating my original neutrality.

'When I came to Wales, I had no intention of getting involved with anything that was going on here. Discovering Hugh Jones like that was an accident of timing,' I said. 'Since then it seems I've been pulled into this . . . situation, and for that you have to bear some of the responsibility. It was you that told Anne I was an inquiry agent, wasn't it?'

'Yes.'

'Why?'

'I owed Anne . . . she needed help and I couldn't give it to her. I thought you might be the solution.'

'What gave you that idea?'

'You came with a reputation, Jay – the Met weren't too complimentary about the withholding of evidence in your previous investigation. They also indicated that you needed to be watched – that you were a potential troublemaker.'

'That's the oldest trick in the book for stitching someone isn't it . . . lay a strong suggestion that there's something dodgy about them and then walk away and let the shit happen. And you bought it?'

'I didn't, actually. I spoke to several people that night and one or two thought that you deserved better treatment from the Met – and some praise for rescuing that woman. It was my boss Pritchard, who took against you.'

'I don't like him.'

He smiled thinly, 'Neither do I.'

He looked at me directly, weighing and judging, and I returned the look. We both knew I was waiting for his side of the story, but he made me ask all the same.

'So go on, then, tell me.'

'What do you want to know?' he asked.

'Everything. Why don't you start by telling me about Mark Haig and why you and Anne were watching him?'

'Like I said earlier, he stole a laptop from OPMA. He was working for them at the time – the tame environmental scientist who was supposed to rubber-stamp OPMA's environmental safeguards – only according to Anne it didn't work out that way.'

'Surveillance operations aren't mounted for small-time theft, so it was obviously the information on the hard drive that was the hot news. What was on it, exactly?'

'I was never told. Neither was Anne.'

'You seem pretty sure about that.'

'I was her boss.'

'Boss?'

Vaughan raised his eyebrows and took a sip from his mug of coffee.

'Anne's job was to get close to Haig, which she did. They became lovers. I didn't know that until after the night it all went wrong and Haig was murdered. An internal investigation led to Anne and myself being disciplined. Anne was required to resign as an alternative to dismissal and I was demoted.'

'Demoted?'

His voice was cold. 'I was in charge of the surveillance operation – an Inspector and well on my way to becoming a Chief Inspector.'

'And you're bitter about that?'

He shook his head. 'Not as much as you'd imagine. I was police barmy, see. It was the most important thing in my life.' He paused and looked around. 'Since then I've reassessed . . . settled for less.'

'Happier?'

He looked away. 'Not that you'd notice.'

'Anne's affair with Haig compromised the operation, then?'

'No. I don't believe it did. Anne was a first-class copper – in the Met before she came to us. She went there straight from university and made an impression right from the beginning. She was seconded especially for the Haig job because she was originally a local and therefore had a good cover . . . coming back to be near her sister. No one besides Julia and the team knew Anne was a detective sergeant.'

'Tell me about Haig.'

'He was older than Anne, early forties. Clever and likeable – and very good-looking. I'd met him once before the investigation.'

'So why did he steal the laptop?'

'The suggestion was that he was going to give it to an eco-protest group.'

'Was he a member of that group?'

'That's what I was told.'

'So what happened the night Anne was shot and Haig was murdered?'

His eyes hardened, 'That's a good question.'

'Tell me what you know.'

'Anne and Haig were in Haig's cottage at Ganllwyd. There was a rumour that he was going to pass the laptop on to someone that night. We didn't know who, but Anne said whoever it was would be there around eight o'clock.'

'So?'

He sighed. 'Eight came and went and when no one showed I eventually made the decision to scale down the operation.'

'What time was that?'

'Eleven. Two of us held on a bit longer, but it looked it looked a dud. Then I made a mistake . . .' He paused. 'I let myself be talked into cutting away.'

'Cutting away?'

His voice became softer and he stared at his hands. 'I went to Julia's, barely five minutes away at the other end of Ganllwyd. We were having an affair . . . no . . . no that's not true . . . we were on the verge of having an affair. I thought—' He stopped for a moment and then sighed. 'It doesn't matter what I thought . . . the point is, when it happened I was somewhere that I shouldn't have been.'

'Go on.'

'I left my mobile number with the guy staying on surveillance with instructions to ring me should anything happen.'

'And it did?'

'Just after midnight. I received a phone call to say that all hell had broken loose and I was to get back immediately . . .'

Vaughan's voice was breaking with emotion and he shook his head. 'I saw the flames as I came down the road. Haig was dead – I pulled him from the house, but it was too late. Anne . . . Anne was naked . . . unconscious and bleeding heavily from a gunshot wound.'

I took a sip of the coffee. 'What was the story?'

'That the guy left on surveillance had had to use the toilet . . . he was gone five, maybe ten minutes. He heard gunshots and came out to find the scene much as I described. Two men were seen fleeing . . . he called for an ambulance for Anne, bandaged her wounds and phoned me.'

Vaughan seemed shaken, as though by retelling the tale he was experiencing it all again. He was still carrying the baggage and it weighed just as much now as the day he'd picked it up.

I was sympathetic. After what I'd been through you'd hardly expect anything else, but I suppressed the urge and concentrated on the questions.

'What aren't you telling me?'

'Sorry?'

'It's all a bit clinical, isn't it? I mean, what did Anne say had happened?'

'She said that she'd been in bed with Haig. They'd made love and were asleep when she was woken by a cry for help. She was aware of a struggle going on in the room – Haig was fighting with two men. She went to help him. It was dark and she couldn't see what he looked like, but as she fought one of the assailants she realised he was wearing leathers and a helmet. Then she was hit and knocked unconscious.'

'Go on.'

'When she came to, the house was ablaze. She managed to get out – she didn't know Haig was still inside. As she ran out she was shot . . . the rest you now know.'

'The laptop?'

'Missing.'

'So we don't know if whoever attacked Haig and Anne got away with it?'

'No. It seems unlikely, though,' Vaughan said pensively.

'Why?'

'Because everyone's still searching for it. Look, Anne never lied about her involvement with Haig and she swore that she'd never seen the laptop. It's possible that her original information was wrong and it was never in Haig's house.'

'Messy?'

'About as bad as it gets. After the tribunal required her to resign, as an alternative to dismissal, Anne disappeared for six months. When she came back she got involved in the campaign to stop the opencast mining.'

'Went native?'

'In a word, yes.'

'And that's why she wanted me to help her find the laptop and wouldn't tell the police about the break-in at her cottage by the guys dressed in motorcycle gear?'

'Do you blame her? She had no trust in the police – and every reason to hate me.'

'Did she? Hate you, I mean?'

'No. No, she didn't.'

He seemed surprised at his own words.

'But you felt guilty. Was that your reason for wanting me to help her?'

'Help her . . . keep an eye on her . . . something like that, yes.'

'And that was all?'

He stared at me. 'Yes.'

'From what you've told me there seems to be a whole string of similarities between Haig's and Hugh Jones's murders – stabs wounds, a burning house . . . two guys on motorcycles in the vicinity?'

'Yes,' he breathed.

'And Jones was about to give Anne information about the laptop. Do you know what Jones's connection was to Haig?'

'They both worked for OPMA, both were locals.'

'Was Hugh Jones a member of the protest group?'

'Looks that way, doesn't it . . . or at least he was sympathetic.'

'And Russell Evans – how does he figure in all this?'

The grin that Vaughan gave was one of acknowledgement, as though I'd finally asked the right question.

'At a guess I'd say he was in it up to his neck. But don't ask me how.'

'Where do James Howard and the military-looking guy fit into all this?'

'Well, I thought I knew. But after what Russell Evans said about Jones's murder I'm not so sure. By the way, the ex-military guy is Sean Murrell.'

'So what's going on with Murrell and Howard?'

He took a deep breath and exhaled slowly. 'When OPMA moved into the area they gave the task of security over to a private firm called Tech-Ops.'

'Who?'

'It's a firm that recruits ex-special forces personnel – SAS, Marines, ex-Paras – though from the research I've done they seem to play the low end of the market . . . mainly going after the people that other firms won't take.'

'What's wrong with them?'

Vaughan shrugged. 'Anything from running up debts to sleeping with other men's wives. Anything, in fact, that becomes an embarrassment to their unit; criminal or violent behaviour usually seems to figure in there somewhere. They tend to end up on the street trained to do just one thing and usually drift into security work.'

'But Howard's sick, isn't he?'

'Allegedly – it's part of his cover. He was here before the mining survey got under way, sniffing out the area.'

'Looks like OPMA were expecting trouble.'

'Opencast mining is as controversial as it gets and this region has a history of protest.'

I swilled the coffee around in my mug, 'I think it was James Howard that ambushed me with Murrell at St Katharine's Dock.'

'That doesn't surprise me. They're after the laptop as well. They're on bonuses if they catch anyone sabotaging Black River Mining Company equipment or attacking their personnel. I imagine that the bonus for the laptop is considerable.'

'Kidnapping and actual bodily harm are still crimes, I take it?'

He inclined his head to one side. 'Where's your proof? You only saw Murrell at St Katharine's Dock. It would be your word against his and you have no witnesses for the kidnapping.'

'And what about Russell Evans's account of Hugh Jones's murder?'

'Well, you can take it as read that as soon I get the chance I shall be interviewing Russell Evans.' He held up his mug. 'Want a top-up?'

'Please.'

He took my cup and walked through to the kitchen to refresh the mugs. I followed him out.

'So why were you in the woods today?

He stopped and turned. 'For the answer to that, I'd need to know where Anne was.'

'Oh?'

'This place has been turned upside down since last Wednesday when someone blew up OPMA's headquarters in London. I need to find her – and quickly.'

Now it was my turn to pause, looking for the words.

'Right now Anne's in a temporary mortuary . . . awaiting

identification. I pulled her body out of the rubble of the OPMA building on Friday night.'

He looked drained.

His mouth opened, but for a minute he couldn't speak. 'Oh, no . . . I . . . are you *sure*?'

'Very. I put her in the body bag myself.'

'But—'

'She's dead! I don't know why and I want to know why. According to Russell Evans she went to London to get the laptop last Sunday. Maybe she—'

'That's not possible,' he said.

'Pardon?'

'I said that's not possible. She gave the laptop to Julia last Sunday.'

36

We tried ringing Julia at Ty Hiraeth, but she'd left half an hour before.

As we left John Vaughan's house the sky was darkening and the early evening air was thick with the coming storm. A breeze had sprung up that blew warm against my skin and moved the tops of the trees; an outrider to the rain.

'Leave your car here. We'll take my Frontera,' said Vaughan, looking up. 'Julia lives on an unmade road.'

Vaughan pulled out of his drive and pushed his foot to the floor, trying to beat the storm. He said that it was a clear run straight down the A470 and then five minutes down the unmade road.

'Fifteen minutes in all,' he replied to my unasked question.

I nodded and watched the first of the lightning snake across the bruised horizon and leave a dull rumble in its wake.

'So how do you know Julia has the laptop?'

'I got a phone call from her this morning, just after you left her at Cross Foxes. She said that she was scared and that she needed to tell someone.'

'When did you plan to tell me that?'

'When I needed to.' He glanced at me and then turned back to the road. 'Listen, Jay – this is a police matter. I know that I—'

'Except you're not playing policemen now, are you?' I interrupted him.

'Aren't I?'

'No, you're not. Do you want to tell me?'

'It's private.'

'*Was* private,' I said. 'Otherwise, what am I doing here?'

Again he snatched a look at me, but this time said nothing.

It was growing hotter by the minute and I lowered the window. Up ahead the sky was darker, with swollen, gunmetal clouds broken only by a slash of gold at the horizon.

Vaughan steered with one hand, pressed the keys on his mobile with the other and handed it to me.

'Julia should be home by now.'

I took the mobile and listened. It rang and rang, but there was no reply.

Another flash of lightning lit the sky, followed by another deep rumble, but still there was no rain. The forest closed in on the road and with the threatening sky it was like driving through a tunnel. Vaughan switched the headlights on and the twin beams cut through the gloom.

Then the rain started to fall.

At first it was big, soft rain, beginning as slow, isolated teardrops as thick as oil that splattered on hitting the Frontera's windscreen. Gradually the tempo increased until they struck with such force that the heavy globules bounced off the bonnet.

Within minutes the incipient fall had progressed to a torrential downpour and Vaughan was forced to slow the vehicle as the wipers battled to shed the water.

'How far now?' I asked.

'Two miles.'

A few minutes later we left the A470 and drove along the track, closely bordered by the forest. Every few seconds the trees were outlined in stark blue-white light as the lightning crackled overhead.

'It's just around this bend,' said Vaughan

Julia's white Suzuki 4 × 4 was parked in the driveway. There wasn't enough room for two vehicles so Vaughan drove on past the house and parked in a clearing just out of view from the cottage.

We knocked on the door and heard Julia call out.

'It's me – John. I've got Steve Jay me.'

There was the sound of a bolt being drawn back and Julia opened the door.

'Oh John, thank God it's you. The phone's been ringing and I was too scared to answer it.'

'That was us.'

'Come in, please.'

We went through to the living room and Vaughan turned to me.

'Tell her.'

I related everything that had happened from the minute I'd arrived in Wales. Julia listened, shaking her head and looking at Vaughan for confirmation. I told her about the OPMA building explosion, but didn't mention Anne and Vaughan didn't prompt me.

When I'd finished he asked Julia for the laptop.

She fetched it and set it down on the living-room table. It was a top-of-the-range Toshiba and I estimated that it probably cost in excess of five grand.

'According to Anne it's protected by a password,' I said.

'It's *Xingu*,' said Julia.

I nodded, plugged it into a wall socket and switched it on.

'You have to type in the name "John Joshua Roth", and then the password,' she added.

I did as she said and the laptop started booting up.

I went into 'My Documents' and up came a series of ten files, all of which were '*read only files*.' The first three related to case studies of mercury poisoning of Brazilian Indians in the Xingu National Park between 1989 and 1992, with particular attention given to the symptoms and the extent of the poisoning.

There was no author's name in the file.

The fourth file dealt with a profile of the drug Pheladone; its molecular make-up, speed of reaction, the fact that it could be taken in pill, capsule or liquid form and its proposed benefits for preventing miscarriage.

The fifth and sixth files dealt with trials carried out on three groups of Indians. The trial period was from March to September 1993.

The next three files dealt with the trial results.

At first I thought I was misreading it and went back to the beginning. I minimised the files on the screen and called up the first, second and third files respectively. Then I maximised the last three files, one after the other.

'What are we looking for? Have you any idea?' asked John Vaughan.

'I didn't, but I think I'm beginning to understand.'

I opened the last file. It was a series of pictures. Some were of groups of Indians – men, women and children. They looked ill and, in the cases of the children, they had deformities. The last four photographs appeared to be different; white men were propping up adult Indians.

'Wait a minute,' said John Vaughan. 'Go back.'

I moved the cursor and we re-examined the last four photographs again. Along the bottom of the photographs were the names of the Indians and the white men holding them.

John Vaughan leaned closer. 'There! The white man helping to hold up the Indian to the left . . .'

I pointed. 'Him . . . Ruddock?'

Vaughan's voice was hoarse. 'Don't you recognise him – it's Bonny!'

37

The more I looked at the photographs the more it was obvious that it was Bonny; younger, thinner, with less hair and a smaller beard, but definitely him.

I looked at Vaughan. 'What happens to the laptop?'

'It's evidence.'

'Oh, it's that all right. But what are you going to do with it?'

'Keep hold of it – for now.'

I smiled. 'That's called withholding evidence.'

His face was impassive. 'I bet those Met boys just loved you, Jay.'

Julia intervened to break the tension.

'Would anybody like a coffee . . . or something stronger?' she said.

'Coffee,' replied Vaughan.

I nodded. 'Coffee would be nice.'

She went into the kitchen and Vaughan went with her.

I switched off the laptop, put it back in its case and peered into the kitchen, intending to ask Vaughan whether we were taking it with us when I caught sight of them in each other's arms.

Perhaps it was just comfort, but to me it looked like surrender.

A few minutes later they appeared from the kitchen, looking like guilty schoolchildren.

As we sat drinking the coffee Julia brought up the subject of Anne and I went into evasive mode. Vaughan helped me out and started asking me questions about the forest fires. In the middle of recounting my tale about the Abergwynant fire Julia suddenly frowned.

'What was that? There was a noise . . .'

Suddenly, there was a tremendous crash and the sound of splintering wood.

Vaughan sprang to his feet and I spun around as three men carrying baseball bats and dressed in motorcycle gear burst into the room. They hesitated on seeing us and Vaughan reacted first by kicking the biggest man between the legs.

I reached for a chair and smashed the smaller man across the head with it and although the helmet protected his skull the force sent him reeling.

The third man swung his bat at Vaughan's head, but he ducked and rugby tackled him.

They were virtually armoured in their leathers and helmets and it restricted the options to damage them. So I kicked the shin of the smaller man and slammed a knee into the thigh of the one that Vaughan had kicked in the groin.

I was aware of movement to my left and saw Vaughan go down under a weight of heavy punches. I rushed to help him, but his assailant picked up a bat from the floor and swung it at me. I stumbled backwards and the bat missed me by an inch.

Julia tried to help, but he pushed her back so hard that she hit the wall and fell to the floor.

I looked left and right for another chair, but he turned back to me and swung the bat again. The only thing that saved me was John Vaughan grabbing his leg and unbalancing him.

Now both the other men were back in the fight and they rushed me.

Vaughan got to his feet and charged them from behind, sending them both to the floor. The helmet of the smaller man flew off and Vaughan shouted at him.

'Evans!'

Evans tried to get to his feet and Vaughan pounced on him, but both the bigger men pulled him from Vaughan's grasp. There was a moment when it could have gone either way, but one of them shouted something and all three turned and ran.

Vaughan went straight to Julia.

She had a cut lip and was groggy, but otherwise okay.

Vaughan grabbed my arm, 'Come on!'

We ran out into the pounding rain and headed for the Frontera.

We jumped in and he threw the vehicle into reverse then backed into Julia's drive before turning the wheel hard and gunning the Frontera down the unmade road. It slewed from side to side like a drunk in an alley and sideswiped a tree.

The motorbikes were just ahead of us and at the junction with the A470 they turned left and roared off down the road. Vaughan barely slowed at the junction and we cut a tight circle as he slammed the accelerator to the floor.

There was a brilliant light overhead and a tremendous clap of thunder vibrated through the vehicle.

'You're going to have to phone this in now,' I shouted above the noise of the storm. 'You can't deal with this on your own.'

'No! I know where they're going.'

'Where?'

'The Williams' mine.'

'Are you sure it's them . . . not Murrell and Howard?'

'It's them.'

'What have the Williams brothers got to do with this?'

'Opencast mining.'

'What?'

'You have to see it to believe it . . . It's large scale – tears the land to pieces – but it's the most efficient way to obtain whatever you want from the ground. In this case, copper.'

'I'm still not with you.'

'Holes are drilled in a pattern, then dynamite, gelignite or sometimes liquid explosive is put in the holes. The explosives are detonated and then the earth movers and trucks get to work.'

'Explosives?'

'Lots of it,' he threw a glance at me, 'in the past six months more gelignite has gone missing than OPMA would like people to know about.'

'How much?'

'Enough to blow a building apart.'

'And you think that's linked to the OPMA bomb?'

He nodded. 'I think that's a fair assumption, don't you?'

'Where would you keep that much gelignite?' But I knew the answer before I said it.

Vaughan nodded. 'That's right – up there, in a mine . . . in one of the hundreds of disused shafts that riddle these mountains.'

'That's why you were up there. You think the Williams brothers are behind the OPMA bombing?'

'Yes.'

If anything the rain was coming down harder and in places water ran off the hillside and cut the road with shallow streams. The sky had grown darker still and was now a black/grey dome split by vivid electrical surges as the thunder echoed around the hills and mountains.

Up ahead we saw the bikes swerve around something and in response Vaughan slowed the Frontera and steered a wide arc around debris washed down on to the road.

'If all that's true then it looks like Bryn Thomas came up here looking for Christ knows what and got too close,' I shouted.

'Don't know about that one, but the timing's right. Bryn goes missing and a few days later the OPMA building gets blown apart.'

'Who have you told about this?'

'No one . . . for the moment?'

I looked at him, flying solo and driving like a madman; what the fuck was going on inside his head?

He turned to me. 'I'm going to warn you now, Jay. Once we get there it'll be hard going. We'll have to follow the track that runs up to the ravine. It's steep.'

'Don't worry about me.'

'There's a spare oilskin in the back, you'd better use it when we get out. You'll have to watch your footing in those trainers – snapping an ankle up there isn't a good idea.'

The Frontera was travelling flat out now, with Vaughan refusing to concede anything to the furious weather. In places the water lay in sheets across the road and when we hit them we aquaplaned and instinctively, I gripped the edge of the seat, expecting to flip over any minute.

If he had doubts they didn't show in his face.

Vaughan suddenly pointed. 'There, up ahead!'

I peered through the rain and in the distance thought I could make out the motorbikes turning off the road.

'That's the bridge!'

'How far up can they get on those bikes?'

'A lot further than we can in this,' he replied.

I tensed, knowing he wanted to reach them before they got away into the cover of the forest and would take any risk to get them.

He waited till the last possible moment and then turned onto the bridge with two wheels lifting clear of the road. I could see the River Eden surging below us, swollen to bursting by the storm.

On the other side of the bridge we were forced to reduce speed as the road metalling ran out and was replaced by a gravel-laid forest track that climbed steeply as it zigzagged up the mountain.

The rain was now falling so hard that visibility was reducing all the time.

'It'll get worse yet,' said Vaughan, 'it'll run off the surrounding mountains and hills and every stream'll become a river and every river a torrent. Going into that ravine will be bloody dangerous.'

Just as he said that one of the motorbikes went over.

The driver pulled the bike up fast and climbed back on, but the pillion rider was slow to get up and as he did so he was cradling his left arm.

Vaughan saw his chance and hit the accelerator, making our wheels spin on the gravel and the Frontera swing from side to side.

The motorbike driver looked back and saw how close we were and signalled frantically to the pillion rider to move. The injured man turned to look at us, only now aware of how close we were. He moved forward, but as he did so he stumbled and with that the biker abandoned him.

Stranded, he looked from the biker to us and then turned and ran up the hillside.

'Have you got a compass?' shouted Vaughan.

'No.'

'Take mine.' He slipped it from around his neck and passed it to me. 'If we get split up go due west, it'll take you to the Eden. Follow the bank in either direction till you hit a bridge. On the other side will be the A470.'

'Right.'

Vaughan brought the Frontera to a halt at the spot where the pillion rider had gone into the forest. We climbed out and I turned the hood of the oilskin up against the slanting rain.

Then Vaughan tugged at my shoulder. 'Come on!'

He ran straight up the thickly forested hillside without looking back.

I ran after him, the ground so slippery beneath my feet that at times I was reduced to scrambling on all fours. At first I stayed with him, but the climb got steeper and I struggled, falling further behind with each stride.

The rain was singing through the conifer branches and the laboured gasps of my own breathing seemed impossibly loud in my ears as Vaughan moved faster and faster, closing on the dark shape of the pillion rider.

It took ten minutes for me to reach the top of the slope and when I got there Vaughan was halfway down the other side.

I half scrambled, half slipped down the rocky hillside, grabbing branches and tree trunks to control my descent. By the time I reached the bottom I was covered in mud and pine needles and my breathing was coming in snatches.

Just short of the base of the hillside Vaughan was waiting for me.

'I think I know where's he's going and it won't be easy with that damaged arm.'

I bent over, my hands resting on my knees. 'Tell me.'

'At the bottom of this slope there's a valley, from there it's a short run to the mouth of the ravine . . . maybe half a mile. The valley's not much off being a ravine itself and it's going to be wet down there, so watch your footing.'

'Got you.'

We emerged from the forest onto a small track beside a surging river that threw up gouts of water as it struck rocks in its path; we crossed it by a series of leaps, dancing from rock to rock.

On the other side we looked up the valley and saw the rider. He'd thrown away the motorbike helmet in the forest and I could see clearly now that it was Russell Evans.

The valley rose steeply the whole way, with a tiny track clinging to the valley wall and the river swelling by the minute, tearing at its banks and threatening to undercut the track.

Vaughan moved off quickly and once again I found myself playing catch-up.

A hundred yards later we rounded a curve and saw a humpback bridge at the top of a series of escalating waterfalls. It looked a short, but fierce climb and the track petered out some way short. There was no other way up except to scramble along the edge of the river.

Whether from fear or desperation, Evans had made some ground on us and I felt responsible. My lungs were like sponges and I was wet from sweat and water and blowing harder still.

The storm was at its height now, with continual flashes of lightning and the rain hammering the rocks around us. Vaughan stopped and hunched down in the shelter of a rock overhang beside a deep pool at the foot of a three-metre waterfall.

I caught up and squeezed in beside him.

'Okay?'

'Hanging in there,' I said.

He grunted. 'Good. We'll catch him. He's putting in his last effort. D'you remember I told you about this bridge?'

'Yes.'

'Well, at that point the ravine begins and then it's half a mile to the falls and the mine shaft where the Williams—' He stopped. 'What? What is it?'

'I thought I saw something in the water up there.'

He glanced from under the rock overhang at the series of cascades above us.

Whatever it was had vanished. As we emerged from the overhang there was a blur of movement from above and a tremendous splash in the middle of the pool.

Then Bryn's body floated to the surface.

38

Bryn's body was bound and wrapped in a tarpaulin. Only the head was exposed with the eyes open and fixed in death and the flesh discoloured.

For a moment I was numb, then anger burned through me, making my heart pound and my fists close tight.

I looked up to Evans, who had stopped climbing and was looking beyond the bridge to where the body had been thrown into the river.

John Vaughan reacted first.

He climbed the edge of the waterfalls so fast a look of panic crossed Evans's face. Evans reacted by climbing up to the humpback bridge and going under the arch. I followed Vaughan as fast as I could, but he was going flat out and reached the bridge before I'd made twenty feet.

Then he went under the bridge and disappeared from view.

I climbed frantically, ignoring the increasing volume of water cascading down the falls, plucking at me and threatening to wash me off the side of the gully.

Several times I slipped, smashing my knees and elbows, cursing and biting back the pain until finally I made the bridge.

There was a shelf that ran above the waterline on the inner face of the arch and I edged along it.

On the other side was the ravine; a V-shaped cleft in the rock with stunted trees clinging to its walls and a jumble of rocks forming a natural staircase to the side of the river. I looked for an alternate route up, but if we were to catch Evans there wasn't one.

I scanned the length of the ravine and saw them.

Vaughan had gained ground, but Evans was still fifty feet above him and shrewd enough to control the pace by throwing rocks down, forcing Vaughan to keep breaking off the chase and take cover.

I started up, warily, dividing my attention between climbing and avoiding the rocks that came bouncing down.

It was impossible to settle into a rhythm and that made the climbing harder, but I pushed on, gaining height and distance gradually and praying that the adrenalin would keep me in there.

Vaughan had said the ravine was half a mile long, but it wasn't the distance that was the problem, it was the incline, it was fierce. My legs were shaking now and I was stopping more regularly. Even Vaughan and Evans seemed to have slowed, but they were only a hundred feet below the mine entrance, half the distance that I had to travel.

I pushed on, determined not to lose touch and leave Vaughan exposed.

The wind was gusting stronger, hurling the rain in our faces and channelling its force down the ravine so that it joined with the river in trying to pick us from the rock.

The next time I looked up Vaughan had gained more ground and was now less than twenty feet below Evans. Then it was head down and climb again, blocking out the pain in the legs and the ache in my lungs, concentrating on the image of Bryn to focus my efforts.

A noise from above made me look up and a rock came bouncing down the ravine, hitting the water two yards to my right. I glanced up and saw Vaughan facing Evans on a small ledge just below the entrance to the mine. Evans had a rock in his hand and his back to the river.

I willed myself to put in a burst and had nearly reached them when Evans went for Vaughan.

They were fighting right on the edge, but I fixed my attention on gaining height. The incline was levelling out and I reached a huge boulder just below the ledge where they were struggling.

I reached up, pulled myself onto the ledge and punched Evans in the face with everything I had. He went down hard and Vaughan rushed forward and stamped on his shin.

Evans bent double from the pain and we both threw ourselves down on top of him, trying to pin him to the rock. He got an arm free and grabbed Vaughan's hair so I slammed my elbow into his jaw and Vaughan kneed him heavily in the stomach.

With that the fight went out of him, though his eyes still burned with hate.

I put my mouth against his ear. 'Listen hard and there's a chance you'll make it off this mountain . . . fuck me about and I will beat the living shit out of you and throw you down that river!'

He looked at Vaughan. 'You're going to let him do that?'

Vaughan, white-faced and barely able to keep his own anger under control, shook his head. 'I'm not even here.'

I grabbed Evans's throat. 'Who blew up the OPMA building?'

'Go to hell!'

I tightened my grip on his throat and slammed his head back against the rock.

'Again – who blew up the OPMA building?'

'I didn't know there was a bomb in the van – I didn't know!'

'*You* did it?'

He looked from one to the other of us. 'He asked me to take her to London—'

'Who did?'

'Ruddock . . . Bonny.'

'Why?'

'He told me she was delivering something to Roth – to make him stop the opencast mining . . .'

'Go on.'

'I had to drive her to the OPMA building – I didn't know that they'd packed the van with gelignite. They gave me a fake ID . . . I was to drive into the basement car park, using the fake ID, and then leave the van for her to bring back.'

'Did Anne know about the bomb – did she?'

'I don't know – the first I knew was when I heard it on the news. I—'

Vaughan smashed him in the face. 'Liar!'

Blood ran freely from Evans's mouth and nose. 'It's true – I swear!'

'Who loaded the van?' asked Vaughan.

'John and Dylan . . . I didn't know about the bomb—'

I pulled him back towards me. 'Why were you at Anne's cottage?'

'I was told to look for the laptop—'

'Who sent you? Ruddock?'

'Yes.'

Vaughan leaned in. 'I want you to think back – two years – to the night when Mark Haig was killed . . .'

Evans's face was flushed, but the wariness kept creeping back into his eyes.

'What do you want to know?'

'It was John and Dylan Williams that killed Haig and shot Anne, wasn't it?'

'No!'

'How come you're so sure?'

'Because it was me that was supposed to pick up the laptop.'

'You?'

Evans nodded. 'Ruddock told me to pick it up at eight

o'clock, but my car broke down. I rang Ruddock and he said that he'd get it picked up. John and Dylan went to get it later, but when they arrived the cottage was alight and there were two other men there—'

'You're a liar.'

Vaughan turned him over and twisted his arm into his back and yanked his hair back. Evans cried out.

'Okay . . . okay . . . Haig refused to hand the laptop over and John and Dylan roughed him up – but it went too far.'

'Too far! They stabbed him, set fire to the house with Haig and Anne inside and then shot her as she tried to escape!'

He shut his eyes. 'No . . . that wasn't us . . . wasn't John and Dylan.'

'Who was it?'

'I don't know.'

Vaughan punched him in the kidneys and I squeezed his throat till his eyes bulged.

'You were there weren't you?' hissed Vaughan.

I slackened my grip, enough for him to reply.

'All right, all right . . . I was there with John and Dylan . . . look, Haig was supposed to hand over the laptop, but he changed his mind . . . John and Dylan were supposed to persuade him – that's why they roughed him up . . . but they were interrupted.'

'Go on.'

'Two men burst in on us. Anne Lloyd was unconscious by then. They had guns . . . they ordered us out of the house and we left. That's it – the truth . . . we didn't stab him or set fire to the house . . . we didn't kill Haig.'

There was the blast of a shotgun and a voice barked out a command.

'That's enough!'

We looked up. Thirty feet above, on the edge of the waterfall overlooking the mine, stood Bonny Ruddock and the Williams brothers. Both the brothers had shotguns.

'Let him go,' shouted Ruddock.

'They made me tell them,' shouted Evans, 'they . . .'

'Shut up!' snarled Ruddock.

John Williams was aiming his shotgun at all three of us. I looked around for an escape route; there was nowhere to go. Our only leverage was Evans and he suddenly looked out of favour.

I dragged Evans to his feet and locked an arm around his neck, keeping him between John Williams and us. Dylan Williams immediately moved to his left and trained his gun from the other side.

There was a small surge of water over the waterfall and I thought I caught a reaction from John Vaughan, but he didn't move or say anything.

I shouted up at Ruddock.

'Why did you kill Anne? What had she done to you?'

'She poisoned Mark Haig against me. He was ready to hand over the laptop, but she persuaded him not to. Then she comes back here – trying to fool us again, pretending she wanted to help our fight against OPMA.'

'She'd resigned from the police. She came back to help the protest,' said Vaughan.

'You're a liar. D'you think I believed that? And you, Jay, you're working for OPMA – you've been after that laptop since you arrived.'

I shook my head and shouted up at Ruddock, 'You're wrong – Anne wanted that laptop, not me. I believe she was going to use it for the purpose that Mark Haig intended. But you had other ideas, didn't you?'

There was another surge of water over the falls and this time Vaughan definitely tensed.

'Get ready to move,' he whispered.

'What?'

'It's going to hit us – flash flood . . .'

There was another surge of water and I saw Ruddock and the Williams brothers turn. Suddenly there was a massive roaring noise as a huge wall of water enveloped them and broke over the waterfall.

I dived down and to my left, wedging myself between the boulder and the ravine wall. Evans hesitated and John Vaughan tried to pull him to safety.

The huge mass of water struck them, swept both up and carried them down the ravine.

The noise was incredible, the deluge hit the ravine wall above me and I tensed, expecting the water to claim me, but the angle of the gully meant that the water plunged straight down the ravine, smashing into the bridge and carrying away its parapet walls.

I stayed tight, not daring to move.

As far as I knew they were all dead. But I had no urge to trade drowning for a plate-size hole in the head so I remained hidden, listening hard and trying to filter out the sounds of the rushing water.

Gradually the flood waned and I started back down the ravine.

I moved slowly, listening to the hissing of the rain as it tattooed the river and tuned for the slightest surge.

The volume of water coming over the falls was still dangerous and I had to pick my way carefully. It helped that the sky had lightened slightly, but the flash flood had scoured away many of the rocks and boulders and in places I had to lower myself down large drops.

I found Evans against the buttress of the bridge.

He'd been smashed to pieces, his neck broken and his limbs bent through unnatural angles.

Ruddock was face down in a pool.

I waded out and pulled him into the side. I wanted to make sure he was dead.

There was nothing from his carotid pulse and when I opened his eyes they were fixed and dilated. I ran a final check and placed my hand over his heart; I swear to God that if I'd had the slightest indication he was alive, I'd have dragged him back out and held him under till the bubbles stopped coming up.

But he was well dead so I settled for rolling him back into the water.

Below me, fifty, maybe sixty feet, I saw something on the edge of the river and moved towards it.

It was John Vaughan.

He was still alive when I reached him. Most of the right-hand side of his face was gone, both his legs were broken and he had internal injuries, but he was conscious.

I wasn't sure that he could see, so I told him who I was and he reacted immediately.

'It . . . was Pritchard . . .' he whispered.

I lowered my ear to his mouth.

'Pritchard . . .' he repeated.

'What about him, John?'

'. . . He said he'd cover for me . . . that I should go to Julia's . . . wanted me out the way . . . bought off . . . by OPMA . . . they . . . shot Anne.'

His mouth moved some more, but nothing came out. Then he died.

I dialled 999 on my mobile and asked for the mountain rescue and the police. I gave them a thin version of what had happened and said I believed that John and Dylan Williams were downstream somewhere, dead, though I couldn't be sure.

Then I walked out of the forest, using John Vaughan's compass, and thumbed a lift back to his house.

I didn't bother collecting my things from the Castell Coch Inn. I just got in the BMW and drove back to London.

39

I reached Alex's at two in the morning.

I drove the whole way without stopping, numb from fatigue and with a cold, black anger weighing like a rock inside me. For the circle hadn't yet been squared. There was still another focus for my rage and I intended that the punishment should be just and irrevocable.

It was that which kept me awake through the long hours of driving, that which served as the stimulant, the drug.

Alex got up on hearing me and came downstairs.

'Stevie—' He stopped. 'Christ, man, the state of you.'

'Is there anything in the fridge? I'm starving.'

'What?'

'In the fridge . . . I'm hungry . . . I—'

And then I cried.

I cried for John Vaughan, for Bryn Thomas and for Anne – especially for Anne.

Elizabeth's prediction had been as accurate as it was possible to be. It was only blind stubbornness that had kept the reaction at bay so long; that, and the love I'd felt for Anne.

I sat on Alex's sofa, my shoulders heaving and great racking sobs tearing through me.

Alex fetched a duvet from upstairs, pulled off my filthy clothes and tucked me in like a child. Then, without further words turned out the light and left me.

There are times when I believe him to be the wisest man alive.

★　　★　　★

I woke at seven, hopelessly conditioned by the seven o'clock wake-up bells, and then drifted back to sleep till gone nine.

Alex was moving around quietly in the kitchen and I walked out to him, wrapped in the duvet.

'How d'you feel?' he asked softly.

'Does your firm have a solicitor, Alex?'

'We have a firm we use . . .'

'Does it deal with criminal cases?'

'Yes – why?'

'I need you to get me an appointment for today . . . preferably this morning.'

'I can try . . . want to talk about it?'

'No. Can I ask you to ring them? Now?'

'All right. Coffee?'

'Please.'

I drank the coffee and Alex got on the phone. He got me an appointment for eleven-thirty. Then I took a shower while he cooked breakfast.

Alex felt the vibe off me and was dying to ask questions, but he also caught my look and held back. Over breakfast, he reminded me that there were other issues that warranted attention.

'I had Jenny on the phone last night.'

'Not now, Alex. I've—'

He interrupted me. 'You have to deal with this, Stevie. I've always fought shy of giving you advice where Jenny was concerned . . . this is different.'

I sighed. 'I'm listening.'

'I broached the subject of a DNA test.'

'You what?'

'It didn't faze her, Stevie. She said she understood the need to—'

My anger erupted. 'What right do you have to suggest anything? How dare you interfere?'

'What right? I've supported you through everything that's happened.' He paused. 'Ordinarily I wouldn't intervene, but I know you – your pride will keep you away from dealing with this matter. And it's not pride that's needed . . . just honesty.'

I stood up. 'I'll move out of here as soon as I've got a place fixed.'

'Oh for Christ sake, Stevie!'

His face spared me nothing and I sat down again.

'I can't deal with this now, Alex. I know there's truth in what you're saying, but there are things that must be dealt with first.'

'How long will you need?'

'Two days, maybe three.'

'And then you'll phone her?'

'Yes.'

'Can I tell her that . . . if she rings?'

I closed my eyes, 'Yes.'

After breakfast I went back to bed for an hour and rested. I couldn't sleep, but I used the time to think through exactly what I was going to do.

My experience in the brigade has brought me many times up against powerful people with the morals and practices of a card-sharp. Such luminaries, when faced with a moral rack brought about by their own duplicity, usually resort to tossing the ball back in the direction from which it came.

Without admitting blame, they look you in the eye and say, 'What is the outcome that you want from this?'

It is a tactic designed to make you expose your true position, so that they can refuse to accept it and dismiss you.

How much more slippery would Roth be; a man of his gravitas, who could move and shake mountains and to whom national leaders extended their hand?

Whilst giant-slaying is a mental hobby of mine, I was only too aware that in the real world giants rarely lose. The best you can hope for is deflection. I had reason to believe, though, that in this case losing and deflection might just amount to the same thing.

I doubted that I could kill this giant, but I could be a pebble in his shoe.

At eleven-thirty I sat down with Alex's solicitor and at twelve I left. In the solicitor's car park I sat in the BMW and rang the mobile number that the kidnappers had given me.

'I want to speak to Murrell.'

'Who is this?'

'Jay.'

'Go ahead, Jay, this is Murrell.'

'I got the laptop.'

'Where are you?'

'A long way from where the laptop is. I want you to get a message to J. J. Roth for me.'

'Don't fuck around, Jay. Where's the laptop?'

'Safe. I want you to give Roth a one-word message: "Xingu". If he wants to meet – and I think he will – tell him to ring me on this number.'

I gave Murrell the mobile number and rang off.

Then I went back to Alex's and waited.

Three hours later the mobile rang. I had a meeting that night at seven. I was given the name of a West London hotel and told to go to reception and give my name in.

I arrived early and sat in the lounge area, observing people who could buy and sell the likes of me without even noticing the difference in their bank statement; not that they would ever have to look.

I think if was Eleanor Roosevelt who said that, 'No one can make you feel inferior without your consent.' But that's what nurture does to you; it conditions. The best the little man can hope for is the balls to rebel.

At seven I was collected and shown up to the top floor of the hotel.

Roth had the entire floor to himself and as I exited from the lift I endured the first of many searches.

I was led down a central corridor and stopped at every set of fire doors and searched again. I eventually got to sit in a small lounge area, with three wired bodyguards who neither spoke nor acknowledged me.

So far I'd counted ten guards since leaving the lift and I had no doubt that another ten were to hand should I throw a strop. Finally I was called through and the three guards took me down the corridor to a door where I was searched for the last time.

I was taken into a huge penthouse suite with views over London that impressed me, despite my determination not to be.

On a sofa as big as a boat sat three men I didn't recognise, but who had the look and shine of American lawyers. Only one spoke, a distinguished-looking character with a New York accent, iron-grey hair, gold-rimmed glasses and a thousand-dollar suit on his back.

Of Roth there was no sign – not that I'd really expected him to appear in person. These people were his proxies, which was fine by me.

'So, Mr Jay, my name is George G Boxleiter. I believe you have something belonging to OPMA?'

'To J.J. Roth.'

'I can't confirm that.'

'You don't have to. His name and personal password access it.'

He nodded. 'What do you want, Mr Jay?'

The man on his right took out a chequebook and placed it on the table.

'I want ten – no – I want twenty-five thousand pounds.'

'The agreement was for ten, I believe,' said Boxleiter.

'It's not for the laptop.'

'Oh?'

'No. I want a letter to go with the cheque. It should thank the recipient for the professionalism, bravery and expertise of Bryn Thomas whilst investigating forest fires for and on behalf of OPMA. It should be on headed notepaper and addressed to Mrs Thomas, 11a Gull Terrace, Barmouth, Wales.'

'Why?'

'Because that's what I want. Don't put the chequebook away yet, please.'

A look passed between the three.

'I want another cheque made out. This one's a bit bigger.' I looked from one to the other. 'How much do you think a detective sergeant – no . . . an inspector in the police earns? Forty? Forty-five thousand? Let's call it forty . . . I want a cheque for forty thousand times twenty . . . I'm tired: somebody tell me how much that is?'

'That's eight hundred thousand pounds,' said chequebook man.

Boxleiter shot him a look and I thanked him.

'Make that cheque out to Mrs Jean Vaughan. I'll write the address out for you. Send her a letter as well. Let's call it an ex gratia payment in recognition for heroism displayed by Detective Sergeant John Vaughan in catching the OPMA bomber.'

It was like someone had just electrified the sofa.

'Can you prove this?' said Boxleiter.

'And much more. Now we come to the hard bit. Sometimes an individual within a company or acting on that company's behalf will go beyond their brief.'

The three of them did well not to let their nervousness show, but chequebook man stole a look at Boxleiter and that did it for me.

'Sometimes that individual will commit a criminal act – or acts. It may be an excess of zeal or it may be what someone tells him to do.'

'Your point, Mr Jay.'

'OPMA employs a security firm called Tech-Ops.'

Boxleiter looked to his right and the other man nodded.

'Okay, we might. What of it?'

'Two years ago, while trying to recover a laptop computer owned by J.J. Roth and again on third of July this year, two operatives employed by Tech-Ops killed an ex-OPMA employee, Mark Haig, and a Black River mining surveyor, Hugh Jones.'

'Wait a minute—'

'They tortured them, killed them and then set fire to the properties where they were.'

'I hope to God you can prove this, Mr Jay.'

'I don't have to prove it, Mr Boxleiter. I know a man who saw it happen.'

Silence.

'What do you want me to do with that information?'

'Tell Tech-Ops.'

'Is that all?'

'And I want an OPMA representative – you, perhaps, Mr Boxleiter – to invite the head of the North Wales Police Force to lunch and explain to him everything that I've told you and say how it would be in everybody's interest if a Detective Inspector Pritchard took early retirement . . . as an alternative to dismissal.'

'I don't understand. Is this Pritchard involved in some way?'

'He took a bribe to look the other way while the Tech-Ops personnel killed Haig and shot Detective Sergeant Anne Lloyd. He probably didn't know that they were going to go that far . . . but you get the picture.'

Boxleiter nodded. He was now studying me very carefully.

'Is there anything else, Mr Jay?'

'I want OPMA to withdraw from their Welsh operation – but still build the Technical Park and the IT Centre. Oh, and the houses.'

He wanted to tell me to go to hell, but he knew now that I had something more.

'If you do this, the contents of this –' I leant forward and handed him the affidavit '– will remain confidential. If you read it carefully, it will tell you the substance of what's in the computer. Namely, that while offering to clean up the mercury pollution in an area of the Xingu National Park in Brazil, OPMA ran a drug-testing programme, passing off the side effects as mercury poisoning. That the drug Pheladone produces side effects that were known about in advance of the testing and that they were so similar to poisoning by methyl mercury as to be virtually undetectable, except by a trained scientist looking for just that.'

'I—'

'And that J. J. Roth knew this when he made his offer to the Brazilian Government.'

40

I moved in with Jenny a week after we received the DNA tests.

Alex gave me a further loan against the money I was owed from the Sheldon case and he and Jenny found a flat for us while I ran around getting our furniture out of storage and buying some extras.

It was an odd feeling, a mixture of the familiar and of otherness. Jenny seemed calmer than before and it might have been my imagination, but I fancied she was already putting weight on.

Three days after we moved in, she cooked a special meal and we christened the flat. As she prepared the food in the kitchen, I put some music on and laid the table.

She called out to me, 'If it's a boy, what do you want to call it?'

'Anything but Alex.'

She laughed. 'I'm sure it's going to be a boy.'

'As long as it's healthy,' I said softly.

Jenny brought the steaks in and I fetched the salad.

We ate and talked of practical things – decorating, budgeting and how we'd now need a car of our own.

She suggested that we toast the flat and the baby. As we did so she gave me a smile and searched my face.

'One more,' she said. 'To us.'

We touched glasses and she turned towards the stack system. 'What is that music?'

'Mahalia Jackson . . . she was a gospel singer.'

PAT O'KEEFFE

THERMAL IMAGE

In his thrilling first novel, London fireman Pat O'Keeffe brings to brutal, authentic life the real world of firefighting and crime in East London.

Steve Jay is a fireman on the edge. Crippling debts and the recent return of his unfaithful partner Jenny have bent him out of shape, getting between him and the job he loves.

But Jay's problems are only just beginning. A horrific fire in an East London fashion store and workshop tests him and his watch to the limit. And when an old friend offers him serious money to investigate the Sheldon family's history of fires, it sounds like the answer to a prayer.

His decision to accept the case plunges him into a nightmare of arson and murder.

NEW ENGLISH LIBRARY
Hodder & Stoughton